Hello! Thanks so much for picking up this book and for choosing to dip into the world that revolves around Fay's Cakes, a little café-cum-cake shop that my heroine Fay has set up in the gorgeous garden of her house that borders the Grand Union canal. It's an idyllic place and since I created it, I've been scouring property sites to see if I can find somewhere that comes close to it! How I'd love to live there.

I'm a big fan of the canal network in this country. I think we're blessed to have this wonderful ribbon of water threading through our towns and villages. The Grand Union passes through Costa del Keynes where I live and I really enjoy walking by the canal. It's my favourite place. I'd always fancied a canal holiday but my partner, Lovely Kev, was adamant that it wasn't for him. White water rafting is more his style than the peaceful, leisurely pace of the canals.

Then, out of the blue, I received an email about hotel boats on the canal – I didn't even know they existed. It sounded perfect. Someone else would cook the food, drive the boat and, if you didn't want to get your hands dirty, they'd even sort out the locks for you. You could literally do as little or as much as you liked. What's not to love?

So I cajoled my dear friend Sue into coming with me and we had a fabulous time. I hadn't envisaged setting a book on the canal at all, but the moment I was on board, I knew it was something I could have a lot of fun with. At every single lock we met a lot of interesting people and some just plain crazy characters. I was in my element. It's a beautiful way to view our countryside and now I'm completely hooked on narrowboats.

And Lovely Kev? He came with us on our second trip.

So I hope you enjoy the book and, if you haven't already, perhaps find some time to experience the wonderful canals in our country and maybe find a little hidden gem like the cake shop in the garden.

Carole ☺ xx

Carole Matthews is the *Sunday Times* bestselling author of over thirty novels, including the top ten bestsellers *The Cake Shop in the Garden, A Cottage by the Sea, Paper Hearts and Summer Kisses, Christmas Cakes and Mistletoe Nights, Million Love Songs* and *Happiness for Beginners*. In 2015, Carole was awarded the RNA Outstanding Achievement Award. Her novels dazzle and delight readers all over the world and she is published in more than thirty countries.

For all the latest news from Carole, visit **www.carolematthews.com**, follow Carole on Twitter (**@carolematthews**) and Instagram (**matthews.carole**) or join the thousands of readers who have become Carole's friend on Facebook (**carolematthewsbooks**).

Also by Carole Matthews

Let's Meet on Platform 8
A Whiff of Scandal
More to Life than This
For Better, For Worse
A Minor Indiscretion
A Compromising Position
The Sweetest Taboo
With or Without You
You Drive Me Crazy
Welcome to the Real World
The Chocolate Lovers' Club
The Chocolate Lovers' Diet
It's a Kind of Magic
All You Need is Love
The Difference a Day Makes
That Loving Feeling
It's Now or Never
The Only Way is Up
Wrapped up in You
Summer Daydreams
With Love at Christmas
A Cottage by the Sea
Calling Mrs Christmas
A Place to Call Home
The Christmas Party
The Chocolate Lovers' Christmas
The Chocolate Lovers' Wedding
Paper Hearts and Summer Kisses
Christmas Cakes and Mistletoe Nights
Million Love Songs
Happiness for Beginners
Sunny Days and Sea Breezes
Christmas for Beginners

Carole Matthews

The Cake Shop in the Garden

SPHERE

SPHERE

First published in Great Britain in 2015 by Sphere
This reissue published in 2023 by Sphere

1 3 5 7 9 10 8 6 4 2

A CIP catalogue record for this book
is available from the British Library.

ISBN 978-0-7515-5215-7

Typeset in Sabon by M Rules
Printed and bound in Great Britain by Clays Ltd, Elcograf S.p.A.

Papers used by Sphere are from well-managed forests
and other responsible sources.

Sphere
An imprint of
Little, Brown Book Group
Carmelite House
50 Victoria Embankment
London EC4Y 0DZ

An Hachette UK Company
www.hachette.co.uk

www.littlebrown.co.uk

To my dear friend, Sue Davie,
who was the perfect companion on my research
trips into the delights of canal living.
So many lovely memories.

Chapter One

I sit on the edge of my mum's bed and take a deep breath. 'I've booked you in for a week's respite care,' I tell her.

She stares at me, aghast. 'But I don't want you to have any respite from me.'

'Things are quite difficult at the moment, Mum. You know how it is. The year's marching on and I need some time to get the café ready for the season.'

She folds her arms across her chest, unconvinced.

I've already brought her a cup of tea and a slice of the new coffee cake that I'm trying out, in the hope of softening her up, but my dear mother has turned up her nose at them.

'I'm not leaving here.' Mum's chin juts defiantly. 'No way, lady.'

For someone who is supposed to be an invalid, my mother has the strongest constitution and will of anyone I've ever met. I knew even as I was making the booking that it was overly optimistic. Even a cake fresh from the oven won't warm my mother's heart.

'There are loads of things I need to do, Mum. I could just do with a couple of days. That's all.' A couple of days without her banging on the ceiling every five minutes, wanting this or that or something and nothing. She has a walking stick by the bed especially for the purpose.

My family have been blessed enough to be able to live in a beautiful home alongside the Grand Union Canal since my parents, Miranda and Victor Merryweather, were first married. Both my sister, Edie, and I were born and brought up here. One of us is more pleased about it than the other. The house is in the pretty village of Whittan, at one time on the outskirts of Milton Keynes, but now being nudged in the ribs by the thrusting city as it engulfs everything in its path.

When I became Mum's full-time carer, I gave up my paid job and, out of necessity, started a small cake shop cum café and tearoom – Fay's Cakes. I'd already started selling cakes from our dilapidated narrowboat, the *Maid of Merryweather*, which is moored at the bottom of the garden. It was a sort of hobby, I suppose, a bit of an ad hoc affair, but it gave me something to do with all the cakes and jam that I so liked to make. Now I run it full-time and it's grown to take over the dining room, veranda and garden of our house. The only problem with running a business that's based in our home is that half of my days disappear with me running up and down the stairs fetching and carrying for Mum while trying to keep things going with the café downstairs. Not that I really mind … it's just that sometimes I do need a break from my caring duties so that I can concentrate on actually bringing in some much-needed money.

'They'll sit me in the corner with the dribblers and shakers,' Mum complains.

'They won't. This is a nice place.' I hold up the cheery Sunnyside Respite Care Home brochure encouragingly, but she averts her gaze, refusing to even look at it. 'It's not a hospital,' I press on. 'You get your own room. I researched it really carefully on the internet.'

2

'Pah.'

'It's more like a hotel – *exactly* like a hotel – but with care. They'll look after you.'

'Just say if I'm too much trouble for you, Miss Fay Merryweather.' There's a sob in Mum's voice and she dabs theatrically at her eyes beneath the rims of her reading glasses.

'You're not too much trouble.' Once again, she makes me feel like the worst daughter in the world. 'Of course you're not.'

She pushes the plate of cake away from her, apparently too overwhelmed to eat.

'I love you. You know that. It's only that I have such a lot to do in the café.' The list is endless. Even the thought of it is making me feel quite dizzy.

'Oh.' She rolls her eyes. 'The café this, the café that. It's all you ever think about. It's all I ever hear about.'

'It pays the bills, Mum.' Just about. The ones that don't go away just because I'm at home and caring for you, I add to myself but dare not say out loud.

My mum took to her bed with a bad bout of flu, four winters ago now. The flu became pneumonia and there's no doubt that she was very poorly at the time. But, several courses of anti-biotics later and when the pneumonia had run its course, she was still in no hurry to get up. Then she slipped in the bathroom and broke her hip. When she came back from hospital, she eschewed the physiotherapy programme that she'd been advised to follow and took to her bed again to convalesce. She made herself very comfortable there and, since then, she's simply refused to get up.

Mum has decided that she's still ill and infirm, no matter how many times the doctor tells her that she's just fine. She's stayed exactly where she is and no one can persuade her otherwise. I've coaxed and encouraged her. Doctors come and cajole her. Mental-health professionals turn up, try to counsel her and are duly rebuffed. Antidepressants were prescribed, dispensed and

3

found, by me, hidden down the back of the headboard. In short, my mother has decided she will be permanently bedridden and, quite frankly, she loves it.

Now, every day Miranda Merryweather sits in her bed, snuggled in a duvet, surrounded by fluffy pillows, holding court like the queen of a very small country. These days, she refuses to let most people enter her domain. Occasionally, our lovely GP, Dr Ahmed, is reluctantly allowed an audience. I think at first she liked the attention. Then, as the months went on, she simply became entrenched until, finally, she was frightened to get up and go out at all. Now it's simply become a way of life.

The friends she once had have all gradually fallen away until, now, I'm the sole person at her beck and call. I cook, clean and run the café. While Mum can still get herself back and forth across the landing to the bathroom, she needs my help to shower, and I wash her hair for her too when she requires it. Though some days I don't have time to wash my own hair. There's an ever-growing cache of tablets that have to be administered at regular intervals – blood-pressure pills, water tablets, sleeping potions, statins. The list goes on. The longer she stays in bed, the more medicines she needs. I change her nightdress every day and her sheets once a week.

'Your sister would never treat me like this,' Mum says.

'She wouldn't,' I agree. 'You'd starve before you got tea and cake from Edie.'

Mum recoils as if I've slapped her, then turns her head to stare resolutely out of the window at the garden and beyond at the canal which meanders past. The trees along the bank are coming into full bud and soon the hawthorn will be in glorious blossom. It's so beautiful out there. Yet she'll stay in this room and miss it all.

'Edie could teach you a thing or two about caring, madam.'

She couldn't. Believe me, she really couldn't.

4

Edie, my younger and only sibling, is the shining girl of the family. Edie, the unemployed, heavy-drinking, recreational-drug user who is currently kept by a married man, can do no wrong in Mum's eyes. As she lives in New York, my mother is unaware that any of this actually goes on. As far as she's concerned, Edie is busily working away at a wonderful career and has a boyfriend who is a fabulously wealthy lawyer. As such, she is a far better daughter than I am. My sister is very scant on detail when she speaks to our mother, and Mum only sees Edie through rose-tinted spectacles. Whereas I am so very often cast as the Wicked Daughter.

The truth of the matter is that Edie rarely rings unless she wants something and never comes home now. She hasn't been back at all since Mum took to her bed – even when she was actually quite ill. And, let's face it, New York is just around the corner these days. You can go there for the weekend. It's not as if Edie's in Australia or New Zealand or somewhere on the other side of the world.

Even though Edie can be a complete pain in the backside, I do miss her terribly. I wish she was here, and not just because I could do with some help with Mum. Though being the sole carer for your parent can be an onerous and thankless task, it would be nice to have Edie here just as a friend who'd know what I'm going through, so that we could, perhaps, share the emotional burden.

I press on, even though I'm beginning to realise that my mission is fruitless. 'I thought I could decorate your room while you're away.'

'I'm not going away, Little Miss Cloth Ears. I told you.'

Goodness only knows this room needs a bit of a makeover. I don't think it's been decorated since about 1972. Some of the pastel-pink, flower-sprigged wallpaper is curling and there's a damp patch on the ceiling that says we may well have a leak in the roof. Not the first. I don't even dare to go into the loft these days. To be honest, the whole of Canal House could do with a bit of tender loving care. It hasn't had any money spent on it in years, simply because there hasn't been any to spare.

I am forty-one years young and this is the only home I've ever known. I was born here, in this very room, and, at the rate I'm going, I will more than likely die here.

'I could bring in some wallpaper samples.'

'Not listening.' My mum puts her fingers in her ears. 'La, la, la. Not listening.'

I wouldn't mind if Mum was actually really ancient, but she's only seventy-seven years old. That's all. She should be out there having the time of her life. Yet the concept of the University of the Third Age has, unfortunately, passed her by. It's so frustrating that she seems to have given up on life and is content just to lie here. Even more frustrating is the fact that she seems to revel in it: she spends her day languishing, watching soap operas and quizzes. Or home-renovation programmes which are never destined to help this particular home.

Before I can remonstrate with her any further, I hear the back door open, and a voice travels up the stairs from the hall.

'Is me!'

That's my assistant, Lija. The café isn't open for a few hours yet but Lija has come in early today to help me scrub down the tables and chairs that have over-wintered in the garden. The first thing on a long list of glamorous tasks that we need to do before we start heading into the busy summer season. Then we won't get a minute to do anything.

'I have to go,' I say.

'My tea's gone cold,' Mum grumbles.

There are times when I'd swear she spends all day thinking up small ways in which to torture me. If she's woken up in a particularly belligerent mood, she often waits until I'm at the bottom of the stairs to call me back for some little instruction she might have forgotten, or to plump up her pillows.

I take her cup. 'I'll bring you a nice fresh one.'

'Not as much milk this time. It tastes like rice pudding when you make it.'

I could suggest that she's perfectly capable of getting up and making her own tea and then she'd have no cause to complain, but I don't. It would be a total waste of my breath as, sadly, I lost that argument quite some time ago. Instead, I scoop up the laundry – the sheets I changed yesterday, the nightdress that was swapped for a fresh one this morning – and head back downstairs.

This is my life, like it or lump it. And I simply have to man up and get on with it.

Chapter Two

When I go into the kitchen, Lija has already stripped off her coat and is taking some eggs from the fridge.

'Morning,' I say as I go to shove the washing in the machine and set it going. I can iron it tonight when I'm watching the episode of *Escape to the Country* that I've recorded. My guilty pleasure. 'Shall we go out and clean the furniture now while it's fine? It's forecast to rain later and we can come in and bake then.'

This afternoon, if all goes to plan, we're going to try out some new recipes.

'Is always bloody raining,' my assistant grumbles. 'Rain, rain, rain.'

Lija Vilks is young, lithe and Latvian. She's not really an ideal assistant for a customer-facing business as she's quite spiky. Particularly with the customers. On the other hand, she's a great and loyal worker who can turn her hand to pretty much anything. She bakes the most wonderful cakes, which, if I'm honest, are far better than mine. You've never had carrot cake until you've tasted Lija's, and I'd swear that her chocolate brownies could win awards. She is a sweary, Goth version of the goddess Mary Berry.

'How is Old Bag today?' Lija throws a disdainful glance at the ceiling, above which my dear mother reposes.

'Not great,' I admit. 'She won't go to the respite-care place, no matter what I say. I'm going to have to ring and cancel it.'

Lija tuts. She's not my mother's biggest fan. But then my mother isn't hers either.

'I've tried,' I say. 'I don't know what else I can do. We'll just have to work round her.'

'Can you get nurse in?'

'I can't afford it, Lija. There's just not enough cash in the pot.' I let out a heartfelt sigh. 'I wish Edie would come back and help. Even if it's for a week or two. Perhaps I'll have another talk with her later.'

'Good luck with that.' Lija gives me a black look.

My assistant's usual colour of choice is black – both for withering stares and for clothing. Today is no different: she's wearing black jeans with a skin-tight black T-shirt and she has her poker-straight black hair yanked back in a ponytail. Only her skin is as white as the driven snow.

Lija seldom wears a scrap of make-up, but she doesn't need it as she's stunningly beautiful without it, despite a slightly vampiric look. Her fringe hangs like a curtain skimming her big blue eyes, and sometimes I wonder how she actually sees through it. She eats cake morning, noon and night and has the skinniest, most sharply angled body I've ever seen. I'm most envious of her tiny frame. She has no breasts, no bottom, no hips, no thighs, no cellulite to contend with. Despite being up and down stairs all day looking after my mother, I run towards curves and only have to look at a cake to form another one.

The other thing I like about Lija is that she's as reliable as the town-hall clock. She lives in the city, not far from our village, and cycles to work along the towpath come rain, hail or snow. Lija has a room in a rented house that she shares with three other Latvian girls. Collectively, they drink like fish and party all night, but she's never once been late in the two years or more that she's worked for me. On the rare occasions that she takes a day off, one of her friends always steps up to the plate to stand in for her, so I never have to worry about cover. The other girls are all similarly black and spiky, but slightly less abrasive than Lija.

I boil the kettle again. 'Mum's tea's gone cold,' I say. 'Do you want one?'

She nods. 'I will take the tea to Old Bag. She won't bang-bangbang on ceiling all day if she thinks it will be me.'

That's another thing in Lija's favour. Despite her grumbles, she really doesn't mind helping out with my mother either. I'm not saying that she's a rival for Florence Nightingale or anything. Far from it: Dr Crippen was probably more charming than Lija. Her bedside manner is somewhat unconventional but she's right, my mother is suddenly a lot less trouble when Lija is looking after her. Lija stands no messing from Miranda. Which is fine by me.

While Lija stomps upstairs with Mum's tea, I fill a bucket with hot, soapy water and find two scrubbing brushes. I slip on my comfy old cardigan, pop the brushes into my pockets and go out into the garden.

This is a large house, strong and sturdy. It was built of serviceable red brick in the 1920s and is hugely proportioned compared to today's modern boxes. We're lucky to have a kitchen big enough to convert into a working one.

We keep Fay's Cakes open during the winter months, but business pretty much only limps along. We still continue to sell cakes from the *Maid of Merryweather* and direct from the kitchen, but it's only when we have a bright and sunny weekend that we see a steady stream of customers. We have a few tables in the spacious dining room, which is done up prettily with pink gingham cloths and bunting, that I made myself, draped around the picture rails. It's a comfortable space that meets the current trend for retro chic, but only because most of the things have actually been here since they were first in fashion. My mother's collection of pink glassware is definitely enjoying a new lease of life.

The back of the house has a pretty ironwork veranda which runs the full length of it. Now it's covered in wisteria, whose blooms will soon be hanging heavily like clusters of grapes. Later in the summer a purple clematis takes over. It's a lovely, sheltered spot and we have a few tables out here too.

I have to say that the main attraction of the cake shop, apart from Lija's cakes, is the stunning garden. It's a generous plot by any standards. Broad and long, it sweeps right down to the edge of the Grand Union Canal.

It's bounded on both sides by tall, red-brick walls which screen it from our immediate neighbour. We don't get a lot of passing trade here as Canal House is situated at the very end of an unmade lane and is generally only discovered by those who are determined to find it. Not exactly the ideal place for a cake shop-cum-café, but then needs must. If I were to try to find premises like this elsewhere, it would cost me a small fortune. A small fortune that I don't have.

As I look down the garden towards the canal, there's a modest orchard of gnarled apple trees. This is protected by the high wall behind it, which is currently smothered with pink clematis that will, later in the season, be followed by climbing roses. On the right, just beyond the veranda, there's an old magnolia which is quite magnificent if the early frost doesn't get it. The wall is hugged by a variety of flowering shrubs, all of which are in desperate need of pruning now.

We've had a terrible year, so far, for weather. This *is* England. It's been unseasonably cold and has done nothing but rain since

11

January. The garden has certainly suffered for it. Though today is dry, the heads of the shrubs are mostly bowed, sodden and heavy with moisture. Further towards the canal, the beautiful cherry trees with their delicate pink blossom have taken a battering from the wind and rain of the last week. But it's still an idyllic spot.

Before Mum took to her bed, she used to love the garden – though all the hard work was down to my dad. He was the one who made the garden so pretty. This was, once upon a time, a humbly priced family home – until several property booms took it to the realms of astronomical. I feel so fortunate that my parents were able to buy it when they were first married, as I wouldn't have a hope of living somewhere like this otherwise. And I love it here. Truly I do. This is my family home and is filled with my memories. Call me unadventurous, but this is my own little slice of paradise and I'd never want to live anywhere else.

There's no denying that I could do with an extra pair of hands to help me maintain it though. It's an overwhelming amount of work for one person. The high winds we had back in February have brought down several big branches and there are mounds of leaves a foot deep against the boundary walls. Thankfully, the cherry blossoms have survived. If I'm honest though, all the paintwork around the place could do with a freshen-up. In the last few years the house has progressed from charmingly weathered to just plain tatty. Today is the first properly sunny day for absolutely ages, even though it's still chilly and rain is predicted later, and I'm so glad to be out in the fresh air. Easter is late this year, at the end of April, and we usually fully open the cake shop that weekend. If we want to be ready for then, we need to get a move on.

Chapter Three

Depositing the bucket by the waiting tables, I wander down the garden to my favourite spot of all on our small jetty at the edge of the canal. My dad loved to be either by water or on it in some shape or form, and this was his preferred place to come and sit too.

Victor Merryweather was born by the seaside in Pembrokeshire and, though his work brought him to this part of the country – which is possibly the furthest away from any coastline – it never quite left his soul. I didn't ever ask him, but I think that's why he and Mum bought this particular property when they married. OK, so it's not exactly the wild beaches and crashing waves that he so loved, but there's a quiet, gentle charm to an English canal that has an irresistible lure all of its own.

I miss my dad. He's been dead for nearly twenty years now, but there isn't a day that goes by when I don't think of him. He hand-built the wooden jetty that runs along the width of the garden overlooking the canal, and I try to come down here every day to sit and look at the water for five minutes if I can. Just as we did together when I was a girl. My earliest memories are of the times when we used to settle down here together, me with my legs dangling over the water, and watch the colourful narrowboats go by, or the families of ducks that are always a feature. Dad taught me to recognise the many birds that live along the canal – terns, herons, moorhens and, if you're lucky, the rare flash of blue from a kingfisher.

Where my mother is difficult, Dad was a gentle soul. Mum's always been demanding and Dad was generous, giving. I don't know how their relationship worked, but somehow it seemed to. Whatever Mum wanted, he agreed to. He was never one for confrontation of any kind. He was the yin to her yang, I suppose. After he died, unexpectedly of a heart attack, she was never quite the same. None of us was.

I pull up one of the wooden garden seats and take the weight off my feet while I watch a timid moorhen dash back and forth to marshal her tiny, fluffball chicks along the bank. On the towpath opposite there's a heron, motionless, eyes fixed on the water, hoping for a hapless fishy snack to swim by. Nothing much ever happens here. Life goes on unchanging, year after year. The canal is always so still and peaceful that it's easy to believe there's no other world outside of this. Two ducks jump out of the water and fluff their feathers on the jetty before waddling in step up the garden. This is my own little universe.

A brightly painted narrowboat putters by. It's one of our local boats – *Floating Paradise* – and the couple who live on it, Mr and Mrs Fenson, often pop in for a sandwich or cream tea.

'Hi, Fay!' Ralph, steering at the back, holds up a hand.

I wave back.

'Open for business?'

'Always,' I call. 'Look forward to seeing you.'

'Get the kettle on! We'll be in later,' he shouts back. 'We need to enjoy this sunshine while we can.'

Ralph and Miriam bought their narrowboat a few years ago when they gave up work. They have a residential mooring at the nearby marina and an apartment in the city that they can retreat to when the weather is too cold. What a lovely way to spend your retirement. It's a shame Dad didn't live long enough to do the same. He would have loved every minute of it.

Unfortunately, their boat is also known along this stretch of the canal as the *Floating Disaster*. I don't think Ralph and Miriam have ever fully grasped the etiquette or the skills required for canal life. They are frequently muttered about as people who leave the sluices open and drain the pound. Or leave the lock gates open. Or rock everyone else's boats as they zoom along the waterways above the usual speed limit, Ralph in his peaked captain's cap and Miriam in one of her many blue-and-white-striped jumpers or T-shirts. Once they had a huge party on board for all of their friends and nearly scuttled their own boat, it was so overloaded. I don't think they go very far in *Floating Paradise* as they're usually moored somewhere close to the marina, which is probably just as well. Lots of the hardened canal folk grumble about them, but they're a delightfully dotty pair and are always welcome in the cake shop as they cheer the day up no end.

The *Maid of Merryweather* is moored here at the bottom of the garden. She's a sixty-foot traditional boat. Dad's pride and joy. He absolutely loved her. There wasn't a day that went by when he didn't come down to see her at some point. It was always his plan to spend more time on her when he'd stopped working.

Mum, of course, hated the narrowboat. She was as jealous of her as she would have been a mistress. (I'm pretty sure that sometimes Mum *did* have to compete with the *Maid of Merryweather* for top spot in Dad's affections.) Much like the Fensons, my parents never went very far in her – though Dad always wanted to. He'd have been quite happy to give up his job and spend his time travelling the canals of England. Mum had other ideas though. She didn't even like to sleep on board overnight as she said it was cramped and she only ever did it under sufferance. With all the delights of the waterways on offer, we only ever used to go as far as Berkhamsted in one direction and Stoke Bruerne on the way to Northampton in the other. That must have driven Dad mad, but he never said so. He just relished every moment he spent on the boat.

Those family holidays were the highlight of my year too. I loved the *Maid* just as much as Dad did and preferred to think of her as cosy rather than cramped. Though being confined to the cabin with Edie when she was little – especially if it was raining – could make it feel like a much smaller space. My sister would be stir-crazy after an hour or two, bouncing off the walls. I've always been the one who could sit quietly with a book.

The narrowboat was Dad's project, a labour of love. He was never happier than when he was on the canal, tinkering away. He was a clerical worker by day in one of the many new firms that settled in Milton Keynes in the 1980s and yet, the minute he came home, he'd strip off his suit and tie to rush down to the canal. Every evening and weekend he was always in his work jeans and a navy sweater, oil on his hands, a smile on his face. Since he died, the *Maid of Merryweather* hasn't moved at all, which makes me feel very guilty. I don't even think the engine works any more. Last time I tried to start it, I couldn't get a peep out of her. Dad would hate that.

The outside of the barge is painted in the traditional colours of the canal – dark green and red embellished with the roses that historically decorate narrowboats. She might look a little bit ragged and worn around the edges now, but I've kept the inside spick and span. It would take a lot of work to make her habitable but, superficially, she's faring quite well. The main living-room cabin and galley are furnished with oak cupboards and a log-burning stove that now stands unlit. There are crocheted lace covers at the windows.

Though the *Maid of Merryweather* might stand idle, she certainly earns her keep. Now she's a vital part of Fay's Cakes. People come to the house to buy our produce, but I think they like the quirkiness of the canal boat and it's a great draw for tourists and the regulars on the canal alike. I stock a nice range of home-made cakes, pies, biscuits and jam. In the summer I make my own lemonade too, which is always popular. A chap in the village, Graham Lovett, paints nice watercolour pictures of the area and I sell them as postcards and small prints as we get a lot of holiday traffic along this part of the canal. The big marina nearby hires out rental boats and we're often their first port of call.

As I've said it was from that humble beginning that the idea of Fay's Cakes gradually grew. I'd see all the boats going by, the people who live on the canal, the tourists on the holiday boats, and watch the families walking or cycling on the towpaths, and realised that they couldn't get a cup of tea or a piece of cake unless they went to one of the pubs dotted along this stretch of water. And you don't always want a pub, do you?

My job as a senior administration co-ordinator wasn't exactly keeping me enthralled. It paid well enough, but it hardly made my days zing with excitement. I'd been mulling over a change of direction for a while, though nothing came to mind that would require only my limited skill set. Then, when Mum decided she was an invalid and was going to stay that way, I simply couldn't carry on working full-time and look after her as well. I'd have ended up in the bed right next to her. I tried having paid help to come in and take some of the strain, but Mum wouldn't let them near her. Plus it was so expensive. Yet to do it all myself was exhausting. In the end I had to give in my notice, and that's when I thought that perhaps I could use the house and garden to expand the business.

So Fay's Cakes and the *Maid of Merryweather* are now both

my sanity and my full-time job. I look fondly at the pretty narrowboat and don't know why my mother has always been so set against her. What's not to love? Even now, when the boat at least brings in some money, Mum's always keen to have a dig at her.

If it was up to Mum the *Maid of Merryweather* would have gone years ago, but it's the one thing I've put my foot down about. The *Maid of Merryweather* is all I have left of Dad and, as long as I have breath in my body, she's going nowhere without me.

Chapter Four

Lija comes to join me in the garden. She stomps up to the jetty wearing yellow rubber gloves and a dark scowl.

'She is evil old witch,' she says. 'If she was my mother, I would put pillow over her face.'

'Sometimes I feel like it,' I concur.

'Next tea I take her, I will spit in it.'

I don't think I'm necessarily a natural carer, but compared to Lija I am Mother Teresa.

'Shall we get started on the tables?' I've sat here musing for too long and now we should get a move on before the forecast rain comes. I brandish the scrubbing brushes in a hopeful manner.

Unfortunately, we don't have a lot of storage space here, so the tables and chairs have to stay out all winter. I stack them and throw over an old tarpaulin to protect them from the worst of the weather, but by the time I uncover them again every spring they're still stained with dirt and green mould.

Lija and I head to the tables. The water in the bucket has gone a bit cold now, but it will have to do as I can't waste time going to boil some more. Together we start to scrub.

The tables out here are pretty, all different pastel shades. I bought them cheaply at IKEA when I started and they were called TWONK or SPLAT or some such. I officially launched Fay's Cakes about three years ago and the first one went in a blur as I learned the ropes. So this summer season I feel as if I'm really getting into my stride. To be honest, as the café sort of evolved rather than came from some kind of cunning master plan, I feel very lucky that it went better than I could have imagined in that first year, particularly in the summer months. I started to have regular customers, people who'd walk along the canal or come by narrowboat. They'd buy something from the *Maid of Merryweather* – a cake, a pot of jam, a bottle of lemonade – and then stay for a cup of tea. The only downside was that being here all day with my mum could not only be testing, but lonely too. I did miss the office environment as I had no one else to talk to, and those customers were my lifeline.

In the second year, flushed with moderate success, I added some more tables in the garden and, just because they are my own favourite, started to specialise in afternoon teas. They proved to be so popular that I soon had to take on an extra pair of hands. I put an advert in the local paper, had fifty people phone me to apply, and interviewed three. I liked Lija instantly. I don't know why, as the other two seemed much more amenable. But she was the only one who brought a home-made cake along with her – a coffee and walnut sponge – and it was simply the best cake I'd ever tasted. So Lija joined me and she's been here ever since.

That year, I turned the dining room into a little indoor space – to many complaints from my mother, who still objects to having the house used for the general public. I keep telling her: if it's good enough for the Queen, then it's good enough for us.

The dining room is a useful addition in bad weather, even

though it only fits four small tables. In the summer we can open the French doors which look out on to the garden. Apart from the few tables under the veranda, the rest of them are at the mercy of the elements. It means that business is very weather-dependent and, as such, a bit erratic, but somehow it works and, just about, keeps the wolf from the door.

I bought two new sunshades at the end of last year which will also provide shelter from a shower, but haven't got round to putting them up yet. I need a man with a screwdriver, and my partner, Anthony, may be a lot of things, but a handyman certainly isn't one of them.

Lija is scrubbing away – with more enthusiasm than me, it has to be said. The sun peeps out from behind the clouds and it feels warm on my back. I hope this year will be a good one and that I can put some money away. I'm trying to save up to renovate the *Maid of Merryweather*, as I know Dad would have liked that. I think, at the very least, she needs a new engine, and that's not going to come cheap.

As I stand up and stretch, I see a narrowboat coming towards our mooring. It's not one that I recognise and it's always nice to have a new customer. Last summer I put up a sign on the canal-side, which attracts a lot of passing trade from the boating community. But this boat I don't know.

Putting up my hand to shade my eyes, I watch it pulling in behind Dad's barge. 'Who's this then?'

The Dreamcatcher. Possibly the most common name for a canal boat, so no surprises there. The boat's a traditional style and, much like the *Maid of Merryweather*, old and a little bit worn around the edges too. But, from this distance at least, the owner of the boat looks to be a young man. He jumps off the stern on to the jetty, mooring rope in hand, in a very athletic manner.

'Looks like we might have a customer,' I say to Lija.

I haven't even opened up yet. All the fresh cakes for sale today are still sitting in the kitchen in their cellophane wrappings. It's normally in the afternoon, when people are thinking about what to have as a teatime treat or for their dinner, that we're at our busiest. Though, if I'm honest, we're never really going to trouble Tesco with our sales figures.

'Humph,' Lija grumbles, still dashing backwards and forwards with her scrubbing brush. 'Tell him we are busy.'

'Nonsense. We need the business, and it won't take a minute to put the kettle on.' I could actually do with a cup of tea myself. 'He can sit on the veranda, if he doesn't mind. The tables there are nice and clean.'

Putting down my scrubbing brush, I make an attempt to look businesslike. Never easy in knitwear products. Efficiently, the man ties up his boat behind the *Maid of Merryweather* and, a few minutes later, is moored alongside the jetty. A little dog, possibly a Jack Russell cross, pops its head over the side of the boat. It's white with brown and black patches and is wearing a red neckerchief which looks unbearably cute.

'Come on, Diggery.' The man clicks his fingers and the dog jumps off the boat, dropping obediently into step behind him.

Canal people tend to fall pretty much into two camps: pensioners and hippies. This man is neither. As he strides purposefully up into the garden, I note that he's tall, very much so, and rangy. Not that I know much about men's fashion these days, but I think he looks quite edgy. He's wearing black skinny jeans and big army boots. These are topped with a black T-shirt and a faded grey denim jacket. His hair is also jet-black, cut short at the sides but a riot on top, going every which way, and ending in some sort of quiff that flops forward.

I would like some sort of statement hair, like Lija's or, indeed, this man's. Instead I have a blonde pixie crop, essentially because it's easy to maintain rather than the mass of bohemian curls tumbling to my waist that I secretly long for. As if I'd ever have the time to look after those.

As he gets closer, I can tell that the sum of the parts adds up to a rather pleasing whole. Without even thinking, I say, 'Oh my.'

Even Lija stands up and stops what she's doing. 'Denim on denim,' is her scornful assessment.

When he's right in front of us, he says 'Hi, ladies,' and treats us to the warmest smile I've seen in a long time. Possibly ever.

That is a smile that would break hearts. Many of them.

'Hi,' I manage.

He takes in the fact that the garden is still very much in winter mode and that we're currently busy scrubbing tables. 'Are you open?'

His accent is soft, Irish and rather sexy.

'Oh yes,' I say and realise that, for the first time in my life, my heart has gone all of a-flutter.

Chapter Five

So I find this rather handsome man a table on the veranda and he sits down, stretching out his long legs. I'm normally quite chatty with my customers, but I feel all flustered and can't think of a word to say. I think he's young, possibly early thirties – a full ten years or more younger than I am. Then I realise that I'm staring.

Perhaps he's used to being stared at, as he seems completely unaware of it.

'I'm Danny,' he offers when it becomes clear that I'm tongue-tied. 'Danny Wilde.' With his big Doc Martens boots and his tatty T-shirt he looks a bit rough and ready, but his voice is cultured, polite.

He gestures to the little dog, which is making itself comfortable at his feet. 'This is Diggery.'

Finally, I find my voice. 'Hello, Diggery.' I bend down to scratch the dog's neck and he leans into my hand, delighted by the attention. 'I'm Fay. I'll get you a menu.'

'I don't need one. All I'd love is a bacon buttie,' he says with a grin. 'A great big one. I've been dreaming of it all morning. I've run out of bread *and* bacon on the boat, so I've been torturing myself.'

'It's not something we usually offer, but I've got some bacon in the fridge. Do you want it on brown or white?'

'White. With lots of ketchup. If you're going to be bad, you might as well be really bad.' His eyes twinkle.

'Tea or coffee?'

'A good mug of builder's tea.'

I don't tell him that our signature crockery is mismatched, delicate vintage china. If this guy wants a mug, he can have exactly that. I can see Lija watching closely, her steady gaze never leaving me.

'It'll be ready in a few minutes.'

As I move away, he kicks back, closing his eyes and letting the sun play on his face. My heart has stopped fluttering now, thank goodness. Unfortunately, it's moved into full-on pounding.

Ridiculously, my hands are actually shaking when I put the bacon under the grill. It's fair to say that we don't get many handsome strangers through our doors. Our day is normally filled with curmudgeonly pensioners or families with hyperactive children who try to pull the heads off all my flowers. Any day of the week, Danny Whateverhesaidhisnamewas makes a welcome change.

I make a mug of strong tea and find a bowl to take some water out for the little dog.

Danny takes his tea with a smile and I put down the bowl of water. Diggery wags his tail in thanks.

'That's kind,' he says.

'I'd love a dog,' I say. 'But, well ... '

I don't tell him that my mum can't stand pets in any shape or form and that I wasn't even allowed a goldfish as a child. Anthony, too, hates dogs, cats and kids. Not necessarily in that order.

'I wouldn't be without him,' Danny says. 'Would I, Digs?'

25

At that, the little dog abandons his drink and launches himself to sit on Danny's lap, and gets a big hug for his trouble. When the dog is sufficiently cuddled – lucky dog – he looks up at me again with those dark, mischievous eyes. 'Are you the owner of this place?'

'Yes – well, no ... sort of.' Stop gabbling, woman, you sound like a gibbering idiot. I take a breath. 'My mother owns the house, but I run the cake shop and café.'

'Pretty,' he says, taking in the garden. His gaze settles on me again and he smiles like a naughty schoolboy. 'And the garden.'

I flush to my hair roots. No one ever flirts with me. Especially not young, handsome men. Especially not when I'm wearing a big cardy.

His face softens when he sees my discomfiture. 'Sorry. I didn't mean to make you feel uncomfortable.'

'I'm fine,' I say. 'Absolutely fine.' Then I realise that I'm fanning my face with the menu.

'You've got a lot on here,' he notes. 'This is a big garden to manage. Do you have help?'

'No,' I admit. 'Not really. I do most of it myself.' Occasionally, if pushed, Anthony will run round with the lawn-mower. But more often than not it has to be done on Monday, when we're usually closed all day, and Anthony is at work. Alternatively, it's done in the evenings when, invariably, Anthony is playing golf. 'We're just gearing up for the season,' I explain. 'And we're a bit behind with our tasks, so we've got our work cut out.'

'Do you need a spare pair of hands?'

'Always,' I laugh.

'I'm serious,' he says. 'I'm looking for some casual work. I can turn my hand to most things. I'm not great with plants and flowers, but I can wield a hammer and a paintbrush. I can work a lawnmower and a strimmer.'

'Really?' Then I remember the bacon under the grill and go into a blind panic. 'Oh my God, the bacon! Let me get your sandwich, then we can talk about it more.'

As I'm dashing back to the kitchen, I think of all the little jobs that are stacking up. Danny could come in really useful for a few days. For a start, he could clear the leaves and branches. The lawn needs mowing, as always, though it's too wet at the moment, and perhaps he could put up those sunshades for me. I bought some nice, retro enamel signs last year too, adorned with catchy sayings, you know the kind of thing: *I don't want to fall in love, I want to fall in chocolate* and *keep calm and eat a cupcake*. Well, they've been sitting in a box ever since. He could put those up too. And there are a few bits of the fence that need repairing. Days could actually be weeks, if I can find the money. I could certainly keep his hands busy for a while. I don't mean that. Of course I don't. You know what I mean. There's plenty of work here to keep him occupied. That's what I mean.

As requested, I put lots of ketchup on his sandwich and take it back outside. Danny, obviously ravenous, bites into it. Diggery whimpers his desire for bacon too, and Danny tears off a morsel and feeds it to him.

'I could do with someone to do the heavier work in the garden,' I say. 'But I'm afraid I can't pay a lot.'

'Perhaps you could make up my wages in bacon butties,' he grins. 'This is great.'

'I certainly don't mind feeding you while you're here.'

'Sounds like a deal. When do I start?'

'Could you possibly stay around now to give us a hand? Lija and I have got a long list of things to do.' None of which is being done while I'm standing chatting. 'We want to do some baking later on if we can, so it would be great to leave you to it.'

27

'Baking? Hmm. I'll work for cake too,' he adds.

I see him eyeing Lija up and down. Why wouldn't he? She's young and beautiful. And, let's not beat about the bush here, so is he.

'That's Lija,' I tell him, following his gaze. 'She works here full-time too. Her cakes are beyond compare.'

He laughs at that. 'Then that's settled. You have a new handyman, Fay.'

'Great.' I'm still stunned at the speed of this. He seems to have morphed very quickly from customer into staff, but I don't think I should look a gift horse in the mouth. 'When you've finished your sandwich, perhaps you could help us finish cleaning down the tables.'

'I'm on it.' Danny wipes ketchup from the corner of his mouth with the back of his hand. 'What do I owe you for this?'

'Have this one on the house,' I tell him. Then I risk a smile. 'I'll make sure you earn it.'

'Thanks. I like the sound of that, Fay,' he says. 'I like the sound of it very much.'

Then he looks at me with those eyes that are so brown that they're almost black. They shine with sincerity and sparkle with mischief at the same time. My breath is in very great danger of being taken again.

'You won't regret this,' Danny says.

But, somewhere deep in the convoluted recesses of my very sensible mind, I wonder if I might.

Chapter Six

'Stinky Stan is here,' Lija says.

'Don't call him that,' I chide. 'It's not nice.'

'He stinks.'

'Only a bit,' I counter. 'He's a little musty, that's all. And when you're ninety-three, you'll smell a bit too. It's what old people do.'

'Then I will never get old,' is Lija's solution.

Conversely, I have a lot more in common with Stan than Lija as, rather too often, I feel old before my time. I'm not one of those young, trendy forty-odd-year-olds that you see on telly and in the glossy magazines. I'm not botoxed or fake-tanned. I've never had my teeth whitened. I'm a forty-one-year-old whom designer labels have passed by.

Sure enough, our most regular of regular customers, Stan Whitwell, is coming through the side gate as he always does at this time of day. Stan lives alone in one of the cottages along the lane that leads up to our house. It's a tiny, two-up-two-down place but it's very pretty, with roses round the door and a postage-stamp garden that Stan keeps filled with fragrant flowers.

'I'll make his lunch today,' I tell her. 'I just came to let you know that the man over there, Danny, is going to help us in the garden.'

She raises an eyebrow at that. 'He could be axe murderer.'

'I think he's OK,' I assure her. 'He seems nice enough.'

'You are too soft.'

'There's so much to do, Lija, and I can't manage.' In fact, the relief that washed over me when Danny said he could stay and help us was palpable. 'He was looking for casual work. I'll see how he does for a couple of days.'

She shrugs. 'Is your business.'

'Will you show him what needs doing?'

'Sure.'

'I'll send him down to you in a minute.'

He'll be fine in Lija's capable if somewhat surly hands, I think. Where lesser mortals might shrink from Lija's acid tongue, Danny Wilde looks as if he can handle himself. So I leave her and go back towards the house to greet Stan.

'Hello,' I say to him. 'How are you doing today?'

'Mustn't grumble,' Stan says.

Which he never does. Ever. I wish he'd give my mother lessons in never grumbling.

'What do you fancy for lunch?'

Stan comes here for his midday meal every single day without fail and has done since I first opened the café. He moved into his little cottage about ten years ago and we've been firm friends ever since. Now he's a customer too, which I can understand as, at his age, it must get harder to be bothered to cook for yourself.

Despite being the ripe old age of ninety-three, Stan's still very sprightly and has all his marbles. I only hope I do as well as I grow older. If Stan's having a bad day, he walks with a stick and sits on the veranda rather than taking on the challenge of the long garden. He has a cleaner who comes in for a few hours a week to keep on top of the housework in the cottage but other than that he's entirely self-sufficient. To be honest, it makes me cross when I think of how well Stan manages by himself compared to how useless my own perfectly capable mum has become. If she had cancer or some terrible illness then I'm sure I'd be a lot more sympathetic to her plight. But, for whatever reason, she's chosen to live like this. The reason she doesn't get out of bed is because she simply doesn't want to.

'Have you got any soup?' Stan asks. As he's a bit deaf, he talks quite loudly.

'A nice fresh tomato and basil.' I speak loudly back to him.

'My favourite,' he says, smacking his lips.

'Do you want to sit down by the canal today?' It's Stan's preferred spot too. Though he also has a penchant for sitting under the cherry trees.

'I'd very much like that.'

'We've just washed the tables. I can get Lija to put one down by the jetty for you. Are you sure you'll be warm enough?'

'I wore my thickest cardigan especially,' Stan says.

There's a hole in the elbow and some unspeakable stain down the front. It's buttoned up all wrong and I resist the urge to do it up properly.

'Look at this glorious sunshine.' Stan spreads his arms as if to embrace the day. 'It's lovely. Nowhere finer than this country when the sun shines.'

Stan was in the RAF for most of his life and he looks like he was. He may be a little bit crumpled and not quite so fragrant now, but he's still dapper. His white hair is swept back and held in place with Brylcreem. He has a bushy white moustache and a matching goatee beard that he trims neatly. His back might be bent, but he's still very sprightly and sharp as a tack. He's had an amazing life and, when I've got five minutes, I like to sit with him and hear of his adventures. Sometimes he reminds me of my dear dad, and I can't help but feel a little rush of affection for him.

On the veranda, Danny stands up and brushes the crumbs from his jeans. 'I can move the table for you, Fay.' I like the way he says my name in his lilting voice. 'You tell me which one.'

'Stan likes the pale green ones.' Needlessly, I point one out. I'm sure he can work out which colour pale green is. Get a grip, Fay. 'He likes to sit right down by the canal. If you put the table down by the blossom trees, there'll be a little bit of shelter from the breeze for him.'

'Danny's going to be helping us out, Stan,' I explain. 'Just for a few days.'

'Jolly good show,' Stan says and toddles off behind our new team member towards the bottom of the garden. Diggery bounds down to the canal and chases the ducks.

'Hello, lovely Lija!' Stan gives her a wave.

'Hello, Stan,' she replies.

I watch them for a moment, as does Lija. Danny takes Stan's elbow to steady him when the path runs out, and gets him a chair to sit on before he goes off to find the right-coloured table. Diggery, already bored with what the ducks have to offer, comes to sit at Stan's feet and Stan obligingly pets him.

'Hello, lad,' Stan says. 'You're a fine boy.' The dog's tail goes into ecstasy overdrive.

Stan had a cat until last year – a manky old thing that would scratch you as soon as look at you. I hated it because he used to jump over my wall and poo in the garden. The cat, not Stan. Now it's gone and is residing under a rose bush in Stan's back garden and, despite it being of evil temperament, I think Stan misses the company.

Disappearing back into the kitchen, I prepare Stan's soup. It's probably about time I took some up to Mum too, or she'll be banging on the ceiling. The smell of cooking bacon must have been driving her mad. For an invalid, she has a very healthy appetite.

I make up a nice tray for Stan with some piping-hot soup, just as he likes it, and a hunk of fresh, crusty bread that came out of the breadmaker this morning. He always has a cup of Earl Grey tea too, no milk, and a slice of whatever cake's on offer. But, if he's having soup, he likes a little gap of ten minutes or so to let it settle before he has his cup of tea.

Stan is nicely ensconced by the canal beneath the cherry trees. I head towards him with his soup, enjoying the spring warmth on my face.

'Here you go, Stan. I hope you like it.'

'I'm sure it will be as wonderful as always.'

Then, as I'm lowering the soup to the table, something catches my eye and I stop dead in my tracks.

There's a half-naked man in my garden.

Danny is moving one of the tables. Where Lija and I would lift one between us, he's carrying it by himself. And he's taken his top off. His T-shirt and jacket are discarded over the back of one of the chairs. I feel a gulp travel down my throat.

'Whoa there!' Stan says.

Turning, I see that I've nearly tipped Stan's soup in his lap. 'Sorry, sorry. So sorry.'

'No harm done,' Stan says.

'I was a bit distracted.'

Stan laughs. 'I can see that, dearie.'

I give Stan his cutlery and napkin, but my eyes keep straying across the garden to where Danny is. It's warm out today but really, it's not *that* warm. Shouldn't he be wearing something?

Eventually, he catches me staring at him. He looks over and gestures at his bare chest. 'You don't mind?'

'Er … I … er … I. No, no, no. No.'

33

Lija fixes me with a deadpan gaze. Stan is grinning like a Cheshire cat at my embarrassment.

'It's fine,' I assure him. 'Really.'

Danny grins at me. 'Cool.'

But I'm not cool. I'm hot. Very hot. And, more worryingly, so is he.

Chapter Seven

By the end of the day all the tables and chairs are scrubbed down and cleaned of their coating of algae. Danny has filled the green wheelie bin with piles of leaves and bagged up the rest ready for me to take to the tip in my car.

We've only had a few customers this afternoon, both pairs for afternoon tea. I settled them on the veranda by the French doors and they seemed to enjoy themselves. Two were ladies who looked like they were from the horsey set in the village and I don't think they'd been to us before, so I made an extra effort for them in the hope that they'll come back and tell their friends we're fabulous. The others were a retired couple who pop in every now and again, sometimes bringing their grandchildren, and I made a special fuss of them too.

Now they've gone, and Lija and I are in the kitchen trying out a new recipe she's concocted. It's a blueberry and lemon-curd cake that she's going to top with lemon icing, and it smells divine. She's made some very delicate pale yellow and lilac sugar-paste pansies to decorate it with. I love to watch Lija when she's baking. The disdainful expression she usually wears disappears completely, and it's the only time her features become animated, alive.

'You are staring,' she complains.

'I'm not. I'm just thinking how clever you are.'

She snorts. Lija doesn't do praise. Give it or take it.

'The cakes smell lovely,' I add.

We're both regarding the rich-looking beauties that she's just lifted out of the oven when Danny pops his head round the door.

'I'm done now,' he says.

'Come on in.' I beckon him inside.

'What about my boots?'

'They'll be fine. Give them a quick wipe on the mat. I'll be running the mop around soon.'

When Lija bakes, she does leave a lot of devastation in her wake. The cupboards and the floor all currently have a light coating of flour.

Danny comes in with Diggery at his heels. Danny lounges against the cupboards, arms crossed, boots crossed. At least he's wearing his T-shirt now. But it's tight and black and stretches across his chest, which I now know only too well is firmly muscled. Oh my. I'm going all jittery again. He seems to fill my entire kitchen even though he's standing in the corner by the kettle and isn't really taking up that much space at all. This is a big kitchen, a working kitchen, and yet his presence is disproportionately large. I don't quite know where to look. He's like the *Mona Lisa*: his dark eyes and his enigmatic smile seem to be following me everywhere.

'I just came to ask if you want me to drop in again tomorrow?'

'Yes, please.' I go to the drawer, take forty pounds out of my cashbox and hand it to him. 'We didn't settle on a rate, but is this OK?'

'It's too much,' he says. 'I only did a few bits and, besides, I'm already in debt for one bacon buttie.' He leaves me with ten pounds in my hand. 'I'll do it for thirty and a nice big slice of that cake.'

I laugh. 'It's a new one we're trying out. Lija's secret recipe.'

'Looks great.'

'Do you want to stay for a minute and have some now?'

'Most definitely.'

'You'll have to have it without the fancy decoration.'

'I can live with that.'

I cut him a slice and hand it to him on a plate. Lija makes a pot of tea and, when it's brewed, slams mugs down next to him and me.

Danny bites into his cake. He looks like a man with a healthy appetite. 'This is good,' he says. '*Seriously* good.'

Lija accepts his verdict impassively. It would be the same if she were found guilty of murder.

While Danny eats, Diggery tucks in close to his feet, hopeful of crumbs. Danny flicks a thumb towards the garden. 'The toilet door needs a new lock.'

We still have the original outdoor loo that was there from when the house was built. It's in a pair of ramshackle brick buildings and it was refitted about ten years ago. It's come in really handy for the café, as Mum would go spare if she had to have people traipsing inside to use the facilities. The old outhouse next to it is used for storage.

'You'll be needing a couple of new fence posts too. There are two, maybe three, that are rotten at the bottom.'

I'd forgotten about those, yet these are things that I've been wanting to get fixed for ages. I'm really pleased that Danny, for whatever reason, has arrived here at just the right time.

'Thank you,' I say. 'If you tell me what I need, I'll get them. It's nice to see the garden looking tidier already.'

Another deadpan look from Lija. She clearly thinks I'm flirting with him. I am *so* not.

37

'What are you doing here?' Lija asks.

I'm glad she has, as I'd never be so bold.

'Passing through?' she presses.

'I'm not sure,' Danny says with a shrug. 'I haven't had my boat for long. Six months, that's all. I'm still really trying out the lie of the land, getting a feel for it.'

'You're living on the canal?' I chip in.

'For now,' he says.

I thought as much.

'I've turned my back on the corporate life,' he continues. 'Seeing whether I like being a freelance vagabond.'

'And do you?' Lija again.

'So far, so good. I'm comfortable with *The Dreamcatcher* now. It's taken a bit of getting used to, but I think I'm there.'

'You're very brave,' I offer. 'I'd never have the nerve to do anything like that.'

'I was sort of forced into a corner,' he admits.

'Oh.'

'It's a long story. Come down to the boat one night and I'll tell you over a couple of bottles of vino collapso.'

'Oh.' The suggestion makes me flush.

'But it's all worked out well in the end,' he adds with a smile.

So rarely are we masters of our own destinies. Would I be doing this if it wasn't for Mum? Not that I don't like running the cake shop and café – I love it – but now I'm tied to it whether I want it or not. Sometimes you just have to fall into the things that life presents you with and make the best of them.

Danny finishes up his cake.

'Thanks,' he says. 'I'm outta here. I'll see you tomorrow. I'll be here about eight, if that works for you.'

'That's fine. I'm always up about six o'clock anyway as I like to get a few things done before I have to see to Mum.' I realise, too late, that my smile is weary. 'No rest for the wicked.'

'I'm planning on staying moored on your jetty while I'm here. Is that all right with you?'

'Yes. It's fine.'

'Have a good evening, ladies. Great cake, Lija.' He winks at her. 'Come on, Diggery.'

And, with that, he leaves. The dog trots along in his wake and both Lija and I watch Danny as he strides down the garden and jumps back on to his narrowboat.

There's something both unsettling and comforting about knowing he's right there at the bottom of the garden.

Lija wrinkles her nose. 'Trouble.'

'He's nice.' There's a warmth inside me that I don't really recognise. 'I like him.'

Her eyes meet mine. 'Trouble.'

Chapter Eight

When Lija goes home, speeding off on her bike along the tow-path, heedless of scattering dog walkers as she does, I turn my attention to making up Mum's evening tray. She likes something light for dinner. Tonight, she's got a little piece of home-made tomato quiche and a green salad on the side. I make sure all her tablets are accounted for, then I double- and triple-check that there's nothing she can find fault with.

I don't know quite when my mum became like this. We've never had the best of relationships, but she was never quite so critical, so judgemental as she is now. Her maternal streak has always been fairly well concealed, and I think it would be fair to say that I don't believe she found motherhood all it was cracked up to be. I guess not everyone does. I know as a mother that you're supposed to be overwhelmed with unconditional love for your kids, but there must be some who fall through the net.

Mum never neglected me or Edie, don't get me wrong. It's just that she was never a touchy-feely parent. If you fell over and wanted sympathy and a plaster, then it was always best to go to Dad.

Out of the two of us, Mum was always closer to my sister. I

think she found me too awkward, too shy. Edie was the outgoing one, the performer, always keen to entertain with a song or dance of some kind. The Drama Queen. I'm surprised she didn't end up on the stage.

I was more of a daddy's girl. Dad was quiet like me. We'd both sit on the sofa and he'd read to me. Or we'd go down to the canal and sit on the jetty, side by side, just watching the world go by for hours on end. Mum and Edie were the ones who wanted to be busy all the time. Which makes Mum's current situation even more difficult to understand. I just wish she'd get out of bed, go and join in with the things that go on in the village – the WI, the church, the sugarcraft guild, the flower-arranging club, the t'ai chi class. There's a whole world of entertainment right on her doorstep. There's plenty she could take part in, but she simply won't.

I climb the stairs, heavy of heart, carrying her tray. It doesn't do to think too much, or I get depressed.

She's propped up in bed, watching television. A couple of years ago, for her birthday, I had a nice flat-screen put in here for her. Before that she'd been using a clunky old portable and I wonder sometimes if perhaps I shouldn't have done it, as now she's more comfortable than ever. Maybe I have become her enabler. If I refused to cook her meals, bathe her, pander to her, would she be forced to get out of her imagined sickbed? She's robust in spirit – more than – but as she doesn't take any form of physical exercise, I can see her starting to waste away, her muscles slowly atrophying. Surely that can't be good for her heart? Yet the doctors seem to be able to do nothing more for her. They keep her topped up with pills, but other than that they've simply washed their hands. I suppose they think they have other, more worthy, cases to attend to.

As I'm virtually her only contact with the world, I pin on my smiley face and say brightly, 'Hi, Mum. Here's your dinner.'

41

It wouldn't do if I was miserable too.

'Thank you, Fay. That looks nice.' She turns off the television. 'Is it from a packet?'

'No, Mum. It's home-made.' Like she ever gets anything from a packet. 'What's on tonight? I've got a pile of ironing to do.'

'Nothing much,' Mum says. 'There never is.'

I fix her pillows so that she's comfortable with her tray across her lap.

'Will Anthony pop round?' she asks.

'Yes. Later, I expect.' He usually calls in during the evening at some point.

'It's about time that man made an honest woman of you.'

'Maybe one day.'

'You'll not get better, you know?'

'Anthony's a lovely man,' I agree. 'But ... well ... we're comfortable as we are.'

My mother harrumphs. 'Don't get *too* comfortable, Fay Merryweather. Men like a bit of spice.'

'Do they?' As if my mother knows anything about the ways of most men. My dad was utterly devoted to her and to the family. Besides, I don't think the relationship between Anthony amd me has ever had 'spice', so we're definitely not missing it now.

Then I try to stifle a yawn, but it burgeons forth anyway.

'This is what I mean, Fay. No one wants to come home to someone who looks like she's been dragged through a hedge and is yawning her head off.'

'Thanks, Mum. I've had a busy day.'

Maybe she feels as if she's been too mean as she softens slightly and asks, 'What have you been up to?'

It's not often that Mum wants to chat, but as she's in the mood I sit on the edge of her bed.

'Lija and I cleaned down all the garden furniture and then we tried out some new cake recipes.' Not the most riveting conversation, but it's the best I can offer. 'We had a nice young chap stop by, someone from the canal.' I don't know why I find myself talking about Danny, but I feel I need to. 'He's going to do a few odd jobs. Things that I can't manage.'

'This house is a burden,' Mum notes. 'It's too big. Too old.'

'It's lovely.' It always makes me panic when she starts talking like this: I fear she's going to want to sell it. 'I can't imagine living anywhere else. It's just that it's had no money spent on it for years and could do with a good spruce-up. The garden's starting to look great, though. The wisteria is amazing this year. You should come out one afternoon, see what we've done.'

'I can see it from the window, thank you very much.' She nods towards the canal. 'And that old heap of junk.'

The *Maid of Merryweather*.

'There's still plenty of life in her,' I counter. 'Dad would love it that I'm using her as a little cake shop. Don't you think?' Though I'm sure he'd be disappointed that she wasn't being used to her full potential.

'You always were a daddy's girl.'

'We were more alike, I suppose.'

She harrumphs at that too. 'All the pair of you ever wanted to do was fiddle with that thing.' Another nod towards the *Maid of Merryweather*. 'It was Edie who was my little princess.'

And I was always well aware of it.

Mum picks up her cutlery and turns the television back on.

That's our cosy chat ended then. 'Well,' I say, 'I'll leave you to it.'

'I'll have a cup of tea when you're ready.'

That means now. So when I get downstairs, I put the kettle on then take her back a cup of tea. This time she keeps her eyes firmly fixed on the television.

Chapter Nine

I have some quiche myself and then get out the ironing board, setting it up in the living room. The bulk of the ironing is bedding, followed by the pink gingham tablecloths for the dining-room and veranda tables. Next it's Anthony's shirts. He's very fastidious and likes me to wash and iron them for him as he says I make a better job of it than him.

Sad old spinster that I am, I record *Escape to the Country* every day. It's my guilty pleasure. I love looking at all the fabulous houses they visit, and the chubby-cheeked Jules Hudson is very easy on the eye too. It's not that I want to up-sticks and move. I *do* love this house. I've known nothing else. But when I look at these places with their swanky interiors and immaculate grounds and I can see a vision of how Canal House could be, given some tender loving care and with a serious wedge of cash thrown at it.

Cup of tea to hand, I start the ironing and let the pictures wash past my eyes. I put Anthony's shirts on hangers, fastening the top three buttons as he likes them. Then, just as the programme and my ironing are coming to an end, there's a familiar knock at the door and I go to let Anthony in.

We've been together for ten years now and, while I'm not sure that Anthony Bullmore is the love of my life, we're happy enough together.

Briefly he kisses my cheek and then breezes past me into the living room, just in time to catch the end credits of *Escape to the Country*.

'What a load of old tosh!' He rolls his eyes at the television.

Anthony and I met at a council planning meeting – the height of romance. The person who was supposed to be taking the minutes was ill and I was asked to step in at the last minute. We stood next to each other when the coffee was served at the end. I don't ever remember him formally asking me out, but we somehow went to dinner a few times and he took me to the theatre once or twice. After that we were a couple, by mutual yet unspoken agreement. We've carried on, without either of us questioning why, ever since.

'Daydreaming again, Fay?' he says as if it's a bad thing.

'Not really. I like looking at the houses, that's all.'

Anthony throws himself into his favourite armchair and loosens his tie. 'I've had a hell of a day,' he sighs. 'You would not believe it.'

My partner in life is a planning officer for the local council. According to Anthony it is the most taxing job on the planet, for which he rarely receives any credit and certainly not enough pay. Anthony – never Tony – believes that he's ambitious, driven. But he's forty-five years old now and isn't even in a senior role in his department. I think he may well have reached the pinnacle of his achievement, but I'm not going to tell him that and burst his bubble.

'Is there a cup of tea going?' He gets the remote and switches channel.

'I'll put the kettle on.'

Some people are old before their time, I think. Anthony is one of them. Me too, I expect. I can see him in years to come – not too many years – mowing the lawn while wearing a shirt and tie. Even when he comes round in the evenings, he's often still in his formal work clothes. Anthony is not a natural embracer of things casual. He's always in trousers and proper laced-up shoes. Jeans have never graced his person. A vision of Danny, long and lean with his jean-clad thighs, comes unbidden to my mind and a warmth rushes over me. Hot flush. Nothing more.

I pull my thoughts away and back on to the safer ground of Anthony. I think my partner should have been born in the 1940s. He would have been much more suited to that time.

He's not an unattractive man. I'd say he's average. Average looks. Average height. Mr Average. And nothing wrong with that. I'm quite probably Mrs Average too. That's why we work well together. His hair is brown and he wears it long at the front to hide his slightly receding hairline and his permanent frown.

He's a little heavier than he'd like to be – mainly due to eating lots of my cake – but he keeps himself fit by playing golf. Lots of golf. Every single weekend without fail, he plays golf. Saturday *and* Sunday. By the time he's popped into the club-house for a few sociable drinks, it's pretty much written off both days. He's currently angling to be captain of the golf club next year, and then I know I'll never see him. But it's an expensive club he belongs to and, well, he has to get his money's worth.

In addition to playing golf, Anthony is the organiser and conductor of our local handbell-ringing team, the Village Belles. Trust me, I know more about handbell-ringing than anyone should in a lifetime. Despite his repeated attempts to involve me in the heady world of handbell-ringing I've so far managed to resist. The Village Belles practise on one, if not two nights a week. Particularly if they've got a 'big' concert coming up, say at the church harvest festival or some such.

I try to be interested, I really do. But there's something about the noise of handbell-ringing that makes me want to tear bites of raw flesh out of people. Anthony finds it relaxing, but I'm afraid it does the complete opposite to me, inciting only a desire to commit murder in a particularly heinous way.

I take Anthony his tea and some of Lija's fresh chocolate tiramisu, as I think he'd turn his nose up at the lemon and blueberry loaf. Too faffed-about, he'd say.

'Thanks, Fay.' Anthony takes his cup and plate then turns back to the television. 'I want to get off early tonight.'

'Fine.' Should it bother me that I'd actually be quite pleased if Anthony just ate his tiramisu and went? I could squeeze in another *Escape to the Country* before bedtime then.

As I fold down the ironing board, I do wonder why we've never thought to move in together. Anthony has a house in Stony Stratford, which is a perfectly pleasant place to live. His home is a 1970s semi-detached residence and there's absolutely nothing wrong with it. But he likes his own space and there's never been a suggestion that I should move in there, he should come here, or that we should buy somewhere between us to live as a couple. I don't think Anthony's in any rush to disrupt his lifestyle. He likes to come and go as he pleases and, while I have Mum to think of, it suits me too.

It's a conversation we've never had and, if I'm honest, it would be really difficult for me now. What if he wanted me to go there? It would make no sense. I couldn't leave Mum to her own devices. How could I do it? I might be putting my life on hold for her, but what other option is there? Plus, in truth, it would break my heart to have to leave Canal House. I'd miss living by the water so much.

Instead, we trundle on as we are. Anthony comes round here on the nights when he's not bell-ringing or at the golf club. He can get nine holes in after work now that the nights are lighter.

When he does come, we rarely do much more than watch television. When we want some privacy to – well, you know – without Mum banging on the ceiling, we go to his house. Occasionally, Anthony cooks dinner for us there. But, now that I think of it, we haven't done that for a long, long time. And I mean a *long* time.

'We should go out one night,' I say to Anthony. 'Do something.'

Sometimes I feel as much tied to this house as my mother. I'm here day in, day out. 24/7.

He glances away from the screen. 'Like what?'

'I don't know.' But I give it some thought. 'We could see a film. Have a pizza afterwards.'

Anthony shrugs. 'If you like.'

I've got the bit between my teeth now. 'What about tomorrow night?'

'Extra ringing practice,' Anthony says. 'We've got the Canal Festival coming up soon.'

'Ah, yes.'

'I'm surprised you'd forgotten.'

'Me too.'

'We need to be note-perfect.'

'It is actually a couple of months away.'

'These things don't happen overnight.' Anthony puffs up his chest. 'We're the main event on the Saturday *and* the Sunday afternoon.'

God help us.

'It's quite a responsibility,' he continues. 'The ladies are going to get new blouses. White ones.'

'Don't they wear white ones now?'

'Yes,' Anthony says as if he's speaking to a small child. 'But these will be *new* white ones.'

In fairness, despite the handbell-ringing interludes, the

48

summer Canal Festival is a very popular affair, one of the highlights of the local calendar. It runs every year and there's a variety of stalls, offering crafts and different foods. There's also usually some very good music that doesn't make me want to kill people in a horribly bloodthirsty way.

Because so many visitors come along, it also brings a lot of business to the cake shop and we normally have a hectic weekend. It being England, we just have to start praying for sunshine now.

Anthony has finished his cake and puts down his cup. He does a mock-stretch, his signal that he's about to depart. After all this time, I know all his little foibles and rituals.

'Did you enjoy your tiramisu?'

'Great.'

'It's one of Lija's new recipes. We've put it on the menu just this week.'

'She has a talent, that girl,' is Anthony's view. 'Shame she's such an irascible character.'

Takes one to know one.

'You're looking tired,' I say.

'Yes. I'll be off.' Another stretch. 'Early night for me.'

He stands and comes to peck me on the cheek again.

'Are we still in love, Anthony?' I ask out of nowhere.

'What?' Anthony looks horrified. 'Of course we are.'

'I just wondered.'

'If this is about going to the cinema,' he says, 'we can go next week. I'm free on Tuesday, I think. I'd need to check the diary. We might need to start putting in some extra practice sessions. Our new member, Deborah, is having terrible trouble coming to grips with some of the tunes. "Congratulations" is a particular sticking point, and that's one of our crowd-pleasers.'

'It isn't about going to the cinema.'

'Then what is it about?'

49

'Nothing.' I'm not even sure I know, myself. 'Don't mind me.'

Anthony glances at his watch. 'I have a lot on tomorrow.'

What he means is that he doesn't want an argument. But then he should know that we never argue, as we never really discuss anything of great import.

'I'll see you tomorrow.'

'I'm playing golf after work,' Anthony says. 'Only nine holes, but I'll eat up at the club. That'll save you a job.'

'Right. Fine.'

He goes to the door. 'You are sure you're OK, Fay?'

'Yes. I'm probably just tired too.'

Mum bangs on the ceiling. She'll be wanting her bedtime cocoa.

'Coming!' I shout.

'I'd better leave you to it.' Another peck on the cheek. 'Bye, Miranda!' he shouts up the stairs.

Anthony turns and waves as he goes down the path. The only thing I can think is, if you were the girlfriend of someone like, say, Danny Wilde, would he be content with giving you the very briefest of brief good-night kisses?

Chapter Ten

I take Mum's cocoa up to her.

'How was Anthony?'

'Fine,' I say.

'He didn't pop up to see me. You know I like to say hello.'

'He wasn't really himself tonight.' He was *exactly* himself. 'I think he was tired. Lots on at work.' Then, from downstairs, I hear my mobile ting that I have a text. 'I'd better see who that is.' Though I can hazard a guess.

Sure enough, when I find my phone buried in the depths of the ironing basket, it's a message from Edie asking me to Skype her. It's ten o'clock here, so only teatime in New York. Have I the strength to speak to my sister tonight? In one way and another it seems to have been an unsettling day, though I can't quite put my finger on why.

I daren't tell Mum that it's Edie or she'll want to monopolise her. I also know what Edie can be like when she phones any time after lunch. Sometimes it isn't pretty.

So I sneak off downstairs and a few minutes later I'm sitting on the sofa with the laptop set up in front of me on the coffee table. Through the miracle of Skype, I connect with Edie. She's right up close to the screen and she's crying. Something I fully expected. Whenever I speak to my sister these days she's weepy. It breaks my heart.

I look as cheerful as I can. 'Hi, Edie.'

'You won't believe what he's done now,' she says without preamble.

My sister has always been a problem child. She was the one who, as a teenager, used to sneak out of the house to go drinking cider with the no-good lads at the bus shelter in the village. She was the one who was smoking – cigarettes and other substances – by the time she was fourteen. She was the one who had an extended Goth phase. My mum either turned a blind eye to it all or was in complete denial about the troublesome, troubled teenager she'd raised. How I missed my dad then. Edie needed his steady hand and I needed some guidance on how to deal with my rebellious sister. I think his death affected me and Edie differently.

He died unexpectedly of a heart attack when I had just turned twenty. Edie was on the brink of becoming a teenager then, and perhaps the blow was much more difficult for her to deal with. Plus with Dad's death we lost our buffer. He was the one who'd step in when Mum was being her most difficult. Without him, we faced the full force of her wrath. Me in particular.

People handle grief differently, don't they? Mum pretty much put her head in the sand and left me to deal with everything. She never talked about the good times they'd had or let us chat about him. Even now, when she mentions him, it's always to complain about some silly slight, often imagined. But they *did* have happy times, I'm sure. It seems as if she'd much rather dwell on their differences now. Mum always resented my close relationship with Dad, and when he went, she seemed to want to punish me more.

Eventually, despite my best efforts, Edie handled her grief by going off the rails. She slept with anyone who asked her and often left me to cover for her staying out all night. She drank too much, smoked too much, swore constantly and generally became a handful. It was only when she started work that things began to change. Thankfully. Though, even at the age of thirty-three, there are still glimpses of that tormented teen.

And me? How did I cope? I had to be there for Edie, to steer a steady course. I think I just retreated into myself and, quite possibly, have been there ever since. I don't like confrontation. I don't like to rock the boat.

I turn back to the screen, where Edie is swigging from a bottle of Bud. You'd never think we were sisters, she looks so different from me. She's tiny and waif-like and the Goth phase is long gone. The hand-cut, dyed-black, spiky crop has since grown into long auburn curls that tumble down her back, and her current style is designer chic. Everything must have a label. Perhaps she started dressing that way as she felt she had to compete in her top law firm. Armani, Gucci and Prada play havoc with her budget though. Champagne taste and beer money, Mum would say. If only she knew.

Once upon a time, Edie used to laugh easily. Now she's looking strained and there are mascara tracks on her face. My heart goes out to her.

'What's happened this time?' I ask, filled with trepidation.

'There's no need to be like that, Fay,' Edie whines. 'I know I can't compete with you and your perfect life.'

I'm not sure I'd view my life as 'perfect', but I let it go. 'I'm just asking, Edie. You're upset. You wanted me to call you.'

When she had just turned twenty-eight, and shortly before our mother took to her bed, Edie moved to the USA. Having flitted from office job to office job since she left college, she somehow landed herself a position as a PA in the New York branch of the law firm she'd been working for in London. It was a great job – a real step up from what she'd been doing previously – and I guess some fancy footwork somewhere must have secured her a green card.

It wasn't much later that it transpired she was in a relationship with one of the senior partners, whom she'd met when he was visiting the London office. Married, of course. I thought it wouldn't last, but here we are five years later and they're still together. Though, if you ask me, in the very loosest sense of the word.

'Brandon told me that he'll never leave his wife,' my sister spits. 'What do you think of that?'

I'm torn. Do I sympathise or do I give my sister a dose of reality? The truth of the matter is that Brandon Ryan was *never* going to leave his wife. He's been stringing Edie along for five years now. That's not the behaviour of a man who's in any rush to leave his marriage, is it?

'He's gone,' Edie says on a sob. 'Back to her. Leaving me alone.'

Every day after work, Brandon goes to see Edie. They have a few drinks, smoke pot, have sex, and then he goes home to his loving wife and children.

'I gave up everything for him.'

To be honest, I think their affair was a poorly guarded secret among their colleagues, but when one day they had a massive row about Brandon's wife slap bang in the middle of the office, Edie was summarily dismissed. No surprise that Brandon Ryan kept his job. That was six months ago and Edie hasn't worked since.

'You could get another job, Edie.'

'I've tried,' she sobs again. 'Really I have. But it's so hard. And Brandon needs me to be around. Everyone here works really long hours. What if I couldn't get home until seven, or even later? He couldn't come to visit me in the evenings then. I'd never see him.'

I do wonder how he manages to get away every evening, if

that's the case. And I don't think it would be a bad thing if he wasn't able to see her so easily, but I don't tell Edie that. If she was less accessible maybe the relationship would fizzle out. Maybe in a new job she'd meet someone else. Someone free, someone with less baggage.

Since she moved to New York, Brandon has helped to keep her in a small apartment in the Lower East Side of Manhattan. I've never visited her, but Edie tells me it's the size of a broom cupboard. It's still beyond affordable on the salary of a personal assistant, and now that she's not working, her lover is picking up the tab completely.

'Come home,' I say softly. 'Perhaps it's time to move on.'

'How can you say that? I love him.'

'You have your whole life on hold, just waiting for him.'

'What else can I do?'

'Come back just for a while,' I cajole. 'Until you get your head straight.' It also worries me that these days, every time I speak to Edie, there's a bottle in her hand. Some days her pupils are too dilated, her movements too animated.

'How can I?'

'I miss you,' I offer. 'Mum misses you.'

Edie tuts. 'Mum doesn't miss me. She wants another carer. If I came back I'd have to look after her, Fay. And I'm not you. I couldn't do it.'

'We could work something out.'

'She's so controlling, Fay. You know that. I escaped from her clutches once. There's no way I'm coming back.'

'Just for a holiday.'

'I don't even have the money for a flight,' she admits.

I wait while she cries some more.

'I rely on Brandon for everything now. He pays the rent, he gives me money for groceries. Everything I want, I have to ask him for.'

'Oh, sweetheart,' I say. 'You sound more like his prisoner than his lover.'

'It's all right for you, you've got Anthony.'

'It's not all plain sailing.' I don't tell her of the dark thoughts I've been having this very evening. 'No relationship is.'

'All we ever do is fuck,' she spits at me. 'We never go out anywhere in case someone Brandon's wife knows sees us together. I bet your whole relationship isn't based around sex.'

That's true, but then Anthony and I so rarely have the opportunity to make love at all. We've never been a hugely passionate couple – Anthony isn't exactly the most tactile of human beings. But I'm beginning to think that the frequency of our intimacy – or complete lack of it – should concern me.

'I'll send you the money for a plane ticket,' I tell Edie. I would be so happy if she was out of that relationship. It seems to bring her nothing but unhappiness. Anthony and I might not be swinging from the chandeliers every night, but we rub along together OK. 'Even a few weeks away from the situation might help you to think more clearly. I have some money saved to renovate the *Maid of Merryweather*. I can dip into that for you.'

'Oh, that goddamn boat,' she groans. As I said before, neither Mum nor Edie shares my enthusiasm for her. 'It just makes me remember how much I hate coming home. I can't bear that house, Fay. It's so shabby. And that smelly canal. I hate it. You and Dad were the only ones who loved that place and that old tub. New York is my home now. It's so vibrant, exciting. And Brandon is here.'

That makes my heart sink. I didn't even go away to university as I didn't want to leave here. Instead, I chose a college that was close enough for me to still live at home. And, for the record, the canal so does *not* smell.

'I don't know what else to suggest, Edie.'

I wish my sister and I had been closer as we'd been growing

56

up, but the eight years between us sometimes feels more like an unbreachable gulf than an age gap. I'm sure she sees me as a stuffy old fart, and sometimes I forget that she's a grown woman and not still a wild child.

'It'll work out fine,' Edie says with a bravado that she clearly doesn't feel. 'I have to keep hoping.' She waves her hand dismissively at the screen. 'He *will* leave his wife. I know it. He just has to wait until his kids are older.'

There'll always be something, I think. Some reason why it can't be now.

'I worry for you.'

'I shouldn't burden you with this.' Edie is maudlin. 'You've got enough on your plate.'

I'm worried about Mum, but I don't tell Edie. There might not have been a great deal wrong with her when she took to her bed, but I feel that, physically, she is beginning to weaken. A visit from Edie would be just the thing to perk her up.

'I've got to go,' Edie says.

'I love you,' I tell her. 'I want this to work out for you. I want you to be happy again.'

Edie softens. 'Love you too, sis. I miss you. You should come out here sometime. I'd love to show you my New York.'

'I will,' I promise.

But I know, in my heart, that there's as much chance of that as there is of Edie coming home to look after Mum. Perhaps I'm as much a prisoner as she is.

Chapter Eleven

I didn't sleep well last night as I was worrying about Edie. I tossed and turned until first light. I'd love to be able to do more to help, but I'm not sure I can.

It's too early to wake Mum. She complains that it's a long day if she's roused before eight. So, when I've finished a quick bite of breakfast, I wrap the fresh cakes that Lija made yesterday in cellophane packaging, adding a bright ribbon and a handwritten label. Then I trundle down to the *Maid of Merryweather* to stock up our shelves. The morning is fresh, with a playful wind in the air. The trees rustle restlessly.

Sliding back the side hatch, I let the breeze freshen the air inside. During all our rain, the window has been leaking and I think the sealant – which has been on the way out for some time – has finally gone. Another job to add to the growing list. It will want taking out and replacing before the winter.

Gazing out of the window, I watch the ripples on the water whipped by the wind. A couple of ducks swim by, pausing to see if there's any bread going today, but I didn't bring anything spare with me. Disappointed, and with a slightly disgruntled quack, they swim on.

I always feel closer to Dad when I'm on the barge, and I wonder what he'd think of Edie's current situation. Perhaps he'd be unhappy that neither of his girls is married and settled down with a family of her own. I know he'd have loved to have had grandchildren and would have been a wonderful grandfather.

Out of the breeze, it's pleasantly warm this morning and, though I'm wearing my trusty cardigan, I'm pretty sure I don't need it. As it's early, there's still a hint of mist hanging over the water, but it will soon be gone. A pair of swans glide along majestically, peering quizzically at me as they go by. How can anyone not enjoy this?

I move away from the hatch and organise the cakes. Then I flick a duster around the galley, which houses the jars of jam and chutney on its shelves. We're getting low on those too; Lija and I should make a batch. Soon it will be time to start making lemonade again and I must make an overdue trip to the wholesaler before we're caught on the hop. Business is starting to pick up for the season now and soon there'll be more regular callers to the *Maid of Merryweather*, people who live on the boats moored nearby, who like to stock up on cakes or jam. Then there'll be the visitors on the hire boats who want something for their afternoon tea or to take home a little souvenir from their time on the canal. It will keep us busy now right through to October.

I have to admit that my dear dad's narrowboat is looking a little worn. She needs to come out of the water soon and have her hull repainted with blacking to stop it rusting, but it's an expense I can do without. There's not enough money yet in my fund to do any major work. I'd love to get this boat going again one day. Although she brings in some money now rather than costing me, and it's a great use of the space, I still feel so sad that she's nothing more than a floating shop. The *Maid of Merryweather* deserves better than this.

Once, I thought her renovation was something Anthony and I might do as a project together, but he's completely hopeless with a hammer or a drill or a paintbrush. Despite living by the canal, I haven't actually been out on a boat in years, and I do miss it. Sitting here on the *Maid of Merryweather* is the closest I get. Sometimes I really wish Anthony shared my dream of languid afternoons on the water, but he doesn't. I can't say I haven't tried, though. We once hired a boat for a week, some years ago now. But instead of it being a relaxing experience, he found driving the barge and working the locks far too stressful. The windlass became his sworn enemy. Anthony likes to be in control and I think he was well outside his comfort zone. But here I am, forever hoping that in time he might grow to love it.

While I'm daydreaming, I see Diggery with his smart neckerchief jump over the side of Danny's boat, *The Dreamcatcher*, and come trotting down the jetty towards the garden. I go out into the well deck. When the dog reaches the *Maid of Merryweather* he stops and wags his tail, waiting to be petted. It seems as if I'm already a firm friend.

I lean over to stroke him. 'Hello, Diggery.'

Following in his wake is Danny.

'Hey,' he says. 'Morning, Fay. Looks like it's going to be a great day.'

'Yes.'

'I like the boat.'

'Come and have a look on board. It's where my business started, really.'

I move out of the well deck so that Danny can climb on board. He squeezes inside the cabin.

'It's great,' he says, taking in my little shop. 'Very enterprising.'

'Needs must,' I say. 'It was either this or face the prospect of selling her. I couldn't have done that. She was my dad's pride and joy.'

'I'm not surprised.'

'She's a shadow of her old self,' I admit. 'The engine doesn't even run now and, much like the house, the list of necessary repairs is growing daily.' I stroke the warm oak of her fittings fondly. 'I'll do them one day, though.'

'I have no doubt about it,' he says.

That makes me smile. 'Then you have more faith in me than I do myself.'

'If I can do anything to help . . .'

'Thanks. That's very kind of you. She means a lot to me. Dad would have loved to live on the canal like you do.'

'I can highly recommend it.'

I sigh, reluctant to leave this little oasis of peace. 'I'd better get back to the house. Mum will probably be awake by now.'

'Give me a list and I'll crack on. I saw some trellis yesterday that needed mending. Looks like the wind's given it a battering over the winter.'

'Come up to the kitchen. I'll put the kettle on and then we can have a look round the garden and see what else needs to be done. Have you had breakfast?'

'Yeah,' he says. 'I'm good.'

He climbs out of the well deck and on to the jetty. He holds out his hand and I take it. The strength and warmth of his grip shouldn't surprise me, but it does.

We fall into step together and walk up to the house. Once he's had a cursory bark at some ducks, Diggery joins us.

When I open the back door, Mum's banging away on the ceiling. 'Fay! Fay!'

'Coming! Coming!' I shout back as I grab her breakfast tray, which I've already prepared.

'Need a hand?' Danny asks.

'No. This is my daily routine. I won't be a minute,' I say over my shoulder to him. 'She gets fractious when she's hungry.'

'Shall I make a brew while you're gone?'

'Yes. Marvellous idea. Put some toast in too, if you don't mind. I could do with another slice.'

I make a noise as I go up the stairs, so that Mum knows that I'm coming.

'Who were you talking to?' she asks as I go into the fuggy air of the bedroom.

She's already sitting up, so I put the tray across her lap. Then I go to draw back the curtains. The thin grey line of the canal meanders by, sparkling in the sunshine, and I open the window to let in some of the fresh morning air.

'Not too wide,' Mum scolds. 'I don't want to catch my death of cold.'

'It's lovely out there,' I tell her. 'It's a beautiful day.'

'Well,' she says. 'Who was it?'

'Oh. That was Danny. The man I told you about yesterday. He's going to do some more jobs for me in the garden.'

She peers at me closely. 'I thought I heard voices last night after Anthony had gone. Was that this chap too?'

'Of course that wasn't him,' I assure her. 'It was Edie. I talked to her last night on Skype.'

'Oh, why didn't you tell me? You are hopeless, Fay. I want to talk to her. I do miss my child.'

'She couldn't stay for long. You know what she's like – places to go, people to see. But she sends her love and I'm sure she'll call again soon.'

I have to nag Edie to speak to Mum as she avoids doing it at all costs.

'She has a very demanding job,' Mum says proudly.

'Yes.' Mum doesn't know that Edie hasn't worked for months now. She doesn't know that she doesn't have any money of her own or that she has a lover who is married and is unkind to her. She thinks Edie's life is a bed of roses.

62

'I asked her if she'd like to come home for a holiday.'

'Oh, I do wish she would. Last time we spoke she said she was going to the Sea Shells.'

'Seychelles,' I correct. 'I don't think that happened.' Mainly because Brandon couldn't give his wife a suitable excuse for a prolonged absence, I assumed. 'She sounded like she needed a break.'

That's the closest I'll ever get to telling Mum the truth.

'That's the trouble when you're a high-flyer. She's always been ambitious, has my Edie.' Then a sob catches in her voice. 'This place was always going to be too small to hold her.'

'Don't upset yourself,' I say softly to Mum. 'You know she'd come home in a heartbeat if she could.' The white lie trips too easily from my tongue. But what else can I do? Tell her that her favoured daughter doesn't actually give a flying fuck? Now I sound like Lija. 'Have your tea and toast. It'll make you feel better.'

I also don't say that if she were to get out of bed, she could get on a plane and go to see Edie. But then the reality of Edie's life would be exposed, and that would never do. Perhaps Mum is better living in blissful ignorance.

'I'd better get on.'

'Don't forget my elevenses!' she warns.

'I never do, Mum,' I reply. I am possibly the most steadfast and reliable person there is. Sometimes, I don't think that's a good thing.

Chapter Twelve

Before I go back into the kitchen, I take care to wipe the weary expression from my face.

Still, as soon as he hears me, Danny says, 'Sit down. I've made us tea.'

I sigh. 'Life saver.' I sit down at the kitchen table and Danny sits opposite. He pushes a plate of hot buttered toast between us.

'Your mum's ill?'

How do I explain this one? 'She's bedridden.' That will suffice. Danny's a stranger here and doesn't need to know the complications of my life. 'I'm her full-time carer now.'

'That must be hard.'

'I'm used to it, I suppose. I've done it for a while. It's one of the reasons why I run the cake shop and café here. It means I can work from home.'

'This is a fantastic house. No wonder you love it so much.'

'I do. I can't ever see myself leaving here. It's the only home I've known. I'm just glad I've been able to organise it so that I can look after Mum here.'

'What's wrong with her?'

'Well ...' I say. 'That's the hard bit.'

'It's none of my business,' he says, holding up a hand. 'I don't mean to pry into your personal life. You don't need to tell me.'

But suddenly it seems like a good idea to share this with someone else. 'Nothing much really,' I admit sadly. I keep my voice low so Mum doesn't hear me. 'She had a bout of pneumonia a few years ago and then broke her hip. Afterwards, she just decided to stay in bed. Now she refuses to get out at all, except to go to the bathroom. She won't even come downstairs any more.'

'That's tough on you.'

'And on her. I've done all I can to persuade her, but she's a very stubborn lady. She's been up there for so long that I'm worried that her health really is failing now. It can't be good for anyone to be trapped indoors all the time.'

Danny shakes his head. 'That's tragic. Particularly when she's got all this on her doorstep.' He gestures out to the garden and the water beyond. 'The one thing I love most about living on the canal is that I'm out in the fresh air every day no matter what the weather is. I don't think I could ever go back to the corporate life now and spend all my time cooped up in an office.'

'You said you'd tell me the story over a bottle of wine one night.'

'So I did.' Danny grins. 'I'll have to see when I can fit you into my busy social calendar.' He looks down at Diggery. 'When are we free, Digs?'

The dog cocks an ear and barks.

'He says any night of the week will suit.'

'Not tonight,' I tell him. 'Anthony's coming over,' I rush on. 'He does most nights.' I flush when I say that.

'Your boyfriend?'

'Hardly a boyfriend at my age!' I laugh. 'He's my partner.'

'A long time?'

'Ten years.'

'Wow. I haven't had a relationship that lasted more than six months.'

'You're young,' I say.

He smiles at that. 'You're not so very old yourself.'

'And you're footloose, whereas I'm not.'

For some stupid reason tears prickle behind my eyes and I quickly force them away. I turn from Danny's gaze.

He focuses it on the now-empty plate between us and looks longingly at that.

'Between us we've snaffled all the toast, Fay Merryweather, and I'd already had my breakfast. No excuse to linger.' He pushes away from the table and stands. 'Well, if not tonight, then consider it an open invitation to drinks and canapés on *The Dreamcatcher*. Just let me know and I can chill the cheap white wine.'

I grin back at him. 'I will.'

He rubs his hands together. 'I can hear power tools calling. Want to come and show me what you'd like me to do today?'

'You just go and make a start. There's a lot to choose from.'

'I'll see what I can do with that trellis first.'

'Yes, good idea. I'll sort the kitchen out and put some scones in the oven, then I'll come out and make a list of things to do.'

'Don't forget to put an extra scone in for me. I'm looking forward to eating my wages already.' He winks at me and then strides out of the door, whistling for Diggery as he goes.

I watch him until he's halfway down the garden and then tear my eyes away from him. I do hope he keeps his T-shirt on today. Flustered, I tidy up our mugs and the plate.

I'm not sure how wise it would be for me to go for a drink on Danny's boat. I'd love to see it, of course. But, well. Well. I don't think Anthony would like it. I don't think Anthony would like it at all.

Chapter Thirteen

Lija glowers at me. 'You take lunch to Hottie Man. I will look after Stinky Stan.'

'Don't call him that, Lija.'

'Hottie Man or Stinky Stan?'

'Both.'

Shortly after ten, the sun came out in full force. Shortly after five minutes past ten, Danny took his T-shirt off again.

It's disconcerting having a half-naked man in my café garden. Even more disconcerting that I'm aware of it. I know my eyes have been drawn to him all morning. I feel like one of those women in the Coca-Cola adverts who can't concentrate because of the undressed gentleman mowing the lawn, cleaning the windows, doing whatever it is he does.

'No, no,' I say now. 'You take it to him.'

We have a few moments of push-and-pull over the plate of cheese and salad sandwiches that I've made for him. Because I am older and wiser, I win. I put my hands behind my back and Lija is left holding the sandwiches.

'Take him a slice of your cake too,' I instruct her.

'Take yourself.' She plonks the sandwiches on the table and

swipes up Stan's soup. Carrot and coriander today. Not his favourite.

Lija flounces out ahead of me. I sigh and pick up the sandwiches for Danny.

'Hello, Stan,' I say as I pass the table. 'Are you fit and well today?'

'Absolutely champion, my dear.'

'Carrot and coriander all right for you?'

'Lovely,' he says. 'My favourite.'

In the end, I didn't find the time to go out to tell Danny what needed doing. He just got on with it. This morning alone he mended the trellis, then he found the strimmer in the back of the garage and, before the first customer arrived, had cut back all the edges of the lawn where the grass had grown tall against the fence. Then he pruned some of the dead wood from the cherry trees. I have no idea if this is the right time of year to do that, but like everything else in this garden, they have to thrive on a certain amount of affectionate neglect.

Now he's stacking the branches behind the shed, and I remember that I've got a little-used fire pit somewhere in the garage. It would be nice if we had some warm evenings this year when Anthony and I could light a fire and sit out under the stars. Something else we haven't done for a very long time.

As I approach, Danny stops working and wipes the sweat from his brow. I'm not sure where to look at all. He's very toned. The only body I've seen since I was about thirty is Anthony's, who is a little bit white and squishy under his shirt. Danny's stomach is firm, muscled and, oh my word, I do believe that's a six-pack. I can't say I've ever seen one in the flesh before.

He pours water from a bottle over his hands and gives them a shake-down, then takes the proffered sandwiches.

'This is marvellous service,' he says as he bites into one. 'I'm not going to go hungry while I work for you. There are great perks to this job.'

For me too, I think.

He sits in the shade of the cherry tree, folding himself down next to the snoozing Diggery, who's already retreated from the sun. The temperature is still rising steadily and it looks as if it will be a glorious spring afternoon.

Danny puts his hands across his eyes and looks up. 'Join me.'

'I can't,' I say. 'Things to do. I need to have a quick word with Stan too.'

'He seems like a great old boy.'

'He is. Stan's ninety-three years young and he's seen a lot of the world. He sees a lot of this café too,' I add. 'He's one of our neighbours.' I nod towards Stan's house down the lane. 'He lives in one of the little cottages. Every day he comes for his lunch.'

'I'd love a long chat with him. You know, if you don't want to come to see *The Dreamcatcher* by yourself, bring Stan along with you. That'd be cool.'

'Oh, it's not that.'

'I just thought you seemed a bit reluctant.'

He's right. But why *am* I frightened to talk to this man? Why does the thought of being alone with him on his barge terrify me so much? He's only trying to be friendly and I'm being completely ridiculous. Living on the canal is a very social existence in one way and yet, if you're a traveller, you rarely see the same people and it must be hard to strike up more than superficial acquaintances.

'I *will* come,' I promise. 'Tomorrow night.'

He smiles up at me. 'Good.'

'If I can get someone to sit with my mum, that is.'

'You'll be at the end of the garden,' he reminds me. His head flicks towards *The Dreamcatcher*. 'If she needs anything, you can be home in less than two minutes.'

69

'Of course.' I'm so bound to the house that sometimes I forget that I *can* actually go out. 'Shall we say a time?'

'Come whenever you're ready. I'm going nowhere.' There seems to be some sort of challenge in his eyes as he says this. 'The dress code is informal.'

'I'll leave my tiara in the wardrobe then.' I throw a thumb back towards the other side of the garden. 'I'd better see to Stan.'

'OK. Thanks again for the lunch, Fay.'

'You're welcome.' My heart is pitter-pattering as I turn away.

Stan has finished his soup as I reach his table. Some of it is down the front of his cardigan.

'Stan,' I say. 'You've dribbled.'

He picks up his napkin and mops himself with it. 'I'm a silly old fool. I'm getting doddery in my old age.'

'Nonsense,' I say. 'You could run rings round someone half your age.'

'You think?' Stan raises an eyebrow. 'I'm not sure I could take on that new young man of yours in an arm-wrestling contest.'

I glance back towards Danny. He's demolished his sandwiches and is now reclining, eyes shut, hand resting gently on Diggery's fur. I'm not a photographer by any stretch of the imagination but, if I had a camera or phone with me, that would make a lovely shot.

'Very few could, I think.' His shoulders, his arms are well defined too. I tear myself away from the merits of Danny Wilde's body and back to the conversation in hand. 'It's good to have some help. I can't keep on top of the jobs, Stan.'

'That mother of yours runs you ragged.'

'She does indeed. Danny couldn't have dropped in at a better time.'

'He's certainly put a sparkle in your eyes,' Stan observes.

I laugh. 'Go on with you. He's done no such thing.'

As we sit there, I see Lija come out of the kitchen with a piece of cake and a mug of tea. She takes them down to Danny, and I watch as he rouses and sits up at her approach. Obviously, I can't hear what he's saying, but I can imagine – all too well – the cheeky Irish charm. Soon they're laughing together, and Lija does not laugh often. In fact, she sees it as an infringement of her human rights if she's forced to laugh.

'Hmm,' Stan notes as he watches them together. 'Looks like you're not the only one.'

I feel a pinch of jealousy. Lija's twenty-five, much closer to Danny's age than me. And she's determinedly single. Yet he has such an easy manner and charisma that, clearly, any woman falls for his chat. I didn't think Lija was so impressionable. Looks as if I was wrong.

Chapter Fourteen

Anthony phones me. 'The ladies have asked for an extra practice tonight,' he tells me. 'I'm going to go straight to the village hall from the golf club.'

'Oh. Then I won't see you.' I don't know why, but I suddenly feel as if I need to be with Anthony. I feel all off-balance at the moment.

'No. But I'll see you tomorrow night.'

'I'm going out tomorrow.' It leaves my mouth before I even think of it. Now I'm committed.

It's Anthony's turn to say, 'Oh.'

'I'm only going along to Danny's narrowboat.'

'Danny?'

'The lad who's doing some odd jobs for me. I'm sure I mentioned him.'

'I don't think you did.'

'Stan's coming along too.' I blush at my lie. I didn't even mention it to Stan. Besides, he won't want to go out in the evening. He likes to settle down with a book after his tea. What am I thinking of? 'I'm sure you could come along too, if you wanted to.'

'Don't let me spoil the party,' Anthony says in a slightly petulant manner.

'I know, why don't I come along to the practice tonight?' I say to placate him.

I want to make up for having too many images of Danny Wilde's toned torso playing behind my eyes. Anthony is a good partner. He's strong, solid, reliable. I should appreciate those qualities more. So what if he has a slightly squashy tum? I'm never going to be mistaken for an élite athlete myself. He might not make me laugh any more, and there's never been a twinkle in Anthony's eyes, but then life isn't all ha-ha-hee-hee.

'You never come to the practice,' he says.

That's primarily because I can't stand the sound of handbell-ringing.

'It's probably time I did, then.'

'Well,' he replies. 'If you really want to.'

I can't say that he sounds overenthusiastic at the thought of my presence. Perhaps he thinks I'll cramp his style.

'Shall I come along about eight?'

'What about your mother?'

'I'll see if she'll be all right for an hour. I should make time for myself. For us.'

'Right.' Anthony sounds mollified. 'I'll see you later.'

I hang up and wonder if Mum's got any spare Valium in the medicine cabinet that I can take.

The village hall always smells of damp. I think it has issues with its drains, roof and many other things. It's small and in need of a coat of paint and has a parquet floor that looks as if it's the original one from when the place was built in the 1920s.

Yet to watch Anthony, you'd think he was in the Royal Albert Hall. Bless him. The Village Belles are already assembled and wait his command with bated breath. He taps his conductor's rostrum with his baton.

'Are we ready, ladies?'

The ladies in question – all of a certain age – stand looking expectantly at my other half from behind a table, bells poised in front of them. Bar one, they're all slightly chubby and have either cropped grey hair or the sort of tight pin curls last seen in fashion in the 1950s. They're all wearing white gloves, except for the one who isn't chubby and grey. She's sporting a fuchsia-pink pair.

Since I'm watching through the glass in the door, I could at this point creep away and no one would ever know that I was there. Instead, vowing to be a supportive partner, I try to sneak in without being noticed. Unfortunately, the door creaks in my wake. Anthony turns round.

'Hello, darling,' he says with a smile. 'Good of you to join us.'

'Sorry I'm late.' By way of explanation, I roll my eyes and say, 'Mum.'

'Not to worry, you've only missed our warm-up. We're just about to get to our practice proper.'

'Hi.' I wave sheepishly to the ladies. They're all rather *keen* on Anthony and I feel as if I'm intruding on their turf.

'Hello,' they say back, a little hesitantly.

'You don't know our new member, Deborah,' Anthony says.

The one with the fuchsia-pink gloves gives me a little wave.

'Hello, Deborah.' She's a well-kept blonde in her early fifties and certainly looks more glamorous than the rest of the ladies. Her fuchsia-pink lipstick matches her gloves. I wonder what the appeal of the hideous hand bells is to her. I also wonder whether she's ever a Debbie or a Debs and not a Deborah.

Anthony taps his rostrum again. I take a chair behind him against the far wall of the hall, careful to be as out of the way as possible, and settle down for my torture.

'Ready, ladies? We'll go straight into "Congratulations" for Deborah.' Anthony smiles indulgently at her. 'Never fear, my dear, we'll crack this for you.'

'Thank you, Anthony,' she breathes.

'Bells against your chest. Nicely vertical. And, here we go. One, two. One, two.'

The familiar jangling tones ring out. I have heard this sound too many times in my life and it always grates on me. But I am Anthony's partner in life, his loved one, and as such I should support him in this. Even though it's as appealing to me as the sound of nails being scraped down a blackboard or the screech of a courting cat. I sit on my hands so that I'm not tempted to claw my own face or rip my eyes out.

Anthony, conversely, is in his element.

'Softly, softly,' he intones. 'Let's tease them. Tease them.'

The ladies clang away. Almost in unison. Two verses in and already my ears feel as if they're bleeding. Who on earth devised this horrible form of music?

'Now build. Crescendo. *Crescendo*. And reach. Reach and circle back. Reach and circle back. Reach! Reach!'

I want to reach, but not in the same way that Anthony means.

'Build it. Build it. Yes. Oh, yes.'

I've never particularly liked this song – sorry, Sir Cliff – it always reminds me now of wet days at Wimbledon. Yet I still hate to witness it being murdered so cruelly. Anthony and his ladies are definitely not ringing my bell.

'Kick out with those bells!' Anthony is experiencing a moment of ecstasy. 'Yes! Yes! Yes!'

He waves his baton with a final flourish and, thank goodness, the bells fall silent. I could jump up and cheer for that alone.

The ladies are giddy with success.

'Well done, Deborah.' Anthony wipes a little anxious bead of sweat from his brow. 'You got through it.'

Deborah is fuchsia-pink-cheeked with pride.

'Well done, all of you. We will *storm* the Canal Festival with that rendition.' Anthony is flush-faced and bright-eyed with excitement. 'Now we'll try "My Heart Will Go On".'

Not if I came back and sprayed you all with bullets from an Uzi 9mm sub-machine gun you wouldn't, I think.

'Bells ready!'

I sneak a surreptitious glance at my watch and wonder when I can go home.

Chapter Fifteen

Though I've left Mum alone for two hours, she seems to have suffered no ills. She looks a little pale, I think, but she's sitting up in bed watching television when I take up her cocoa. The freshly baked cookies I left for her have all gone.

'How was Anthony's rehearsal?' she asks as she sips at her bedtime drink.

'Great.'

'He's so clever, that boy.'

'Yes.'

'You should snap that one up, you know, Fay. At your age there won't be many more chances for happiness.'

'No.' She's right, of course, yet the thought of it makes me feel chilled inside.

Perhaps it's because I've just come back from that mind-numbing rehearsal that made me want to eat my own eyeballs, but sometimes I look at Anthony and wonder why we're together. Is he the love of my life? Or are we in this relationship purely out of habit? I contemplate my parents' marriage and wonder whether they were blissfully happy together. Are many people? They were never lovey-dovey, but they didn't fight like cat and dog either. Is love really just a matter of finding some-one you can mostly rub along with? I've never yearned for a love life that's full of fireworks and high drama. I know I'd hate to have a relationship like Edie's, which always seems so angst-ridden, the lows far more common than the highs. Anthony and I bimble along together. And that's fine by me.

Bimbling is good.

I think.

When Mum's finished, I take her cup and tidy her plate on to the tray ready to carry downstairs. She snuggles down in the bed and I tuck her in as you would a child. I kiss her forehead and smooth her hair.

'Don't fuss.' She bats my hand away.

'I love you,' I tell her. 'I want you to be comfortable. Are you sure you're all right?'

'I'm fine,' she says. 'Just tired.'

'Good-night, Mum.'

She turns over in bed.

I pick up her tray and head for the door. Then, before I leave, I turn back. 'Did you love Dad?'

Her head snaps up from the pillow. 'What sort of a question is that?'

'I don't know. Were you happy together?'

'We were married for over forty years.'

'But were you happy?'

'What's that got to do with anything?'

'Nothing.' I wonder whether it is possible to stay delirious and in love when you've been together for a long time. 'Good-night, Mum.'

I should go to bed myself, but I can't settle. Instead, I make a mug of hot chocolate, take two cookies from the tin and, shrug-ging on my cardigan, go out into the garden. It's a mild evening.

The sky has darkened to indigo and a few grey cotton-wool clouds obscure the stars. Away from the night-time glow of the city, we suffer from very little light pollution here and I love star-gazing – another thing I used to do with Dad. I pull my cardy around me and head for the jetty.

Sitting on the wooden boards, I put my back against the grassy bank and, while I sip my rich chocolate, I think about this evening. If I'm really honest, Anthony seemed like an alien being to me. I've known him for so long, and yet I think I know him so little. I'm not sure he knows who I am, either.

The feeling of my hands around the warm mug is soothing and I hear myself sigh as I start to relax. What is there in life that a hit of chocolatey sweetness can't solve? There's a slight breeze teasing the leaves in the trees and I hear the hoot of an owl, but other than that, all is quiet on the canal. Occasionally, the moon peeps out from behind the clouds and dances on the water.

Further down the jetty, I look to where *The Dreamcatcher* is moored. The lights are on inside, shining out invitingly into the night. When I focus, I can hear the gentle hum of the generator in the stillness.

A second later, I hear a thump and out of the darkness comes the squat shape of Diggery, trotting towards me. He comes to nuzzle my lap.

'Hey, Diggery,' I say, ruffling his fur. 'Come to see what I'm doing?'

His tail wags against my leg. I should get a little dog, it would be company for me. Then it occurs to me: I have a partner, a sister, a mother who need me, and yet I'm lonely.

'I'm feeling sorry for myself, that's what,' I tell Diggery. He sits up and looks at me, head cocked. 'Want a little piece of my biscuit?'

I'll swear that he nods. So I break off a bit of cookie. His jaws snap down on it enthusiastically, nearly taking my finger with them. He shuffles expectantly.

'Do you think that's the key to happiness, eh?' I ask his hopeful face. 'A faithful hound who'll love you whatever?'

The sound of Danny's voice pierces my musings.

'Diggery! Digs! Where are you, boy? Diggery!'

'He's here,' I call back. 'Just come to say hello.'

I hear the echoing thump of Danny's boots on the jetty and my heart starts to thump too.

'I'm feeding him biscuit,' I confess as Danny comes towards me. 'Just a little.'

'No wonder you're his new best friend.' Danny sits down next to me and strokes Diggery, who is then content to wriggle in between us and doze with his head on his paws. 'Nice night.'

'Yes.'

'Though you do look like you have the weight of the world on your shoulders.'

'I couldn't settle,' I confess. 'Too much going through my mind. I thought I'd come out here for a while. I love just sitting and staring at the canal, the stars.' I shiver. 'Though I am getting a bit cold now.'

'Come back to *The Dreamcatcher*. I have a wood burner, central heating and everything. All mod cons. It's toasty in there.'

'It's very tempting,' I say, noticing that he's wearing only a thin shirt. He's so close to me that in the clear night air I can smell the fresh scent of soap on his skin. 'But I need to go to bed. I have a lot to do tomorrow.'

'It will all still be there waiting for you.'

'How true. I think that's what worries me.'

'You know, Fay, life's too short to spend it worrying.'

'Is this something you discovered when you started your new life on the canal?'

'Yeah.' He laughs softly. 'It took me a while to get there, though.'

'My dad would have loved your kind of lifestyle. He was never more at home than on the canal, steering the *Maid of Merryweather*. He loved to come out here and watch the stars too. It was him that made me see the beauty in it.'

'I must be mellowing in my old age, since it's something I've started to do as well.' Together we stare at the heavens. 'I know absolutely nothing about the night sky.'

'I could probably point out a few constellations, if pushed.' I extend a finger. 'That's Orion. He looks like a hunter.'

'Only if you have a very good imagination.' Danny screws up his eyes, which makes me giggle.

'It's supposedly the most recognisable constellation. Its brightest stars are Rigel and Betelgeuse.' Danny leans in closer to follow the line of my finger. Our arms brush together and neither of us move. We sit stock-still, staring upwards, not acknowledging that we're touching. 'The three stars across the middle are known as Orion's Belt. My knowledge is a bit rusty. Dad taught me quite a lot though.' I'm so distracted by Danny's closeness that I can hardly form coherent thoughts. 'I'll have to see if I can dig out his telescope.'

'You miss him.'

'Every day. He was a great dad.'

'There's no better accolade. I hope one day someone will say that about me too.'

'Do you have a girlfriend?' The question nearly sticks in my throat. Why? I don't like to pry, that's why.

'Nah. I've become a bit of a loner since I set off on *The Dreamcatcher*. But I needed to put some distance between me and my past life.'

'Sounds intriguing.'

'I could tell you all about it now.' He gently ruffles Diggery's fur as he talks, but his arm stays close along the length of mine. It's as if there's static electricity crackling between us. When I do move away slightly, there's something that draws me right back. 'I promised I would, and I've got a decent bottle of red that's calling to me. I was just thinking of opening it.'

'I couldn't.'

'The night is young.'

'For you, perhaps. But it's way past my bedtime.'

'Don't make me drink alone, Fay Merryweather. There's nothing more cruel.'

I laugh too. 'It's very tempting, but I really can't. Save it until tomorrow. I *will* come along in the evening when I've seen to Mum.'

'Promise me?'

'Yes. Of course.'

'It's nice to have stopped here and found a friend,' he says, gazing out over the water.

'I'm glad too,' I admit. 'You've saved my bacon.'

'I've *eaten* your bacon,' he corrects me.

I laugh at that. Danny is a man who's very easy to be with. Perhaps too easy.

His face in the moonlight looks even more beautiful, and I feel a yearning deep inside me that I haven't felt for such a very long time. So long, in fact, that for a few moments I don't even recognise it as desire. My membership of the passion club has been lapsed for some years.

Danny goes to stand. 'I'll say good-night then.'

His face is close to mine as he turns, and for one crazy moment it looks as if he might kiss me. I hear myself gasp. Then he either thinks better of it or I'm very much mistaken.

'I'll see you in the morning,' he adds. 'Thought I might put up the sunshades as my first job.'

I can hardly find my voice. 'That'll be great.'

'Come on, Digs. Bedtime for us too.' He clicks his fingers and the sleepy dog jumps up. 'Good-night, Fay.'

'Good-night.' I can't even trust myself to say his name.

'You *will* come tomorrow night?' he asks again.

'Yes.' The thought both terrifies and excites me. When he's near me, everything I previously knew as certain seems somehow skewed. But I want to be alone with him on *The Dreamcatcher*. So very much. And everything inside me tells me that I shouldn't be. I must never put myself in that position.

I watch him and his long, lean frame as he lopes back to his boat. I hear him jump on board, Diggery close behind him. He shuts the cabin door and bolts it.

Then I sit here and finish my hot chocolate and, despite not wanting to, I find myself wondering what it might be like to spend the night in the arms of a man who is ten years younger than me.

Chapter Sixteen

The next morning, I'm tired, troubled and tetchy. I didn't sleep well last night and when I did sleep I can't even begin to tell you what I was doing in my dreams. It wasn't handbell-ringing, let's put it that way.

When I take Mum's breakfast in to her, she doesn't look too good either. I thought she was perhaps looking a little pale last night, and now I'm sure she is.

'Is everything all right, Mum?'

'I feel poorly,' she murmurs.

'Where? What's wrong?'

'I don't know. My heart's racing.'

'Do you need the doctor?'

'No,' she says weakly. 'I don't think so.'

For once, I don't think she's playing to the gallery and I'm genuinely concerned. There's a grey pallor to her skin and a dullness to her eyes.

'I'll phone Dr Ahmed right away.'

'I don't need a doctor.'

'You do.'

'If you think so ...'

I realise that she really is feeling very unwell when that's the extent of her protest. Helping her to sit up, I ask, 'Could you manage some toast?'

'Not now.' Mum shakes her head. 'Maybe later.'

So I go downstairs, phone the doctor and, with much huffing and puffing from the receptionist, organise an emergency home visit. Then, rather than throw it in the bin, I eat Mum's toast myself. Although I can't say that I actually taste it.

Minutes later, Danny arrives. 'Hey,' he says.

Perhaps I look as stressed as I feel because he adds, 'Everything OK?'

'Mum's not well,' I tell him without hesitation. 'I just called the doctor.'

'Anything I can do?'

I shake my head. 'I don't think so.'

'I'll get out of your hair then,' he says. 'Just come and tell me where you want these sunshades and I'll get on with it.'

'Thanks.'

He reaches out and touches my arm tentatively. 'You'll let me know if there's anything you need?'

I look at his long, strong fingers on my arm. It's such a small gesture, but an enormous comfort. 'I will. Thank you.'

So I follow Danny outside and quickly show him where the new sunshades are stored and whereabouts they need to go in the garden. Then I come back inside to bake some cupcakes while I wait for the doctor. I'd like to go and sit with Mum until he comes, but I'd better get on. As soon as I do get baking, I find the stirring of the mixture soothes me, taking the edge off my anxiety.

Lija arrives.

'Mum isn't well,' I tell her.

She rolls her eyes. 'Old Bag is pretending again?'

'I don't think so. Not this time.'

'I will look after cake shop and café today,' she says. 'Even Stinky Stan. No worries.'

I kiss Lija's cheek. 'I love you.'

She grimaces. 'You love everyone.'

So I fuss, fidget and fret until Dr Ahmed arrives. I check on Mum every five minutes, but she's dozing now and I don't want to wake her. We have a trickle of customers throughout the morning and the café is filling up for lunchtime – two couples in the dining room, another three in the garden – but Lija is coping with it all wonderfully.

When Dr Ahmed finally turns up, I take him straight upstairs. He's been our family doctor for many years and his calm presence is always reassuring.

'I'm worried about her,' I confide. 'I think there might really be something wrong with her this time.'

'I'll give her a good check-over,' he promises. 'If you don't mind me saying, you look tired too, Fay.'

'Run ragged,' I admit. 'As usual.'

'Throttle back a bit,' he says. 'I don't want to see you in my surgery as well.'

We swing into Mum's bedroom.

'Good morning. Now then, Mrs Merryweather,' he says gently, 'what seems to be the matter?'

Mum rouses herself. 'Oh, doctor. I'm not feeling quite myself.'

'Let's have a look at you then.' He sits beside her on the bed and takes her temperature, her pulse. Then he uses his stethoscope to check her chest and her heart.

Eventually, he lets out a sigh. 'Well,' he says. 'I can't see anything specifically wrong. However, you know, Mrs Merryweather, it isn't doing you any good lying in bed all day.'

'But I'm ill,' she insists.

86

'We've done many tests for you in the past,' he says. 'We couldn't find any underlying problem. There's no reason why you couldn't be up and about if you wanted to.'

'My heart was racing.'

'It seems fine now,' he assures her. 'But when you're bed-ridden, any little movement will put it under stress. Your temperature is a little elevated and your blood pressure is on the high side too. Are you still taking your medication?'

'Yes.'

'I make sure she does,' I chip in.

'You know, poor Fay must be exhausted.'

'Fay doesn't mind.'

'We can get you some help, Mrs Merryweather. There's no need to be like this. With the right support, you could be on your feet again in no time.'

'I'm very weak.'

'The longer you stay in bed, the worse you'll get. You're not helping yourself. Your heart will be under terrible strain if you continue to lie here. It will waste, like any muscle. We don't want that, do we?'

Mum looks as if she doesn't give one jot about her poor heart.

'You need fresh air and some gentle exercise to get you moving again. That's what I'd prescribe for you. You have this beautiful canal. A little stroll along the towpath is just what this doctor would order.' Dr Ahmed puts his stethoscope away and stands up. 'I'll call again tomorrow to see how you are. If your blood pressure's still as high, I'll need to adjust your medication.'

With that, I show him from the room.

'What can I do?' I ask him at the top of the stairs.

'Nothing. If she won't help herself then we're stuck. All I can do is give her more tablets.' He looks at me with what might be pity. 'I'll come by tomorrow.'

'Thank you. I'm sorry to take up your time.'

'Never feel like that, Fay,' he says. 'As I said earlier, don't run yourself into the ground either.'

'Thank you.' But I'm not entirely sure that I have much option.

Chapter Seventeen

I see Dr Ahmed to the door. When I go back into the kitchen, feeling bone-weary, Lija is dashing about making sandwiches and cutting cake. Danny is brewing up.

He holds up his hands. 'I washed them first.'

That makes me smile.

'I am rushed off fucking feet,' Lija complains. 'Are you done with Old Bag?'

'Yes. I'm sorry I was so long.'

'Don't apologise. Is not your fault.' She nods at the counter. 'Take soup to Stinky Stan.'

Doing as instructed, I pick up Stan's soup and put a nice hunk of granary bread on his plate. He shouldn't really have granary bread as he once cracked a brittle tooth on it, but I know he loves it, so we let him have it every now and again.

Stan's settled in his preferred place down by the canal. Although Lija complains about him, I know she's secretly fond of him too. With a smile, I note that Diggery has made himself comfortable at Stan's feet.

'Hello, Stan.'

'Hello, lovely,' he says. 'Glorious day.'

'Beautiful. I see you've found a new friend.'

'Nice little fellow.' Stan pats Diggery's head. 'Looking after him while the young man's busy in the kitchen.'

I put down his soup. 'Broccoli and Stilton today.'

'Oh, my favourite.' He rubs his hands together.

'And a nice hunk of granary bread. Be careful with your teeth.'

'Right-oh!'

Then, as I turn back, I notice for the first time that Danny has put up the sunshades. 'Look at those, Stan. Don't they look smart?'

'Wonderful,' he says. 'Marvellous. Wish we'd had these when I was out in Egypt.'

'What did you do out there, Stan?'

'Oh, this and that. Tootled around, that sort of thing. Tremendous fun. Hot as Hades though. Some days I thought my boots would melt.'

Stan never says very much about what he did in the war, but sometimes he'll tell you a little more. He was a bomber pilot for some of his time, I know that much.

'That young man is proving to be quite helpful,' he says.

'Yes.' I realise it sounds more wistful than I'd like.

'I hope, for your sake, that he'll stay around.'

'You know what canal folk are like, Stan. I'm sure he'll be moving on soon enough.'

'That's a shame, Fay,' he says. 'I fancy he's put a little spring in your step.' He winks at me and, obligingly, I flush. 'If I was a few years younger, I might have done it myself. I was quite the boy in my time.'

'That doesn't surprise me one bit, Stanley Whitwell.'

That makes him chuckle.

'Don't let your soup get cold.'

'Lovely. What is it today?'

'Broccoli and Stilton,' I say again, patiently.

'Oh, my favourite.'

'Mind those teeth.'

Leaving Stan to tuck in, I go back to the house, collecting some empty dishes on my way and taking an order for two afternoon teas. In the kitchen I take over from Danny and he goes back into the garden.

We're so busy that the next time I look up it's five o'clock. The café is empty now, the last customer just gone, and Lija is sitting having a well-earned cup of coffee and a somewhat over-due lunch. No wonder she's so very thin.

Danny comes back in. I haven't had a chance to catch up with him all afternoon.

'Thanks for helping out earlier.'

'No worries,' he says. 'I just made a few cups of tea and a few sandwiches.'

'He's good,' Lija says grudgingly. 'Quick learner.'

'I got the sunshades up too.'

'I saw. They look great.'

'And the signs. I'm not sure they're where you want them, but I can always move them again. I also fixed the lock on the loo. I rummaged around in the garage and found a spare bolt.'

'I think I bought one for it last year and never got round to doing it.'

'Well, it's done now.'

'Thanks, Danny.' I can't believe quite how much he's man-aged to accomplish.

'Am going outside for ciggie,' Lija says, grabbing her pack from the windowsill.

'I've given up, but I could kill for one now. Old habits die hard,' Danny says. 'Mind if I join you?'

She shrugs, so he takes that as a yes and follows her outside.

I sit at the kitchen table, catching my breath with a cup of tea, and watch them standing on the drive by the garage door. The house is difficult to get to. Access is either via the canalside or by a narrow, rutted lane just after a steep humpback bridge. Our location has both pros and cons. It probably deters a lot of customers, but we have enough to get by, and when they get here they always fall in love with the garden. In front of the house, there's parking for about six cars on the drive, and a double garage, covered in ivy, which is useful for extra storage.

Lija lets Danny light her cigarette and then leans against the garage door in her usual insouciant way. Danny stands close and I can see him chatting away. Lija is doing her best not to laugh, but even she cracks and is soon smiling back at him.

I envy their youth, the casual way they have with them, their easy chatter. I envy them. Oh, how I envy them.

Getting up, I busy myself with the washing-up. I must go to check on Mum in a few minutes.

Soon Danny and Lija come back inside, still laughing.

'I'll be off now,' Danny says. 'Will I still see you later, Fay?'

Lija's head snaps up at that.

'I'm not sure.' I can feel my face burning furiously. 'It depends on Mum.'

'I understand. I hope you can make it. That wine is still calling for me.'

'Don't wait on my account. You go ahead.'

He shrugs and I think he looks disappointed.

'I'm sorry.'

He gives a casual wave and whistles for Diggery, who appears from behind a bush, and together they stride off down the garden.

Lija fixes me with a stare. 'What is this?'

'Nothing,' I say, feeling guilty.

'Did not sound like nothing.'

I cave under her scrutiny. 'I was going to see Danny tonight, on *The Dreamcatcher*. Just for a drink. But I can't leave Mum while she's not well.'

'She is *always* not well,' Lija notes. 'Go. I will babysit Old Bag.'

'I can't.'

'Go. She won't bangbangbang while I am here.'

My heart starts an uneasy patter and I realise that I do want to go. I really, *really* want to go and drink wine on *The Dreamcatcher* with Danny Wilde.

'You don't mind? You're not doing anything tonight?'

'Nothing especial. Besides, you will pay me and I need money.'

'I'll pay for a cab home too.' I'm not planning on being late, but I don't want Lija cycling home on the towpath in the dark.

'Is not problem. I will sleep in Edie's room,' Lija says. 'I always keep spare pants and toothbrush in handbag.'

I look at her, astonished. 'Why?'

She shrugs. 'Emergency Shag Kit. You never know when good opportunity for love might arise.'

By 'love', I'm assuming Lija means sex. With someone she might just meet in passing. Yikes. I could never dream of doing that, and that makes me feel so terribly old-fashioned.

'Is good to be prepared,' she adds.

'Right.'

And, thinking that in my whole life I've never, ever needed to be prepared in that way, I start to worry about my coming evening with Danny Wilde.

Chapter Eighteen

I call Anthony before I leave. It does not go well. He's having to deputise for a colleague at a planning meeting and he's very grumpy about it. He's even more grumpy when he remembers that I'm going out for the evening and there won't be a hot dinner waiting for him when he calls in to Canal House on his way home.

'I'm sorry,' I say to Anthony. 'I'll be at home as usual tomorrow night. I'll make your favourite.' He likes a good home-made steak and kidney pie, does Anthony.

'Humph,' he says. 'I was thinking of calling another handbell practice. I'll have to see if the ladies can make it.'

I'm sure they will. It looks like I'm getting the brush-off for tomorrow night, favourite dinner on offer or not.

'I'd better go,' I say, with a glance at my watch. I didn't give Danny a specific time, but I don't want to get there too late and appear rude. I'm tempted to call it off, but I've inconvenienced Lija now and I couldn't face her wrath if I were to tell her I'd changed my mind.

'Don't let me keep you,' Anthony says and hangs up.

I sigh at my phone. You know the saying, 'You can't please all of the people, all of the time'? That.

Before I head off towards *The Dreamcatcher*, I quickly nip upstairs to see Mum. She's looking a little better now, I'm sure of it. I think when she realised that she wasn't getting very much in the way of sympathy from the medical profession, she forced herself to rally a bit.

'I won't be late, but Lija's staying here,' I remind her. 'Anything you want, just call her.'

'She never comes when I do,' Mum complains.

'Don't call her every five minutes,' I tell her. 'You'll be fine.'

'Why do you have to go out tonight?' she whines. 'What if Edie wants to Skype me?'

'Lija can set that up if you like.'

'You went out last night.'

'That's twice in about six months, Mum, and I'll only be at the end of the garden.'

'Hardly seems worth the effort.'

'I'd like to see his narrowboat, that's all.' I'm sounding defensive.

'Why? You've seen hundreds of them. They're all the same.'

'I'm being sociable. Danny's been working very hard in the garden for me and I'm going to take an hour to get to know him a little better. I'm being neighbourly.'

I do wonder why I want to know more about him when, as sure as eggs is eggs, he'll be moving on again soon. Still, it's better than yet another night in front of the telly with only the lovely Jules Hudson for company.

'I won't be long.' I kiss Mum's dry, papery cheek, but she brushes my hand away. Not a big one for displays of affection, my mother.

In the living room, Lija has a bowl of Kettle Chips on her lap and *Emmerdale* blaring out of the television.

'I'm going now,' I say to her. 'How do I look?'

She turns and gives me a frosty appraisal. 'Like tramp. Comb hair. Put on make-up. Change top.'

'I'm only going for a quick drink.'

I get a death stare in return.

'OK,' I say. 'But I'm wasting my time.'

'I will be judge of that.'

So I trudge back upstairs and do as Lija says, grumbling as I go. Comb hair. Put on make-up. Change top. Then I catch sight of myself in the mirror and am quite startled by what I see. Though it wasn't in Lija's list of instructions, I've put on clean jeans too and, I have to say, for an old girl I've scrubbed up quite well. Perhaps I should do this more often. It's really no wonder that Anthony doesn't actually look at me – in *that* way – any more.

Back downstairs, I give Lija a twirl. 'Better?'

'Yes. Now he might be overcome with lust for you.'

I laugh and it sounds loud, shrill. 'Danny?'

'You should take Emergency Shag Kit just in case.'

'I'll do no such thing.' My blood is heating at the very thought of it.

Lija puts her Kettle Chips to one side. 'I have made this.' She leads the way into the kitchen. In the cake tin there's a lemon drizzle cake. 'The way to man's heart. Take bottle of wine too.'

There's no point arguing, so I pick a bottle of white from the fridge. It's one that's been in there for an aeon, waiting for an excuse for Anthony and me to drink it. This is as good an excuse as any.

'I'd better take a cardigan.'

'You don't need cardigan.'

I snatch the one that's on the back of the kitchen chair. Lija snatches it off me.

'Go out without fucking cardigan for once. See what happens.'

'I like a cardigan.'

'You are not having it.' Lija clutches it to her skinny chest.

No cardigan then.

'Just give me a ring if there are any problems with Mum. I can come straight back.'

'I will turn television up loud so I don't hear. She will be fine.'

But, despite her words, I know that I can trust Lija to look after her.

She wags a finger at me. 'I don't want you back before midnight. Earliest.'

'It's only a drink, Lija.'

She mimics my face.

I hold up a hand. 'Fine, fine, fine! I'm out of here.'

'Laters,' she says. '*Much* laters.'

Chapter Nineteen

My heart is positively pounding in my chest as I make my way down the garden in the twilight and towards *The Dreamcatcher*. I really never knew that my heart could be so easily influenced. I thought it only pounded if you ran for a bus or got into an argument with a cashier in a bank. I don't think I've felt like this since I went on my first proper date, at the tender age of sixteen. Now that I know that life begins at forty, you'd think it could cope with the sudden appearance of a handsome young man. But clearly not. Snap out of it, for goodness' sake, Fay.

I'm clutching a cold bottle of wine in one hand and the cake tin in the other. I think I feel like this because I'm so rarely alone with a man who isn't Anthony and, to be perfectly honest with you, it's been a long, long time since Anthony made my heart race. I wish I had my cardigan too.

I walk along the jetty and, as I reach the narrowboat, I stop and take a few steadying deep breaths. Inside, Diggery starts barking and scratching excitedly at the cabin door.

'Calm down, Digs,' I hear Danny say. 'We've got company, that's all.'

Timidly, I knock on the door with a knuckle, and Danny opens it.

'Come on board,' he says, holding out a hand.

I hand him the wine then take the outstretched fingers while I climb over the sill. The feel of his touch surprises me yet again. His hands are soft, not callused as I'd expected them to be. Diggery barks another welcome and wags his tail.

Inside *The Dreamcatcher*, it's exactly as I'd expected. It's cosy and warm and not exactly state-of-the-art as boats go, but it has a slightly bohemian feel to it. In the main cabin there's a multi-coloured rag rug on the floor and the seating area has a squishy, well-worn chocolate-brown leather sofa which faces a log-burning stove. The sofa is covered with a colourful crocheted throw and there are two Union Jack cushions at either end of it. Beyond that there's a small galley kitchen all done out in a light, natural wood. There's a microwave and a proper kettle on the stove, but not much else. It's not very smart, but it's certainly homely.

A narrow corridor leads further down the boat to what I assume must be Danny's cabin and the bathroom.

'This is wonderful.' I do love the cosy confines of a canal barge. Even though everything must have its rightful place, it's all so manageable, and it makes me realise just how much hard work the big, rambling house that I live in has become.

'Thanks. She's still a work in progress.'

'I brought wine and cake,' I manage. 'Though the cake's from Lija.'

'I have a bottle of red open. Shall I put this in the fridge?'

'Of course.'

When he takes my gifts, I find that I'm hugging myself.

'Cold?' he asks.

'No.' Then I sigh. 'Frightened. Nervous.'

He laughs. 'Of me?'

'Yes.' I can feel my cheeks reddening. 'I don't do this kind of thing.'

'We're just going to have a chat and a glass of plonk, Fay. I thought you might like to see *The Dreamcatcher*. I'm not planning on abducting you or holding you here against your will.'

'No,' I say, feeling foolish. 'Of course you're not.'

'You have a partner. Anthony?'

I nod.

'I know that.' He pours a glass of wine for us both. 'I thought we got on well together. Nothing more.'

'Thank you.' I take the wine he's holding out and am glad to see that my hands don't look as shaky as they feel. 'My social skills are very rusty, I'm afraid. I don't have much of a life,' I admit. 'It revolves round my mother and the café.'

'And Anthony.'

'Not even Anthony, if I'm honest.'

He clinks his glass against mine. 'Then here's to a more exciting life.'

That makes me smile. 'I'll drink to that.' I sip the wine and it's good. Fruity, rich and far too drinkable.

'I walked into the village earlier,' he says. 'Bought some cheese and biscuits. Would you like some? I hope you say yes or I'll be eating it for days.'

'That would be lovely.' I realise that I haven't actually eaten any dinner this evening and am suddenly ravenous.

'Make yourself at home. Kick your shoes off,' he says. 'It'll take me a minute to rustle it up.'

Self-consciously I slip off my shoes and settle on the sofa, having a little plump of the cushions to distract myself. I don't know if it's the smallness of the space or the way Danny fills it, but this all feels so very intimate.

A few minutes later, Danny brings a platter from the galley and puts it on the coffee table in the middle of the living area.

Outside, the sky is dark, the night closing in on us. He lights the wicks in a couple of hurricane lamps by the stove and turns off the bright one overhead. Then he sits down next to me on the sofa. The big boots have gone now and he's barefoot. I never thought I liked men's feet before, but now I think I do. He's wearing faded, ripped jeans and a white T-shirt. Round his neck is a grey scarf, the sort that you'd normally see pop stars sporting. Round one wrist there's a chunky watch that looks expensive and beside it a black bracelet of plaited leather. On the other there's a silver identity bracelet and he's wearing two silver rings, one on each hand. It seems exotic, edgy. Anthony is not a jewellery wearer. He has a Rolex watch with a worn brown leather strap that his father bought him for his twenty-first birthday, and that's it. Consequently, he's not a jewellery buyer either.

Danny must have showered just before I arrived as his hair is still damp and I'm so close to him that I can smell the musky soap he's used and a hint of aftershave. Has he put it on especially for me? I wonder. I take a glug of wine to steady my nerves. Despite his reassuring words, the mood feels charged, seductive. It must just be me. This man is years younger than me. He's more suitable for Lija or my sister, and yet I'm sitting here with butterflies in my stomach.

'Well, Fay Merryweather,' Danny says, his charming smile in place. 'Now we can get to know each other better.'

Chapter Twenty

'Don't stand on ceremony. Tuck into some cheese,' Danny says. 'This is dinner for me.'

'Me too,' I admit.

'Then let's kick back and enjoy.' He pours more wine for me and then hands me a plate. We both fall quiet as we help ourselves to the food.

There's some music coming from an iPod in the corner: Ed Sheeran, I think. I don't really have time to keep up with current trends in music but sometimes Lija has the radio on in the kitchen and I pick up bits and pieces. I like this song. Leaning against the wall is a battered guitar. After some fussing, Diggery goes to curl up in his bed next to it and instantly falls asleep.

My plate is heaped with a lovely selection of cheeses – Brie, Stilton, Wensleydale. There are some nice crackers, and grapes too. I wonder if Danny did pick these up at the village shop, or whether he made a special trip into the city centre? Though I don't know when he'd have had the time. 'You shouldn't have gone to so much trouble.'

'You're my first proper guest on *The Dreamcatcher*,' he says. 'I thought it would be nice.'

'You haven't had her for long?'

'Six months. Maybe a bit longer.'

'I thought you were a seasoned canal dweller.'

He laughs. 'I'll take that as a compliment. But no. She was a total impulse buy. I'd never even been on a canal boat before.'

'Seriously?'

He nods. 'I know. Madness. But sometimes the planets or something just align and you know something's meant to be. Don't you ever feel that?'

'I can't say I've ever experienced it myself,' I admit.

God, even to my own ears I sound so crushingly dull. I've always aspired to a quiet and ordinary life, one without any high drama. And, with the exception of a few outbursts from my mother, I've managed to achieve it. I'm realising it doesn't make for exciting dinner conversation though.

'Well, I hope it does happen to you one day, because it's an amazing feeling. You know right deep down in your bones, your soul, your whole being, that what you're doing is absolutely right.'

'Wow.' I feel quite envious.

'I said I'd tell you my story, didn't I?'

'It's the only reason I'm here,' I tease.

He laughs. 'Are you sitting comfortably then?'

Recklessly, I curl my legs up on the sofa and settle back against the cushions. 'I am now.'

Danny's eyes sparkle in the candlelight as he tops up our drinks and I nestle my glass in my lap. I'm not usually a drinker, yet already, in one night, I've exceeded my usual monthly quota of booze, and it feels rather nice. Two glasses of wine in and I'm feeling a mellow glow that I haven't experienced for many months. It's something I've missed. I seem to be as taut as a bowstring these days, and a glass or two of drinkable red is helping take the tension away. Perhaps it's also because I've

103

been forced to stop dashing around for a few hours. Whichever way, my limbs feel heavy and my eyelids are pleasantly so too. There's the occasional gentle swaying movement of *The Dreamcatcher* as another boat goes by on the canal, the odd call of a bird settling for the night, the lap of the water on the hull, but, other than that, we're cocooned in a world of silence.

'I worked in commodities,' Danny starts. 'In the City.'

'You don't look like your average City trader,' I note, taking in his ripped jeans and worn T-shirt.

He grins. 'It's fair to say that I've turned my back on it now. All my Armani suits went straight to the local charity shop. Well, except one.'

That makes me smile.

'I loved it at first, I can't deny it. The London buzz, the adrenalin rush of doing deals, all that crap. But it's a life that you can only live for so long. I was never at home; the few relationships I started foundered because I couldn't give them enough attention. I was working all hours, had more money than I knew what to do with and no time to enjoy it.' He shrugs. 'Same old, same old.'

He pauses to take a drink.

'I was dealing mainly with Russians and was over there a lot. More than I wanted to be. I started to find myself in situations that I wasn't comfortable with. There was a lot of drinking.' He holds up his glass. 'And I'm Irish. I'm someone who doesn't mind a good drink. But it was more than that. There were drugs too. And I'm not talking the odd spliff. Heavy stuff. Then one night, I'd taken out a party from a big corporation. There was an important deal riding on it. They were horrible blokes, out for all they could get. All through dinner they were pushing, pushing, and I got a queasy feeling in my gut. These weren't the kind of people I wanted to be dealing with and yet it was becoming more the norm. So, we finished dinner, went back to the hotel. So far, so good. Instead of staying in the bar, we went up to a suite. There were girls waiting for us. Hookers. Young ones. Too young. My boss told me that he'd organised them to make sure we closed the deal. And I looked round at these fat, sweating, disgusting men, and the women – girls – they were exploiting, and just knew that I didn't want to be there.'

'I don't blame you.'

'I made an excuse. A lame one. I walked out, hailed a cab straight to the airport and jumped on the next flight out. I texted my boss my resignation from the departure lounge.'

My eyes widen. 'Really?'

He nods.

'What did he say?'

'He went ballistic. Of course. I was his golden boy. His wing-man. He hadn't seen it coming at all. But then, neither had I.' He shrugs. 'I didn't like the way the business was going, but I didn't think I'd turn my back on it in an instant. My boss came back the next day and texted me to say he'd done the deal despite my abrupt exit. As soon as he hit the office, he sum-moned me to a meeting and demanded to know what was behind my resignation. He was convinced I was being poached by another firm, but that couldn't have been further from the truth. I simply wanted out.'

Danny's eyes meet mine.

'I'm not a saint, Fay,' he says. 'In fact, far from it. There are things I've done that I'm not proud of. Both in my work life and my personal one. I've done deals that have been sharp. I've trod-den on people because I could. There are women that I've hurt. I'm not holier-than-thou or even taking the moral high ground here, but something about that situation just floored me. It overstepped the mark. I was supposed to be a professional busi-nessman and yet I found it all too sleazy.'

'Did they ask you to go back?'

'Yes, but I'd left my stomach for it in that Russian hotel room. It was like a wake-up call. I knew if I carried on like that, I'd turn into a person I didn't want to be. I needed a clean sweep. My boss thought I was going to turn whistle blower and go running to the *Daily Mail* with the story or something.' He raises an eyebrow. 'I thought he might have known me better than that. In the end, he got me to sign a confidentiality agreement and gave me a massive pay-off.'

He stands and goes to the galley, coming back a few moments later with the bottle of white wine. I pick again at the cheese and biscuits to try to soak up the unaccustomed alcohol. Checking my watch, I realise it's getting late. I'm hoping Mum is all right with Lija, but with a jolt I realise that I haven't really thought about her all evening and I feel a stab of guilt. But I don't want to go back. Not yet. I want to hear Danny's story out.

He tops up his glass and I cover mine. 'Not for me.' I'll never get up in the morning if I drink any more.

Danny carries on where he left off. 'I was there with money in the bank, no job, no desire to get a job. Then I went out for a farewell drink with an old friend who was going off on a long-term contract overseas. After some back-slapping and a few beers he told me he was selling his narrowboat. He'd had it for a while and hardly had time to use it. He said he didn't want to keep the boat sitting unused in a marina, paying all the fees for the next three years. We had another pint or two, shook on a deal and the next day I was the owner of *The Dreamcatcher*. Bought and not even seen.'

I laugh. 'You didn't even go to look at it?'

'No.' Danny shakes his head. Even he still seems amazed at his naivety. 'It could have been a complete old tub, I suppose. But I trusted him. He didn't try to rip me off and it sounded like the perfect way to embark on my new life. It hadn't even crossed my mind before that it was something I could do. As I said earlier, sometimes everything just comes together and feels right.' He looks round at his boat proudly. 'I knew, with everything that I am, that this would be for me.'

'You're so brave.'

He smiles. 'Stupid, maybe.'

'But it's what you want.'

'It hasn't all been plain sailing, pun intended. Being trapped, unable to move because of the ice this winter, was something I hadn't anticipated. It was just a good job that I got stranded within walking distance of a Tesco Express.'

'I'm sure living on a boat must have its challenges.'

'Yeah. But they're far outweighed by the benefits.'

'We only ever had holidays on the *Maid of Merryweather*. It was Dad's thing. Mum didn't really like her much at all. I loved her though, and still do. One of my dreams – if I have any – is to get Dad's narrowboat working again.'

'One day,' he says. 'If you want it enough.'

I think of all the things that need to be done before then, but don't voice them.

Danny sits back. 'I've done nothing but talk about myself all evening. How rude of me.'

'No, no,' I say. 'It's very interesting.'

'So that's my story. What's yours, Fay?'

Then a text pings into my phone. Diggery pricks an ear. 'Sorry, can I get this? It might be Mum. I've left her with Lija.'

But it isn't Mum, it's Edie. *Skype me*, the text says. *Urgent.*

Sadly, I hold up my phone. 'This is my story,' I tell him. 'A mum and a sister who are both dependent on me. I'm really sorry, but I have to go.'

'No worries,' Danny says. 'It's been nice to have your company.'

I wonder when the last time was that someone said that to me.

I'm flustered now and more than a little bit tipsy. I hope Edie's OK.

When it's clear that I'm leaving, Diggery jumps out of his basket and comes to be patted. I bend to stroke his head and, when I stand up, Danny is right in front of me. Close, so close.

He puts his hands on my shoulders and leans in. His warm lips, his soft stubble, brush against my cheek.

'Shall I make sure you get back to the house safely? Me and Digs could walk you home.'

'I'll be fine,' I say. 'Really. I'll just say good-night.'

'Good-night then,' he says. 'I'll see you tomorrow.'

'Thank you for the lovely wine, and food,' I say. 'It was very nice.'

His dark eyes challenge me. 'If it was "nice", Fay Merryweather,' he teases, 'does that mean you might consider doing it again?'

Chapter Twenty-one

I make my way back to the house, hurrying as much as I can in the consuming darkness. The city of Milton Keynes is bathed in the orange glow of street lighting but here, out in the village, down by the canal, the darkness is still dense and I should have brought a torch. Thankfully, as I reach the halfway mark up the garden, the light from the house guides me.

It's past midnight when I'm opening the door. I'm normally in bed at ten o'clock on a 'school night'. I don't even push it much past half-past ten at the weekend. I text Edie to say that I'll be online in a few minutes.

There's no light on in the kitchen, but there's one in the living room, so Lija must still be up. When I push the door open, she's lying full-length on the sofa watching some sort of chick flick.

'Hey,' I say and make her start. I think she might have been asleep. She's wearing baggy football shorts and a tiny camisole and still looks like a cover model.

'What time is it?' She rubs her eyes sleepily.

'Just after midnight.'

'Why are you home soon?'

'Edie texted me. She needs me to Skype her.'

Lija rolls her eyes. 'Tell her you are busy on hot date.'

'You know what she's like.'

'Pain in bloody arse,' Lija says.

'Well, yes. But she's my sister. And, stating the obvious, I wasn't actually on a hot date.'

Lija tuts at me. 'I will go to bed.' With a stretch and a yawn, she hauls herself from the sofa.

'Is Mum OK? She wasn't too much bother?'

'Bangbangbang,' Lija says. 'I gave her cocoa at ten o'clock. I put poison in it. She is sleeping now.'

'She *will* wake up tomorrow?'

A shrug. 'Probably.'

'Thank you,' I say. 'It was really kind of you to stay. I appreciate it.'

'You are my friend,' she says. 'Plus you owe me extra ten pounds.'

'It's worth every penny, and more.'

Lija risks one of her rare smiles. 'Want tea?'

'I'll make it myself in a minute.'

'Sometimes,' Lija sighs, 'people can do things for *you*.'

'Sorry, sorry. Yes, I'd love a cup of tea. Thank you. Thank you very much. That's very kind.'

She stands and regards me, hands on hips. 'So. Tell. How was *not* hot date?'

'Our *evening of socialising* was very pleasant.'

'Pleasant!' Lija makes a strange, dismissive noise in her throat.

'*The Dreamcatcher* is lovely inside. Danny and I had a nice chat.'

'*Pleasant. Lovely. Nice*,' Lija mimics. 'Gah. Did you do shagging?'

'Lija.' I give my assistant my sternest look, which doesn't even register with her. 'We had cheese and biscuits and a few glasses of wine.'

'Sounds dull.'

'It wasn't. It was lovely.' It was more than that, but I've run out of adjectives to describe it that won't involve Lija pouring scorn on me. I drift back to being curled up on Danny's sofa on *The Dreamcatcher* and reflect that I hadn't felt so relaxed for a long time. I flush at the thought.

Lija grins. That girl misses nothing. 'I would shag him,' she states.

'Would you like me to tell him that?'

Her signature shrug. 'Maybe I tell him myself.'

I feel myself frown at that, even though I know Lija's only joking. At least I think she is. Anyway, even if she went straight down to *The Dreamcatcher* with her Emergency Shag Kit in her handbag, what is it to me? Both she and Danny are free agents. If they want to do that kind of thing, that's entirely up to them. 'I'm going to Skype Edie.'

'Don't let her see you are little bit pissed,' Lija advises.

'I'm not.' Then I laugh. 'Yes, I am.'

Chapter Twenty-two

I set up the laptop on the coffee table and moments later Edie's face is in front of me. She's clearly been drinking. And much more than me.

'Brandon's threatening to cut off my allowance,' she sobs the minute we're connected. 'He says he can't afford to keep me here.'

'Hi, Edie,' I say.

'What am I going to do?'

'You could get a job.'

'We've had this conversation before.'

'Many times.'

'It's not that easy,' she continues.

'You could come home and help run the cake shop and café with me.'

'And look after Mum? No way. You do too much. We both know there's nothing wrong with her.'

'If you can't stay there, then what else can you do?' I think I'm a little too tired and a little too tipsy to be as sympathetic as I normally am.

'I am *not* coming home, Fay. I'd rather throw myself off the top of the Empire State Building.' Then she stops and peers closely into her computer. 'Have you been drinking?'

'Yes. Just a little.'

She scowls at me. 'Where have you been?'

'Seeing a friend.'

'Who? You don't have any friends.'

'Thank you, Edie.' But, in the back of the more sober part of my mind, I fear she may be right.

'Which friend then?'

'There's a nice man who's been helping out doing some odd jobs around the garden. I went to see him.'

'You've been out with another guy? Does Anthony know?'

'Yes, of course he does. And we didn't exactly go out. I went to see his narrowboat, which is currently moored on our jetty. He lives on the canal.'

'Oh, God.' Her eyes disappear into the back of her head. 'You and that stinking bloody canal. You're obsessed with it.'

'I'm not. I just love living here, that's all. It might not be Manhattan, but it's a nice place, Edie.'

'I hated growing up there and I'd hate it more now. You should try getting a life, Fay, then you'd know what I mean.'

'If you've only called me to be mean, Edie, I think I'm going to go now.'

'Don't,' she pleads. 'Stay. I need you to help me.' On the screen she pouts and makes doe eyes. It's a look she perfected at the age of three, yet I'm still not immune to it. 'I'm desperate and there's no one else I can turn to. You're everything to me, Fay.'

I know what's coming next.

'Can you send me some money, sis? A loan.'

'It's difficult at the moment.' I try to help Edie out whenever I can, but there's a limit to what I can do. 'I'm paying Danny to do the work that needs to be done here.'

113

'Danny?'

'The bloke from the canal I just told you about.' I think back to our evening and how, in a few moments, Edie has managed to wipe out all my feelings of peace and contentment. If I'm not wrong, I'm stone-cold sober now.

'What if Brandon doesn't pay the rent?' Edie breaks down and cries. 'I'll be homeless.'

'Don't cry,' I tell her. 'Please don't cry.' I hate to see Edie like this and she knows it.

'Help me then,' she pleads.

It looks as if I'm going to have to dip into my meagre fund for the renovation of the *Maid of Merryweather*.

I crack and hold up my hands. 'All right. I'll send you what I can. Just this once. It might not be much. But I can't keep bailing you out. If you can't rely on him, Edie, then you *have* to do something to make yourself less dependent on him.'

'I love him,' she says as if it's the answer to everything. 'I love him *so* much.'

And I wish he could love her back, but I don't believe he does.

'I have to go,' I tell her. 'It's late here. But I'll put some money in your bank tomorrow.'

'Do it now,' Edie urges, drying her tears. 'Before you go to bed. A couple of grand would be great.'

'I'm not sure I can manage that much.'

'I'll love you for ever,' she coos.

I sigh. Perhaps that's the problem with Edie: people very rarely say no to her and she's addicted to Brandon because he does. Frequently. 'OK. I'll see what I can do.'

'Love you to the moon and back,' she says and blows a kiss at the screen.

'I love you too. *Please* ring Mum,' I say. 'Around teatime is the best. She's desperate for a call. You haven't spoken to her for over a week now and she misses you.'

'Yeah, yeah, yeah,' Edie says.

'Good-night, sis. I miss you too.'

But the screen has already gone blank.

Chapter Twenty-three

Anthony pops in on his way home from work. We've had another really busy day at the café. The Fensons popped in again at lunchtime, as they'd had yet another disaster aboard *Floating Paradise* – something to do with a plastic bag tangled around their bow thrusters – and were in need of restorative tea and cake. There's been a constant flow of people buying cakes from the Maid of Merryweather too. But all the customers have finally gone now and I'm just finishing up in the kitchen. Lija wanted to bake some cakes for tomorrow, but I've already sent her home as she's worked so hard today. It will, however, mean a dawn start tomorrow.

Anthony is looking all hot and bothered. And a bit vexed. He's still wearing his work suit and his shirt is crumpled, but at least he's loosened his tie.

'Managed to sneak off early for once,' he says.

'What a nice surprise,' I say. 'Cake? We've not much left, but I can rustle up a piece of lemon drizzle.'

'That'll do,' he says.

So I slip a slice on to a plate and hand it to him. In return, he kisses my cheek.

'Been to see an extension that's twice the size it should be. I don't know how these people think they can get away with it.'

'Is it nice?'

He looks at me askance. 'Nice? What's that got to do with anything? They're flouting planning laws.'

'Oh.'

'Cost them quarter of a million quid.' He pushes cake into his mouth. 'But it's going to have to come down.'

My eyes widen. 'All of it?'

'Every single brick.' With the back of his hand he wipes his lips. Which, now I look at them properly, are quite fleshy. Have they always been like that?

'Can't you come to a compromise?'

'Compromise?' He laughs at the thought. 'No way!'

'What a terrible shame.'

'There are rules, Fay. Where would we be without them?'

'I can't help but feel a bit sorry for them. It's their home.'

He shrugs. 'They should know better than to mess with the Bullmore.'

Perhaps they have gone beyond their permission, but it seems such an awful waste of money and resources to ask them to destroy it. Surely it would be better if they paid a fine or made some modifications or something? I say nothing. Matters of planning are very much Anthony's domain.

'It's a lovely evening,' I say. 'I could finish up here quickly and we could have a walk down the towpath to Cosgrove, have some dinner at the pub. I'm sure I could leave Mum for an hour.'

'Hmm,' he says, clearly indicating that it's not such a great idea. 'We've got handbell practice tonight. I have to be at the village hall for eight o'clock.'

'Oh.'

'You know what it's like, Fay,' he says tetchily. 'Deborah's still not up to speed.'

117

'She seemed OK to me.' If anything she added a bit of colour to the ensemble. Even if they make her wear a boring white blouse and black trousers for performances, I think she'll still manage to look bling-de-bling.

Anthony looks at me as if to say, What do you know?

'It's not a problem.' I don't want Anthony going off in a grump. 'We can have a quick dinner here. There's some pasta in the cupboard. Maybe we can eat in the garden. It's all looking lovely out there.'

Anthony strides to the back door and looks out to admire it. Then his mouth drops open.

'There's some rough-looking man lurking out there.' Anthony yanks open the door. 'Hey! Hey, you! This is private land! Clear off! I'll go and sort him out.'

Before he can rush out, I'm at Anthony's side and searching the garden for our intruder.

When I see where his eyes have fallen, I laugh out loud. 'Oh, Anthony, that's only Danny,' I tell him. 'The guy who's been doing some handy jobs for me. I told you about him.'

'Oh,' Anthony says, wind gone right out of his sails. 'Oh.'

By now Danny has turned round and I wave. He gives me a wave back, hammer in hand. My stupid heart skips a beat as it always does. I do wish it would stop this nonsense.

'He's been doing lots of little repairs in the garden,' I explain. 'Looks as if he's mending some more of the broken trellis.'

'He looks an unreliable sort.' Anthony sounds disgruntled.

'He's been brilliant,' I counter. 'He's already fixed the loo door, and put up the sunshades and some new signs.' I point them out. 'And a dozen other little things. I don't know what I would have done without him.'

'You know I don't have time for all that, Fay.' Anthony has gone from disgruntled to tetchy. Clearly, I've hit a nerve. It's a very rare occasion when Anthony lifts a finger to help out here – unless you count being chief cake taster as helping out. 'I have a very busy job.' Then he corrects himself. 'A demanding *career*.'

'I know you do.' I stroke the lapel of his suit, placating him. 'But these things don't fix themselves. I've been very glad of the help. He's a nice bloke too.'

Anthony snorts. 'He looks like a typical canal scallywag.'

I don't point out that looks can be deceiving. Instead I say, 'I'll put the kettle on. Slip your jacket off for a little while.'

He makes a big fuss of doing so and then puts it over the back of a chair, smoothing out the shoulders. Anthony doesn't do crumpled if he can help it.

'Would you mind very much popping up to say hello to Mum? She's been so grumbly today. I think it's because the weather's been warmer. She always likes to see you. Ask if she wants a cup of tea.'

'Very well.' He climbs the stairs and I hear him shout, 'Hello, Miranda. How's my favourite girl?'

Anthony's good with my mother and she thinks he's wonderful. Hence her constantly telling me how disappointed she is that he's not yet officially her son-in-law.

I set about making tea.

As soon as he's gone, his phone tings that he has a text. A second later, there's another one. While the kettle boils, I dig into his jacket pocket and find his iPhone. I flick into the text messages and open them up in case it's anything important about work.

One is from someone called John. *Sorry I had to cancel golf @ last minute. C u Fri?*

So that's why Anthony is here early, because his round of golf was cancelled. I shouldn't be disappointed, but I am. I thought that for once he'd come straight here from the office just because he wanted to see me.

I scroll up. The next one is from Deborah. *C u at 8. Can't wait. xx*

Wow, she is keen on her handbell-ringing. I smile to myself. Well, it takes all sorts.

I leave Anthony's phone on the table for him. At least the texts weren't anything to worry about.

Chapter Twenty-four

The weeks go by and the weather breaks. Suddenly, as is the way with the British climate, the temperature soars to twenty-five degrees and we enjoy unbroken sunshine every day. It's like living in the Mediterranean rather than Milton Keynes.

Lija and I are run off our feet. I haven't had time to turn around, let alone do anything else. I've hardly seen Anthony as he's been making the most of the weather by playing as much golf as is humanly possible. There are also the handbell sessions to fit in before the big Canal Festival which is approaching quickly. I know it's important to them, but to hear Anthony talk, you'd think they were performing at Wembley Stadium in front of a capacity crowd.

Since the Easter weekend, we've had an increasing stream of visitors to Fay's Cakes. Everyone and his brother, it seems, wants to try our afternoon teas. Soon I'll need to go off to the car-boot sales or the charity shops to see if I can find a few more tiered cake stands and some extra china, as once or twice we've come close to running out. The cakes, jams and lemonade for sale in the *Maid of Merryweather* have been flying out to visitors along the canal too, and all day long there's always another barge tied up alongside her and *The Dreamcatcher*.

Lija is a cake-making machine and, at the moment, her cakes aren't so much made with love, but with lots of swear words.

'Fucking Victoria sponge,' she mutters darkly as she slams yet another one into the oven.

'I'll take Stan his lunch,' I say, and scuttle out of her way before I'm treated to some of her four-letter abuse.

Down the garden, Stan is installed under one of the new sunshades that Danny fitted a few weeks ago. Diggery is asleep at his feet. It's nice to see that the little dog has become as much a feature of the café as his owner has.

'Minestrone soup today, Stan.'

'Oh,' he's says, smacking his lips. 'My favourite.'

I sit down next to him and help him put his napkin on his lap. 'How are you doing, Stan? I feel as if I haven't had five minutes to talk to you in the last few days.'

'Champion,' he says. 'Just champion.'

Again I think how different he is from my own mother. He's many years older than her and, though he might well have more cause to grumble than Mum, he never has a bad word to say about anything.

'Nice to see business is booming,' he says.

'Yes.' It's bringing in some much-needed funds; ostensibly for my *Maid of Merryweather* project, but most of it seems to be trickling – no, haemorrhaging – Edie's way.

'That young Danny is making a marvellous job of the garden.'

Stan nods towards where Danny is working away. Now that most of the repair jobs have been completed, he's turned his hand to painting and is touching up the badly weathered window frames in the outhouse.

'It's all looking shipshape. I expect you'll miss him when he's gone, Fay.'

That hits me like a hammer blow. *Gone?*

My mouth's dry when I ask, 'Has he said anything about leaving?' He hasn't spoken to me about it at all. But then, since our lovely evening together, we've hardly had five minutes alone to chat. It's always been fleeting conversations about what needs doing in the garden, and usually with Lija in attendance. He hasn't invited me to spend an evening on *The Dreamcatcher* again. Perhaps he didn't enjoy it as much as I did. Consequently, I haven't dared to invite him into the house for dinner. Besides, what would Mum think? What would Anthony think? I can't imagine the three of us sitting cosily round the kitchen table with a spag bol.

'He mentioned that he's off up to London to see some friends,' Stan answers.

'Oh.'

I knew that Danny would be leaving eventually. There's nothing much to keep him here now. As Stan says, the garden is looking in tip-top shape. Pretty much everything that was broken is now mended and, unless Danny starts working on the house, there's no real reason to detain him further. I've also paid out quite a lot on repairs, which I'm really grateful to him for, but it has made a significant dent in my bank account. That, combined with helping out Edie, has left me somewhat strapped. I transferred yet another thousand pounds into Edie's bank account this week as her situation isn't improving. But it means I'm having to watch the pennies a lot more carefully.

I give Stan his cutlery and he tucks into his soup, his spoon shaking slightly as he lifts it to his lips.

'I haven't been into London for a long time,' Stan muses as he sips. 'I used to work for the British Museum many, many years ago, cataloguing their Egyptian collection. We should take a train up there, Fay. You'd like it. It would be nice to see some of those treasures again. I went on quite a few digs for them back in the day.'

'I didn't know that.'

'Oh, there's a lot you don't know,' he chuckles. 'I've had a full and rewarding life, Fay. The things I've seen! The things I've done! If God chose to take me tomorrow, I wouldn't mind a bit.'

'Don't say that, Stan.'

'It's true. I haven't wasted a moment. After the war I was a test pilot. I've led expeditions in Nepal and one to the North Pole. I've worked in films, doing flying stunts. One or two that you might even have heard of! I spent two summers hunting for Nessie.'

'The Loch Ness Monster?'

'Can you believe it! A friend of mine was running the project. We had a few interesting whispers on the sonar, but that was all. Immense fun though. Drank a lot of very good whisky too.' He dribbles minestrone down his chin and I help him to wipe it away.

He sighs, spoon poised, and looks across at me. 'What I'm really trying to say, in my hugely ineffective way, is that you only get one life. We pass this way just once, Fay. Make the most of it.' He pats my knee in a fatherly way and it brings tears to my eyes. 'I've said yes to every single opportunity that's come my way, and it's taken me to some very interesting places, I can tell you.'

Stan laughs out loud at his memories.

'I'm not sure I'm going to get the sort of offers you've had while I'm running a little cake shop by the canal.'

'Sometimes there are opportunities right under your nose that you simply don't see.' Stan glances over at Danny and my gaze follows his.

I'm not sure what Stan means by that, but I know that I don't want Danny to go and I can't even give voice to that.

'Don't get to my age and be filled with regrets,' Stan advises. 'That's what makes you old and bitter.'

I stand up and kiss his cheek. 'Well, you're the most lovely and sprightly ninety-three-year-old I've ever known, so that must be excellent advice.'

'Take it,' he says, earnestly. 'Grab it with both hands.'

'I promise,' I say. 'If I ever get the opportunity, then I promise I will.'

I wander back to the house, pensive and unsettled. My life is small and I try to tell myself that I'm not discontented. I love the house, the cake shop, the customers who come here. Anthony. Is that so wrong?

'What is matter?' Lija asks, brushing flour from her pale cheek. 'You look like woman who has lost fiver and found pound.'

'Just having a talk with Stan.'

'Is enough to depress anyone,' Lija concludes. 'War, war, war. Move on, old man.'

I laugh. 'He's not like that at all. You should take time to sit and chat with him one day. Stan has lived a full and interesting life, Lija. We should be so lucky to do the same.'

'So why sad face?'

I lower my voice. 'Stan said that Danny's leaving. I guess it had to happen, but I have to admit that I've liked having him around.'

'*Liked?*' Lija scoffs. '*Liked!* Listen to you.' Crossly, she pulls at my knitwear. 'Take bloody cardigan off and shag him before he goes. He looks like he would be good shag.'

'Will you stop talking about me shagging him, Lija Vilks!' I look round furtively, just in case Danny is within earshot. It would be just my luck. 'You are totally outrageous. What sort of woman do you think I am?'

'Frustrated old woman.'

'I'm *so* not. I'm a woman of a certain age, I agree. But, even if I was ... *frustrated* ... Danny's very much younger than me.

125

I don't think of him like that at all.' I ignore the fact that my heart is racing. 'He's just a friend.'

She looks totally unconvinced. 'He would be good. I know these things. I can tell.'

I splutter at her brazen assessment of his virility. '*And*,' I remind her, 'I also happen to have a very nice partner, thank you.'

'Anthony looks as if he has small dick,' she observes.

'You say the most terrible things,' I tell her with an exasperated shake of my head. 'It's a good job you make wonderful cakes or I'd sack you.'

At that moment, of course, Danny comes in. 'You're not making trouble, are you, Lija?'

'No,' she says, face all innocent. 'I am trying to help.'

I hold my breath in case she decides to let Danny in on our conversation but, when she sees the frozen terror on my face, she clearly thinks better of it.

'I came to have a quick word,' Danny says, and he gestures with his head that we should move away from Lija's bionic ears.

With one last warning glare at her, I follow him outside and on to the veranda. There are two couples having lunch and a table of three elderly ladies who will need some fresh tea in a moment, so I can't talk for long. He walks to one end, beneath the canopy of the wisteria, and lounges against the wall.

Despite the warmth of the day, I feel a shiver go through me as I stand in front of him and wait to hear what he has to say.

'I've finished in the garden now, Fay,' he says. 'I don't think there's anything else for me to do.'

'No,' I agree. 'You've been brilliant. You've really worked hard to make it look good.' All it needed was some tender loving care. Perhaps that's all any of us ever need to make us flourish.

'This is hard,' he says, and I'm sure I hear a catch in his voice. 'Harder than I thought.' He lets out a steady exhalation of breath.

'I'm going to be moving on, Fay. For a while. One of my old friends is getting married and he's asked me to be his best man. I'm heading back to London so I can help him to get it all ready. I don't even know what that entails. Suits and stuff, I suppose.'

'That's nice.'

'I've never done it before, so I want to make sure I'm there and up to speed. With the stag do and everything, I'm going to be gone for a few weeks at least. Maybe longer.'

'But you're coming back?' My voice sounds too anxious, too needy. I could kick myself.

'I don't know,' he admits. 'Part of my wandering-existence idea is supposed to be that I can go wherever life takes me. I'll have to see what happens.' He laughs uneasily. 'I can't spend the rest of my life moored up here.'

'Right.'

'But, I didn't want to just go,' he says, and a troubled look comes over his usually sunny face. 'I wanted to ask you if you'd come out with me for the day on *The Dreamcatcher*.' He seems shy, uncertain, and the words rush out. 'I thought we could head back up the canal towards Leighton Buzzard. If you want to. I came past some places on the way that looked grand. I've been having a glance at the map and, I know you've got your mother to think about, but we could grab a pub lunch or something and get back early evening.'

'That would be nice.' I realise that I'm agreeing before he's barely got the last sentence out of his mouth.

'Would Monday suit you? When the café's closed?'

That's probably the only day I could do. 'I think so. I'll have to ask Lija to look after Mum.'

'Fay,' he says softly. 'We might not get the chance to do it again.'

And suddenly, I can't bear that thought. I can't bear it at all.

Chapter Twenty-five

'I am not having that horrible foreign woman looking after me!' my mother cries. 'She's rude to me.'

'Lija's rude to everyone, Mum.'

Who knew that organising one day out – *one day* – would be this difficult?

'She keeps me waiting.'

'Not on purpose. It's just that her service isn't as exemplary as mine.' I have it down to a fine art due to years of practice.

Mum turns her face to the wall. If I want praise in this house, then I have to give it to myself.

'You won't have a nurse,' I remind her. 'You spat at the last one.'

'She looked mean,' Mum says. 'She looked like she'd pinch me given half the chance.'

'She was nice. She was very upset that you sent her away.'

'You can't be too careful,' Mum warns.

I check my watch. 'I'm going to be late.'

'Why do you have to go out? Again. You're always going out these days. You never used to.'

'I want a life beyond these four walls,' I say to her. 'You should too. The weather is fabulous. The garden is looking beautiful. You should see the clematis. It's a treat. I could help you downstairs and you could sit out there.'

'I'm too weak,' she says.

If there's one thing that my mother isn't, it's weak.

'I'll see you later. Be good for Lija.'

'You speak to me as if I'm a child,' she says haughtily.

Only because you behave like one, I retort silently.

'Love you.' I kiss her cheek. 'Shall I put the television on for you?'

'There's never anything worth watching.'

'I won't be long,' I promise. Though I know, God willing, that I'm likely to be out for the whole day.

As soon as I'm outside her bedroom and on the landing, I hear the television turn on. She'll be fine, I tell myself. Just fine.

Downstairs, I give Lija her instructions. 'I've left her lunch in the fridge,' I tell her. 'If you could put it in the microwave. But she doesn't like it too hot.'

'Or too cold.'

'No.'

'I have done this many times,' Lija says, hands on hips. 'Is she dead?'

'No.'

'Then she will not be dead today either.'

'That's very reassuring.'

'Leave now,' Lija says. 'Or I go with him instead.'

'Right, right. Don't forget Stan, and be nice to him.'

She gives me a look that says that might be a step too far. But as Stan comes for lunch every day, even when the café is officially closed on Mondays we still feed him. I usually pop down the lane to take his lunch to him then, as I can't bear to think of him going hungry. Lija is totally reliable, there's no

129

way she'll forget, but he won't have to mind having his lunch banged down in front of him. He rarely has more than soup and a sandwich, a piece of cake, but at least I know he's had something to eat every day.

'I will not kill Stinky Stan either,' Lija assures me grudgingly.

'How do I look?' I've put on the only sundress I possess, which, due to the inclement weather in the last few summers, I haven't worn for ages. It's very flowery, a bit sticky-out and most unlike me. I'm only pleased that it still fits. Though I had to give the zip a bit of a tug. I give Lija a twirl.

Lija shrugs. 'OK.'

'Thanks.' That's Lija's equivalent of saying I look a million dollars. Then I hesitate and chew my lip. 'I'm nervous,' I admit.

'Drink lots of vodka,' is Lija's advice.

'You will call me if there's anything wrong with Mum?'

'No. Enjoy your day. Whatever is wrong with her can wait.'

'Right. I'll see you later then.'

She makes a shooing motion with her hand and, picking up the cake tin, complete with chocolate and ginger cake, and my sunhat, I head for the door.

'Don't forget old-lady cardigan,' Lija says.

'Oh, no.'

She holds it out for me. 'I don't want you to have panic attack.'

'Thank you.'

Slipping my cardigan on to my shoulders, I head out.

I feel vaguely nauseous as I head down the garden and towards *The Dreamcatcher*, and I don't know if it's with excitement or fear. There's something about Danny: perhaps it's his youth or his easy confidence, but he always makes me feel tongue-tied and like a gauche teenager.

As I walk out on to the jetty, the customary welcoming party trots out to meet me. Today Diggery's wearing a smart black neckerchief decorated with white skulls-and-crossbones. He barks a cheery greeting.

'Hello, boy.' I ruffle his ears and send him into ecstasy. If only men were so easily pleased.

'Hey.' Danny is standing at the bow of *The Dreamcatcher* ready to welcome me. There's an expression on his face that might be relief, and he says, 'I thought you might not come.'

'I wouldn't miss it for the world,' I tell him. 'It's such a long time since I've been out on a narrowboat. Which is ridiculous, given that I live alongside a canal.'

'Totally,' he agrees. 'There's some fresh coffee on the stove.'

'And I've brought a cake.'

'That's why I love you,' he says, and then we exchange an embarrassed glance.

We go inside, all polite and you-go-first-no-you-go-first, and when we finally make it to the galley, Danny pours us coffee. I put the cake on the side and then we do an awkward little dance around each other in the tight space. When he's so close to me I go weird and become all clumsy. I drop things and walk into stuff. I don't do this normally. I nearly knock over the mug that he slides towards me, but Danny catches it.

'Sorry,' I say. 'Sorry.'

'Let's take the coffee outside on to the stern as it's a lovely day. I had a look on the internet and I've found a nice pub with a garden. Depending on the locks, I'm hoping we can stop there for lunch.'

'Sounds great.'

'I want you to have a chilled day, Fay. *The Dreamcatcher* has been eating up all of my money and you've really helped me out the last few weeks. I want this to be your treat.'

'That's very kind.'

So we make our way to the stern of the boat and Danny undoes the ropes on the way. Diggery trots behind us. It's such

131

a long time since I've actually been cruising on a boat that I've forgotten what to do. At the back of *The Dreamcatcher* there's enough room for both of us to stand comfortably, though in very close proximity. We balance our mugs on the hatch cover and Danny fires up the engine. Then he jumps off to take in the last rope.

'Come on, Digs,' he says, and the little dog bounds on to the boat with him and comes to stand at our feet, nose sniffing the air.

I feel self-conscious standing next to Danny in my prissy sun-dress, hat and, of course, my much-derided cardigan. He looks so much more casual and edgy than me. Perhaps I should have got Lija to choose my outfit. Today he's wearing a baggy grey T-shirt and ripped blue jeans. His big boots are back in place and I sort of miss the glimpse of his bare feet that I got last time I visited *The Dreamcatcher*. Why didn't I wear jeans too? Dress down a bit. But then I so rarely get a chance to dress up, I might as well.

'You look great,' he says as if reading my thoughts.

'Thank you.' I feel myself blush, unused to compliments. 'It's just something old.' Then I feel foolish and vow to keep my mouth shut.

Danny opens the throttle and we move away from the tow-path, a thrill running through me.

'This is exciting,' I say.

He smiles across at me and my insides turn to water. 'You can take the tiller in a minute, if you want to.'

'I haven't driven a boat for years.'

'It's like riding a bike,' he assures me. 'You'll remember in no time.'

So we cruise away from the café, passing the *Maid of Merryweather* as we go. There's a freshness to the air, though the morning is warm. As we cut through the water, the slight breeze lifts my hair. We head out through the village, past gardens that, like my own, sweep down to the water's edge. Weeping willows hang low, dipping their leaves into the canal, and we're accompanied by a flotilla of ducks which Diggery barks at enthusiastically.

Before long, though, we're out into the countryside and there's nothing but open fields on either side of us. The gentle Buckinghamshire landscape rolls away into the distance. The throaty putter of the engine is the only noise to break the silence.

All along the towpath there are pretty boats moored, and I do think it's lovely that something that was once an industrial lifeline has become such a treasured part of our heritage. For so many people, the canals are still a way of life.

There are no other boats moving at this hour and, as there are no locks on this stretch of water, we make steady progress. But the canal is all about slowing down, and something about it forces you to take the day at a more sedate pace.

'This couldn't be more different from your city life,' I say to Danny.

'No. And I'm glad of that.' He eases the tiller gently as we take a curving bend. 'I've only been doing it for a short while, relatively, but I love it.'

'I'm sure I've already told you that my dear dad would have loved to live on the canal,' I say, nursing my coffee. 'This would be his idea of heaven. I was never happier than when we had our family holidays on the *Maid of Merryweather* too, but my younger sister, Edie, and Mum never liked it. Particularly Mum. She'd stick it out for a week, if necessary. But she was really more of a hotel type of person.'

'I don't know what I'd do now if I found a partner who didn't like this lifestyle.' Then he adds hastily, 'Not that I'm looking to settle down.'

'You don't think it would be nice to share this with some-one?'

'Yes. I suppose so.' He sighs. 'I've probably become too self-sufficient over the years. Or maybe I mean selfish.'

'You don't strike me like that at all.'

'A lot of the women I've had relationships with have been pretty shallow. They've been the sort who've been chasing money and good times. Just as I did.' He swallows. 'Maybe I'm looking for more than that now.'

'Tastes change as you get older.' I can't even meet his eyes. 'What you want in a partner in your twenties is very different from what you look for in your thirties.'

'What about you?' He gazes ahead at the canal as he asks, 'Are you and Anthony ever going to tie the knot?'

'I don't know,' I answer candidly. 'We've been together for so long, it seems as if the moment has passed.'

'It's only a piece of paper.'

'Yes,' I agree.

But is it? I still believe in all that's behind that piece of paper. The willingness to commit to sharing your life with someone. Till death us do part. And, in my heart of hearts, do I actually want that with Anthony?

We've fallen into a habit of togetherness, but do we *really* want to be together? Is he the right man for me, with his plan-ning issues and his golf and his damn ding-dong bells? Anthony and I are anchored so firmly in middle age and, as I look at this handsome young man next to me, I'm not sure I'm ready to be there yet.

Chapter Twenty-six

The sun is climbing higher now. It's even warm enough to discard my cardigan-cum-comfort-blanket and give my bare shoulders a rare outing. I pull my sunhat down slightly to shade my eyes. Danny dons mirrored aviator shades and looks even more cool, if that's humanly possible. He cuts a fine figure on his boat, a dashing cove among the amiable pensioners and the dreadlocked swampies – as Anthony calls them – who usually populate the canal. I try not to look too much.

Diggery is curled up asleep in a sunny spot, his front paws occasionally twitching in his dreams. There's not a cloud in the sky and the towpath is getting busier now, with a sprinkling of dog walkers, joggers and cyclists.

'Here,' Danny says. 'Take a turn at the tiller.'

'Yikes. I'm a bit worried.'

'You'll be fine. I've got you.'

He eases out of the way, and hesitantly I move in front of him. As I do, his hand grazes my waist. I get hold of the tiller, mouth dry.

'Just think ahead,' he says. 'Slow, steady movements.'

Immediately, the tip of the boat starts to drift. He puts one hand on my arm to guide me, the other covering my own hand. His fingers are hot against my skin.

'Easy does it,' he purrs next to my ear.

To be honest, at this moment, I can only just about stand upright. Every fibre of my body is tingling. And I'm afraid that this sort of thrill doesn't come from having control of the tiller of a narrowboat, much as I'd like to think it does. He feels so tall, so manly against me. Instead of watching where the boat is going, I'm looking at the way the strong muscles of his forearm move.

'Concentrate, Fay,' he says. 'There's a lock not far ahead and I want you to take the boat while I work the gates.'

'Right,' I say. 'Right.' Focus, Merryweather. Focus.

He laughs. 'Don't look so terrified.'

'It's not like riding a bike.' Though I do think I'm one step up from the Fensons when it comes to navigation skills. 'I've forgotten everything.'

So Danny keeps his hands where they are and together, carefully, tentatively, we steer *The Dreamcatcher*.

Chapter Twenty-seven

When we reach the first lock, Danny takes up the rope and his windlass for opening the paddles. 'Will you be OK?'

'Fine,' I assure him. 'I'm not a nervous wreck at all. You can totally trust me with your home and all your belongings.'

Winking at me, he jumps on to the towpath. Diggery starts awake and then follows him. 'You'll ace it,' he says. 'Just take it slowly.'

He opens the gates and, with slightly damp palms and a heart that's palpitating with anxiety, I ease the narrowboat into the lock. I chant to myself, 'Don't crash into the wall. Don't crash into the wall.' It shows how long it's been since I've done this: at one time, I could have driven *The Dreamcatcher* in my sleep.

Danny closes the gates behind me, slowly opens the sluice at the top pound and lets the water flow into the lock chamber. *The Dreamcatcher* rises sedately on the foaming water. I adjust the tiller to keep her from bumping the sides, though I'm relieved to see she is amply supplied with fenders.

When the water has reached its level, Danny opens the gates ahead. Then he waves me forward and I drive *The Dreamcatcher* out. With a bit of panicked manoeuvring I manage to come alongside the towpath. Danny and Diggery jump back on.

He grins at me. 'That wasn't too bad, was it?'

'It was great,' I admit. There's something inside me that loves being on the water, and I realise just how very much I've missed this.

I take the tiller as we carry on. Danny goes inside to refill our coffee cups and Diggery, clearly experiencing separation anxiety, leans against my leg for comfort. I look along the boat, watching it glide smoothly through the water, leaving barely a ripple in its wake. People on the towpath wave a greeting as we pass. This ribbon of water that traverses the length and breadth of our country feels like a watery green corridor of peacefulness. I feel so happy and contented and I wonder why I've stopped doing this.

My life has got so small, so humdrum. What with the demands of my mum, and Edie to counsel, and Anthony to please, and the café to run, I don't ever seem to have time to do what I want for myself. In fact, until today, I think I'd completely lost sight of what I want.

There are only a few locks on this stretch of the canal, so we make good time. I manage each one without incident, Danny and I working well as a team, and I'm slowly getting back into my stride. Ahead of the lunchtime crowd, we moor up beside the towpath on the opposite side of the canal to what is obviously a popular pub. One that I've been meaning to try for a long time. It's a smart place, a gastro pub, and my tummy rumbles in anticipation.

There's a flight of locks just ahead of us. At the weekend this area is normally busy with tourists who like to sit and watch the steady stream of boats as they go through. But now, on a Monday lunchtime with all the visitors back at work, it's pleasantly deserted. It's always more nerve-racking to attempt the locks when you've got a party of critical spectators.

I step off with Danny and, taking one rope each, we tie up *The Dreamcatcher*. Diggery runs backwards and forwards between us, checking that we're making a good job of it. Then we walk over the lock gates together – Diggery adeptly leading the way – and go into the pub garden. We bag a table, the nearest one to the water, in full sunshine. Danny fills the metal bowl beneath it with fresh water for Diggery from a nearby tap while I browse the menu. After this morning, I'm now more comfortable, more relaxed in Danny's company. My hormones have stopped doing strange things when he's near me. Well, not quite.

I choose a Caesar salad and Danny has lasagne. He goes in to order it and insists on paying. I wait, feeling chilled and a little decadent. My Monday is usually spent cleaning, tidying, running to the wholesaler for supplies and generally trying to catch up with myself. So this is certainly a welcome change. Even though it's hard, I resist the urge to phone Lija to see how Mum is. She'll be fine. Absolutely fine.

At the next table a young couple sit down. They don't choose seats opposite each other; instead they sit on the same side, so close together that you couldn't get a piece of tissue paper between them. She rests her head on his shoulder while they look at a shared menu. He toys with her hair while murmuring into her ear. Whatever he's saying, he makes her flush and laugh huskily. Beneath the table, their feet are entwined as if they can't bear to be separated for a second. When he looks at her, his eyes shine.

Have I ever been so in love? I wonder. Have I ever played footsie with Anthony beneath a table in a restaurant? I can't recall that I have. He'd wonder what on earth I was doing. Has there ever been the urge to press my body close against his, unable to stand even a millimetre of space between us? No. I don't think so. I wonder what it feels like to be so cherished, so adored.

Danny brings me a glass of chilled white wine, even though I forgot to order a drink. It's perfect and I relax back in my chair as it hits the spot. Danny swigs Peroni from a bottle. He stretches out his long, jean-clad legs and tilts his face to the sweltering sun. I watch the condensation drip along the bottle as he tips the neck to his lips and gulps thirstily at it. On his chin there's more stubble apparent, as if he hasn't shaved for a few days, and the trace of a dark line of moustache appearing over his full lips. The hair looks soft and I wonder what it would feel like to kiss a man with a moustache, to have that brush against my mouth. Anthony shaves so religiously, twice a day, that his skin is often raw, red, dotted with little spots of angry dried blood. I never knew that I liked stubble, but I do.

The pub slowly fills up as we wait for our food.

'It's been a lovely morning,' I tell him. 'I do so love the canal.'

'Me too. I can't wait to get moving again,' he says. Then he shrugs apologetically. 'You know what I mean.'

'Yes. I do. I have to say, it sounds very appealing.'

'You do a lot for other people, Fay.'

'Oh, not really,' I protest. 'Mum mainly. And Edie. She has a tricky time with her relationship. But that's what families are for, aren't they? We have to look out for each other.'

'I've no family left now,' Danny says. 'No ties. My mammy died nearly five years ago and I don't have any contact with my stepfather. We never did see eye to eye. Once Mammy had gone, we dropped the pretence.'

'That's a shame.'

'Sometimes your family are the people who hurt you most,' he says.

'Tell me about it.'

'Who's looking after your mother today?'

'Lija,' I tell him with a grimace.

He laughs.

I continue, 'She's a great girl. I admire her. She has her own individual style.'

'She does that,' he agrees. Then his face softens. 'I like her too.'

I look up, perhaps too sharply. I get a nip of jealousy. Something that I'm not used to. How much does he like her? I wonder. If he was staying, would he be asking Lija on to his boat with her emergency spare pair of pants and toothbrush? She's more his age. More his style.

'Why the frown?'

'Nothing,' I say. 'Nothing at all.' And I shake the thought away. I don't want anything to spoil this day for me.

'I wanted to invite you back to *The Dreamcatcher*,' he says. 'I sat there every night on my own, wishing you'd just call in and keep me company.'

'But you didn't tell me that.'

'I thought it would make your life too complicated and you have enough on your plate.'

'I would have liked it,' I admit. How can I confess that most nights – after I've finished in the café, seen to Mum, ushered Anthony home – I sit on my own feeling exactly the same?

He glances up, but I can't see what's in his eyes because of his shades. 'Me too.'

Then our lunch arrives and it's delicious. We linger over it, steering the conversation on to safer ground. We talk about books and films and I listen to him reminisce about all the places he's travelled to and his adventures, while realising that I have been nowhere, done nothing. Danny gets me another glass of wine and I feel really spoiled.

When we're finished and can find no more excuses to stay longer, we make a move to leave.

'Thank you, Danny. No one looks after me or fusses over me like this.' Certainly not Anthony. 'It's very nice. I could get used to it.'

'You deserve it.'

'I think you're right.' I giggle. 'Oh God, two glasses of wine and I'm as giddy as anything. I'll have to watch my step or I'll end up in the canal this afternoon.'

'Do you think you'll always run the cake shop and café?'

'I think so. In some ways I'm tied to it by Mum, even if I wanted it to be otherwise. Plus I did have a career at the local council before starting the café but, if I'm honest, I hated it. Like you and your corporate life, I'd loathe to go back to that kind of job. I love running Fay's Cakes. I love the house. It's always been my home and the only way I can afford it now is to make it work for itself. It's never going to make me a millionaire, but it suits my needs.'

'Is that what you want? To be a millionaire?'

'No,' I laugh. 'Not really. I just want to be happy.'

Over his sunglasses, Danny's eyes meet mine. They're as dark as jet, unreadable. 'And are you happy, Fay Merryweather?'

Suddenly, tears blur my vision and my throat threatens to close. 'Yes,' I manage. 'I'm very happy.'

But something in Danny's expression, and something in my heart, says, Are you sure?

Chapter Twenty-eight

Danny Wilde is a bad influence on me. By the time we get back to *The Dreamcatcher*, I'm feeling very mellow and more than a bit squiffy.

Together we untie the ropes and Danny starts the engine. This time, I jump on last. We go through the first lock with me at the helm, then Danny takes the tiller and I stand by his side.

'I keep meaning to get a seat fitted here,' Danny says. 'It's on the list of jobs to be done. But I don't often have guests. Well, never,' he corrects. 'I might invest in a "pram cover" for the stern too. People tell me it's not real boating if you do, but I don't mind sacrificing some of my credibility for a degree of comfort.' He grins across at me. 'There's still some of the soft City boy left in my soul. Don't get me wrong, I love to be out in the elements, but I've already stood out in too many heavy downpours to make me want to do it for ever.'

'I don't blame you.'

But today, there's no chance of a shower. The sun is so hot now, high in the sky, the mood very relaxed. We lingered for a long time over lunch and now it's much later than I anticipated.

I had an early start today and my eyes feel heavy with sleep. I stifle a happy yawn.

Danny glances at me. 'Why don't you go and lie down for an hour?' he says. 'You look very sleepy.'

'I am,' I admit.

'You can use my bed in the cabin or, if you want to stay out in the sunshine, there are some cushions that you could put on the seats in the well deck.'

I'm not sure I could cope with being in Danny's cabin, on his bed. 'I'll sit out on the front, if that's OK?'

'I'll pull over. I don't want you to risk walking along the gunwale while you're under the influence,' he teases.

Many a true word spoken in jest. 'Probably for the best.'

So he steers *The Dreamcatcher* to the bank and I hop off on to the towpath. 'I'll have forty winks, then I'll make us some tea and we can have a piece of Lija's cake.'

'Sounds like a plan,' he says. 'Do you want Digs for company?'

'What a lovely idea.'

'Go on, Digs. Go with Fay.'

Obediently the dog jumps off the boat and trots after me and we both get back on at the bow.

There are already comfortable cushions set out along the bench-like seats in the well deck. There's a plastic scratch cover over it too, for inclement weather, but that's been rolled up out of the way today and the sun is blazing down. I kick off my shoes, grab the Union Jack cushions from the sofa inside and prop them up on the bench seat. Then I lie down on them, legs stretched out, feet resting on the inner edge of the boat.

Diggery settles down on the floor next to me, head resting on his paws, and is instantly asleep.

A tall heron stands on the bank, looking intently into the murky water for his supper. When *The Dreamcatcher* approaches, he lifts his wings reluctantly and, with something like a scowl in our direction, majestically takes flight.

I tip my sunhat over my face and, letting my eyes close and my limbs grow heavy, give in to the sensation of sleep. I wish I could strip off all my clothes and lie here naked, letting the sun, the breeze, the water tingle my skin. Then I catch myself. I don't know what happens to me when I come aboard this boat. I start to think weird thoughts, have very strange emotions. Perhaps it really is a dreamcatcher, filtering out all bad thoughts and dreams and leaving only good ones in their place. I certainly feel a sense of self when I'm here, when I'm with Danny, that I don't get anywhere or with anyone else.

I drift off, only vaguely aware of the puttering of the boat, the occasional shift in position from Diggery.

It seems like moments later when I'm rousing but when I glance at my watch, an hour has passed. It's nearly five o'clock and I don't know where the afternoon has gone. I can't think of a time when I've had such a lazy day. I feel refreshed, but still a little drowsy. Diggery is awake too and nuzzles my hand. I pop my head up out of the well deck and wave to Danny, who's still driving on the stern. He indicates that he'll pull over to the grassy bank and then makes a tea sign with his hands. I give him the thumbs-up and pop inside to the galley to put the kettle on.

As we manoeuvre over to the bank, I jump off and help to secure the boat. We're not far from home, as Danny's moored up by Manor Park in Great Linford. Another hour should do it.

'This is my favourite place,' I tell him as I let my feet sink into the lush grass. 'I'm so glad we've stopped here.'

'I thought it looked like a nice area on the way down. It's not the sort of place you'd normally associate with Milton Keynes. From what I've heard of it, anyway.'

'Ours is a much-maligned city. It has some really lovely areas tucked away.'

'I'm going to miss it here. It's a beautiful stretch of the canal.' He takes in the park, the pretty church, the mellow stone manor that was once the country seat of the Lord Mayor of London, and nods contentedly. 'I've enjoyed it, Fay.'

Hesitantly, I say, 'It's been nice having you around too.'

Then he asks, 'Did you have a doze?'

'Yes. Thanks for that. It was just what I needed. Too much to drink at lunchtime, I think.'

'Sometimes it does you no harm.'

'I should embrace the concept of the siesta more often.' Fat chance of that.

The kettle whistles, and while Danny and Diggery potter about on the grass together, I go inside to make some tea. I cut us both a slice of Lija's cake and get a pang of guilt that I've left her alone at the café for so long. I text her to let her know where I am and that it will be a while yet before I'm back.

She texts back: *Mother still alive. Complaining about tea.*

That makes me smile.

Thanks Lija xx I return.

In the park, Danny has laid out a rug on the grass in the shade of an old oak tree and I take the tea to the well deck, handing the cups out to him. Then I get the cake and climb on to the bank myself.

We stretch out on the rug and, despite our hearty lunch, both devour Lija's cake in a nanosecond. Poor Diggery barely gets a look-in.

'This is where the Canal Festival will be held soon,' I tell him. 'It's a big event for us. Loads of narrowboat people come from all over the country to moor up for the weekend. There are stalls and bands. All kinds of music.' I don't tell him that Anthony's handbell-ringing ensemble will be making an appearance; for

146

reasons that I don't want to probe too deeply, I actually don't want to mention him at all today.

'Sounds great.'

'You should come.'

Danny turns on to his stomach and looks up at me. He looks as if he doesn't know how to broach what he's about to say and I brace myself for the inevitable. 'I'm probably going to be leaving first thing in the morning, Fay.'

'Oh.' I knew this was coming. Of course I did. But, if I'm honest, that doesn't make it any easier to hear. 'You'll be back this way sometime?'

'I'm sure I will,' he says hurriedly. 'Definitely. And I'll drop in and see you.' He tries a laugh, but it sounds forced. 'I have to get my cake fix.'

'You'd be very welcome,' I say, and then a traitorous tear escapes from my eye and rolls down my cheek.

Danny frowns at me and I can't fathom the emotions on his face. His thumb gently traces the line of my tear down my cheek and, unable to help myself, I close my eyes and lean into it.

All he says is, 'Oh, Fay.'

Chapter Twenty-nine

Danny moors *The Dreamcatcher* next to the *Maid of Merryweather* and, when I've helped him to tie up, I fuss with putting on my shoes, my old-lady cardigan, my sunhat. I bend down to snuggle against Diggery, stroking his soft fur, and try to bite back the tears that are still threatening.

We've been a bit subdued for the last hour. All of us, even the flipping dog. I always knew that Danny was to be a transient feature, someone who was just passing through, so why am I feeling so sad?

He stands on the towpath while I climb off the boat.

'Well,' I say. 'I've had a really lovely day.' A big fat ball of emotion is lodged in my chest. 'Thank you so much.'

'I'm glad we've had this time together.'

'Oh, me too.' I sound too bright, false. 'It was a nice idea. Very nice.'

'This won't be goodbye for long,' Danny says. The word 'goodbye' stabs me in the heart. 'I'm sure of it,' he adds.

'It would be really lovely to see you again.' I try to keep it light. 'If you're passing.'

'That clematis of yours will want cutting back again next year.'

Next year. So long. 'Yes.' I try a laugh. 'Yes, it will. I'll save it especially for you.'

'You'd better,' he jokes. 'Don't let just anyone get near it with the secateurs.'

'No.'

Then we're both awkward.

'I should get back to Mum. I expect she'll be worried.'

'Of course.'

But neither of us move.

'I didn't think this would be so hard,' he says, a catch in his voice. He puffs out a breath through pursed lips. 'The downside of living a nomadic lifestyle.'

'I guess so.'

'Hug?'

I want to say no. I want to tell him that, for some stupid reason, I'm barely holding it together and that if he holds me I might fall apart completely. I want to say that, in the short time I've known him, he's become very special to me. I want to let him know that he's made me question who I am and what I want from my life.

But I don't. Of course I don't.

Instead, I stand there while he moves forward and takes me in his arms. And they're as strong and as comforting as I knew they would be. We fit together perfectly and he holds on to me so tightly.

He sways and squeezes me and I hear him suck in his breath. My arms twine round him and my fingers stroke his back as we cling together. Then, suddenly, he breaks away and his dark eyes are troubled. 'I'm not sure this is doing either of us any good.'

I can still feel the heat from his body on my skin, even through my dress.

'I won't come up to the house,' he says. 'Say goodbye to Lija for me.'

'Enjoy the wedding.'

'Thanks.'

He might meet someone there. Someone younger, someone more sparkling. Someone who isn't tied down with commitments, who can sail away into the sunset with him. Probably one of the bridesmaids. Isn't that the way?

'Bye, then.' Too bright. Way too bright. My silly façade isn't stopping the dull ache in my stomach, my bones.

I set off down the jetty and Diggery trots after me.

Bending down, I stroke him. 'Bye, Digs.'

I walk on, but still he follows.

'Diggery.' Danny calls him back. 'Let Fay go. We're not staying here.'

The dog, head hanging, goes to stand by Danny. Christ, they both look so forlorn. I bite down on my lip.

So I give a last perky wave to them both and force a happy smile. Then I make my way up the garden, walking briskly, not daring to look back.

I hear Danny whistle and the thump of Diggery jumping on to the boat. Then, when I think it's clear, I glance over my shoulder and, as I thought, they've both gone below decks. So I turn away from the path and go to hide behind the old apple tree in the corner of the garden. I slump to the grass, back against the rough bark, and cry as if my heart will break.

Chapter Thirty

When I finally pull myself together, I wipe my face on the skirt of my dress and go back to the house.

In the kitchen, Lija has the juicer out and is squeezing lemons. The wonderful scent sharpens the air and I guess she's decided we were running short of our popular home-made lemonade. The counter is also covered with batches of scones and two fresh cakes. Despite having to keep an eye on Mum, it looks as if she's been busy while I've been gallivanting with Danny Wilde.

'Hey,' I say, trying to sound a lot more jolly than I feel.

She frowns as she takes in my face. But then Lija always frowns. 'Good day?'

'Yes, lovely.' It sounds false. Ridiculous. I steady myself against the table. 'How's Mum been?'

'Evil,' Lija says, deadpan. 'That woman is total witch.'

'Lija, that's my mum you're talking about.'

'"Lija, is too hot. Lija, is too cold. Lija, is not right at all,"' she says in the style of my mother. A shrug. 'I have not killed Old Bag. But was close thing.'

'You're so fabulous,' I tell her. 'I really appreciate all that you do for me, for her. What would I do without you?'

Then suddenly I break down and cry again.

'What?' she says. 'What?'

But I can't even speak. Lija tuts, wipes her hands on her T-shirt and comes to hold me while I sob great racking sobs against her inadequate, bony shoulder.

'I'm being stupid,' I snivel, my breath wavering. 'Just stupid.'

'What is this about?' She glowers at me. 'This is because I called Old Bag evil witch?'

'No, no.' I wipe my nose on my cardigan. 'Danny's leaving in the morning. And we've had such a lovely time.' More sobbing.

'Then why are you here?' Lija asks. 'Go to him.'

'I couldn't possibly.'

'Now.' She says it as if it's the most uncomplicated suggestion in the world. 'Go.'

I shake my head. 'That would be silly. You don't even know what you're saying.'

'You have until tomorrow. Make most of it.'

'I have Mum to look after.'

'Excuse. Is all. I will stay. I will let her boss me more.'

'No, no, no.' I shake my head in a very empathic way. 'I couldn't ask you to do that.'

'You are not asking. I am telling.' Lija gives me a piece of kitchen roll and I wipe away my tears.

'I'm just being ridiculous.' I dab furiously at my leaky eyes. 'I don't even know why I'm being like this.'

'Because you love him.'

I laugh, and it sounds hysterical. 'Of course I don't.'

Lija rolls her eyes. 'Sometimes you can be very stupid woman.'

'I love Anthony.' As if to reassure myself, I repeat it more forcefully. 'I *love* Anthony.'

My disdainful assistant snorts.

'I do.' I pull in some deep breaths. My lungs hurt. Everything hurts. There's a pain behind my eyes. 'What would I possibly see in Danny? He's young, single, free. Flighty. Here today, gone tomorrow.' Another sob escapes. 'He wants to live an itinerant lifestyle, unencumbered by ties and responsibilities. And I don't blame him.' I wipe my eyes, but still the tears come. 'What would he see in me? I'm old. Old and worn out. I have things, other people to think about. My future is here. I could never leave. I have Mum to consider. The cake shop. Anthony.'

Lija pulls a face.

'Besides, I'm happy with what I've got. Perfectly happy.'

'Yeah.' Lija folds her arms and stares at me. 'You look ecstatic.'

Chapter Thirty-one

'I suppose *you* had a nice day, miss,' Mum says.

'Yes, I did. Thank you.' With two strong cups of tea and some withering glances from Lija, I've managed to get my pathetic emotions under control. I take the tray from my mother's lap.

My lovely Lija gave her some home-made chicken soup for dinner and she's finished every drop.

'That was terrible.' She points at her empty bowl. 'I've been stuck here all day with that rude girl.'

'That rude girl' has gone home now with an extra twenty pounds tucked in her purse as a sign of my unstinting gratitude.

'No need to be stuck here,' I say. 'I can get you up tomorrow, if you like. The weather is fantastic. The garden is looking very pretty. Sitting on a deckchair under the cherry tree would do you a world of good.'

Mum switches on the television. She flicks it to *Holby City*. That's me dismissed then. I turn and head to the door. 'Just shout if you need anything else.'

'I spoke to your sister this afternoon.'

'Edie?'

'Do you have any other sisters?'

'Was she all right?'

'Yes,' Mum says. 'Very concerned about me, obviously. She's *so* caring.' I get the evil eye.

I can't ask Mum if Edie's got a job yet as my mother is convinced that she's running the entire USA single-handedly and isn't relying on a controlling married man for her income.

'She wants you to ring her.'

I glance at my watch. This is early for Edie. I hope nothing awful has happened. 'I'll Skype her now.'

So I go downstairs, text Edie to say that I'm home and set up the laptop in the living room. Moments later, she's on the screen.

'Mum tells me you've been out all day,' she says without bothering with such pleasantries as 'hello'.

'Yes.'

'Again?' Her eyes are glazed; I'd like to blame it on the poor internet connection but in all honesty I think she's a little bit slurry.

'Just with a friend.'

'That same bloke again?'

'Yes.' I don't want to talk about Danny, to Edie or to anyone. As it is, I'm keeping a very tenuous grip on myself and I don't want to be interrogated. 'Mum said you rang this afternoon.'

'I didn't ring,' Edie corrects. 'She got that bloody grumpy Goth girl you employ to set her up on Skype.'

'Oh.'

'I don't know why you keep her on.'

'Because she's a great worker and she helps me out with Mum.'

'Mum hates her.'

'Mum hates everyone, Edie.' Except for Edie, of course.

155

'That girl looks like something out of a horror movie. She must frighten half of your customers away.'

'They love her.' I think, technically, Lija does frighten the customers, but I won't give Edie the high ground on this.

'Look,' Edie says. 'I've got a bit of a problem.'

As always.

'What now?' As if I need to ask. I've had a great day with Danny and I want to hang on to that or I'll be blubbing all over again. I really don't need Edie to bring me down.

'The money you sent me was great. Thank you. Thank you *so* much.' Her voice goes all girly and pathetic. 'I don't know what I'd do without you, Fay.'

I wonder if she's like this with Brandon. It must be exhausting for him. Perhaps there's a good reason he's tiring of her. But then I think that's very unkind of me. You can't help who you fall in love with. And, for some reason, that thought makes me want to weep again.

'But it's gone,' my sister says. 'All of it.' On the screen, she has the good grace to look contrite.

'Edie, it was a thousand pounds.'

'I know. It's expensive to live here.'

'Then maybe you can't any more.'

'That's your answer to everything,' she snaps.

'It seems like the most logical one and, quite possibly, the *only* one,' I retort. 'What else do you want me to offer you?'

She looks taken aback at that. I don't want to fight with Edie. Not now, not today.

'Come home,' I say more softly, even though this is a well-worn record. 'Perhaps if you come back, he'll miss you. Absence can make the heart grow fonder.'

'Or perhaps he'll be glad that I'm out of his *fucking* hair.' She plays with her own long curls and then wheedles, 'Just send me one more payment, Fay. Whatever you can manage. I've got an

156

interview tomorrow. Everything could change. Once I've got a job, once I've sorted things out between me and Brandon, then I'll come home. I'll come home for a visit.'

'I can't keep bailing you out, Edie.'

'I love you.' She pouts at me. 'I need your help. Just this once.'

How can I turn her down? I know how important this is to Edie. I can't see her suffer like this. I cave in, as my sister knows only too well that I will. 'A thousand. That's it, Edie. Then you've cleaned me out completely.'

'Transfer it tonight,' she says, more briskly now. 'I've got the rent to pay.'

'OK. Night, Edie.'

'Night, sis. Love you!'

Closing the laptop, I sag back. That's some more money gone from the *Maid of Merryweather* renovation fund. I look at the worn couch, which also sags. What I couldn't do in the house with that money! Never mind. Edie's need is greater than mine. Or at least more pressing.

I make the bank transfer. A thousand pounds whooshes overseas with the push of a button. My heart sinks as I think how long, how hard I had to work to make that. Still, that's what families do for each other. They help each other out in times of crisis.

It's late now and I can't be bothered to see if there's anything on television. I feel weary, still emotional, when I climb the stairs to my bedroom.

As I pass Mum's door, I see that she's fallen asleep with the television on and I tiptoe in to turn it off. In her sleep, she looks younger, more content. The hard, puckered lines that mar her mouth have softened somewhat. I wish, for her sake, that she could be so relaxed when she's awake.

In my own bedroom, I don't turn on the light. Instead I

wander over to the window and gaze out. The moon is high and bright. My eyes grow accustomed to the dark and as I scan the garden down to the canal, I see that the lights are still on inside *The Dreamcatcher*. When I look closer I see that Danny is sitting outside on the seat in the well deck, strumming a guitar that's slung across his lap. There's a bottle of booze – possibly Jack Daniel's – at his side.

Carefully, quietly, I slide open the window. Diggery's head swivels round at the noise and his tail wags, but Danny doesn't look up. I can hear his guitar now, him softly singing 'The Man Who Can't Be Moved'. Thanks to Lija, I recognise the tune. He has a lovely voice and, though I know nothing much about music, it sounds like he plays well too. I slide down to the floor and curl up, laying my head on the windowsill so that I can stay here for a while and listen.

I could go to him, I think. Just share a drink. Listen to him play his guitar. Nothing more.

Then I realise that, since coming home, I haven't even called Anthony. In fact, until now, he hasn't crossed my mind at all. Not once.

In my mind's eye I see a snapshot of myself, sitting here, moping like a lovelorn teenager. This is nothing but foolishness. I have someone here who loves me. Someone who has loved me unstintingly for a long time. I stand up and close the window. Abruptly, Danny stops playing and looks up. He peers into the blackness, but I don't think he can see me. Diggery, the traitor, barks. I twitch the curtains closed.

Danny will be gone tomorrow and then everything can get back to normal.

Chapter Thirty-two

So, Danny leaves. My world doesn't end. It might be a little less bright without him in it but, on the whole, it carries on much as it did before. Mum continues to grumble. Edie still stiffs me for cash. Lija continues to bake fabulous cakes. And Stan comes every day for lunch.

The only thing that has changed is that I try to be nicer to Anthony. He's my future and I'm trying to see only the positive things in our relationship. When you've been together for as long as we have, it can be very easy to let things drift. Well, no more drifting for me. Now I have my hand very firmly on the tiller – if you'll pardon the expression. I'm trying my hardest not to think of Danny Wilde. And I'm sure, as the days go by, that I'm starting to forget him. I am. Really.

Anthony is just as lovely in his own way and has a lot of qualities. I'm focusing on those. In fact, I'm thinking of taking up handbell-ringing. I know: shoot me. But it's what couples do, isn't it? They have shared interests, passions. And perhaps if I somehow develop a passion for handbell-ringing, then a passion for other things might blossom again. A couple that plays together stays together, right? Even if it's with hand bells. I haven't mentioned this to Anthony yet, but I'm sure he'll be thrilled. I might even take up golf. Who knows? I could do with the exercise.

Anthony is coming round tonight and I'd like us to go out. To whit I haven't made us any supper. There's a nice pub in the village, the Two Barges. It's right on the canal, so we wouldn't have to go far. I know he's always tired after his busy days at work, but I hope he'll be up for it. A change is as good as a rest. Isn't that what they say?

The summer is upon us now and the weather is glorious. Which is never a given in England. My lovely cake shop and café are busier than ever, so I don't get much opportunity to enjoy it during the day, which means I really can't bear to spend every evening sitting indoors watching television. In the few leisure hours I have, I want to get out and live a bit.

I've just come down from giving Mum her tea when Anthony arrives. She looked a bit pale again, I thought, but she hasn't grumbled any more than usual, so I'm assuming she's feeling OK.

Anthony is wearing a harried expression. 'What a day,' he complains. 'What a day.'

I twine my arms around him and kiss him. 'I thought we could go out tonight. For a change.' I've put on a skirt and prettied myself up in anticipation.

He sighs. 'Do we have to? I'm cream-crackered. Sometimes I don't think you understand the pressure I work under.'

'I'm sure I don't,' I agree pleasantly. 'That's why it'll be nice to have a wander along the canal to the Two Barges, a glass or two of good red, unwind a little.'

Anthony looks slightly mollified.

'It can be my treat,' I say.

That goes down even better.

'I'll have to go like this,' Anthony says. He's wearing his second best work suit, which is old and slightly rumpled.

'You look just fine.'

'I don't want to have a late night,' he adds. 'You would not *believe* what I've got on tomorrow.'

'We don't have to stay for long.'

'What about Miranda?'

'She'll be all right for a couple of hours. I'll make sure her mobile is to hand. If there's anything wrong, we can be back in a few minutes.'

Put any obstacles in my way and I vault them effortlessly.

'OK.' He holds up his hands in resignation. 'The Two Barges it is.'

Anthony looks resigned rather than enthralled, but I can live with that. 'Lovely. I'll be two minutes.'

So I grab a cardigan and, with a brief kiss, say goodbye to Mum, who doesn't complain too much because it's Anthony I'm going out with, for once. Then we walk down the lane and over the humpback bridge that spans the canal, and on to the towpath. I link my arm through Anthony's as we stroll.

Because of the glorious weather, the towpath is busy with joggers, cyclists, dog walkers and people like us who are just out for a pleasant meander to the pub. There's a throng of narrowboats moored up along the bank. A couple of the boats have their barbecues out on the bank and the smell of steak and sausages drifts on the air. Their owners sit, waiting in anticipation, on deckchairs by the side of their boats. What an idyllic life. It would be lovely to think that one day Anthony and I could do that with the *Maid of Merryweather* – just take off somewhere, chill out, relax. He'll be retired in another fifteen years, that doesn't really seem so long to wait, does it?

A family with two young children have a picnic spread out by the lock, watching the boats as they pass through. In a few weeks this stretch will be full of barges of all shapes and sizes due to the Canal Festival, and my little café will be overflowing with visitors.

Anthony is quiet as we walk, lost in thought. But that's fine. That's nice. We've been together for so long that, sometimes, there's no need for us to speak. I squeeze his arm in mine.

'What's that for?' he asks.

'Nothing. It's just nice to be out with you. We don't do this often enough.'

'No,' he agrees distractedly.

The pressures of Anthony's work weigh heavily on him. He's not the sort of person who can leave his troubles behind in the office, and I admire him for his dedication and drive. Anthony would never walk out on his job, buy a narrowboat – unseen – on a whim. Then I realise where this train of thought is taking me and stop. I stop it at once.

The Two Barges is a nice pub, old-fashioned – one that hasn't been troubled by a makeover with chalkboards and stripped wooden floors. The 1980s blue-patterned carpet is still firmly in place at the Two Barges. But the food is excellent, straightforward pub grub – you won't find couscous or polenta on the menu at the Barges, oh no. Its main attraction, though, is the garden, which runs down to the canal, a favourite with visitors.

I used to know the owners here really well, but they've retired now and, after many years of gazing longingly at the canal – much like myself – have also opted for a life on a narrowboat. The pub is run by a new, young couple and, as they're still getting to grips with the business, they don't seem to have the time for chit-chat. I hope they don't rip out the carpet any time soon.

I'd like to sit out in the garden, and there's one last table empty right by the canal, but Anthony decrees that it's getting too breezy. So, as a compromise, we bag a table just inside the French doors, with Anthony tucked in the corner and me sitting by the doors in the fresh air. Anthony slips off his suit jacket and hangs it on the back of his chair. He loosens his tie. We spend time perusing the menu, choosing our food. Anthony opts for steak and chips. I think I'll have lasagne.

'Why don't you order for us?' he says. 'I just need to check my emails.'

So I go to the bar, place the order for our dinner and get us two large glasses of house red. By the time I get back to the table, Anthony is sliding his phone into his pocket.

'Everything OK?'

'Fine,' Anthony says. 'Nothing that can't wait until tomorrow.'

'What have you got on at work at the moment?'

'This and that,' Anthony says. 'It's relentless.'

He clearly doesn't want to talk about work.

'Golf?' I venture. 'Are you playing at the weekend?' It's a silly question really, as Anthony always does, unless there's a gale-force wind or torrential rain – and for the next week or so the weather looks set to be fine.

'Yes,' Anthony confirms. 'On Saturday and Sunday.'

'Oh.'

'There might be a trip away coming up soon too. Some of the lads fancy heading off to the Belfry or somewhere for a few days.'

'That'll be nice.'

'It's not confirmed yet,' he says. 'It's only an idea.'

'Sounds like a good one. Perhaps the partners could come along too? I haven't seen your golfing buddies or their wives for ages. It would be nice to catch up with them again.' It's been so long, in fact, that they've quite possibly forgotten who I am.

'Wouldn't that be difficult?' Anthony says. 'With the café and your mum?'

'It depends when you go. It won't be easy, but I'm sure I could work round it given enough notice.' Though any idea of Mum going into the Sunnyside Respite Care Home has been

163

kicked into the long grass. 'I could get Lija and her friends to step in for a day or two.'

Anthony tugs absently at his loosened tie. 'Probably best if it's just for the boys.'

Then we sort of run out of conversation and sit in a slightly awkward silence while we wait for our food. I didn't plan for the evening to be like this. I thought Anthony and I would have fun relaxing together, but there's some kind of atmosphere between us and I don't know why.

As I sit there trying to look absorbed by my surroundings, Deborah from the Village Belles comes into the pub.

'Oh, look,' I say, glad of the distraction. 'It's your new young lady.'

I suspect she's actually quite a bit older than me, but relative to his other ladies, she's definitely young.

'What?' Anthony's head snaps up and, when he sees Deborah, his face falls. 'What's she doing here?'

'Having dinner, I expect.' I have another glance. 'Hmm. And with a rather handsome man.' I lean in. 'Is that her husband?'

'No.' Anthony scowls at them both. 'It's someone she just met. He's not even a proper boyfriend. She got him off the internet.'

'Wow. Good for her. Looks like she hit the jackpot.'

'It's interfering with her practice,' Anthony says crisply. 'The Canal Festival is only a few weeks away and she still can't dampen her bells properly.'

I gather there is no worse crime.

'They could join us, if you like.' I hate to admit this, but it would be nice to have some company and Deborah looks like she's fun to be with.

'No, no, no.' Anthony is clearly horrified by the thought, though I assumed he liked her.

Deborah sees us and waves cheerfully in our direction. I wave back.

'Don't,' Anthony says. He pretends to study the menu even though we've already ordered.

'Why not? It would be nice for me to get to know her.' I could be a fellow handbell-ringing devotee soon.

Despite Anthony trying to pretend he's not there by hiding behind his inadequate disguise, Deborah heads straight to our table. She looks lovely. Bright. I'm not sure the Two Barges has ever seen such glamour. She's wearing a tight, pink body-con dress with matching heels, lips and nails. There's a lot of her squeezed into it. I would love to be able to rock that much va-va-voom.

'Hiya,' she says, all gushy. 'Fancy seeing you here.'

Anthony is tight-lipped. 'Fancy.'

'You look fabulous,' I tell her.

She pats her hair and goes all coy. 'Thanks.' From under her fake eyelashes, she glances at her stylish companion. He's younger than her, I think, tall, and is wearing a fashionable blazer. 'This is Ed.'

'I'm Fay,' I say to Ed.

'Hey,' he says, raising his hand.

Anthony stares at him in a slightly open-mouthed way and is in danger of being quite rude. I have to resist the urge to kick him under the table. Why is he being like this? Anthony is normally the bastion of good manners.

When he fails to speak, I add, 'And this is Anthony.'

Ed grasps Anthony's hand and shakes it vigorously.

This is the moment when we should ask them to sit with us. We're on a table with seats enough for four, but still Anthony stays silent.

Just as it's about to become embarrassing, our meals arrive.

'Oh, here's our food,' Anthony says in a theatrical manner.

'Well.' Deborah looks a little bashful. 'We'll leave you to it.'

'Lovely to see you,' I say. 'I might see more of you soon. I'm actually thinking of taking up handbell-ringing.'

'What?' Anthony spins towards me and his face darkens.

I'm caught off-guard. 'It's just a thought.'

'How nice. We could do with some young blood,' Deborah says. 'Couldn't we, Anthony?'

Anthony doesn't look at all happy that we're making unilateral decisions about *his* ensemble.

'We'll have to see,' he says cagily and then, somewhat pointedly, picks up his knife and fork, holding them poised.

'I'll see you at practice, Anthony.' Deborah slips her arm rather possessively through Ed's and, with a beaming smile to us, goes off to find another table.

'They could have sat with us,' I offer.

'You wanted a night out together, Fay.' He saws crossly at his steak. 'That's what you're getting.'

'And that's nice.'

'Then just drop it.'

'Wouldn't you like me to take up handbell-ringing?'

'I don't know if you have the aptitude for it.' My eyes widen at that. 'It takes patience,' Anthony continues. 'Lots of patience.'

I think I have that. And I have a white blouse. Beyond that, how hard can it be? I don't voice these thoughts, obviously. Instead, I concentrate on my lasagne.

Across the room, I hear a laugh and, at the same time, Anthony and I both look up. It's Deborah, who seems quite absorbed by her companion.

'They seem to be getting on well,' I quip.

'She knows nothing about him,' Anthony says darkly. 'He could be a serial killer for all she's aware.'

'He's a very smartly attired one.'

'All she's seen is a young man with a pretty face and her head's been turned.' I feel myself flush guiltily. 'She missed practice this week,' Anthony continues. 'Hasn't known him for five minutes and yet she's ready to sacrifice everything for him.' He shakes his head, clearly filled with disappointment in his new team member. 'I'll get us another drink, shall I?'

Before I can answer, he grabs our glasses and heads to the bar.

Chapter Thirty-three

Anthony seems a little bit more mellow as we walk home along the towpath, arm in arm. Maybe a ten-ounce rump steak and three glasses of red have done the trick.

And now, with a bit of prompting, he's telling me about the round of golf he played yesterday. 'If I hadn't missed two putts,' he says, 'I could have had a birdie.'

To be honest, I've probably heard more about this round of golf than anyone needs to. I've had it replayed stroke by stroke over dinner. That was after the blow-by-blow account of the last handbell-ringing session, 'Bridge Over Troubled Water' proving particularly tricky with the ladies. The more I think about it, the more I'm sure that handbell-ringing isn't for me. It's good for couples to have separate interests.

The boats on the canal are settling down for the night; the lights inside are coming on. I can't help my thoughts drifting towards Danny. I wonder where he is now. I wonder if he's moored up for the night, settling down with Diggery – and maybe someone else. I think back to the day we spent together, my evening on *The Dreamcatcher* with him. He's a stranger to me and yet he's so very easy to be with. I look at Anthony in the gathering darkness and know that there's something not right between us. But how can things be right when I seem always to have another man on my mind? I wish I could scrub my brain out with bleach and remove all trace of Danny Wilde. What good can come of continually dwelling on him?

We retrace our earlier steps across the bridge and make our way down the lane. I wish I'd thought to bring the torch, but I didn't. Stan's lights are off in his cottage, so he must have retired for the night.

Though it's only just past ten o'clock, our house is in darkness too when I let us in. 'I think Mum must be asleep.'

'Put the kettle on,' Anthony says, flopping into the sofa rather than his usual armchair. 'I'll see if there's anything on telly.'

I do as instructed and then stand in the kitchen waiting for the kettle to boil. I can hear the sound of laughter coming from the next room, and wonder what Anthony's watching.

Opening the back door, I lean on the frame and gaze out at the canal. It's picked out in the moonlight and the trees that border it sway gently in the breeze. I feel as if Danny's name is in the air, blowing on the wind. I can almost hear it. I take in a lungful of air and try to breathe the thought away. But it's a persistent little beggar. Perhaps he's still in London, having fun with a younger, hipper crowd. Maybe he's already forgotten his time with us at Fay's Cakes. Wherever he is, I'm pretty sure he won't be spending his evenings discussing the finer points of handbell-ringing or the perfect execution of a bunker shot.

Tears spring to my eyes. I'm trying so hard to forget him, I am, but I can still feel the caring touch of his hand on my arm, the thrilling brush of his lips on my cheek. It's too much to bear. I miss him. Dear God, I miss him.

'Is that tea ready yet?' Anthony shouts above the noise of the television.

Wiping my eyes, I lock the back door, make the tea and take

two mugs through for us. Anthony had a generous portion of crème brûlée following his steak, so I'm assuming he doesn't want any cake.

I sit down next to him and put his mug on the coffee table. To my surprise, he slips his arm around me.

'All right, old thing?' he says and gives me a brusque squeeze.

'Yes. Fine.' I hope my voice doesn't give away my inner turmoil. 'Absolutely fine.'

'There's nothing on the telly.'

'I thought I heard you laughing at something.'

'Load of old twaddle,' he says.

Even more surprising, Anthony takes the mug of tea out of my hands and puts it on the coffee table, placing it carefully next to his. Then he moves in to kiss me. And I'm so shocked that I almost shy away. It's a proper full-on kiss, though we're not a snoggy couple. I can't think of the last time we smooched like this. We've been together for so long, yet it feels as if I'm kissing a stranger.

Anthony's lips move against mine. He tastes of stale wine and food. He presses against me and his body is heavy, unyielding. I can feel my heart pounding, and it's not with passion, it's panic. I want to push him away and yet I know we need to do this, we need to reconnect on a level that's been sorely missing.

'Let me get comfortable,' I say, and adjust myself on the sofa. I take a minute to gather my senses and then we kiss again.

'I could stay,' Anthony says huskily. 'It's been a long time, Fay.'

'Well ...'

'Your mother's asleep.'

When exactly did we last make love? So many months ago that I can't remember. It's difficult now. My mum's always around when we're here and we hardly ever go to Anthony's place, also due to Mum.

170

When we do get round to it, our sex has always been fairly pedestrian. A choice of two positions. One up, one down. You know what I mean. Even in the early days. But I've liked that. I'm not a person who's comfortable naked. And Anthony is happy with under-the-duvet-lights-off sort of sex too. If he asked me to dress up in a nurse's uniform/use handcuffs/wear a gimp mask, I'd probably pass out. I like to make love in a bed. A comfortable one. I'm not a back-of-a-car or an up-against-a-wall type of person. I've never ever had sex outside.

'Let's go upstairs,' Anthony urges.

'Yes,' I make myself say. 'That would be nice.'

So I take the mugs and pop them into the dishwasher while Anthony turns off the television and the lights. I set the bread maker for tomorrow so that we'll have a nice fresh loaf. I check the back door is locked one last time and try not to glance towards the canal.

Anthony has already gone upstairs by the time I come back into the living room, so I tiptoe up after him, careful not to wake Mum.

He's already in the bathroom and I know he'll be borrowing my toothbrush, which freaks me out a little. I hate to share my toothbrush, but equally we both need to be nice and clean before we make love. I'd actually prefer to take a shower first, but I'm worried that if this takes too long I'll be tired in the morning.

I fuss with turning down the bed while I wait for Anthony to finish his ablutions and try to find my nightie. Anthony doesn't really like me wearing pyjamas, so I keep something a bit more flimsy in the bottom of the drawer especially.

Eventually he comes out of the bathroom in his boxer shorts, a little tummy burgeoning over the top. His shirt and trousers are draped over his arm. Again, it's some time since I've seen Anthony naked and I'd forgotten how very pink his skin is. His

171

chest is freckly and there's a smattering of fuzzy, sandy hair that's flecked with grey.

'I'll have to get up early so that I can go home and change,' he says. 'It wouldn't do to go into the office in last night's clothes. Do the walk of shame.'

'No,' I agree. 'I'll set the alarm for six?'

'Yes. That'll give me plenty of time.'

'I can make you breakfast too.'

Then I take my nightie and head to the bathroom. I strip off and give myself a good wash with a flannel, run my toothbrush under the hot tap for a minute and then clean my teeth. I slip on my nightie and take a good look at myself in the mirror. I feel silly in this nightie. It's black and strappy with a little bit of lace at the top, a bow and a loop of Swarovski crystals. It's not me at all. But Anthony likes it.

I wonder whether I'm still a desirable woman. I'm not slim, not fat. My hips are full, but so are my boobs – maybe one cancels out the other. I'm not as pretty as Edie. She looks more like Mum, whereas I've always taken after Dad. My hair could have something a bit more exciting done to it, if I ever had the time. I've got good skin, eyes, my own teeth. I'm young. Ish. In my prime. But I don't feel it. I feel middle-aged, bowed down with responsibility. And a little strappy nightie isn't going to change that.

When I go back into the bedroom, Anthony has already got into bed. His boxer shorts are on the chair with his shirt and trousers. I slide into bed beside him. I normally sleep on the right of the bed, but so does Anthony. As he's in bed first, he's bagged the best side.

'Well,' I say. 'This is nice.'

In unison, we wriggle down under the duvet. I turn off the bedside light. Then I turn it back on again and sit up. 'Forgot to set the alarm.' I fiddle with the clock.

Light off and I wriggle down again. We turn to face each other and Anthony snakes an arm around me and kisses me again. I lost my virginity at the age of eighteen, yet I still haven't learned what to do with the arm that's beneath me. Where are you supposed to put it? I've never worked that out. In the meantime, with a decade of doing this between us, we struggle to find out how we fit together.

Anthony moves to kissing my neck.

'Shall I take my nightie off?' I ask.

'If you want to.'

'It's up to you.'

'Go on then.'

I sit up and, as I go to lift the hem, I hearing Mum banging her stick.

'Fay,' she shouts. 'Fay!' More banging. 'I've forgotten to take my tablets.'

'It's Mum,' I say pointlessly.

'Fuck,' Anthony says. And Anthony never swears. He flops back on the bed.

'She'll need a cup of tea to take them with,' I say apologetically. 'But I'll be quick.'

I jump out of bed, tug on my dressing gown and pad across to Mum's room. 'I'm here, Mum,' I say. 'I'll go and put the kettle on. I'll be back in just a minute.'

But if I'm honest, I've never been more relieved to hear Mum banging for me. Sorry to be vulgar, but the other sort of 'banging' was holding no appeal for me at all. And when I've given her tablets to her and got back to my own room, I'm even more relieved to find that Anthony is fast asleep.

Chapter Thirty-four

In England, we have waited a very long time for a decent summer and now here it is in all its luscious glory. The flowers in full bloom are ablaze with colour, the bees sate themselves on an abundance of pollen, the sky is boldly, brazenly blue.

Last year was one of the wettest on record. This year it's already the hottest, and every day Fay's Cakes is teeming with visitors. Some weekends we've even had a queue waiting for tables. We've extended the opening hours and Lija has helped to put a spring in my step by creating some new cake recipes. We've had a lovely time baking together in the evenings and now have some new cake delights on the menu – apple and cinnamon, sticky ginger and orange, an old-fashioned seed cake and, now that they're in season, a strawberry dessert cake.

It's well over a month since Danny's been gone and, though I try very hard not to notice the time too much, there isn't a day that goes by when I don't have a fleeting moment when I think of him. Sometimes it hurts less when I do.

This is the weekend of the much-anticipated Canal Festival, and today the café is super-busy. We've made lots more cakes for sale in the *Maid of Merryweather*, and have even, for the first time, pre-packed some sandwiches to go in the narrowboat shop too. I think we should make this a regular thing as they've been very popular.

Both of Lija's friends whom she shares her house with, Krista and Evelina, have been drafted in to help us out. Krista has been left to man the *Maid of Merryweather* for the last two days and is doing really well. Takings have soared and I've asked her to stay on for the festival weekend. If it carries on like this, I should think about employing someone for the rest of the summer. I'm sure we'd sell more if there was a permanent assistant on board.

To be honest, I've earned so much more than usual in the last few weeks that I might even be able to send Edie some extra money. No doubt she needs it, as her situation hasn't improved. She's still in the apartment, just about, but I can't see it lasting. And there's still no sign of a job on the horizon.

I do a turn of the garden, collecting empties and seating a family. In the kitchen, I stack the debris of an afternoon tea for two in the sink.

'Stinky Stan's soup is ready, Fay.'

'Lija.' I tut at her. I'm sure she does it for effect sometimes.

She turns from the stove to give me one of her rare sardonic smiles.

'You'll go straight to hell,' I warn.

'I will be able to look after your mother there too.'

I laugh as I take the tray she offers me and trot out into the garden. Stan is on the last table down by the canal. He's wearing a white short-sleeved shirt with a V-neck Fair Isle slipover and a Panama hat that looks as if it's done at least two turns round the globe.

'Hello, Stan.'

'Hello, dearie,' he says. 'Haven't seen you for days.'

'I'm sorry. I've been so busy.'

175

'No mind. Lovely Lija has been looking after me very well in your absence. She's a super girl. Sparky.'

'She's that all right.'

'Talented too. I told her she should do more with her skills.'

It's something I've tried to encourage her to do too. Without much luck. 'What did she say to that?'

'She told me to naff off.' He laughs.

'It's a good job you're family, Stan, and not just a customer.' I shake my head in despair. 'But that's too rude.' Even though it's one step down from what Lija would normally say. 'I'll have a word with her.'

'Don't,' he says. 'I love her just as she is. She keeps me on my toes.'

'And me.' I put down his tray. 'Here's your lunch. Pea soup with fresh mint from the garden.'

'Oh, lovely,' Stan says. 'My favourite.'

I check that no one else needs my attention and slip into the seat next to him for a second. 'Are you going to walk up to the Canal Festival later?'

'I wouldn't miss it for the world. It's the highlight of my calendar.'

'Not very thrilling for someone who's been a test pilot and a film stuntman.'

'I take my excitement where I can now, dear Fay. I'm just glad that, at my age, I can still walk at all.'

'Do you need any help getting up there?'

'No, no,' he says. 'I'll take my time. Enjoy the sunshine. I can stop and sit on the lock if I need a rest.'

'Let me know if you change your mind. I can zip you up there in the car. It's no trouble.' I pat his hand and smile.

'I'll be fine,' Stan assures me. 'Will you go up when you've finished here?'

'Yes, for an hour.' Strangely Lija is keen to go to the festival

176

and won't be able to keep an eye on Mum for me, so it will have to be a brief visit. 'I want to be there to support Anthony. He's there with the Village Belles again.'

Stan grimaces.

'I know.' I give a laugh and lower my voice. 'It's a terrible noise, but it keeps him out of trouble.'

'No news from that young lad, what was his name, Danny?'

'Noooo. He's long gone.'

'I'm surprised,' Stan says. 'I thought he'd be back this way again.'

'Maybe one day.' I stand up.

'Perhaps he'll come back for the festival.'

'I'm not sure it's his style.'

'There are boats from all over the country that come to it. You never know.'

Despite saying it doesn't hurt to think about Danny, it does, and I don't really want to be drawn into a conversation about him. He is much better out of sight, out of mind.

'Must get on.' I stand up and stretch my tired back. 'Enjoy your lunch, Stan. Lija's made a wonderful sticky ginger and orange cake. I'll bring you a bit in a while.'

'Champion,' he says and rubs his hands as he peers at his soup.

I can't bear to think that one day I won't see Stan in the café every day, telling me that whatever soup we serve him is his favourite. The thought of it brings a lump to my throat and, on impulse, I peck his dry cheek.

'What's that for?' he says.

'Nothing,' I tell him. 'Have a nice time at the festival. I'll catch up with you later, Stan.'

Chapter Thirty-five

Lija has been banging pans around for an hour now. Finally she crashes the last one to the draining board. My nerves stop jangling as she wipes her hands on her T-shirt.

'Right,' she announces. 'I am off. Laters.'

'Is there something I'm missing?' I say. 'Why such a rush to get to the festival?'

Lija gives her usual shrug. 'New barman at Two Barges.' She holds up her handbag. 'Emergency pants and toothbrush at ready.'

'Oh. Good luck with that.'

Perhaps I should have taken more notice of today's outfit. Black vest top, skimpier than usual, with a hint of lace even. The briefest of denim shorts with black tights and her very best red Doc Martens. Lija is clearly out to impress.

'Don't forget to come into work tomorrow,' I remind her needlessly. 'The forecast is fabulous and we're going to be rushed off our feet.'

'Have I ever let you down?'

'No,' I say truthfully. 'You never have.'

'Are you coming to festival?'

'Yes, yes. Anthony's ensemble are playing. I want to be there to support him.'

Lija pulls a face.

'Don't say a word. Nothing!'

For once, she actually laughs.

Taking a twenty-pound note from my purse, I press it into Lija's hand. 'Have a drink on me. You've earned it today.'

'Thank you, Fay.' Even though it's a small gesture, she seems genuinely moved.

'I couldn't manage without you. You know that.'

'Don't get mushy,' she says with a scowl. Lija slings her backpack on her shoulder. 'Don't be long or you will miss fun.'

'I'm just going to tidy up here and then I'll be with you. Did you pay Evelina and Krista?'

'Yes,' she says. 'I took money from biscuit tin.'

Soon we'll need to get a proper digital till and everything, but I'm trying to put off that fateful day.

'Can you check that Krista's all right on your way out, please? If she needs any help or any more cake, phone me.'

Lija nods and heads out.

I watch her walk down the garden, swinging her hips with all the confidence of youth, and let out a sigh. Hurriedly I wipe down the work surfaces, put some of the pots and pans away and unload the dishwasher ready for the next day.

Then I go upstairs to change into my one and only sundress, which has taken a battering this summer. As I'm ready to leave, I pop into Mum's room and wonder, once again, what on earth she is doing confining herself to a small life like this when it's so very unnecessary. Even if she was in a wheelchair we could get her down to the festival for an hour or two. If Stan can manage it, then I'm certain she could. And I'm sure she'd enjoy it, if only she'd try.

Even I've caught the sun this year; there's a sprinkling of

freckles over my nose, and my arms are a golden brown. But Mum seems to be getting paler and paler. Her grey hair is turning white and thinning at a shocking rate. I wash it for her once a week and, though I'm as gentle as can be, I seem to leave more and more in the sink each time.

The room is both stuffy and stifling. 'Shall I open the window, Mum? It's very warm in here.'

'No,' she says. 'I'm feeling chilly.'

'You can't be. It must be over seventy degrees out there.'

'I can hear music,' Mum says.

'It's the Canal Festival. I'm going to pop along there for an hour.'

She looks me up and down. 'That's why you're all dressed up.'

'Anthony's playing there with the Village Belles.' He isn't quite headlining, as he's been saying, but he is on soon and I need to get a move on or I'll miss him. Then there'll be hell to pay.

'I'd like to hear that.'

'If you'd get up, Mum, you could do.'

She waves a hand irritably. 'I'm too tired.'

I don't have the strength to argue with her. 'I won't be long. Your phone's right here if you need to ring me.'

'Where's Lija?'

'She's gone to the festival too.'

'Oh. Well, you have fun then,' she says grudgingly. 'Don't you worry about me.'

'I'll be home before you know it.'

I leave her looking miserable and me feeling guilty. But if I don't go, then Anthony will be upset. Whatever I do, I'll make someone unhappy, and I'd rather be at the festival with everyone else than here.

So, vowing to make it up to Mum later, I make a rush for the

180

back door, collecting my sunhat on the way. Moments later I'm on the towpath heading down towards the park at Great Linford. Colourful boats of all shapes and sizes have been arriving since yesterday. All the moorings by the café, as far as the eye can see, are taken. It will mean a busy week, I expect, as people will stay for a little while and then slowly drift off over the course of a few days. Perhaps we should open on Monday. It would be foolish not to. I'll see what Lija thinks.

As I get nearer to the park, I can hear that the festival is in full swing. I haven't walked down here since the last day I spent with Danny, when we stopped and had our picnic before going home. It makes me feel melancholy to think of it.

The music that has been drifting down towards the café is rocking now. Some sort of indie band are on the stage that's been erected in front of the manor house. There are plenty of craft stalls on the towpath side of the canal, many of them selling narrowboat-related paraphernalia – traditional rose-painted canalware, rope fenders, rag rugs, lace cabin dressings. Some of the boats themselves are selling food, as we do on the *Maid of Merryweather*. There's the *Cheddar Cheesy*, a boat selling all kinds of tasty British cheeses, which I know is a regular up and down the canals. There's also someone selling the ubiquitous cupcakes. A few boats are advertising rentals and canal holidays. I can see that, across the water, the area in front of the alms cottages has been given over to food stands. There is, of course, the requisite burger van, which has a long queue, but there are some more inventive food stalls too – a vegetarian curry stall and one with wonderful, spicy-smelling Caribbean food. The Two Barges has set up a beer tent which is doing a roaring trade, and there's a huge crush outside it.

This is a big crowd by any standards. It's a very popular event on the local calendar and the glorious weather has brought out more people than ever. The festival always has a diverse range of musical styles, but I feel that the Village Belles sit uncomfortably here. I check my watch. Half an hour until Anthony is due to play. I feel quite nervous for him.

If I don't get a move on I might miss it altogether. I still need to go over the bridge to get into the park, and time is pressing. I'm about to put a spurt on when I'm stopped right in my tracks.

Ahead of me there's *The Dreamcatcher*, and Danny, smile on his face, is hammering pegs into the bank to tie her up. He's the last person I expected to see, and my mouth goes dry.

After all these weeks, long, long weeks, he's here. And I didn't know. I didn't think he'd come. I couldn't have hoped for it.

I'm frozen to the spot, unable to move. From behind him Diggery barks a welcome and bounds towards me.

Then Danny turns and sees me. His smile widens. 'Fay!' he shouts with delight.

And I could weep. Weep for joy.

Chapter Thirty-six

'Hey. It's so good to see you,' Danny says, animated. 'I hoped you'd be here.'

He's right in front of me now and I want to hug him or something, but in my ridiculously shy British way, I just stand here tied.

His dark eyes rake me and I could melt under his scrutiny. 'You look fabulous,' he rushes on, excited. 'All tanned and stuff.'

'It's been a hot summer,' I say, scraping the barrel of inane comments.

'It sure has.'

He looks fantastic too. Sun-kissed, relaxed and even more muscled than I remember. His dark hair is longer, but still messy on top, with a random quiff. He's wearing a black T-shirt and faded grey jeans. My eyes could feast on him for hours.

I bend down to fuss over Diggery, who is going into paroxysms of ecstasy. It seems the little dog hasn't forgotten me.

'You've had a good time?' I ask.

'The best,' he says. 'The wedding was amazing. And then, well, I sort of stayed on a bit. I didn't mean to be in London for so long. But I saw a lot of old friends and it was good to hang with them again.'

'That's nice.' I wonder if he's hankering after the excitement of his previous life.

'Some of my old buddies have come up for the weekend. I'd been telling them all about my new lifestyle on the canal – which they all just take the piss out of – then I remembered the festival and it seemed like a good excuse for a party.'

'That's nice.'

'Come on,' he says. 'You've got to meet them.'

I follow him the few steps back to *The Dreamcatcher*, wondering if he's told his friends all about me too. Then I think, why would he? I was probably a passing moment in Danny's life. I bet he hasn't mentioned me at all.

As I reach the barge, a young girl steps out of the cabin and Danny holds out a hand to her, which she takes before climbing out of the boat.

The girl's slender, long-legged like a colt. She's wearing a white strappy top and denim shorts that are even briefer and tighter than Lija's. Her long blonde hair is straight and shiny. Her teeth are so dazzlingly white that the sun pings off them.

'This is Sienna,' Danny says. 'I used to work with her in the City. I'm introducing this strictly city chick to my new life.'

She giggles.

'This is Fay,' Danny says. 'I worked for her for a bit in the spring, doing odd jobs and stuff.'

'Wow,' Sienna says, as if she can't believe Danny would lower himself thus.

Clearly he hasn't talked about me, and I try not to notice that he doesn't introduce me as a friend.

Another two people come from the back of *The Dreamcatcher*, more obviously a couple. The man has his arm slung round the girl's shoulders.

184

'This is Henry and Laura. Also old work colleagues.'

'Nice to meet you,' I say shyly.

'They love my old tub,' Danny says proudly.

'Totes amazeballs,' Sienna says.

Danny laughs as if she's the funniest person in the world. 'Come and get a drink with us, Fay. We were just about to hit the beer tent.'

'Anthony's playing in a few minutes.' I gesture towards the stage in front of the house on the other side of the canal. 'I should go and listen to him.'

'I'll come with you,' he offers. 'I need to know what you've been doing all summer.'

'But your friends . . .'

'They can look after themselves for a while.' He turns to them. 'Hey, Sienna, guys. Go on ahead of us to the beer tent. I'll catch you up in a while. I want a few minutes with Fay.'

'Sure,' Henry says. 'Want us to get one in for you?'

'No. But don't get too far ahead of me. I don't want you falling into the canal on the way back to the boat.'

They wave and join the steady stream of people wandering in the direction of the park.

Danny turns back to me and grins. 'Sorted. I'm all yours.'

'The handbell-ringing is about to start,' I tell him anxiously. 'I have to get going.'

'Then I'll come with you.'

'You *really* don't want to listen to it, believe me.'

'I do,' he insists. 'If we've not got time to grab a drink first, let me get a couple of beers out of the fridge on the boat, though. Want one?'

Suddenly, there's nothing I need more in life than a cold beer. Well, not quite.

'Yes, please.'

He jumps back on to the boat and reappears seconds later

brandishing two bottles of beer. 'This should see us right for a while.'

We make our way along the towpath, then over the bridge and into the park. It's slow going through the bustling crowd there, but we pick our way carefully through to the main stage, where the rock band are just about to finish their set.

'Good,' Danny says, nodding his appreciation at them.

We find a space on the grass near the front of the crowd and park ourselves. The band belt out the last tune and receive rapturous applause from the audience. A gulp travels down my throat. Poor Anthony has a hard act to follow.

In the brief interval between acts, Danny swivels to face me. 'So, tell me everything. How's it all been going?'

'Fine,' I say.

'Café busy?'

'Very.'

'How are Lija and Stan?'

'The same as ever. They're both up here somewhere, but I haven't seen them yet. We could try to find them later.' Then I remember his friends. 'Oh, but you'll want to get back to your mates.'

'No, no,' he says. 'It's a great idea. They won't mind. What else have you been doing? You haven't upped and married your man while I've been away?'

'No,' I say. 'You?'

He shakes his head. 'Footloose and fancy-free as ever.'

I wonder if Sienna's aware of that.

'Tell me about the wedding.'

'Good crack. Especially the stag weekend. Traffic cones were worn on heads, that kind of thing. I haven't done that in a long while.' He swigs his beer. 'Nothing much else to say. The bride looked beautiful. We all got wasted. Typical wedding. I guess I didn't realise how much I'd missed my friends. Don't get me

186

wrong, I love the canal, *The Dreamcatcher*, but it *is* a lonely life. I think I just needed to let off a bit of steam.' He laughs. 'I took some stick from that lot.' He gestures with his bottle towards the beer tent where his friends are. 'That's why I persuaded them to come up this weekend. I picked them up at Leighton Buzzard Station last night. They couldn't believe it had taken me a week to get there on the boat when it had only taken them half an hour or so on the train.'

'They've enjoyed it though?'

'Yeah.' Then he shrugs. 'It's OK for a day or two. But they're party animals. Still like the fast life. As I did once.' Those dark eyes fix on mine. 'I lived on *The Dreamcatcher* while I was in London, which was nice. But I couldn't stand the pace of the partying any more. Three or four nights in a row and I was desperate to get back to the peace of the canal. I'd had my fill of pubs and clubs. I think I've got all that out of my system once and for all. I just needed time to take another look.'

There's a smattering of polite clapping and I realise that Anthony and his ladies are all up on the stage and ready to perform.

'This is your other half? The guy at the front?'

'Yes.'

He subjects Anthony to close scrutiny but says nothing.

'I can hardly bring myself to watch this,' I confess to Danny.

'Not a fan of the old hand bells?' he teases.

'A long way from it. But I really want it to go well, for Anthony's sake.'

'It'll be fine,' he assures me. 'Most people look drunk enough not to care what's on.'

Unfortunately, I'm not one of them.

A few people drift away before the Village Belles even start. The ladies are looking very smart in what I know are new blouses. I smile to myself. Deborah still stands out a mile from

187

the rest. I knew she would. Her blouse fits tightly over her curvy shape and has a plunging neckline showing her ample cleavage. Where the other, more elderly ladies are wearing comfortable shoes, Deborah is in leopard-print numbers with spiky gold heels. Good for you, girl. Bringing some much-needed glamour to the sedate world of handbell-ringing.

Anthony lifts his baton. He looks like a haughty headmaster and so much older than his years. He's wearing ill-fitting black trousers and a boring white shirt. I suddenly feel embarrassed for him, and then I'm ashamed that I feel like this. He's my partner and I should be proud of him. But I'm not. Is it wrong that I want to run away and hide?

On Anthony's instruction, the women start to clang out 'Tie a Yellow Ribbon Round the Ole Oak Tree'.

It's the most hideous noise on earth.

It seems that my companion thinks so too: Danny turns to me, eyes wide, and says, 'Wow. Seriously?'

'Yes,' I answer. 'Seriously.'

Chapter Thirty-seven

We sit and listen to the Village Belles as Anthony encourages them to slaughter the Beatles' classic song 'Yesterday', followed by the brutal murder of Elvis's 'Are You Lonesome Tonight?'

It's bad. Very bad.

I keep my eyes fixed forward.

In fairness to Anthony, he might not be thrilling the entire crowd, but there's a hardy group of pensioners at the front who are lapping it up. I think they're quite probably the husbands, sisters and brothers of the ladies of the Village Belles. There are also some appreciative children dancing too. The sort you see at weddings, rushing all over the dance floor like mad things to Status Quo hits.

The thing I have to admire is that Anthony is in his element. This is his moment, his Royal Albert Hall, his O2 Arena. It's what he loves. *This* is his passion. Who am I to take that away from him?

Danny, I think, has been stunned into silence.

After one more song, he puts a hand on my arm. 'I can't do this,' he whispers. 'We *have* to leave.'

189

I smile despite myself. 'I can't,' I whisper back. 'What about Anthony?'

He grins at me mischievously and those eyes that I have, against all reason, grown to love, twinkle at me. 'Fuck Anthony.'

I laugh when I really shouldn't. 'OK.'

So he takes my hand and I follow him.

There's a terrible crush at the bar in the beer tent but, with a bit of judicious pushing and shoving, we squeeze to the front. Our bodies are pressed close together as we wait to be served.

'Good Christ, Fay,' Danny laughs as we're squashed up against the bar together. 'That was terrible.'

'He loves it,' I say. 'I feel really awful for sneaking away. Anthony will be so disappointed in me.'

'It made me want to commit bloody murder.'

I pull a disapproving face and then admit, 'Same here.'

'If it floats his boat.' He shrugs, but is clearly unable to comprehend.

It floats his boat more than anything else in the world. Even golf. Even me.

'You should never criticise a man's choice of wife or musical instrument,' Danny concludes.

Then the barman comes and Danny orders half a dozen bottles of beer and a bottle of red wine. 'That'll keep us going for a little while.'

We fight our way out again, arms loaded with our booze stash and some plastic cups. By the time we emerge into the sunlight, Anthony's performance has finished and they're already preparing the stage for the next act.

Danny scans the crowd; his young eyes must be better than mine as moments later he says, 'Ah! There they are.'

'I should leave you with your friends,' I say. 'You'll want to spend time with them.'

'Nonsense,' he replies. 'You're not going anywhere.'

He shifts all his beer to tuck it under one arm, then takes my elbow with his hand and we're off and moving through the crowd.

Danny's friends have found themselves a space under one of the old chestnut trees to the side of the stage and the manor house. They're sprawled out, relaxing, on the grass.

'Hey,' Danny says and flops down.

I sit beside him and Danny hands round the beers and cracks open the wine.

'Good timing, mate,' Henry says. 'We were just running dry.'

Danny pours some wine into a plastic cup for me and then tops up Sienna's.

'This festival is so quaint,' Sienna says. 'So old-fashioned.'

She's probably more used to Glasto or Download or something. I say this as if I know anything about festivals at all.

As I sip from the white plastic cup, a text pings into my phone. It's Anthony.

Just giving one of the ladies a lift home. Will be back later.

My return one says, *Well done. You were great. xx* Then I cross my fingers before I send it so that it's not really a lie.

'We should all go to Fay's fabulous cake shop tomorrow,' Danny says to his friends. 'For lunch or something. She runs a great place. Her cake is the best on the planet.'

'Sounds marvellous,' Henry says. 'But we're thinking of heading back first thing in the morning.' He grimaces. 'I've got a flight out of Heathrow, early evening.'

'Where to?' Danny asks.

'States. Two days in New York. Brinkley Corporation. Back-to-back meetings.'

'Oh, man,' Danny throws back his head and laughs. 'I don't envy you that.'

191

'Yeah, think of me when you're doing whatever it is you do on the canal.'

'Nothing,' Danny says. 'I do *absolutely* nothing.'

'Fuck off, waster.' Henry throws the stack of remaining plastic cups at Danny, who dodges them expertly.

I feel out of place here, on the edge of their conversation. They're young, bright, hungry, and I've got nothing to talk about. Mum is back at the house alone and I wonder if she's OK. And, of course, that's my cue to leave.

Finishing up my wine, I say, 'I should be getting back.'

'No.' Danny takes my cup and refills it. 'Stay. You can't go now. Look, there's another band coming on.'

So, with that tiny amount of persuasion, I stay.

The next group are very good. A riot of people who punch out soul hits into the mass of bodies as the sky starts to darken. Lights come on in the trees around the park and the party mood picks up.

Sienna and Laura kick off their shoes and dance barefoot in the grass. Henry wanders off in search of more booze, as everything that Danny and I brought from the beer tent has already been consumed. Danny and I are sitting close together, just watching the band, not speaking.

Then, as they start up with 'Respect', he turns to me and says, 'I couldn't go back to the City, Fay. Not now. Probably never. I listen to how Henry talks about his life and it makes me shudder. The canal has turned me into a boring old fart.'

'You couldn't ever be that,' I tell him. And I have a degree in being a boring old fart.

'I just hope I can keep funding this lifestyle. It's not a particularly cheap way of living. I've still got money, but it'll run out fast if I don't supplement it in some way.'

'I can probably find you some more work, if you want to stay around here.' I don't know where that came from. I would so love Danny to stay, but quite where I'd get the money is another thing. My dear sister, Edie, is still using me as her personal cash machine.

'I thought you were pretty straight at the café.'

'There's always something to do.' That's certainly not a lie. 'I also thought one day I'd like to get Dad's narrowboat going again.'

'The *Maid of Merryweather*?'

I nod. 'It does a great job as a shop, but I'd love to see it back on the water and working properly. Maybe you could help with that?'

'I'm a dab hand with diesel engines now. I've learned more about them in the last six months than I ever thought I'd need to know. I'd definitely be up for it.'

'I'm strapped for cash at the moment,' I admit. Danny doesn't need to know that Edie has all but emptied my meagre renovation fund. 'So it depends on how much it would cost.'

'I can look into it for you.'

'I'd like that.'

Danny nudges his beer bottle against my plastic cup. 'Cheers, Fay,' he says. Then his eyes hold mine. 'It's great to be back.'

My heart pounds when I reply, 'It's good to have you back.'

Chapter Thirty-eight

So I sit and talk to Danny for a while and then I catch sight of my watch and am alarmed to see that it's nearly ten o'clock. Mum will be frantic at being left alone for so long, and she'll need her cocoa and tablets. I make an excuse to visit the ladies' and, while I'm queuing up outside the line of Portaloos, I ring her.

'Where are you?' she says petulantly.

'I'm still at the festival.'

'When are you coming home?'

'I'd like to stay for a while longer,' I tell her. 'Can you manage?'

The truth of the matter is that I might not see Danny again. He might say now, after a few beers, that he'll stay around for a while, but by tomorrow he could have changed his mind. Sienna might bat her pretty little eyelashes and he could head straight back to London after her. Whatever the reason, he may well be moving on and, if he does, goodness only knows when he'll be back this way again. Is it wrong of me to spend as long as possible with him while I can?

Mum doesn't answer me.

'Is that all right with you?'

'I'd rather you came home.'

'Did you eat the sandwiches I left on your bedside table for you?'

'Yes.'

'And you still have some tea in your flask? Could you take your tablets with that?'

'There's only one cup left. What will I do after that?'

'You're normally asleep by now, Mum.'

'Come home, Fay. I don't like it when you're not here.'

That tugs at my heartstrings. 'Settle down. Leave the television on while you fall asleep. I won't be long. An hour at most,' I promise.

Then I'm at the head of the queue for the Portaloos, so I say, 'I have to go now, Mum. I'll be home soon.' And I head for a cubicle before I'm barged out of the way.

Sitting on the loo in the smelly plastic cubicle, I contemplate my life. I'm so tied, so bogged down with commitments. I can't even have a night out without worrying about someone else. I should have got a nurse in to sit with Mum, and hang the expense. It might be of her own doing, but it can't be nice to be stuck in the house alone while everyone else is out having fun.

I wish Edie would come home. I know she doesn't want to help look after Mum and I can fully understand that – the caring gene definitely bypassed my sister – but it would be good to have her here for support, to feel that I wasn't doing all this alone.

Still feeling racked with guilt, I head back to the park. Tonight, I've let Anthony down and I've let my mum down. I've let myself down.

On my way back to the stage area, I see Lija, hand in hand with the barman who was in the beer tent earlier.

'Hey,' she says. 'Why long face?'

'I'm worried about Mum,' I confess.

'Stop it,' she says. 'You are allowed a life.'

'I know.' Quickly, I change the subject before Lija berates me further. 'Are you having fun?'

She gives a surreptitious glance at her man. 'Oh, yes. This is Ashley.'

'Good to meet you, Ashley.' He looks very nice, as fair as Lija is dark. His face is open, friendly. Perhaps I should warn him that he'll have his work cut out with Lija. 'Have you seen Stan?'

'Yes. He's in pub. I bought him drink and crisps.'

'Is he all right?'

'Is fine,' she shrugs.

'He's not on his own?'

'No. He has plenty of company.' Then she holds up her handbag and shakes it at me. 'We must go. Things to do.'

'Oh, yes. Right. OK.' I imagine that the emergency pants and toothbrush are about to be put to good use. 'Mustn't keep you.'

'See you in morning, Fay,' she says and they both give me a wave.

Watching them walk away, Lija sashaying her non-existent hips, I feel a pang of jealousy. Oh, to be so young, so carefree, so confident.

I wonder also whether I should go up to the pub and check on Stan, see if he needs any help getting home. Then I remember that, despite him being of a great age, he is perfectly capable of handling himself. He has my mobile number and I know that if he needed to, he would call me.

So, instead, I head straight back to Danny and his friends. When I get there, I see that Danny is up and dancing. Sienna is strutting her stuff in front of him. What do they call it? Twerking? Whatever it is, she's good at it. He's laughing and mimicking her, hands in the air, beer bottle aloft, shaking his hips.

When he sees me, he shouts, 'Come and dance, Fay! Let's see what you're made of.'

But I'm made of doubts and insecurity, fear and self-consciousness.

'I need to go home,' I tell him.

'Noooo,' he says, taking my hands.

I think he's a little bit drunk. Well, quite a lot drunk.

'You have a great time,' I reiterate. 'Enjoy the rest of your evening. It's been really lovely to see you again.'

He steps away from his friends and frowns at me. 'With these guys here, with the music, we haven't had a chance to talk,' he says. 'Let's have some fun.' He makes it sound so easy. 'Please. Don't go yet.'

'I have to.'

'Then come to me tomorrow,' he urges. 'They'll be gone then. Come to *The Dreamcatcher* tomorrow night.'

'I can't do that either. It's my birthday,' I confess. 'Anthony's taking me out.' He's booked his favourite restaurant. I find it a little pretentious, if I'm honest, but it's where we go for all our special occasions.

Sienna comes up to Danny, still breathless from dancing. She slips an arm possessively around his waist and rests her head on his shoulder.

'Dance with me,' she pouts.

I can take a hint. I know when my presence is no longer required.

'I'll see you, Danny,' I say, and then, with a wave, I start walking away. I ignore every fibre of my being begging me to stay, and put one foot in front of the other, one foot in front of the other, and just keep going.

I leave Danny with his friends, with the pretty young Sienna, and head back to the café, to Anthony, to my mum. And that's exactly how it should be. All I have to do is convince my breaking heart.

Chapter Thirty-nine

When I got home last night, Mum was fast asleep. I texted Anthony and called him a dozen times, but there was no reply. Thwarted, I went to bed and lay with the window open, listening to the music from the festival drift into my room. I had a book open on my lap and I attempted to read, though the same sentence went past my eyes time and time again, while all the time I was brooding. What would have happened if I'd done this? What would have happened if I hadn't done that? How would my life have been different? All the way back to my childhood. Every little thing. It was exhausting.

Now, this morning, I'm tired and accepting. This is my life and there's nothing very much I can do to change it.

I go into Mum's bedroom and throw back the curtains. 'Morning!' I say brightly.

She scowls at me. 'Shut that out!'

'You're not a vampire, Mum. It's a glorious day out there. And it's my birthday.'

'Oh, yes,' Mum says. 'Happy birthday. I haven't got you a card or a present. How could I?'

'It doesn't matter. There's nothing I need.' I smooth the duvet. 'Here's your breakfast.'

'Is Anthony taking you out tonight?'

'Yes.'

'Another night out?'

'Yes,' I confirm. 'That'll be nearly into double figures for this year.'

'I suppose you're leaving that Russian tart here?'

'She speaks very highly of you,' I tell her, keeping my fingers crossed so that it's not a lie. 'And she's Latvian.'

'Hmph.'

'We've got a madly busy day today, what with the Canal Festival. So I'll come back as soon as I can.'

'That music kept me awake tossing and turning all night,' Mum complains.

I don't bother to point out that she was sleeping like a baby when I came home, as she will only disagree with me.

When I've settled her, I go downstairs to get my own breakfast. I'm still in my dressing gown, carb-loading for the day ahead with a plate of toast in front of me, when Lija comes in through the back door, flinching as it creaks. Then she leans heavily on the counter, unmoving. When she has steadied herself enough, she makes it to the kitchen table. She stands, braced, clearly waiting for the swaying to stop.

'Emergency pants and toothbrush used?'

She nods, a barely perceptible motion. She looks at me over the top of her dark glasses and then takes a piece of my toast without speaking.

'Was it good?'

The same minuscule inclination.

Getting up, I make her a thick black coffee and heap two sugars into it.

She pours the scalding liquid straight down her throat and pushes in more toast after it.

'Am I going to get any work out of you today?'

One bleary eye tries to focus on me. 'Wait until toast hits spot.'

I pull out a chair and she winces at the noise of it scraping on the floor. Then she sinks gratefully into it before she lapses into pained silence once more.

After a while, I can bear it no longer. 'Lija,' I say, hesitantly. 'What does it feel like to sleep with so many different men?'

'Fucking A,' she mumbles, slumping forwards.

'Doesn't it feel . . . weird?'

'If good is weird, then yes.'

'Even the ones you don't really know?'

'Yes.'

'Was this one nice? He looked lovely.'

'Was OK.'

I think that's Lija-speak for fantastic. She's very probably in love with him. I sigh wearily. 'I'm not sure I could do it.'

She pushes herself upright again, her face as white as the tiles on the wall. 'I couldn't shag Anthony.'

'Oh.' Then I think about it. 'Fair point.'

'Is there reason for this?'

'No,' I say. 'Just thinking.'

'You think too much,' Lija says. 'Sometimes you should just do.'

'Do you still get . . . um . . . *satisfaction*? Especially with the ones you don't know?'

'Yes,' she says, and suddenly a little light sparkles in her bloodshot eyes. 'Four times.'

'Wow.' I'm not sure that I've had . . . um . . . *satisfaction* with Anthony four times this year.

Lija drains her cup. 'Now, enough with the questions. I need to make some fucking cake.'

Chapter Forty

Anthony rings me at lunchtime. He sounds very sheepish. I do too.

'Sorry for running out last night,' he says. 'We were on such a high after the concert that I ended up going for a drink or two. Quite forgot the time.'

'That's fine,' I say, trying to hide my own guilt at sneaking away and not seeing the end of the Village Belles' performance. 'You were pleased with how it went?'

'It was a triumph,' Anthony says proudly. 'We've been booked for a guest slot at the Olney Dickensian Christmas on the back of it. They only want the best in Olney.'

'Wonderful.'

'We're race-fit now for our performance at the St Andrew's Church fête in two weeks.'

'Lovely.'

This is where Anthony and I differ. He is supremely confident of his abilities. He wouldn't let a little thing like the crowd drifting away or the mere smattering of polite applause break his stride. Whereas I would focus on that and nothing else. I could learn a lot from Anthony.

And that's what I've got to remember. My future is with Anthony. Solid, dependable Anthony. Not with someone, anyone, who lives a nomadic lifestyle, here today, gone tomorrow, popping in and out as he's passing. What sort of future would that be?

'Are we still on for tonight?' I ask.

'Oh, yes. I nearly forgot. Happy birthday, darling. Twenty-one again? Hahaha.'

Forty-two, I think, with a sinking heart. Though it's a betweeny birthday, it somehow feels like a milestone. Perhaps it's me officially hitting middle age. Despite what they say about forty being the new thirty, it so isn't. I am *forty-two* years old today and feel every single year of it. In my case, forty feels like the new fifty.

'The table's booked at the Manor,' he says. 'Your favourite.'

Your favourite, I want to say to him. But I let it go.

'I'll pick you up at seven o'clock. I don't suppose you want to drive on your birthday, do you?'

He sounds hopeful until I say, 'No. Not really.'

'Oh, right. See you later then. The planning world awaits me.'

'I love you, Anthony.'

'You too, old thing,' he answers and hangs up.

Old thing. I sigh to myself. The trouble is, he could well be right.

Chapter Forty-one

Lija, still wearing her dark glasses, is juggling a dozen different lunch orders. Despite her clearly hungover state, her efficiency hasn't dropped an inch. The orders are stacking up simply because we've had so many customers this morning. The Canal Festival has certainly been driving some very welcome business our way.

'You haven't forgotten you're babysitting for Mum tonight, have you?'

'No,' she says. 'But when rush has gone, can I go home for clean clothes?'

'Of course.' It's been something I've been meaning to address with Lija for a while. 'Why don't you bring some things back here? You can use Edie's old bedroom as if it's your own. I never go in there now except to waft the duster around.'

'I don't know.' Lija wrinkles her nose. 'What will Edie say?'

She knows only too well that Edie, like my mother, can be tricky.

'I don't think she'll be coming home for the foreseeable future,' I admit. 'Don't tell Mum though.'

'Is she still with shitty boyfriend?'

'Yes.'

'Fucking idiot,' she mutters.

I don't know if Lija means my sister or Brandon, aforementioned shitty boyfriend, but I think the term could apply equally to both of them.

'Think about the room though. You could easily move in. You like it here.'

'I will think about it.' Lija flicks a look over her shoulder. 'Stinky Stan's soup. He has been waiting long time.'

'I'll get it straight to him.'

Loading up a tray, I add the sandwiches that are ready for another table and make my way down the garden. I deliver the sandwiches to a couple, then go to see Stan.

'Hello, Stan.' I kiss his cheek. 'Sorry for the wait. Here's your soup at long last. Roasted onion with goat's-cheese toasts.'

'Oh, my favourite.'

'We're rushed off our feet today.'

'I'm not going anywhere in a hurry, Fay,' he says. 'Just happy to watch the boats go by on the canal. There are a lot of them on the water today. Some nice ones too.'

'It's the people going backwards and forwards to the festival. I'm sorry I didn't see you there last night. Did you enjoy it?'

'Very entertaining,' Stan chuckles. 'I was up way past my bedtime.'

I wish I could say the same.

'Ended up playing poker with a group of very nice biker chaps in the Two Barges. I've had a motorbike or two in my day. Brought back some lovely memories, chatting about them. They put me in a taxi home. Very kind.'

'They didn't take all your money off you, did they?'

'Quite the contrary,' Stan assures me. 'I still have my eye in. I came away fifty pounds up.'

That makes me laugh too. I don't know why I ever worry about Stan. 'I'm glad to hear you had a nice time.'

'I enjoyed Anthony's little show too,' he says. 'Very nice.'

Possibly Stan is Anthony's target audience.

'I saw you sitting with that young man. It's nice to see *The Dreamcatcher* is back.' Stan gestures down the canal to where Danny's boat is moored.

As far as I can tell from this distance, it's all shut up still, no sign of activity yet. I thought Danny's friends were leaving early, but perhaps they're all still in bed. Then I urge my brain to move on before I start to dwell on what the sleeping arrangements might have been.

'Yes. It was good to see Danny at the festival too.'

'I knew that boy would be back.' He winks at me.

'I'd better get on, Stan.'

'Before I forget.' He reaches down to the side of his chair. 'A little something for you.' He hands me a card and a box of hand-made chocolates from a nice boutique store in the shopping centre. Bless him, Stan must have gone there on the bus to get them. 'Happy birthday, Fay.'

I take the present and kiss his cheek.

'It's not much. But you and Lija are very kind to me.'

'Oh, thank you, Stan. You didn't need to.'

'Hope that young man of yours is taking you out on the town tonight.'

'We're going to the Manor,' I confirm.

'That posh place?'

'Yes.'

'Very hoity-toity.'

'I'll have to put a frock on.'

'You deserve it. No one works harder than you, Fay. It will be nice for someone to spoil you for a change.'

'I'm really looking forward to it.'

And, even though I see that one of our younger customers has just hurled a scone into the flowerbed, there's a spring in my step as I walk back to the house.

In the kitchen, I let out a puff of breath. 'Phew. That was a rush, but I think there's a lull for a few minutes now.'

'Good,' Lija says. She goes to the larder and whips out a cake, already set out on a plate. There's a candle on the top.

'For me?' I'm taken aback.

'Happy birthday.'

It's a beautiful Victoria sponge, but decorated with an abundance of summer fruits – strawberries, raspberries, blueberries – and a sprinkling of pretty fresh flowers. Cream oozes out of the sides.

'This is lovely. Your best creation yet. Have we got time to have a piece now?'

Lija does a quick check that all the customers in the garden are happy. 'I think so.' She pulls a cake knife from the drawer and hands it to me.

'I'm so excited,' I say.

'Make a wish,' she instructs.

I close my eyes and am still trying to quieten my mind so that I ask for something good, when there's a knock at the door. Opening it, I see Danny standing there, lounging against the frame.

'That was quick,' Lija quips, assuming she knows what my wish would be.

He has a bunch of wild flowers clutched in his fist.

'I have no idea what these are.' Danny offers his flowers. 'But they were picked by my own fair hands. I hope that counts for something.'

'They're beautiful.' His strong hands are brimming with a profusion of summer blossoms – tansy, cow parsley, feverfew, sorrel, meadowsweet, some buttercups and even dandelions. 'I love wild flowers. Much better than any formal florist's bouquet. That's so kind of you.'

'And you are in time for cake,' Lija says.

'Hey, you,' Danny says to her.

'Hey, you, yourself,' she retorts.

'You look like something the cat sicked up,' he notes.

'You too.'

'I did have a heavy night,' Danny admits. 'It was almost dawn before we went to bed.'

Again I try not to dwell on whether that was alone.

'I've just seen the guys off at the station. We were all a bit green when the taxi came for them.'

'Did they enjoy the festival?'

'Yeah. Though I think it was a bit low-key for them.'

'Cut cake,' Lija says. 'We don't have all day.'

So I ease great big slices out of her beautiful cake and she produces plates for us all.

'You'll have some, Danny?'

'Try and stop me. That looks amazing.' He bites into the slice of cake I hand to him. 'Uh. That's heaven.' He winks at Lija. 'I should snap you up before some other underfed bloke gets you. Would you do me the very great honour of marrying me, Lija?'

'Fuck off.' She flicks her head towards me and says, 'Marry her.'

While I flush furiously, Danny laughs. 'I think Fay's already spoken for.'

'I'll take some cake to Stan too,' I say, hastily cutting another slice.

'Give to me.' Lija holds out a plate. Only she could do it in such a surly manner.

I pass her some cake for Stan. 'I can take it to him. You have things to do.'

'*I* will take.' She throws me a pointed look and bears the plate high. 'I might be some time,' she announces loudly. '*Quite* some time.'

Then she stamps out of the door and, with only a slight recoil as the rays hit her, goes into the sunshine.

I pull a puzzled face as she disappears. 'What was that all about?'

Danny grins at me. 'Do you think it was a subtle hint that I should use the time wisely to give you a birthday kiss?'

'Oh.' I hadn't thought of that.

'I'm guessing I shouldn't waste the opportunity.' Danny puts down his cake and moves towards me. I can't go anywhere as I'm backed up against the kitchen table.

'I think I'll disarm you first.' So he takes the cake knife out of my hand and puts it down.

My heart is beating double time. He stands in front of me, close, so close.

'Happy birthday, Fay.'

Slowly, tentatively, his lips find mine and they taste of summer and sunshine. He kisses me softly, tenderly. His fingers move into my hair and he cups my head, tilting my face up towards his. The intensity increases and I feel as if my feet are floating above the ground. This kiss is reaching corners of my being that I didn't even know existed.

Oh God. Oh God.

Then I hear bangbangbang. It's Mum rapping on the floor with her stick. 'Fay! Fay!'

Danny breaks away from me.

'Phew,' I say, too overwhelmed to even think about playing it cool.

'Phew indeed,' Danny says, and he too looks a little bit stunned.

Bangbangbang.

'Mum,' I say.

'You'd better go.'

'Yes.' I want to touch my lips. Touch his lips.

'Have a lovely time tonight.'

'Tonight?' I'm dazed, light-headed. There must be something in his kiss that has addled my brain.

'Your meal out with Anthony?'

'Oh, yes.'

His lovely smile lights up his face. 'You know what we were talking about last night, Fay?'

'Yes.' I have no idea.

'I think I might stay around here for a while.'

'Oh, right. Good. That's very good.'

'Happy birthday.'

Bangbangbang. 'I'm coming!'

He grins at me again, grabs the rest of his cake and heads for the door. He waves as he goes out into the garden and I wonder if that was just his normal standard of birthday kiss, or something much more.

Chapter Forty-two

While I'm getting ready to go out for my birthday meal, Edie Skypes me. I take the laptop into the bedroom and talk to her while I'm putting on my make-up.

'I think things are getting better,' she says. 'Brandon's talking about leaving his wife again, and he's given me this month's rent.'

How this is an improvement on anything, I'm not sure, but I say, 'I'm glad for you. If that's what you want.'

'Of course it is,' Edie snaps. 'He's my life.'

I wonder if the feeling is reciprocal though. At least today Edie seems sober and isn't tearful, but then it is only lunchtime where she is. There's a whole lot of day to get through yet.

'I thought about my job situation too,' she continues. 'I think I'm going to try for media positions. Law is so terribly dull.'

I try to put on my eyeliner while balancing a mirror on my knee. 'Uh-huh.'

'I don't think you're even listening to me,' Edie complains. 'What are you getting all dolled up for, anyway?'

'It's my birthday,' I remind her.

'I know,' she says shirtily. 'That's why I Skyped you. Happy birthday.'

'Thank you.'

'I didn't send a card,' she adds. 'You know what the post is like.'

'It doesn't matter. I'm not sure that I want to mark birthdays any more, now I'm the wrong side of forty.'

'Surely Anthony is taking you out?'

'To the Manor,' I say. 'I'm as nervous as I'm excited. It's very formal there. I'm always worried that I'll use the wrong fork.'

'That is so typical of you, Fay. You should loosen up, live a little.'

'I am going to try,' I admit. 'It's something that I've been thinking about.'

'I wish I was there,' Edie says. 'I'd make sure you had some fun.'

I laugh at that. 'I'm sure you would!' Then I glance at the clock and note that time is marching on. 'I'm sorry, Edie, but I have to finish getting ready. Anthony will be here in a few minutes and he'll be cross if I keep him waiting. Our table's booked for seven-thirty.'

'I won't keep you then.' Edie sounds a little miffed.

'Do you want a quick word with Mum? She'd like it.'

'No, no. Not now,' Edie says. 'She'll keep me on here for ever and I've got stuff to do. Important stuff.'

'I'd better log off,' I say. 'I'm really glad things are working out for you.'

'Yeah. Have a good dinner, sis. Don't get too drunk.'

And then the screen goes blank.

Chapter Forty-three

It's half-past seven and I'm all ready and raring to go, yet Anthony still hasn't appeared. Which is most unlike him. Punctuality is Anthony's middle name. If he's fifteen minutes early, then Anthony thinks he's late.

I try his phone, but it goes straight to voicemail. Then I text him and wait and wait, but nothing comes back.

Lija has gone home to get some new clothes and is coming back to babysit a little later. If she was still here we could at least break out a bottle of wine together and have some more of her excellent cake.

When it gets to quarter to eight, I ring the Manor and tell them that we're going to be late. Obviously. The man at the end of the phone tuts at me and tells me they can only hold our table until eight o'clock. I text Anthony again and then turn on the television. *Coronation Street* wanders across the screen. I try to watch it but I can't settle.

When it hits eight o'clock, I have a fresh bout of trying to contact Anthony. We've clearly missed our table now and, when I still get no response from him, I call the Manor and apologise profusely for failing to show up. They're not best pleased, I can tell. People can wait over a month for a weekend booking.

My mother bangs on the ceiling. 'Fay! Fay! Have you not gone out yet?'

'Anthony's late,' I shout up the stairs. 'I hope he won't be long now.'

'You've probably got the wrong day,' she says, continuing her assumption that Anthony is infallible.

Then I ring Lija and tell her that we've missed our table and I won't now be going out for my birthday. She tuts down the phone at me and calls Anthony something very bad in Latvian.

'I'll see you tomorrow,' I say.

'I will come with bottle of Lambrini.'

'Don't. I'll be miserable company. Just be thankful you've got a night off from my mother.'

'So should you,' Lija says. 'I will spit in that man's tea next time he is in café.'

I actually don't mind if she does. I make very few demands on Anthony and I'm disappointed that he's not here and hasn't called to say why. He was probably playing a few holes of golf this evening, but surely he would have let me know if he was delayed. He can't have forgotten it's my birthday since he called at lunchtime. Can he?

Another hour ticks by. Now I'm anxious. Anthony wouldn't have wanted to miss the table at the Manor. He loves it there. It must be something serious to keep him away. I start to have visions of him upside-down in a ditch, the wheels of his car spinning in the air. I'm feeling really panicky and stressed and have stopped attempting to watch television and have resorted to pacing the living room, interspersed with visits to the front window to look out down the lane for any approaching cars. Nothing.

Then, just as I'm getting to the point where I'm thinking of getting into the car and going to Anthony's house in case he's collapsed, or phoning round hospitals to see if he's been admitted due to some hideous accident, I get a call from the man himself.

'Where are you?' My heart is racing as I answer my phone.

'At the hospital,' he says, slightly breathlessly.

'Oh God. Oh God.' Instantly, all my mean thoughts dissipate and I feel terrible for even thinking badly of him. 'Are you hurt?'

'Of course I'm not,' he says crossly.

Instantly, all my mean thoughts rush back.

'What are you doing at the hospital then?'

'Deborah's fallen,' he explains. 'Quite badly. She's in a terrible state. Broken wrist. And it's only two weeks till St Andrew's Church fête. What will we do? How will we manage without one of our key players?'

'So why are you at the hospital with her?'

'Er . . .' he says. 'I was her first port of call.'

'Oh.' There's a little pause when one of us ought to say something. Something like, Why didn't she call the handsome man she got off the internet instead of you? After a while, I fill the yawning gap by saying, 'We've missed the table. I called the Manor.'

'We'll have to celebrate your birthday another day,' he says without apology.

'How long are you going to be there?'

'Hours yet,' he grumbles. 'She's only just had her X-ray. Now we've got to wait for it to be plastered.'

'Oh.'

'What do you expect me to do, Fay?' he says tightly. 'I can't just leave her.'

'No. Of course not. You must stay. Tell her I'm sorry she's hurt herself.'

'I'll call you tomorrow,' he says.

'I could wait up, if you want to pop by.'

'Go to bed. You could probably do with an early night.'

And he hangs up.

I look at the phone in my hand. I'm very sorry that Deborah's hurt, though I'm still not sure why Anthony is the one she's turned to to act as her chaperon. Couldn't he have told her it was my birthday and we had a special celebration planned? Couldn't he have called one of the other ladies and asked her to go with Deborah? It seems such an imposition. Beyond the Village Belles, he hardly knows her.

So, with all my lovely plans in disarray, I slump on to the sofa. I could take a bottle of wine up to Mum's bedroom and share a small glass or two with her but, if she's not asleep already, she soon will be. Plus she would only tell me how wonderful Anthony is for helping out a friend in need, and perhaps she'd be right. But what about his *girlfriend* in need? Sometimes I'd like to be at the top of Anthony's list, and today is one of those times. Mum would make out that it was somehow my own fault that Anthony had missed my birthday. He could never possibly be at fault. And he is. This time he very much is. I could have a drink by myself, but that's never much of a celebration, is it?

There's one thing that I'm absolutely sure about: I *don't* want an early night. I want to do *something* to make this a night to remember. It's my forty-second birthday, and so far I've had gifts from Lija, Stan and Danny. Nothing from my mum or Edie or Anthony. My supposedly nearest and dearest have done nothing for me at all.

Some bloody birthday this has turned out to be.

Chapter Forty-four

I go and sit on the veranda, feeling so very sorry for myself. I had to come out here as I couldn't stand the thought of my mother bangbangbanging on the ceiling, asking why I still haven't gone out. If she's asleep, I hope she stays that way. I'm hungry and should have something to eat, but I can't actually face food now. Well, what I can't actually face is making it for myself.

The night is warm, sultry. The sky is as clear as crystal and filled with shining stars. How lovely it would have been to sit out on the terrace at the Manor after our meal – which, no doubt, would have been delicious – with a coffee and a brandy. Still, there's no point crying over spilt milk. What's done is done.

When my eyes become accustomed to the darkness, I can make out the shape of a boat moored up behind the *Maid of Merryweather*, and my heart skips a beat or two when I recognise it as *The Dreamcatcher*. Danny must have moved her back up here late this afternoon sometime.

It feels ridiculously comforting simply knowing that he's down there, close to hand. A moment later, I hear the sound of a guitar being strummed and realise that Danny is sitting out on the seats in the well deck at the front of the boat. I strain to hear what he's singing, but can't quite pick it up.

Then I think, What am I doing here alone when I could have company? I don't want to be by myself on my birthday and why should I? Didn't he ask me to call at his boat yesterday? He said that his friends – Little Miss Sienna included – had gone back to London. I know it's late, but perhaps Danny would appreciate a visitor.

Before I can think better of it, I dash back inside. I snatch up a cardigan and the remains of Lija's lovely cake and, without even letting Mum know that I'm going out, I head down the garden. Trying to block all those thoughts that are making me feel that I should turn back, I walk purposefully towards *The Dreamcatcher*.

When I get to the jetty, Diggery barks and Danny's head snaps up. He stops playing his guitar.

'Hey,' he says when he recognises me in the twilight. 'What's wrong?'

'I'm having a really crap birthday.'

'Come for some tea and sympathy?'

'I was thinking more Jack Daniel's and sympathy.'

Danny laughs. 'The Jack's all gone. Last night was a heavy one. But I can do vodka.' He holds up a bottle that's still two-thirds full.

'That would work too,' I say.

'Hop on board then.' He holds out a hand and helps me to climb on to the boat.

He budges Diggery out of the way and finds me a place on the seat next to him. The little dog curls at my feet.

'What happened to the fancy dinner?'

I sigh. 'Anthony's at the hospital. With a friend. She's broken her wrist.'

'Bad timing.'

'The worst. I do feel bad for her though. She's a nice lady and, from a very shaky start, she seems to have become Anthony's star ringer.'

He laughs again. 'Faint praise.'

'Don't,' I say, with a guilty laugh. 'They take it all very seriously. They couldn't practise any harder if they were playing to twenty thousand people at the O2.'

'Good on them.' Danny stands. 'Let me get you a glass.'

So he gets another shot glass from the galley and puts it down next to his. He pours us both brimming measures. 'Shots are the way forward,' he says.

'If you say so.'

Then, when we both have them in hand, he clinks his against mine. 'Here's to drowning your sorrows.'

'I'll drink to that.'

We each knock back our shot, but only one of us shudders, unaccustomed to this style of drinking. One of us might even give a bit of a spluttery cough.

'OK?' Danny asks.

I nod, my voice having been burned away by the strength of the vodka.

'I'm a little ahead of you,' Danny says. 'You need to catch up. Go again?'

I giggle. 'If you insist.'

'I do.' He fills my glass. 'This one is for a happy birthday.'

'It's getting better already,' I tell him, coughing a little less after this one.

He tops us up once more and, with a toast of 'Happy birthday', together we knock them back.

Anthony would be furious if he saw me. He hates women who drink and get all silly. That's probably my major motivation for doing it.

Danny hits us both with another one and I have a warm burning in my chest. I don't need my cardigan, let's put it that way. One more shot and then Danny gets the Union Jack cushions from his sofa and passes them to me.

'Might as well be comfortable if we're having a session,' he says.

I put the cushions behind my back and kick off my shoes. Danny, also barefoot and clad in jeans and a Guns N' Roses T-shirt, slings his guitar across his lap and strums at it. I stretch out my legs on the seat so that our toes are almost touching, and even that small intimacy brings a flush of heat to my face. Leaning my head back, I watch the stars and listen to his soothing voice.

After a few moments, Danny stops and looks over at me. 'There's nothing between me and Sienna, you know,' he says. 'Not now.'

'Was there? Not that it's any of my business.'

'I'm making it your business. We had a few nights together. That's all. When we were colleagues. If we used to stay over somewhere, then sometimes – usually – we'd hook up.' I'm shocked at his frankness. 'We're past that now though. When she was on board last weekend, she took my bed and I slept in the well deck with Digs.'

'That must have been cramped.'

'Cramped but less complicated,' he concedes. 'Sienna's not my type.'

I don't know where my courage comes from, maybe it's the drink talking, but I ask the burning question, 'What is your type?'

'My thoughts on that have altered, Fay. Quite significantly. I love Sienna, she's a great girl, but I don't want a relationship with someone like that any more. These last six months have changed me as a person. I'm looking for something different now. Something more. I want someone with depth, warmth. Someone loyal. A woman who cares about others. And who shares my values, my interests.' He looks as if he's about to say something more, but he stops himself. Instead, he picks up his guitar and starts to sing again.

I sit back and listen, trying to absorb what he's just said.

'You don't know you're beautiful,' he croons softly into the night.

'That's lovely,' I say when he's finished. The lyrics are very moving. 'Is it Bob Dylan?'

'One Direction,' he says, and we both chuckle.

'Well, it was very nice.'

A pause for another shot for both of us.

'Did you ever want to be a musician? A full-time one?'

'Nah,' he says. 'I can hold a tune, strum a bit, but I'm not good enough to make it professionally. Since giving up my job, I'm not sure what my forte is going to be. I might be good enough to get a few pub gigs, if I'm lucky. My money won't last for ever, so I'll have to think of something.'

'You strike me as a very resourceful person.'

'You too,' he says.

'Oh, no.' I shake my head. 'Not really. I've just fallen into running the cake shop out of necessity. I had a job in administration at the local council, which I hated. It wasn't too difficult a decision to become a full-time carer for Mum. Now I love having the cake shop and café, but there was no big master plan.'

'Sometimes that's the best way. Just see where fate takes you.'

That's all very well if fate takes you where you want to be. But what if fate always seems to pull you in the wrong direction?

While I'm musing on the vagaries of fate, Danny glances up at me. 'I bet you haven't eaten. Are you hungry?'

'Starving,' I confess. My stomach gives a sudden rumble now it's been reminded that it hasn't seen food since lunchtime.

'Give me five minutes.' He abandons his guitar and instructs Diggery, 'Look after our company, Digs.' Then he ducks into the cabin.

As I lie back on the cushions, Diggery snuggles in next to me and I tickle his tummy. The sounds of the canal settling for the night wash over me. There's the hoot of an owl, the leaves rustling on the trees, the background hum of the generator running.

A few minutes later, as my eyes are growing heavy, Danny comes back out. He's carrying a big dinner plate loaded with cheese on toast cut into small triangles. They're arranged meticulously around a coloured glass tea light that's burning in the centre.

'Happy birthday to you.' He serenades me slowly, melodiously. 'Happy birthday to you. Happy birthday, dear Fay. Happy birthday to you.'

He offers the plate to me and says, 'Make a wish.'

And, as I blow out the candle, I do. Then I worry that it might just come true.

Chapter Forty-five

'Are you feeling more chilled now?'

'Yes.' Tipsy, I think, is the actual word.

The cheese on toast that Danny very kindly made me has gone some way to minimising the effects of the vodka shots, but I've had two more slugs since then. I've certainly lost my inhibitions about being here. And why shouldn't I get a little merry on my birthday, for heaven's sake?

'I have a little something else too,' Danny says and he pulls out a spliff. 'I don't normally partake these days, but it was a parting gift from Sienna. Do you mind?'

'No, no.'

I'm actually not sure what I feel. I'm one of those people who were too late for the sixties and too soon for the current lax attitude to soft drugs. I've never smoked pot, or anything else, in my life. I've never had any interest, and you already know enough about Anthony to realise that he would never, ever touch an illegal substance. I don't particularly like the idea of recreational drugs either. I think the law is far too soft on the use of them and, in my somewhat sheltered existence, I've never had anything to do with them other than try to stop my teenage sister from dabbling.

While my addled brain is trying to organise all of this information, Danny lights up with an old Zippo and takes a toke. He lets his head fall back, his eyes close. Then he holds it out to me.

I don't know whether it's the drink or whether I don't want Danny to think that I'm an old bore, but despite my previous and very recent thoughts on the evils of cannabis, I find myself taking it and putting it to my lips. Perhaps it's something that at the age of forty-two I should try the once. Hoping he's not watching me, I pull it deep into my lungs. It instantly makes my head spin.

'OK?' Danny asks.

'Yeah.'

While Danny gently strums his guitar, we pass the joint back and forth between us until it's gone. By now, I'm feeling more relaxed than I've done in years. There's a lightness and a heaviness in my body at the same time. I want to laugh and I want to cry.

We do another vodka shot, clinking our glasses together enthusiastically and dribbling the vodka down our chins. I don't know how much time has passed.

Danny's singing again and I think his voice is the best one I've ever heard. Ever. Really. I don't often find my singing voice but, tongue loosened by the vodka, I feel bold enough to sing along with him and I join in softly by his side.

When we've run through a few songs, filling the night air with our tunes and laughter, I stand up in the well deck and, using the empty vodka bottle as my microphone, dance along to our music. I lift my arms, sway my hips and only feel the very slightest bit unsteady.

Danny grins at me. 'You've got the sweetest voice.'

And I'm glad it's dark, or he'd see me blushing. Above us, the sky is a velvet shade of indigo and the stars pulsate and sparkle.

I can't see the Milky Way but I know it's up there, marvellous and mysterious. This is a beautiful planet. Really. I feel myself shiver with pleasure.

'Cold?' Danny asks from somewhere far away.

'No. Happy.' My senses are all alive and numb at the same time. I start to laugh.

'Come here.' He puts down his guitar and our eyes meet as he reaches out, gently pulling me towards him. His hands are hot, burning on my cool skin. His arms wrap round me and my head rests on his chest. It feels as if I've lain like this with him for all of my life. It feels as if it's where I've always belonged. Then somehow our legs are twined together, our bodies pressed close. Here, nestled into the crook of his arm, I know that I can come to no harm. The breeze from the water teases over us and tingles my skin.

'I've wanted to do this since I met you, Fay,' he says, softly kissing my hair. 'Just lying out with you on *The Dreamcatcher* under the stars. I've dreamed of this.'

'Me too,' I confess.

'I know you're with someone else . . .'

I put my finger to his lips. 'Not now. Not tonight.'

We move together, our lips meet and his kiss explodes in my head. Stars burst overhead. And I'm falling, falling, falling.

Chapter Forty-six

We kiss until our lips are bruised and my senses are scattered. He kisses my face, my lips, my neck, my hair. Then Danny stands and opens the cabin door. He takes me by the hand and, urging me from my seat, leads me inside.

'Stay, Diggery,' he says.

Much to the dog's dismay, he's locked outside.

The kissing starts again and I know I should stop it. I know I'm drunk and my inhibitions are low due to the weed, but I wouldn't have the nerve to be doing this otherwise and I so, so want to.

We're holding on to each other tightly, and slowly Danny unzips my dress. I tug at his T-shirt and, with his help, pull it over his head. In the moonlight, his naked body is so strong, so defined that I don't mind if I just stand here all night and look at him.

Tentatively, I run my hands over his chest and he shudders with pleasure. Oh my God. What a heady feeling that is. This man, this young, this beautiful man, is thrilling to my touch.

He eases the straps of my dress from my shoulders and continues to let it fall down my body, running his hands over my breasts as he does. Someone gasps out loud with ecstasy and I think it might be me. His mouth follows his hands and he traces kisses over my chest and my tummy, and for once I don't even care about sucking it in. He's treating me with a reverence I've never known before and I feel like a queen, a goddess. All any woman ever wants is to be desired in this way, and I've never known this before.

He feasts his eyes on me while he undoes my bra, eases off my knickers. And I'm glad I was due to go out as at least I'm wearing nice underwear. I think of Anthony in the hospital with Deborah, and that should stop me in my tracks, make me think exactly what I'm doing, but it doesn't. This is my night, my moment. For once, I don't want to think about other people before myself, I don't want to dance to their tune any longer. I want to be me. I want to do what I want to. Whatever the consequences.

Then, in the velvety darkness, Danny pleasures me in a way that no one has before, and my legs tremble with delight. I tug off his belt, his jeans, his underwear until we're both naked and I do things to him that I've never done with anyone. I can't even bring myself to say what, but I'm doing it nevertheless. He lays me down on the rag rug in front of the log burner and he makes love to me. He loves me as I've never been loved before. He loves me tenderly. He loves me hard. He loves me in every delicious way that I can imagine. And I can't get enough of it.

The Dreamcatcher moves with us, echoing our rhythm in the elements. It feels pagan, raw, organic and all of those things that I don't normally give the time of day to. I imagine myself drifting, drifting as if I'm borne by the water, the canal carrying me away. The gentle rocking of the boat sends me deeper into bliss.

Danny moves above me and I think he has truly been sent from heaven to show me what I've been missing for all of these very long years. He makes love to me again and again. He loves

226

me until our senses, emotions, bodies are blurred and I no longer know where I end and Danny begins. There's a sexy, wanton woman writhing in rapture beneath him and I don't know who she is, but I like her.

When finally we're sated, he takes me by the hand and leads me to his cabin. In the bed, he pulls the sheet over us, our skin still damp and warm with lust. Our legs wrap together, my body spoons into his.

His dark eyes look into mine and he murmurs, 'I love you.'

He strokes my face and it's enough to make me yearn for him again. 'I love you too,' I say.

We make love once more, tenderly, slowly, and then, in the shelter of his arms, I fall into the deepest sleep I've ever known.

Chapter Forty-seven

I wake at dawn as the light is tentatively pushing in through the porthole window in Danny's cabin. I look around, disorientated, and then the realisation of where I am hits me with full force.

Danny is still sleeping soundly next to me. If possible he looks even more beautiful in repose. His arm is thrown back over his head on the pillow and his hair is even more tousled than usual. The expression on his face is soft, angelic. He's sprawled across his side of the bed, the sheet rucked up round his thighs, showing long muscled legs that dangle over the edge. A fine line of dark hair runs down his stomach and disappears beneath the bedding. It's all I can do not to trace my fingers along it.

There's a thrilled and anxious knotting in my stomach when I think of what we did last night. I can't believe how shameless I was. It was the most passionate, exciting night of my life and it has left me wanting him even more. I didn't even know I was capable of such ardour, or how much I had been missing by not having it in my life.

Back in reality though, I can't imagine what I must look like.

My mouth feels like the bottom of a birdcage and I have a pounding headache to match. It feels as if someone has my brain in a vice and is squeezing it tightly. I wonder whether it's the weed or the vodka that's responsible. Or it could be a deadly combination of the two – unaccustomed as I am to the use of recreational drugs overlaid with binge drinking.

An early-morning boat putters past *The Dreamcatcher*, which rocks in its wake. There'll no doubt be a steady stream of barges leaving the festival today, heading to their home territory. Then I remember that we're opening the café today to catch the last of the extra traffic the festival has brought to us, and I realise that I need to get a move on. How I'm wishing that we'd stayed closed now.

I want to kiss him awake, to feel my lips on his again. I want our bodies to be entwined, making love, but I lie here not knowing quite what to do while he sleeps on contentedly. I should leave, I think. I have things that I should be doing and they won't get done if I stay here, dreaming, drinking in the sight of my lover.

Easing myself out of bed, I tiptoe across the cabin so that I don't disturb Danny. I grab my clothes as I go. In the bathroom, I try to wee as quietly as I can and then I splash water over my face in an attempt to wake myself up. The shower looks complicated and potentially noisy, so I leave that well alone even though I think standing under a torrent of soothing hot water is definitely the way forward.

If my mouth is the bottom of a birdcage, then my hair is the bird's nest. I pull my fingers through it in an attempt to make it look better, then I pinch some of Danny's toothpaste and rub it round my teeth and gums with my finger to freshen my breath. I can now see the benefit – if you are like Lija and get this kind of offer on a regular basis – of carrying emergency pants and a toothbrush. I dampen a piece of loo paper and use it to wipe away the smudges of mascara beneath my eyes. The rest of my make-up has been kissed or caressed away, and the thought makes my stomach thrill once more.

Dressing hurriedly in last night's clothes, I go back to the cabin, where Danny is still blissfully cocooned in deep sleep. I don't know what to do. Should I wake him? Or should I creep out and leave him to it? I've never had a one-night stand before and I'm unaware what the etiquette is. For heaven's sake, I'm even awkward with Anthony in the morning, and I've been with him for ten years.

I wonder what Danny will think about last night – we were both drunk, not to mention high. When he wakes, will he be regretting having me spend the night with him? We both said things that perhaps we wouldn't mean in the cold light of day. He told me he loved me and I told him that I loved him too. I so want to wake him and see if he still feels the same.

Last night I felt like the most adored woman in the world. This morning I'm the most insecure one. Is this come-down from the pot? Is that how it even works? Or is it just the result of being so intimate with someone who, essentially, I don't really know? I wonder whether this will be nothing more than a one-night stand for us, and it's a conversation that I don't want to have.

While I stand and dither and stress, Danny sleeps on unawares. I should leave him to it. Perhaps he'll come up to the house later when he wakes. He might be the sort of person who does this a lot; he might be grateful that I'm up and gone when he rouses.

Then I think of Edie and Brandon. She says that to have sex with her he likes to be drunk and stoned. Is that the only reason why Danny and I made love? Would we have done this had we both been stone-cold sober? I know that I wouldn't. Without the fortification of several well-aimed vodka shots, I would have panicked and fled. Am I turning into Edie by forming an attachment to someone unsuitable? If only I hadn't got a monster hangover then I might be able to think more clearly.

I look at Danny and I so want to make love to him now, but I'm too frightened to wake him. Even I realise that doing a row of vodka shots at this hour might not be the right way of getting up the necessary courage. My stomach roils at the thought of it.

The best thing I can do is go home, have the hot shower that I crave and some tea and toast, and a handful of Nurofen. Perhaps then I'll be ready to face the day.

Taking one last lingering gaze at Danny, I fix the snapshot in my brain. Despite my many and varied anxieties, I'm leaving with a warm glow in my tummy. I blow a silent kiss to him from the doorway and whisper 'Thank you' to his sleeping form.

Then, as silently as I can, I make my way out to the well deck. When I ease open the doors, Diggery cocks an ear and jumps up to greet me. His tail goes into overdrive and you'd think he'd spent a month abandoned in the wilderness rather than one lonely night in the bow of the boat.

I rub his ears and he leans in to my legs. 'Sorry to displace you, boy,' I murmur apologetically. 'I don't know if it will ever happen again.'

He whimpers that dogs need their breakfast.

'Stay out here,' I tell him. 'I don't want Danny to wake up yet.'

I want him to drift in his dreams for as long as possible because when he wakes up reality will flood in again. And I'm not sure that I want to deal with what it will bring.

Chapter Forty-eight

I pop my head into Mum's bedroom and, thankfully, she's still asleep. With a bit of luck and a following wind, she might not have realised that I've been out all night. Being as quiet as the quietest mouse, I ease the door closed again.

'Fay! Fay! Is that you?'

I lean against the wall and count to five. 'Yes,' I say, hoping I sound more chirpy than I feel. 'Just a minute.'

From the back of my bedroom door, I quickly grab my dressing gown and pull it over my dress before she spots that I'm still wearing the same clothes I was in yesterday evening. Then I open her door again. 'Morning.'

'I didn't hear you come home last night,' she says.

'You must have had a lovely sleep then.' I am forty-two years and one day old. A more than grown woman. Should I have to lie to my mum like this? I know that some women can tell their mothers everything. Mine, not so. I don't think I've ever had a frank conversation with her in my life. And I certainly don't want her to know where I spent the night. 'Are you ready for your breakfast?'

'I don't want an egg today,' she tells me. 'I'm not feeling all that well.'

'Some toast?'

'Just one piece.'

'It will be with you in five minutes.'

So, in my dressing gown and last night's dress, I make Mum's tea and toast and take them straight back up to her.

'I'll be in the shower, if you need me.'

But she's switched on her breakfast telly and isn't really listening.

I make my escape, peel off my clothes and set the shower going. Before I step in, I look at myself in the full-length mirror in the bathroom – something I normally try to avoid doing at all costs. I take in my full breasts and equally full hips. It's not in bad shape, but it is without doubt the body of a middle-aged woman. Despite what he murmured sweetly to me last night, could Danny *really* love this? I wonder. How does this creased and careworn carcass stand up against the likes of the lean and lithesome Sienna? Is this body more suited to the Anthonys of this world?

Then I get my first searing pang of guilt. I have betrayed Anthony and he doesn't deserve it. He is solid – sometimes to the point of being stolid, but, nevertheless, I shouldn't have done this. I'll call him as soon as I've showered to see how he got on with Deborah at the hospital.

But then my stomach clenches and I don't know if I can even bring myself to speak to him. How will I face him after this? I have always been unfailingly loyal and now I'm not. From this day, there will always be a secret between us, something that I must keep locked in my heart. What future do I have with him if I can't be entirely honest? Can I even contemplate a future with Anthony after last night? How can I not compare my experience with Danny and find shortcomings in our relationship? Will I ever be able to make love with Anthony and not think of someone else – someone more beautiful, more virile, more enthusiastic, more perfect in every way – moving inside me? I know that, in sleeping with Danny Wilde, I have crossed the line and, whatever happens, things will never be quite the same again.

What have I done? What *exactly* have I done?

I can't bear to look at myself any longer, so I step into the shower and let the water cascade over me. It feels wonderful, cleansing. It would be lovely if the water could wash away the memories of last night but, as I soap myself down, I can smell his scent on my body and I relive every single moment of his hands on my skin. As I do, I tingle with pleasure once more. I can't help myself. Despite my guilt, my remorse, every fibre of me wants to be with him again.

By the time I get downstairs, Lija has arrived.

'Hey,' she says. 'How was crap birthday?'

'Er ... Not quite so crap, as it turns out.'

She raises an eyebrow. Should I confide in Lija? No. Definitely not. I should keep this to myself. I know I should. My night with Danny is a secret that I should take to the grave. Discretion, I think, discretion.

Then I can't help myself. I *have* to tell someone or I'll go stark staring mad. *Someone* has to know that I'm capable of such reckless passion. And I can hardly tell my mother or confess it to one of our customers over their cream scone.

Lija has folded her arms and is waiting impatiently.

In for a penny, in for a pound. I take a deep breath. 'I got stoned on pot, drunk on vodka and was shagged ragged on a rag rug all night.'

Lija's face doesn't even register a modicum of surprise. But then I think that Lija probably does this every weekend. If the way she usually turns up looking on a Monday morning is anything to go by.

'With Danny?'

'Of course with Danny,' I whisper. 'Who else? It's hardly likely to be Anthony.'

She grins at me and I get a rare glimpse of her perfect white teeth.

I frown at her. 'What?'

'Good for you,' she says.

'I could have done with emergency pants and a toothbrush.'

She laughs out loud at that. 'I am your role model.'

'God help me.'

'It was good. I know,' she says smugly. 'I can tell by your face. I knew he would be.'

'I shared a joint with him,' I confess, still not quite able to believe it myself.

'Half a joint? I don't think you are in danger of becoming crack whore.'

I hope Lija is right. It's a slippery slope. Then I have to ask her something that's niggling at me. 'Is sex always better when you've had too much to drink or smoked some dope?'

'No,' she says. 'It has to be good sex first of all.'

'I hoped you'd say that.' I wouldn't want the way I felt to be purely down to that.

'So it *was* good?' she asks with a smirk.

The giggles grip me again. '*Fucking brilliant!*'

Then we laugh together until we cry and Lija, my skinny, spiky girl who never initiates affection, comes to hug me warmly.

When we've calmed down, she says, 'This is not like you, Fay.'

'I know.'

'What about Anthony?'

'That I don't know,' I admit. 'I feel terrible. I've treated him so very badly.'

Lija's usual shrug. 'He treats you like doormat.'

'Two wrongs don't make a right. I'm not proud of this.'

She starts to laugh again and I can't help but join in.

'I'm *not* proud,' I insist. 'It's not like me.'

'I think I like this you better.'

'If I'm honest, I think I do too. But don't tell anyone, Lija,' I beg. 'Please don't tell anyone.'

'Fay,' she says. 'I do not think you should be ashamed of this.'

I'm not sure I agree with her, but I know that, however wretched I feel, I'm going to struggle to keep the satisfied smile from my face today.

Chapter Forty-nine

It's lunchtime when Anthony phones me. 'It was midnight by the time Deborah had her arm plastered. Midnight. That's the state of the NHS these days for you.'

I try to sound as solicitous as I can. 'Is she all right?'

'In a lot of pain,' Anthony says. 'Six weeks she'll be done up like this. She's not going to be ready for the performance at the church fête, and she might not be back up to speed for the Dickensian Christmas. I can't have someone substandard on show in Olney. It could be the end of her handbell-ringing career.'

It seems as if Anthony can think of nothing worse.

'I didn't realise it was so bad. How did she do it?'

'Falling out of bed,' Anthony says. 'As easy as that.'

I can't help but laugh at that, which makes me feel evil all over again. 'Nooo! What was she doing? Having an enthusiastic session with Internet Man?'

'She was not,' he says tightly.

'Well, good job you were able to go round so quickly and take her to A and E.'

'Er ... yes,' he says. 'Yes, it was.'

'Please send her my good wishes.' And I do mean that; she seems to be a lovely lady.

'I can't believe we missed the table at the Manor. What awful timing,' Anthony complains. 'I had to call weeks in advance for that booking.'

'We could go another time.'

'It's hardly worth it now, is it?'

I'm waiting for him to apologise for leaving me alone on my birthday, but nothing is forthcoming. Thankfully, he doesn't ask me what I did instead as I still haven't formulated a suitable explanation.

'I'll come by on the way home from work,' he says. 'Will you cook something?'

'Yes. What do you fancy?'

'Nothing too exotic,' Anthony says.

And, I think, that, right there, is the problem.

The cake shop is busy all day, filled with people who've stayed on after the festival has finished. It takes so long to get any-where on a canal boat that some have decided to make a holiday of their trip.

Lija is producing a steady stream of sandwiches and cakes. I'm rushed off my feet with orders, so I barely have a chance to chat with Stan. Which also means that I don't have time to think about Danny or why he hasn't been up to see me yet. He must be up and about by now. I glance over at *The Dreamcatcher* and, although the curtains are open, there's still no sign of life. I wonder if he's popped out and I've missed him. I thought – hoped – he might get up and come straight to see me. We need to talk about what happened last night, and the more time passes, the more difficult it will become.

I try to keep busy and not think about it. But every now and again, I get a flashback to our tangle of limbs and him moving

238

above me, beneath me, and it's all I can do to keep upright. My insides go liquid at the thought of it.

Yet by late afternoon he still hasn't been up to see me. I wonder why. It's not like him. I don't think so anyway. Now I'm feeling anxious. Is he waiting for me to go to *The Dreamcatcher* later? Perhaps.

I distract myself by talking to the Fensons, who managed to run *Floating Paradise* aground earlier. They are still clearly traumatised and need two pots of tea to get the colour back into their cheeks.

Soon the last of our customers are finishing up their cream teas, and the minute they've gone I'll be free. Will I be able to go down to the boat to see Danny before Anthony arrives? I'm not sure. It will have to be a quick visit. I didn't realise that being deceitful would be so very complicated.

Pushing my thoughts aside, I take Mum her tea and some of Lija's cake. But, when I see her, I decide she's not looking very well at all. Since this morning all her spark seems to have gone. Her face is the colour of putty and her eyes look slightly glassy.

'Are you all right, Mum?' I stroke the wispy hair from her forehead. 'Are you tired?'

'I don't feel so good,' she admits.

'Shall I give Dr Ahmed a call for you? Perhaps your blood pressure is high again. I think he should drop in if he's passing.'

'Might be for the best,' she says without argument. Which is most unlike Mum.

'Is there anything else I can get you?'

'I just need to rest, Fay.'

Reluctantly I leave her and come downstairs. I phone the surgery straight away. The receptionist says that Dr Ahmed will come out to her as soon as he can, but it won't be for a couple of hours.

239

When I go back into the kitchen, I tell Lija, 'Mum's not very well. I've phoned the doctor.'

Perhaps she can see that I'm more worried than usual as she doesn't make one of her quips. 'Sorry, Fay.'

'I'm sure she'll be fine. I just want him to have a look at her.'

'Everyone has gone from garden and I have wiped down tables,' Lija says. 'Shall I close up now?'

'Might as well.' I force myself not to run out of the door and down to *The Dreamcatcher*. 'I'll make some tea for us.'

Then, as I'm filling the kettle, there's a loud thump from upstairs.

'Mum,' I say.

Dropping the kettle, I bolt for the stairs and take them two at a time. Lija is close behind me.

In the bedroom we find Mum slumped over in bed. She's knocked the pile of books from her bedside table and upset the cup of tea I've just delivered. Her face is deathly white.

'Call the ambulance, Lija,' I say. 'Call the ambulance *now*. Please.'

Chapter Fifty

In the ambulance on the way to the hospital, Mum has a stroke. All those years of lying bedridden have finally taken their toll.

Anthony, thank heavens, turned up at the same time as the paramedics and went into organisation mode. I leave Lija to lock up the house and I jump into the car with him. The ambulance sets off at a startling pace and Anthony drives after it to the hospital, keeping up as best he can.

Mum's taken on a trolley to Accident and Emergency where she waits – too long, in my opinion – to be assessed. Eventually she's found a bed on the general ward and we go up there with her. She's white and frail and has lost movement down her left side. At the moment she can't speak and one side of her face has drooped alarmingly.

I can't stop crying and Anthony has his arm round my shoulders.

'Will she be all right?'

'We'll have to wait and see,' he says, his face grim. 'You've done all that could be asked of you, Fay.' He pats me in a comforting way. 'No one could have cared more.'

'I'm glad you're here, Anthony.'

'Where else would I be?'

Together we sit in the waiting room until Mum's settled in her bed. Then the duty doctor comes to see us.

'I'm afraid your mother is quite poorly,' he explains, and goes on to list a host of complications to Mum's condition. I'm not sure I take it all in.

When he's finished, the nurse takes us to the ward, where we're allowed to see her for a few minutes.

She looks so tiny swaddled in her hospital sheets and so very old, much older than her years.

I sit down at her bedside and take her hand. 'How are you feeling, Mum?'

She manages a nod and a tear squeezes out of her eye.

'Have a good sleep,' I say to her. 'We'll be in to see you as soon as we're allowed tomorrow. Try not to worry. You're getting excellent care now.'

She goes to say something, but no words come and she can only manage a grunt.

'You'll be back home in no time at all,' I lie hopefully.

Her eyes close and I take that as our cue to leave.

'Bye, Mum.' I kiss her cheek and her skin smells sour.

Anthony gently pats the papery skin of her hand. 'Take care, Miranda.'

Slowly we walk out of the hospital and back to the multi-storey car park. Anthony keeps his arm around my shoulders as we go. It's late, gone eleven o'clock, and we're both bone-weary. Hospitals are never going to be conducive to relaxation. It's another warm evening, but I feel cold inside.

'She'll be all right,' he assures me.

'I knew all this lying in bed and doing absolutely nothing would come to no good. She's hardly old at all. Why can't she be out there enjoying her life like Stan?'

'Your mother is a stubborn woman, Fay. I'm sure she'll fight this.'

'I hope you're right.' I turn to Anthony as he feeds his parking ticket into the machine and am filled with affection for him. He has been all I needed tonight: steadfast, unflappable in the face of adversity. I touch his arm gratefully. 'Thank you for coming with me, Anthony. I couldn't have managed alone. I bet you didn't think you'd be spending two consecutive evenings at the hospital.'

'No,' he concurs.

'I'd better Skype Edie when I get back,' I say with a weary sigh. 'She'll be so shocked, and I'm sure she'll want to come home as soon as possible.'

Chapter Fifty-one

'I'm not coming home,' Edie says, a look of horror on her face. 'How can I? I've got a job interview tomorrow.'

'Mum's very poorly, Edie,' I reiterate at the screen. '*Very* poorly. That's what the doctor said.' I could reel off all the things he said were wrong with her, but my brain is too tired and scrambled.

'She'll be fine,' Edie says. 'You know what she's like.'

In the kitchen, I can hear Anthony murmuring into his mobile phone and I wonder who he's calling at this hour. A few minutes later, he brings me a nice hot cup of tea and a couple of biscuits in lieu of dinner, and then he sits in the armchair opposite. If Edie was on the phone, I could cover the mouthpiece and tell him how the conversation has gone so far. But, of course, with Skype, my dear sister can see everything.

'It would be nice if you came to see her,' I press on. 'You know she adores you. It would give her a real boost.'

'Look, Fay . . .' Edie sighs at me. 'Things are going well for me. Brandon's being great again. I think he really will leave his wife this time. Everything's looking up. I believe I'm on the verge of getting a job too. I can just feel it.'

'She's your *mother*. She needs you here.'

'Oh, Fay ...'

'A few days, Edie. That's all I ask.'

'You're putting too much pressure on me.' Edie hugs herself. 'I hate this.'

'I don't mean to worry you, but I have a bad feeling about this.'

'Oh, Fay. You're such a drama queen.'

I am?

'I'll send you the money. You know that.'

'Don't blackmail me,' Edie whines.

'I'm not blackmailing you, but I am begging. I'm frightened that Mum won't pull through this, Edie, and I'd hate anything to happen while you're still in New York.'

'Hey, Edie,' I hear a male voice call out in the background, and can only assume it's the much-talked-about Brandon. I hope he's not waiting for her in bed, but I fear he might be.

'Look,' she says to me. 'I have to go. Keep me posted. I'll Skype you tomorrow. Or the day after. Mum'll be fine. Trust me.'

'Edie—'

'Love you,' she says, and then the screen goes blank.

Heavy of heart, I log off.

'Your sister is a complete nightmare,' Anthony says.

For once, I don't disagree. 'I don't know what to do,' I tell him.

'Sleep on it,' Anthony suggests. 'I'll stay with you tonight. It'll all look better in the morning.'

I should go to see Danny. I *want* to see Danny. But Anthony has been so very kind this evening. He's rallied to my aid without complaint. He's been there for me to lean on and I can't thank him enough. And, if I'm perfectly honest, I'm frightened to be alone.

Chapter Fifty-two

I call the hospital the minute I get up and they say that Mum's had a comfortable night. I don't know what 'comfortable' means. Does it mean that she's getting better or does it mean that she's really ill and this is the best they can hope for? I'm not up with hospital terminology and it only serves to make me more anxious. Visiting time isn't until ten o'clock, so I can't go on the ward before then.

I see Anthony off to work, fussing over him. I didn't sleep at all. Obviously. The previous night I'd been with another man, and, try as I might, I couldn't get him out of my mind. I lay in bed alternating between fretting about my mum and then going over every single moment of my night with Danny on *The Dreamcatcher*. Anthony slept on innocently ignorant, snoring loudly. My eyes are red and sore. I stifle an exhausted yawn.

'I'll call later,' Anthony says. 'If I get time, I'll drop by the hospital and see her.'

'Thank you. I do appreciate it.' I wind my arms round him and hold him close. I get another rush of affection for this uptight, unemotional man. When he's needed to pull it out of the bag for me, he has.

'Nonsense,' Anthony says all gruffly. He kisses my cheek. 'Don't worry.'

But I do.

I'm still worrying when Lija arrives.

'How is Miranda?'

'Poorly,' I tell her. 'She had a stroke last night on the way to the hospital.'

I get my second cuddle in two days from Lija. 'So sorry.'

'I've got to go to see her soon. Can you hold the fort?'

'Of course.'

'Thank you.'

'Have you seen Danny?'

'No,' I tell her. I'd like to say that he's the very last thing on my mind, but he isn't. 'Anthony stayed last night. I couldn't go to Danny.'

'Awkward.'

'Anthony's been great. He couldn't have been more helpful.'

'So he should be.' Then Lija fixes me with one of her stares. 'You could go see Danny now. I will get on with preparations for lunch.'

'I don't know what to say to him. I feel really awkward now.'

'Best to get it over with.'

I chew at my fingernail. 'Do you think so?'

'Absolutely.'

But I really don't know what happens next. Will he laugh at me, shrug it all off as a bit of fun? Or will it be the start of something new? What of Anthony, who has been so very good to me? He deserves better than this. Whichever way, it has rocked my world and nothing seems to be quite as simple as it was a couple of days ago. I suppose Lija is right: I should go and find out one way or the other.

I think I should check on Mum first – and then it hits me that she's not even here.

'It seems weird not to be running up and down stairs after Mum,' I admit. 'I feel a bit rudderless.'

'Then go to him. Use time wisely.'

It's no good putting it off any longer.

So I head out into the garden, nerves making my heart race. It's another beautiful day. One in a long unbroken line of beautiful days. It's years since we've had such a glorious summer. I can't remember when it last rained, and the garden is looking in sore need of water. The grass, which needs mowing, is crisping up to a nice shade of brown.

The nearer I get to the water, the more my spirits lift. I can't wait to see him. I need him to hold me, to tell me that everything will be fine. But when I reach the jetty, I'm stopped in my tracks and can barely catch my breath. The mooring behind the *Maid of Merryweather* is empty. *The Dreamcatcher* has gone, and Danny with it.

Anxiously I scan the canal, but there's no sign of a boat of any kind in either direction. It's quiet, still, the water unruffled even by a breeze.

He's gone. Danny's gone.

I stand there not knowing quite what to do. When did he go? I wonder. Last night? This morning? What if he realised that our night together – the night that I thought was so very wonderful – was all a terrible mistake? What if he can't face me and has made his escape as soon as possible? He could have realised that his future lies with the Siennas of this world after all. Who in their right mind – of course – would hook up with a dull, middle-aged woman ten years older than themselves? It might be commonplace in the world of celebrity, but it doesn't happen to people who run a café by the canal. Why did I even think for one stupid minute that it would?

I'm so disappointed that Danny would run out on me without

even saying goodbye, without saying anything at all. I thought he was a better man than that.

Yet, deep in the centre of my soul, I know he's gone for good. He let me fall in love with him and now he's left. There's a terrible pain in my chest and I realise that it's my heart breaking in two.

Chapter Fifty-three

Mum's heart is also breaking. Slowly, piece by piece. During her second night in hospital, she had a cardiac arrest, and another just before dawn. I got a call at seven to tell me that I should come to the hospital as soon as I could. I'm dressed and in the car on my way in minutes.

When I get there, the unfeasibly young doctor tells me that two chambers of her heart have been damaged.

'It's not what we'd hoped for,' he tells me. 'I'm very sorry. She's resting now, but you can go through to see her.'

Armed with Lucozade and grapes that I bought yesterday and a clean nightie for her, I follow a nurse on to the ward. Before I got here, she'd been moved up to the Cardiac Care Unit, so I know she's in the best possible place. Here there's an air of serious silence and subdued lighting. It's as different from a busy, bustling general ward as it could possibly be. A few well-spaced beds hug the walls and, not that I can see very much, the handful of patients are all hooked up to a myriad softly beeping machines.

My mother looks tiny in her bed and very ill.

'Mum,' I say. 'I'm here.'

Her eyes flicker but she struggles to open them.

Before I can say anything else, one of her machines flatlines, an alarm goes off and Mum cries out in pain. I don't even have time to respond before all hell breaks loose around me and the crash team comes running to her bed. The curtain is whisked around her and I'm ushered back into the waiting room.

Where I wait, and wait, and wait.

An hour later, I'm still waiting when Anthony arrives. He gives me a hug. 'The nurse said she's had a setback.'

'Heart attack. Three of them. The last one very serious.'

'She'll be fine.'

'I don't think so, Anthony.'

'Have you seen her yet?'

'Not properly. I arrived as the last one happened.'

'My poor love,' he says.

He sits down next to me and I lean my head against his shoulder. 'I have to ring Edie. Let her know.'

'Wait until the doctor's been,' he suggests. 'Let's see what he says. There's no point in worrying her unnecessarily.'

I'm not convinced that Edie is worrying at all.

'I'll cancel my appointments for the rest of this afternoon,' Anthony says.

'You don't need to. Really. Not if they're important.'

'I will,' he says. 'You need someone here with you.'

I go to protest as I know how busy Anthony is, but I really don't think I can face this alone and I'm fed up of being stoic.

'Thank you,' I say. 'I'd like that.'

'Give me five minutes.' Anthony goes outside to make his calls.

So I sit and, without really seeing anything, read all the magazines that are ten years old and ripped to shreds, and wonder how many germs are breeding on them.

Eventually another doctor comes in. She's also young.

Terribly young. She's Chinese and looks about fourteen. I wonder if all these child-doctors are really old enough to know what's going on. 'Mrs Merryweather?'

I nod and stand to shake her hand.

'Where's your husband?'

Before I get the chance to explain our marital status and that I'm not actually a Mrs, Anthony comes back in.

'I'm here,' he says. He's carrying two white plastic cups of coffee.

'I'm afraid it's not good news,' the young doctor says solemnly.

I brace myself for the worse and it's what I get.

'Your mum's sustained major damage to two chambers of her heart. Her condition is very unstable.'

'But she will recover?'

'That's very difficult to say, Mrs Merryweather. We will do our best to keep her comfortable.'

That word again. *Comfortable.*

'She may have a week or more. Or it could be a few days. It might even be today.'

'She'll die?'

'I'm afraid that your mother is critically ill.'

Somehow I find my voice. 'Is there anything I can do?'

'I'd plan on not going too far,' she advises. 'We'll let you know if there are any changes. It's just a waiting game now. I'm sorry.'

'I need to call Edie, right away,' I say to Anthony. He nods in agreement.

'You can see your mother,' the doctor says. 'But she might not recognise you. You can spend as long as you want to on the ward. There's a kitchen where you can make tea and toast, heat up some soup. If you want to stay overnight, then we can put a sleeper chair for you alongside the bed.'

'Thank you, doctor. I'd like that.'

'I'll get one of the nurses to organise it for you.' She touches my arm. 'I'm terribly sorry that it's not better news for you.'

'Thank you,' I say. 'Thank you for all that you're doing.'

I call Edie then Anthony and I go through to the Cardiac Care ward, which is still in semi-darkness. Mum is in the corner bed and she looks like an alien with so many tubes running in and out of her. It's unbearable to see. After all these years of crying wolf, of lying in bed when she could have been out living her life, she's now truly, desperately ill.

Anthony and I sit beside her. I carefully stroke the fragile skin on her hand on the only clear patch between the tube that runs into the back of it and the monitor or whatever it is attached to her finger.

'I'm here, Mum. I'm here.'

Her eyes flicker but fail to focus. 'Edie?'

'Fay,' I correct. 'It's Fay.'

'Oh.' The disappointment is palpable.

'She'll be here soon,' I promise.

And I can only pray that I'm right.

Chapter Fifty-four

Edie comes home. Reluctantly. I meet her at Heathrow Airport, where she's flown in on the red-eye.

We hug each other at the barrier. She looks thin. Too thin.

'It's good to see you,' I tell her as I take her case. 'I'm glad you came.'

'What choice did I have?' she says. 'I'm still not sure what I can do.'

'You can be here for Mum. She's desperate to see you.'

We head back to the car park, Edie trailing after me. I was so looking forward to seeing Edie, despite the circumstances, but it's obvious that there's an atmosphere between us.

'I had to cancel an interview,' she complains. 'It was a great job too.'

'I'm sure Mum will appreciate how much trouble you've put yourself to.'

She looks at me to see if there's any sarcasm lurking. There is.

Stopping, I turn to face her. 'She's dying, Edie.'

My sister looks as if I've slapped her. Then she recovers herself and says, 'You know what she's like, Fay. With all the fuss and attention, she'll rally.'

'I don't think so, Edie. Not this time. We should get to the hospital as soon as possible.'

Chastened, she drops into step behind me again.

My sister is all kitted out, as usual, in designer gear, but she's so small now that she looks like a child. She's wearing a white T-shirt with a pink and white spotted skirt. They're accessorised with a yellow belt and matching kitten heels. She's clip-clopping along the pavement like a little pony.

Despite just coming off a night flight, she also looks immaculate. Her auburn hair, just like Mum's used to be, is glossy and curls down past her shoulders. Her skin is flawless, her manicure equally so.

I slept all night in the chair by Mum's bed and, even though I went home to shower and change, I still feel as if I've been dragged every which way through a hedge. Edie and I seem to have so little in common now that it troubles me.

I have to confess that, in the brief time I was in the house, I found five minutes to walk down the garden to the canal, ostensibly to clear my head, but *The Dreamcatcher* hadn't returned. It was too much to hope for. I want to be able to tell Danny what's going on, why I couldn't come back to see him. What would he be like in this situation? I wonder. I'm sure his presence would be comforting too.

Edie and I find the car in the short-stay car park. She climbs into the passenger seat while I put her case in the boot. I pull out and we head for home. My sister stares blankly out of the window, face impassive. Perhaps she's just tired, and I certainly don't have the energy to make small-talk.

'It feels weird to be back,' Edie says eventually, as we negotiate the slip-road on to the motorway. 'It feels like a foreign country to me, not home. I realise I haven't missed this place at all.'

My sister has been gone for years now and though New York

255

is but a hop, skip and a jump away, she hasn't visited us in all that time. Yesterday I transferred nine hundred pounds for her flight, which was the best price she could get at such short notice. Which is a sizeable sum, though it's hardly astronomical. She could have come home once, couldn't she? That wouldn't have been hard to manage. You can get cheaper flights if you book ahead. Yet she's never been back for anything – birthdays, Easter, Christmas. They all go unmarked by Edie. And, due to looking after Mum and running the café, I haven't been over there either. Though we've kept in touch by Skype – and thank God for technology – it's not the same, and I feel as if the distance has driven a wedge between us.

She perks up a bit as we settle into our journey. She prattles on about how wonderful Manhattan is and I get the latest download on Brandon, but I can't really process it all now. The only thing I'm thinking about is Mum and how I don't want to leave her alone for too long. What if something happens – the unspeakable – and we aren't there? As difficult as she can be, I can't imagine a life without my mum in it. Perhaps it's because Edie has been away for so long, because she doesn't see Mum on a daily basis, that she seems less concerned.

I tune out and concentrate on my driving and holding it all together, just hoping that I say yes and no in the appropriate places.

An hour and a half later, despite the morning rush of traffic, we're bumping our way along the lane to our family home.

'God, I hate this place,' Edie says with a dramatic sigh. 'It really is the arse end of the back of beyond.'

'I love it,' I reply. 'I can't think of anywhere I'd rather live.'

'You sound like Dad.'

It's true. He loved this place too.

'Have you still got that knackered old barge thing of his?'

'Of course I have. Nothing would make me part with her.

256

The *Maid of Merryweather* is still moored at the bottom of the garden. She doesn't run these days. I use her as a shop, selling cakes and stuff to the people on the canal.' I glance at my sister. She's twizzling her long curls round her finger and gazing out of the window. Her lack of interest is palpable. 'But I've already told you all this.'

'Oh, yeah,' she says distractedly. 'It's probably quaint and all that, but I like the excitement of the big city. New York rocks all night long. The city that never sleeps.' I can't think of anything worse. 'I wouldn't want to live anywhere else now either.'

We pull into the driveway and I have to admit that the old house does look a bit shabby, a little frayed around the edges. I'd love to have the money to bring it back to its former glory, but it's been like this for as long as I can remember. Its former glory was obviously long before Mum and Dad bought it.

'We can't hang around for too long, but I thought you'd want to freshen up and have some breakfast.'

'Fine.'

'Then I'll take you straight to the hospital.'

She wrinkles her nose at that.

'I know it's difficult, but I really don't like to be away from Mum.'

'You know I don't do ill,' Edie says petulantly. 'Will we be there for ever?'

'Mum is very sick.'

'I know. But we won't make her better by sitting there all day, will we?'

'What else have you come home for, Edie? Do you want to go shopping? Get a manicure?'

She stares at me, startled by my retort.

'I'm sorry,' I say. 'I don't mean to snap at you, but this scenario is as bad as it gets. You just don't seem to understand that.'

'I'm trying,' Edie insists.

'Let's see how we go.' I'm hoping that when Edie gets there and the full reality of Mum's situation hits her, she might feel more compassionate.

Placated for the moment, she jumps out of the car and heads for the house. I lug her case out of the boot and follow her.

Lija is in the kitchen and already busy. The homely smell of baking fills the air. It's so welcoming that it makes me want to weep.

'That smells divine,' I say.

Lija wipes the flour from her hands on to her T-shirt and eyes Edie suspiciously.

'How is Miranda?'

'Not good, I'm afraid,' I tell her.

'Hey,' Edie says, over-bright.

'Hello,' Lija says and keeps her arms resolutely folded.

'So this is the infamous Lija.' Edie raises an eyebrow. 'I've heard a lot about you.'

None of it good from Mum, I'm guessing.

Lija scowls darkly.

'You've got this place looking nice, Fay.' My sister wanders to the window and takes in the garden, which is still looking very pretty. Thanks to Danny's hard work. Tables and chairs in pastel shades nestle among the rambling roses; the clematis which is in full and vibrant bloom sprawls along the wall. 'It's not as bad as I remember it. Are those sunshades new?'

'Yes.'

'Fab. And you're busy?'

'We've had a very good summer, haven't we, Lija?'

My assistant nods, face impassive. I'm not sure who'd win in a staring-out competition, Edie or Lija.

'I've aired your room for you,' I say to Edie, relieved that Lija hadn't got round to moving her stuff in. That would have been tricky to explain.

My sister heads upstairs and I follow with her case.

'I'm pleased that business is booming,' Edie says.

'I wouldn't say that. But we get by. Every year it gets better, and I can't ask for more than that.' Enough to keep sending you money, I think unkindly. 'It's hard work though. I couldn't manage without Lija.'

'She looks like a moody mare.'

'She's great,' I say in her defence. 'She's looked after Mum for me more than once.'

Edie seems unimpressed that Lija has this skill on her CV.

'My old room,' she sighs.

She picks up an ornament from the dresser. A hideous china cat.

'It took me years to escape from here, Fay.' She fixes me with a cool stare. 'Wild horses wouldn't drag me back.'

If Mum survives this, which I'm hoping against the odds is possible, then it's obvious that I can't rely on Edie for any help with her care. But then, I'd already worked that out.

Chapter Fifty-five

Mum dies. We only just make it to the hospital in time.

When we got back from the airport, Edie had a long bath, washed her hair, picked at her breakfast. Then she enjoyed a long, whispered transatlantic telephone call with Brandon, even though it must still have been pre-dawn in New York, while I paced up and down in the kitchen tearing my hair out.

I could barely contain my frustration and helped Lija to knead some dough in a particularly aggressive manner while I waited for Edie, impotent. Just as I was thinking that I'd go back to the hospital alone and Edie could follow in a taxi when she was ready, the phone rang.

It was a nurse from the Cardiac Care ward. She told me that Mum had taken another turn for the worse and they thought I should come in right away. It then took me another ten minutes to persuade Edie to bring her phone call to an end and get into the wretched car.

'Brandon's having problems,' Edie says, chewing her finger-nails as, not before time, we zoom towards the hospital. 'He's lost his job. How can that be? He's a partner and they've asked him to leave. Whoever heard of that? I think there's more behind it. He's vital to the company. They must have wanted him out for some reason.'

I really don't care about Brandon's issues. Not now.

'What will that mean for me?' she wails. 'Until he gets another partnership or something, he'll be reliant on his wife's money. How will he pay for my apartment?'

'I don't know, Edie,' I say. 'But I can't think about it now.'

'Thanks for the sympathy.' She tuts and, folding her arms, turns to stare out of the window.

'The hospital says that Mum's gone downhill quickly, Edie. This is serious.'

By the time we're racing along the dual carriageways of Milton Keynes, I'm literally pulling my hair out. I screech in to the multi-storey to park and, tugging Edie along, run as fast as I can along the maze of corridors to the ward. I just knew, knew it in my bones, that this would be the day.

I'm almost frothing at the mouth by the time we reach the serious stillness of the Cardiac Care ward. All the colour has drained from Edie's face and, now that we're here, I think the reality of this has finally hit her.

We go to Mum's bed and her eyes light up as she sees Edie sit down next to her. That's all I needed to witness. Mum knows that Edie has come for her, that she's here.

'Hi, Mum,' Edie murmurs softly. 'I came as soon as I could.'

Mum's too weak to talk, but Edie holds her hand tightly.

Both of her daughters are by her side and that's all that matters to me.

Then, as our mother takes her last breath, she whispers, 'Oh, Edie.' And that's all.

Chapter Fifty-six

Edie and I are sitting here in the hospital, stunned, holding each other tightly and not knowing quite what else we should do.

'She's gone,' Edie says, sobbing. 'I should have been here sooner.'

'You were here just in time,' I offer. 'That's all that matters.'

I'm amazed at how quickly they come to take Mum away from the ward, but then I suppose there's someone else who is also very poorly waiting for her bed. They disconnect all the tubes and wires with a brisk efficiency that is borderline cruel. Then Mum is loaded onto a trolley and wheeled away. It seems as if there's nothing left for us to do here, so we walk away from the ward, bereft.

I don't know how I drive home. I probably shouldn't: we should have left the car and got a taxi home, but it didn't occur to me at the time and Edie didn't say anything. It starts to rain as I negotiate the traffic, and for a moment I can't remember where the windscreen wipers are.

When we reach home, Lija can tell from our tear-stained faces that it's not good news. Without me needing to say anything, she hugs me fiercely. 'I am so very sorry, Fay.'

'Thank you.'

'I am here for you.'

'I know.'

I call Anthony's mobile but he doesn't pick up, so I leave a voicemail to let him know what's happened and that we're now at home. It would be horrible for him to drop into the hospital, only to find that Mum's no longer there.

Lija makes us both tea.

Edie sits sniffling at the kitchen table. I can't deal with her pain right now; I need a few minutes to myself. Despite the heavy rain, I need to get out. I knew this moment was coming, but it's still a heavy blow when it does.

'I need some fresh air.' I feel chilled to the bone, so I pull on my cardigan and take my tea out into the garden.

Huddling under one of the sunshades that Danny erected for me, I watch the rain pour down. The drops patter on the canal, creating pretty circles, and, oblivious to my pain, the ducks splash happily on the water. I take as much pleasure from it as I can. The heads of the flowers are bowed low with the weight of the raindrops. My own heart feels as heavy as lead.

Because of the weather, very few people have come to the café today, which I'm thankful for. I wouldn't want to have left Lija in the lurch. Not surprisingly, the garden is completely empty, but there are a few hardy folk ensconced in the dining room. The French doors are firmly closed against the elements. There's no sign of Stan either, and I wonder whether Lija has taken his lunch to him at home today. Sometimes we do that if the weather is too bad for him to venture out.

I wish Danny was here so that I could talk to him. He'd want to know about Mum. I'm sure he would. He was so very easy to chat to and I could tell him my worries, my fears. I realise that I don't even have a mobile number for him. He's gone and that's that.

Looking at the *Maid of Merryweather*, water puddling on the cratch cover, I wonder what will happen now. That's Dad and Mum both gone. Edie and I are all that's left of the family. We'll have to stick together, just the two of us.

For all her cantankerous ways, I'll miss Mum. I wish our relationship had been better, but I'm sure she loved me the best that she could. For all her faults, she was my mother and, as such, will be sadly missed. Having spent so much time with her, she'll leave a big hole in my world. Her death was quick and unexpected, but I'm glad for her sake that she didn't have a long, lingering illness. But, I'm ashamed to say, there's also a feeling of relief at her passing. It means that, for the first time in years, I'll be free to devote my attention to my own life, to the café, to things that I want to do but have never previously had the time or the freedom for.

I'm thinking that Mum will have left the house to both me and Edie. I want to carry on with the cake shop, of course I do, but that will mean buying Edie out of her share as I'm sure she'll want the money. It would certainly help her current situation. Will I be able to arrange a mortgage to cover it? The banks are notoriously difficult about lending in the current climate, and that's going to be a sizeable amount of money. Still, the house is a good asset. It may need a bit of a makeover inside, but it's structurally a good, sound place and in a very desirable location. Canalside properties always attract a premium. We haven't ever had it valued, but I'm sure it's worth a tidy sum.

Softening my gaze, I let it wander along the canal again. I wonder where Danny is now and why he went without saying goodbye. I know I need to put this behind me, but thinking about our night together brings some much-needed warmth to my heart in this time of darkness. It was wild, reckless, inappropriate. And a lot of fun. I should regret it, but I don't. Not one minute of it. It's something I won't forget for a long time. For once in my life I was spontaneous, adventurous, crazy. Perhaps having one wonderful night locked in my memory will help me to cope with a life that is destined to be otherwise very mundane.

Chapter Fifty-seven

The rain has eased slightly and my mug is empty, so I stand up, stretch my tired back and head into the house. The wisteria which cascades over the veranda has taken a battering and most of its petals are scattered on the patio.

When I open the door to the kitchen, Anthony has just arrived. He wraps his arms around me and, not for the first time in these last few days, that gives me a great deal of comfort.

'I'm sorry, Fay,' he says. 'I know you were close.'

But *were* Mum and I close? I wish with all my heart that we could have been more so. 'Thank you, Anthony. It's nice to have you here. You've been very good to me.'

'I'll call the funeral director too,' he says. 'It's a terrible job. I did all this for my mother when she died. I know what has to be done.'

'Thank you.'

Then he does what Anthony does best. He goes into organisation mode. It's awful that, at a time when you least feel like doing anything, there is so much to think about.

'I want nothing to do with the arrangements,' Edie says. 'You do what you like. Jet lag is catching up with me, I'm going to go to bed for an hour.'

So Edie retires to her room. While she's still sleeping, later that afternoon, Anthony and I go to see the funeral directors and make the necessary arrangements. I sit like a zombie while Anthony works it all out with them, only requiring me to nod my consent in the appropriate places. Then he takes me to the registrar to record Mum's death. After that it's the florists to choose her floral tributes. I choose white roses as, I now realise, I don't know what Mum's favourite flower was – and that makes me cry again.

There won't be a wake, as such. Since Mum took to her bed, all her friends have fallen away, so anyone who does come along to the small service at the local crematorium will be invited back to the café. That was Anthony's suggestion too, and an excellent one.

A few days later, her ashes will be buried with Dad's in the cemetery there. When Dad died, I wanted to scatter Dad's ashes on the canal, as was his wish, but Mum wouldn't hear of it. Perhaps it's just as well, as they can be together again now. Mum wouldn't have taken kindly to being scattered on the canal.

When Anthony and I get home, I'm so very weary that I could lie on the floor and weep. Lija has gone for the evening, but she's left us a shepherd's pie that we can pop in the oven. How very thoughtful of her. That small kindness nearly has me in tears again.

Anthony sets the table for the three of us and, just as the potato topping is browning nicely, Edie appears.

She looks pale, washed out, her eyes red-rimmed.

'How are you feeling?'

'Like shit,' she says. 'You?'

'Much the same. Lija's left us a shepherd's pie.'

'I'm not hungry.'

'You haven't eaten all day, Edie. Try some.'

She shrugs. 'I could do with a drink.'

'Tea?'

'I was thinking of something stronger.'

'There's a bottle of white in the fridge,' Anthony says. 'Shall I open it?'

'Not for me,' I say.

'Yes,' Edie says. 'That'll do.'

So Anthony pours her out a glass, which she necks quickly, topping it up herself.

Without even realising what I'm doing, I somehow manage to take the shepherd's pie out of the oven, put it on the table and serve it. There's no veg. I didn't even think to open a packet of frozen peas, but no one comments.

The shepherd's pie is lovely. Anthony and I make a valiant attempt at eating, while Edie pushes the food around her plate.

'I've booked Mum's funeral for next Tuesday,' I tell Edie.

'That's nearly a week away.' She looks aghast. 'I hadn't planned on staying that long.'

'It's the earliest they could do it,' I say tightly. 'Normally you have to wait a lot longer than that. We only got this slot because someone else had to move their relative's funeral.'

Edie sighs.

I don't know if she's thinking of skipping straight back to the States, but I say, 'You can't miss the funeral, Edie. She's your mum. You need to be there.'

'I know,' she bites back. But she pouts anyway.

'Plus we've got a lot to sort out while you're here. We need to go to the solicitors to talk about Mum's will. I'm sure you'll want to get the house sorted out.'

'Yeah,' she says. 'I suppose so. But I'm not really interested in it.'

'Half of it will be yours.'

She brightens up at that. 'Really?'

'Of course. Why wouldn't it be?'

'Wow. Do you think we can see the solicitor tomorrow?'

I see the pound signs flicker in Edie's eyes. She'll be through her half like water. 'I'll ring him.'

I suppose the sooner we get the ball rolling, the better.

When dinner's finished, Anthony and I clear up. Edie takes her wine on to the veranda and lights up a cigarette. I can't see from here, but I hope it's just a cigarette: I'm sure not even Edie would risk coming through customs with anything stronger.

'Do you want me to stay tonight?' Anthony asks.

I shake my head. I know he doesn't like to be here too often in the week, but it's nice of him to suggest it. 'I should spend some time with Edie. There's a lot of tension between us, and I don't get to see her very often.' I put my hand on his arm. 'I appreciate all that you've done today. Really I do. I couldn't have managed without you.'

'I don't want you to struggle on your own.'

'I love you,' I say. But even saying those words sets me off crying again.

I feel so very dreadful about betraying him so horribly, about my night of reckless passion in the arms of Danny Wilde. It was so unlike me, so out of character. I resolve here and now to be a better girlfriend to Anthony. From this moment on, I'll be the woman he deserves. We'll have a long and happy future together and I promise myself that I'll never again look at another man.

'Shush, shush,' Anthony says and tenderly kisses my fore-head.

This is why I first fell in love with him. I know where I stand with Anthony. He might not set the world alight, he might not turn me inside-out with excitement and ecstasy, but who needs that on a daily basis? He is a solid, dependable man. He's organised. He's here for me when I need him. It would serve me very well to remember that.

Chapter Fifty-eight

Edie and I sit on the sofa together. I've put some music on the iPod. It's the stuff that Lija downloads to play in the café and I'm usually running about so much I don't have time to listen to it properly. Whatever it is, it's nice, soothing. Then one of the tunes that comes on is the one that Danny and I were singing together in the well deck of *The Dreamcatcher*, and I allow a spark of warmth into my traumatised heart. Yet I promised fealty to Anthony not a few hours ago, so I'm going to have to stop referring everything back to how I was feeling that night, even if it is helping to sustain me at the moment.

My sister has carried through the bottle of white, which doesn't have much left in it. She brought me a glass too and I squeeze the last vestiges out of the bottle just to be sociable. We sip our drinks in quiet contemplation. The wine, to my surprise, hits the spot in a way that the copious cups of tea I've consumed today haven't. I could open another bottle.

We're both in our pyjamas now and, as the night is cool after the rain, I've lit the fire. This can be a cold room and the flames from the hearth give it a warm glow. I note that Edie's pyjamas are a lot more slinky and skimpy than mine.

'It's nice to spend some time together,' I say to Edie. 'Even though the circumstances are awful.'

'Yeah,' she agrees absently. 'It's been too long.'

Because of the age difference between us, we're not as close as some sisters might be, and I wonder, not for the first time, why Mum and Dad left such a big gap between us.

'Anthony's been very good today,' Edie says.

'Yes,' I agree. 'I'm very grateful to him.' In fact, I don't think I'd actually have been able to manage without him. I was so relieved to be able to lean on him, to rely on his strength. He knew just what to do and my mind seemed to have gone completely numb. 'He liked Mum, and she thought a lot of him too.'

'I doubt she'd have liked Brandon,' Edie says. 'He's not the sort of man that mothers approve of. She'll never meet him now, anyway.' Edie glugs her wine. 'Never thought about tying the knot with Anthony? You've been together for ever and yet, unless I'm mistaken, I still can't hear wedding bells?'

'You sound like Mum.'

'Why the reluctance? You must be sure of each other by now.'

'I don't know,' I confess. 'I assumed we'd always be together, but then I had a bit of a wobble.' Much more than that, I could add, but I'm unsure how to articulate what I've been feeling over the past few months. 'We've been having a bit of a tough time recently. I began to doubt that Anthony really was the one for me.'

'I used to think he was a total wanker,' Edie says. 'But he's OK. In fact, I wish my man was more like him. If Anthony says something then I bet you can rely on it. It's not the same with Brandon. I can't guarantee that he'll be around from one day to the next.'

'It must be tough to live like that.'

She gives me a wry smile. 'Better than living without him.'

'You'll go straight back to New York as soon as the funeral's over?'

Edie nods. 'It's sad, isn't it, but I don't want Brandon to get used to me not being around. He might find he likes it.'

'Can't you find yourself someone nicer, Edie? I hate to see you being treated so badly.'

'He'd have to be the one to end it. I love him too much to walk away. He'll need me more than ever now he's lost his job. That will be a terrible blow for him, and he gets no support from his wife.'

I wonder if said wife sees it quite like that.

Edie curls her feet up on the sofa. 'I feel like my insides are bleeding when I'm away from him. Have you ever felt like that?'

'No – no,' I bluster. 'Anthony and I aren't like that.'

'You're old before your time, woman. There should still be a spark between you, the undeniable, irresistible sexual chemistry.'

'I'm not sure we've ever had that, if I'm honest.'

'That's a shame,' she says. 'I wish you could understand how I feel.'

Maybe it's the wine loosening my tongue, or maybe it's because I get so little time to talk frankly to my little sister, but I say, 'There was someone. Recently.'

Edie raises an eyebrow and grins. 'Oh, sis!'

'It was nothing really,' I lie. 'He was just passing by on the canal.'

'Not one of those fucking hippies that don't realise the sixties are over?'

'No,' I laugh. I think of Danny, young, bright and vibrant. 'He's definitely not a hippy.'

'How far did it go?'

'Oh, not far.'

272

'Longing looks? Tongues? More? I need details.'

After a pause, I confess, 'I spent one night with him.' One fantastic, one brilliant, one passion-filled night.

'You dark horse, Fay Merryweather! I don't suppose you mean playing Scrabble?'

I feel myself blush under her interrogation. 'We definitely didn't play Scrabble.'

'I take it Anthony doesn't know?'

'No.' It's a secret that I'll take to my grave.

'Wowsers!' Edie guffaws. 'I didn't think you were capable of such skulduggery. You're the Good Girl. I'm the one who's supposed to be the black sheep of the family.'

'It was just the one night.'

'That is so *totally* out of character for you.'

'I know.'

'And it was only the one time?'

'It was the one *night*. I didn't say it was the one time.' I'm trying to make light of this but my stomach flutters with pleasure, with unresolved longing, when I remember how we loved each other all night long.

'God almighty!' Edie is wide-eyed with shock. 'I'm not sure I know you any more.'

'I don't know if I know myself.'

'So what happened? I bet you kicked him out of bed in the morning, you evil minx.'

'Not quite.' I might be in confessional mode, but I still can't bring myself to tell Edie the circumstances of our parting. So all I say is, 'He left the next day.'

'And that's it? Is he ever coming back?'

'I don't know,' I admit.

'Now I'm jealous,' she says. 'How fucking romantic.'

It was. It was spontaneous and sexy and tender. And I wonder if I'll ever feel that way again.

'And you're sure he wasn't some unwashed, dreadlocked bloke with flies circling round his head?'

'No,' I say. 'He wasn't that.'

'Bloody hell.' Edie bounces from the sofa. 'I need another glass of wine after that revelation. Is there any more in the fridge?'

'Yes. There's a bottle of Chardonnay.' Anthony put it there earlier for us. And, to be honest, I need some more too.

'Fab.'

'Edie,' I call after her as she pads towards the kitchen. My voice sounds uncertain. 'You won't tell Anthony, will you?'

'What kind of a sister do you think I am?' She frowns at me. 'Of course I won't. You've kept my secret from Mum for years.'

All of your secrets, I think.

'How could I forget that?' Edie makes a locking gesture on her mouth with her fingers. 'My lips are sealed.'

Chapter Fifty-nine

So life must go on, I guess. Fay's Cakes still has to open, and thankfully Lija comes in as usual. She's currently tiptoeing around me and isn't as rude as she normally is. I think it's a big effort for her though.

Edie is still asleep. It was gone two o'clock when we went to bed last night as her body clock is all over the place. I'm completely exhausted now, but it was nice to be curled up on the sofa, gossiping with her until late. I think we could become close again, given enough time.

'Fay.' Lija breaks into my thoughts.

'Yes?'

'Do you want to take cakes for today down to *Maid of Merryweather*? I baked some more lemon drizzle loaf yesterday. I think we are low on that.'

'Of course.' So she loads me up with a tray of half a dozen lemon drizzle loaves – one of our best sellers – and then opens the back door for me.

The day is sunny, summer restored once more. The grass is still damp though, and my feet get wet as I walk down to the *Maid*.

I concentrate, balancing the cakes carefully, as I climb into the well deck and unlock the cabin. There'd be hell to pay if these ended up in the canal. I'd have to go into hiding.

The cabin is cosy inside and the warmth of the sunshine has brought out the natural scent of the wood. Sometimes I even catch a hint of my dad's smell. I wonder wistfully whether this old boat will ever be fully functional again. After I've loaded up the shelves with Lija's baking, I check that we're not low on anything else.

As I'm making my inventory, I hear a narrowboat coming in to moor behind the *Maid of Merryweather*. An early customer, perhaps. I carry on counting the cakes, making a note of what's missing. We could do with some more strawberry jam, I think. The summer-fruit season is upon us and people just can't get enough of it.

Then, as I'm dwelling on the delights of strawberries, there's the thump of boots on the jetty and my heart skips a beat. It can't be, surely? Yet a moment later, I hear the welcome pitter-patter of a dog's claws on the wood and an unforgettable bark. I stand frozen to the spot.

'Diggery,' I hear Danny say. 'Here, boy.'

I could weep. Weep for joy. He's back. Danny's come back.

Then I'm gripped with apprehension. What if he's not alone? I'm fully expecting to see him lifting the lovely Sienna from *The Dreamcatcher*, and I can't move.

Footsteps are coming towards the *Maid of Merryweather*, but still I stay where I am.

A second later and Danny is there, as large as life, crouching down on the jetty next to the cabin doors, peering inside. 'Hello,' he says cheerily. 'Anyone at home?'

I step into the sunlight.

His face splits into a grin and he swings himself on to the boat and comes to lean against the doorway.

'Hey.' He smiles at me and my insides turn to water. 'Good to see you, Fay.'

I try to stop my heart fluttering, try to resist flinging myself into his arms. 'You too.'

He cocks his head to one side. 'That's very cool.'

'Sorry,' I say. 'I don't mean to be. This is a pleasant surprise.'

'*A pleasant surprise?*' He mimics me. 'So, is that how we're going to play it?'

He folds his arms and settles in. As always he seems too big for the space, his presence taking up every atom. I'm finding it hard to breathe. Anxiety stabs me in the chest.

'I have some news for you,' Danny says.

'What?'

'It's good,' he says. 'Don't look so stricken.'

It's a long time since I've had good news, so I guess panic is my default reaction.

'I met a guy up on the three locks at Leighton Buzzard. He was trying to get rid of a spare engine. I thought maybe you could use it for the *Maid of Merryweather*.'

'Sounds great. But how much does he want for it?'

'If you want it, I'll sort it out,' he says. 'Everything can be horse-traded for a bit of work. By all accounts it's in a bit of a state. Needs reconditioning. But I reckon I could get it to run, given a bit of luck and a following wind. It's worth a try.'

'I'd love it. That's very kind of you to think of me.'

'No worries.' His eyes meet mine. 'But you know that's not why I'm really here.'

I don't know what to say, what to do.

'Now we could carry on indulging in this genial yet slightly awkward chit-chat,' he says, 'or we could cut straight to the difficult conversation.'

'Chit-chat,' I opt for.

'Difficult conversation,' he counters.

I can't help but smile in return.

'I had to come back, Fay. I wasn't going to,' he says. 'But I couldn't stay away.'

I think that's a good thing.

'I had to see where things stood between us. You left, in the morning, without saying anything,' he continues. 'Not a word. Even "goodbye" would have been better.'

'I'm sorry.'

'We spent the whole night ...' He falters. 'Well, you know *exactly* how we spent the night. I thought we really connected. Did you not enjoy it?'

'Oh, Danny.' I can feel myself burning up under his intense and troubled gaze. 'Of course I did.'

'Then what?'

'I've never been in that situation before,' I admit. 'I didn't know what to do or to say. I needed time to think. I thought you'd come up to the house later.'

'I did,' he says. 'I came up after the café closed. I didn't want to bother you while you were busy. I thought you might tell me it had all been a mistake and that I should clear off. I didn't want to hear that with an audience there. But, when I did come back, there was no one at home.'

'Oh.'

'Then I came back later that night when I saw the lights come on. But you were with Anthony. In your bedroom. It didn't look like you'd welcome a visitor.'

'It wasn't what it looked like,' I assure him. Then I rub my face in my hands. There's been too much to take in during the last day or so. All the highs and lows have left me feeling like a wrung-out dishcloth. 'My mum was taken ill that afternoon,' I explain. 'She had a stroke on the way to the hospital.'

'Oh, Fay,' he says. 'I had no idea.'

'How could you? I don't even have your mobile number.'

278

'I'm really sorry to hear it.'

'Anthony's been brilliant. He came to the hospital with me. Then he stayed over. I didn't want to be alone, Danny. What else could I do?'

'God,' he says. 'What awful timing. Is she OK now?'

I shake my head. I'm not sure how to break this news. 'She had a heart attack and died yesterday.' I just about manage to hold it together without breaking down.

Danny rubs his hands over his face. 'I'm so sorry.'

'You weren't to know.'

'Christ. Now I feel like a total shit.'

'I did come down to see you,' I tell him. 'But you'd already gone. I thought *you* were the one who'd run out.'

'I figured I was a complication that you could do without. You've got the café, a nice settled existence. Anthony. You've been with him for a long time. I didn't want to come along and mess that up. You're better off without me, Fay. Your life is here.' He lets out a weary breath. 'What can I offer you? I don't have a proper job. I'm living an itinerant lifestyle on the canal. I have no money to speak of.'

'That's not what matters.'

'Having reached warp speed to escape from city life, I'm not ready to settle. I can't stay here permanently. Not yet. I'm enjoying my freedom. I want to spread my wings while I can.'

My mind is in too much turmoil to process anything. Even with Mum gone, I'll still be tied here. There's Lija to think about, Stan, Anthony. Edie too, now. The weight of all these commitments crushes down on me. No wonder Danny isn't eager to sign up for that.

When I don't speak, he asks, 'So where do we go from here?'

'I don't know. Mum's funeral is next week. Edie's come home. I can't even think straight.'

'And I'm putting more pressure on you.'

'No. I'm pleased to see you. Really, I am. But it's difficult to concentrate on anything with all that's going on.'

'I feel as if I'm messing up your life, Fay. What can I do to help?'

'I just need some time,' I say. 'We need to get through this in our own way.'

'I should go,' he says. 'I should stay away. I'm not what you need right now. Easy to say. Not so easy to do.' His face is dark with anxiety. 'God, all I want to do is kiss you.'

He pulls me to him and it's a joy to be in his arms again. For a moment, the pain in my heart melts away.

Then a voice shouts, 'Fay! Where are you?'

Diggery starts to bark.

'That's Edie,' I tell him. Instinctively I step away from him again, and he lets his arms fall by his sides. I don't want Edie to catch us in an embrace. If I'm honest, I don't really want her to see us at all. I wanted to savour a few moments alone with Danny.

'Want me to make myself scarce?' Danny asks.

'No. I told her about you. About us.' I flush. 'She knows everything.' I hear her footsteps on the jetty and look at him ruefully. 'Besides, I think it's a bit late to make a break for it now.'

Chapter Sixty

'I've come to look at this rotten old piece of junk,' Edie chirps as she pops her head around the cratch cover. 'I still have night-mares about the wretched, rain-sodden holidays we had on this vile thing—' She stops dead when she sees that I'm not alone. 'Oh,' she says.

'Morning, Edie.'

My sister gives Danny an open appraisal. 'Who's this then?'

'I'm Danny,' he says, and holds out a hand to help Edie on board.

She's still wearing her skimpy pyjamas and has borrowed my dressing gown, which she lets fall open. The sparkly flip-flops on her feet are wet from the grass.

'I'm sorry for your loss,' Danny says.

'Thanks,' she answers dismissively. Edie is still looking from me to him, from him to me.

Edie and I went to bed as friends last night, but I feel as if some of the tension between us has returned this morning.

I can tell that Danny's uncomfortable now too. 'I'll leave you to it, Fay.'

I want to tell him not to go, but how can I, with Edie here?

281

It's for the best that he leaves again. My life is too complicated and Danny wants to be free to go wherever *The Dreamcatcher* may take him.

I want him to stay and never leave my side again. Instead I say, 'It's been good to see you.'

'I meant what I said,' he tells me, eyes fixed on mine. 'That night on *The Dreamcatcher*. Every word. It still stands.'

His eyes say it again. *I love you*.

Then he leaves. He clicks his fingers and Diggery falls into step next to him.

We watch him go. Then Edie turns to me. 'Cute.' She widens her eyes. 'And I don't mean the dog.'

That does make me smile.

'Who's he when he's at home?' she wants to know. 'If I'm not mistaken, there's more than a little chemistry going on there, sis.'

'That's Danny,' I tell her. 'The guy I was telling you about.'

'The one you spent the night with?'

I nod.

'You. Are. Kidding. Me.' She's gone from wide-eyed to seriously agog. 'You had casual sex with *that*?'

'With *him*,' I correct.

And why do they call it 'casual sex'? It seems to have made my life considerably more difficult than it was. For me, there's nothing casual about it at all.

There was no doubt that I was attracted to Danny before I spent the night with him, but I could, in time, have dismissed it as no more than a silly crush. He's kind, he's charming. Not to mention handsome. But now that I've slept with him, it's taken it to a level that I hadn't even thought possible. That one act has changed everything. He's under my skin. I've become part of him and he's become part of me. And I can't go back to how it was before.

Also, he makes me a different person when I'm with him, and I like that person very much. She's not a boring frump, old before her time, ground down by life. She's fun, slightly frivolous and brimming with passion.

'Good God, no wonder you succumbed to his rather obvious charms. I *so* would.'

Edie definitely would. I know that. And she wouldn't be racked with guilt as I am.

'I thought it was the manifesto of the *Maid of Merryweather* to repel all boarders?'

'Hilarious,' I say. 'He came to talk to me about a reconditioned engine for her.'

'Is that code?'

'No.'

'Wow. How very romantic of him.'

'He's kind. Funny.'

'And everything else.' She frowns at me. 'Yet you're letting him walk away?'

'I'm with Anthony,' I remind her. 'I couldn't hurt him.'

'*Fuck* Anthony!' she says.

I don't, actually. Not very often.

'This is about what *you* want, Fay. Do you even know?'

'I can't give up everything for Danny,' I tell her. 'Look at him. He's young, he's single, he's free. Why would he want to be saddled with someone like me? He'd tire of me. Of course he would.'

'You need to work on your self-esteem issues,' Edie says.

'I don't think I'm the only one,' I snap.

Edie looks as if I've struck her.

'I'm sorry,' I say.

'You're saying that Brandon's not appropriate for me.'

'Yes. No.' I take a steadying breath. 'You have to decide that for yourself, Edie.' I back down in the face of her steely glare.

283

'We all have to decide what's right for ourselves when it comes to love. Danny and I are different people. We want different things. Anthony is a more appropriate man for me. I have given him ten years of my life. Some of the best ones. How can I throw that away?'

'Have you heard yourself?'

'I have the café to run. I have Lija to think about. I have responsibilities. I can't simply turn my back on them because I've had one night of fantastic sex.'

Edie's face breaks into a slow grin. 'So it was fantastic, was it?'

'Yes.' I feel beaten into submission.

'I can see what you feel for him. And what he feels for you.' Edie's suddenly serious. 'Love like that doesn't come along more than once in a lifetime, Fay. Don't let it pass you by.'

But that, I fear, is easier said than done. I can't turn my back on all I've worked for, all I've nurtured.

My sister sighs at me. 'What I came out to tell you was that the solicitor has phoned. He wants to see us both the day after Mum's funeral. I begged, but he wouldn't see us any earlier, so I said that would be OK.'

'It's fine.'

He'll want to sort out Mum's will, I'm sure, and that's much more critical to my future than matters of the heart.

Chapter Sixty-one

It's Mum's funeral. We're all assembled in the kitchen and we make a meagre little group. Edie appears to be channelling Audrey Hepburn. She's looking very sleek in a new black dress of tightly fitted taffeta. It's sleeveless and has a diamanté belt and a skirt that kicks out to skim the knee. She's wearing bug-eye sunglasses and high-heeled patent stilettos – also newly purchased – and looks far too glamorous for a low-key service at the local crematorium. But my dear sister likes to put on a show whatever the occasion.

Edie bought her entire outfit, including matching clutch bag, courtesy of my credit card in Coast. Whereas I, of course, have dragged something not too tatty out of the back of the wardrobe to be pressed into service.

Lija is here too, wearing a sombre black dress that she's borrowed from one of her friends, and black Doc Martens. She might not have been Mum's biggest fan, but I know that she wants to be at the service for my sake. She currently has an apron over her dress and is making some sandwiches for us to eat when we return home.

We've closed the café today as I didn't know what else to do.

I suppose I could have asked Danny to stay and hold the fort. I know he would have done that for me. But I didn't think of it soon enough and now he's gone. Instead, I wandered up to the lamppost at the end of the lane and stuck up a note that I'd written on an A4 sheet of paper in a plastic sleeve that read *café closed today due to unforeseen circumstances*.

I've opened up the *Maid of Merryweather*, as people can still buy cakes and the like from the canalside. They'll just have to use the honesty box, or steal them. Today, I couldn't care less.

Stan's here too. He and my mum used to be quite good friends before she took to her bed on a permanent basis. After that, she wouldn't allow anyone to visit her and, in time, all her WI friends and people like Stan gradually gave up trying.

He looks very smart today. Our dear friend is wearing a smart black suit, with a crisp white shirt and a tie. On his chest is a row of shining medals.

'You look lovely, Stan,' I tell him, brushing his lapels unnecessarily. I point to his medals. 'What are all these for?'

'Oh, a bit of this and that,' he says. 'I like to give them an airing every now and again. Thought I'd show Miranda a bit of respect.'

I have a closer look. I'm not a great aficionado of military medals, but there's one that seems familiar. 'Is that a Victoria Cross?'

Stan looks a little bashful. 'Oh, that? Yes. Yes, it is.'

'That's the highest award for valour there is in this country. I'm right, aren't I? What were you given it for?'

'Nothing much,' he says cagily. 'Just doing what anyone else would do.'

I kiss his cheek. 'I'm sure it was much more than that, but I'll let it go for now. I didn't know you were a war hero.'

'Oh, hardly that,' he insists.

Dr Ahmed is also kindly joining us at the crematorium, and the only person we're waiting for now is Anthony.

We've only booked one funeral car to follow the hearse as the funeral director has assured us that we can all fit in there. We're now waiting patiently outside and we need to leave in a few minutes if we're not going to miss the very tight slot.

I'm just thinking about texting Anthony to find out where he is when I hear his car turning into the drive.

'Sorry,' he says, dashing into the kitchen. He's pink and a little bit breathless. 'Sorry I'm late.'

I kiss his cheek. 'You're just in time.'

'Ready?' Edie asks.

'As I'll ever be,' I say.

Chapter Sixty-two

The service is perfectly adequate, I think. The vicar from St Anselm's in the Field leads six self-conscious people in a mumbled version of 'All Things Bright and Beautiful'. Mum hadn't been to church in years – we've always been a high-days-and-holidays-only type of family anyway – but when she did go, it was to that one. There's a picture of Mum projected on to a screen as she was when she was in her thirties. It was one that Edie looked out in the box of photographs that's kept in the sideboard in the dining room.

I look at her smiling into the camera. She looks slim, strong, happy, as if the whole of a wonderful life is ahead of her. She's a woman who appears not to have a care in the world – and I speculate sadly on what made her retire to a self-imposed prison years before she needed to. When she was that age, what were her hopes and dreams? Did she really ever love my father? Sometimes I do wonder.

The vicar recites a pleasant eulogy, ignoring the fact that she was a difficult, cantankerous woman who had no friends left to show for her seventy-seven years on earth. He makes only the briefest of references to the fact that she was bedridden through her own choice.

For so many long years, she opted not to venture beyond the four walls of her bedroom when, with a little help and support, she could so easily have done so. Was she tired of life? Did she want attention? In spite of the doctors' best efforts was there really something wrong with her that they never discovered? My eyes fall on the coffin at the front of the room and I realise that we'll never know now. With a few more words from the vicar, it moves off through the curtain.

Anthony grips my hand. Edie sobs noisily at my side, but I find myself dry-eyed and regretting that, despite being her full-time carer for years, I didn't know my mother better.

An hour later, the service is over and we're back at the house. Dr Ahmed went straight back to his surgery from the crematorium, so it's just the five of us.

Edie is still tearful. 'I should have been here for her more. You take people for granted, don't you?'

I couldn't agree with Edie more, but today's not the day for recriminations. I pat her hand. 'She knew that you loved her, and she adored you.'

Tears roll down my sister's face. 'I'm going to miss her.'

This also isn't the time to remind Edie that she didn't actually ever want to come and see Mum when she was alive.

Anthony is being very solicitous. He's fussing around me like a mother hen, which is very kind of him. His hand rests on my shoulder. 'Do you want more tea, dear?'

'I'd love another cup, please.'

The sun is high and we're all sitting out in the garden. Lija pulled two tables side by side so that we could all sit together. There's a platter of sandwiches and some of Lija's specially made cake, and we're downing copious cups of tea. Lija is being really nice to everyone, which is rather disconcerting.

I keep thinking I should pop upstairs and see how Mum is,

but then I remember that she's not there and that there'll be no more banging on the ceiling with her stick now. No more tablets to administer. No one to shower. No one's hair to wash and comb. I'm free to come and go as I please now and, strangely, that's going to take some getting used to.

There's still a sense of unreality about it all. Tomorrow the sun will come up, the cake shop will open again, Edie will no doubt book her return plane ticket to New York, and life will go on.

'I'm just going to sit by the canal for a few minutes,' I say to Anthony.

'Want me to come?'

'No. I'll be fine.'

'I could do with getting back to the office. Do you mind?'

'Not at all.' I touch his arm. 'You've been brilliant today. Thank you.'

'I'll leave you with Edie tonight, but I'll pop by tomorrow after work.' He kisses my cheek.

As Anthony heads off, I take my tea and wander down to the jetty. I sit by the edge of the water and take off my shoes, letting my bare feet dangle over, my toes barely an inch from the water. Even though it's been Mum's funeral, I find myself thinking about Dad. I very rarely visit the crematorium where his ashes were buried, which makes me sad. But then, I always feel closer to him here, down by the canal. This is where I like to remember him, not in the cold ground where he didn't ever want to be. I wonder what he'd think if he could see me now. Would he be proud of what I've achieved, or would he think I'd wasted my life?

A few minutes later Edie wanders down to stand beside me. She looks at her posh new dress and the dusty dirt on the jetty, then, with a resigned sigh, sits next to me.

'You love it here, don't you?'

'Yes. It's my little slice of heaven.'

'It's hell on earth to me.'

I turn and smile at her. 'We've always been very different.'

'I sometimes wonder if they picked up the wrong baby in the maternity ward,' she says. 'I'm just so unlike you and Dad.'

'But you are like Mum.'

'God,' Edie says. 'Don't say that. I'm too like her by half. It terrifies me. I don't want to end up moody and lonely, locked in my own bedroom. You got the best genes.'

I laugh at her. 'Your future is in your own hands.'

'Yours too,' she counters.

'I'm worried about what'll happen here,' I confess. 'If I have to raise the money to buy you out of your share, I'm not sure how I'll do it.'

'It won't come to that,' Edie says. 'There's only the two of us now. Just you and me, sis. We'll sort something out. We're family.' She leans against me, resting her head on my shoulder. 'And families stick together.'

Chapter Sixty-three

A few days later Edie and I sit in the waiting room at the solicitor's office. We're not really talking. My sister woke up in a very strange mood today and I can't put my finger on why. Currently, she's pretending to read the copy of *Country Life* that she's grabbed from the coffee table and is studiously ignoring me.

I've left Lija in charge today, so I don't need to worry about the café. I'm taking advantage of a few moments' peace to think about Danny. I let images of the way he looks, the way he moves, wash in front of my eyes. I see him standing on the back of *The Dreamcatcher*, turning to smile at me.

'Misses Merryweather,' a male voice says, and I snap back to the present.

Edie and I look up.

'Would you like to come into my office?'

We have very little call to use a solicitor, but Mr Crawley has always dealt with family business when the need has arisen. I think he's about seventy or more now. He certainly looks it.

He shuffles into the office ahead of Edie and me. When he takes his place at his desk, Edie and I sit opposite him, straight-backed and well-behaved. I feel as if I'm in the headmaster's office.

'Now then,' he says in his kindly manner. 'I'm very sorry to hear of your mother's passing. And we're here today for the very necessary business of executing her will.'

I can't think that Mum had much. There was very little in her bank account and only a few personal possessions. The major topic will be the house and its contents. I wonder if Mr Crawley is aware that I now run it as a café. I don't know when Mum last revised her will, but he has visited her at home once or twice in the last couple of years.

Mr Crawley makes a show of organising and scanning the papers in front of him, while Edie and I, both with our hands cupped in our laps, try not to fidget.

Finally he takes off his round glasses, pops them in his top pocket and peers at us both, pursing his lips. 'I'm afraid this is a little difficult.'

When he doesn't enlighten us any further I ask, 'Is there something wrong with Mum's will?'

'No,' he says. 'It's all present and correct.' He glances from me to Edie and back. 'Were you aware of your mother's wishes?'

I shake my head. 'No.'

Edie echoes my sentiments. 'No.'

'Oh dear.'

Then I have a moment of clarity. What if Mum has left the house to me and cut Edie out of the will? I know she hated the fact that Edie never came home to see her; what if she's been vengeful and shown it in the cruellest way she possibly could? I wouldn't put it past her. She could certainly be like that if she put her mind to it. That would be dreadful. I turn to Edie, my face bleak.

'What?' she says. 'What?'

'Whatever's in the will,' I tell her, 'we'll sort it out between us.' I couldn't bear to see her cut out like that.

293

'Right,' she says uncertainly. Edie is obviously as worried as I am now.

Mr Crawley clears his throat. 'Shall we?'

He goes through the rigmarole of getting his glasses out of his top pocket again, unfolding them and putting them on. He reads out the legal formalities of the will while we wait for him to get on to the stuff that matters to us.

Then he pauses, clearly not wanting to break the bad news to us. With a heartfelt sigh, he glances over the rims of his specs as he says, 'To my daughter, Edie Merryweather, I leave Canal House and its entire contents.'

Both Edie and I gasp, but for different reasons.

'To Fay Merryweather, I leave the narrowboat, *Maid of Merryweather*.'

Then he blah-blahs on for a little bit about what's in the bank account and an insurance policy worth just over four hundred pounds, which also goes to Edie. I sit there, stunned into silence and numb from head to toe. Mum has left everything to Edie. Everything. And I've no idea why.

Why? I think. Why on earth has she done this?

Mum's solicitor rests his hands on his desk. 'Not what you expected?'

'No,' we say in unison.

My face feels as if it's gone completely white, while Edie has little high spots of pink on her cheeks.

'She left a letter for you, Fay,' Mr Crawley says. 'I'm not aware of the contents, but I hope that it may go some way to explaining what she was thinking.'

'Thank you.' Standing, I take the small pale blue envelope from his gnarled hands. The tension in my stomach is like cramp.

I look at Edie, the new owner of my home, my café. She's beaming widely and not even trying to hide it.

Chapter Sixty-four

'Let's go for a coffee,' I suggest when we're back out on the street. To be honest, I don't feel capable of driving. My legs are barely supporting me and my head is spinning. Mum has cut me out of her will. Completely.

Edie glances at her watch. There's nowhere she needs to be.

'OK.' She couldn't look more reluctant if she tried.

'I need to know what this letter says.'

'Maybe you should read it by yourself,' my sister suggests.

'Don't you want to know why she's left everything to you and nothing to me?'

'She left you the boat,' Edie counters.

'You've got half a million pounds' worth of house. Which is both my home and my business,' I point out. 'She's given me a forty-five-year-old narrowboat that doesn't even run.'

I march off down the street and Edie totters along in my wake in her silly yellow kitten-heeled shoes.

When we hit the first coffee shop that we come to, I dive inside. It's busy, but there's a table free by the window and I head for it, sitting down straight away. I'm not sure I could have stood upright for much longer.

'I'll have a latte,' I say to Edie. If she thinks I can manage to go to the counter then she's got another think coming. I peel a ten-pound note out of my purse and hand it over.

'Anything else?' She can hardly meet my eyes.

'No.'

My sister heads to the counter and I hold the envelope that I've just received with shaking hands.

I don't know what to feel. Anger, rage, despair, humiliation, disappointment. All of these things. Everything is going round inside my head at once and I'm powerless to stop it. Why has Mum done this? What reason could she possibly have to treat me so shabbily, to favour Edie over me? I think of all the hours of care that I've lavished on her. Do I really deserve to be slighted like this? Perhaps it's all a terrible mistake. Maybe Mr Crawley is so old now that he's lost his marbles and misinterpreted the will, or read out someone else's.

The sun is beating against the window and I feel quite queasy and clammy. I can barely bring myself to read her letter, but I know I have to. My hands are shaking so much that I almost drop it on the floor, and I have to clutch it tightly. When I manage to still the tremors for a moment, I slip my finger under the flap and rip it open. It's Mum's distinctive neat handwriting sure enough.

Dear Fay

I've been meaning to tell you this for a long time. I don't know why I haven't. Probably because I promised your father that I wouldn't.

I've left everything to Edie, because she is my only true daughter. You were just a year old when your father and I courted. He was recently widowed, left alone with a baby, and I took you in as if you were my own.

He didn't have a penny to his name. All he came to me with was that boat of his. It was something that he and his

*first wife, your mother, both loved, and that's what I'm
leaving to you. This house was bought for me by my own
family on our wedding and that's why I'm bequeathing it to
Edie. It needs to stay in the family. My family.*

*You've been very kind to me over the years, but you're
not my flesh and blood. You were always your father's
daughter.*

Yours

Miranda

I'm trembling all over by the time Edie comes back with our cof-
fees. My history has just been rewritten and I don't know how to
handle it. The woman who I have loved all my life is not my natural mother and I never, for a minute, for a second, saw this
coming.

'What?' Edie says when she sees my ghostly, drawn face.

I hand over the letter and she scans it quickly.

'Oh, shit,' she says. 'You're not even my sister.'

'I *am* your sister,' I insist. 'What about this changes that?'

'Well . . .' Edie's sentence trails away. 'I didn't even know Dad
was married before. Did you?'

'No. I didn't.'

Then her head flicks up. 'He *is* my dad, isn't he?'

'Of course he is,' I snap. 'It's only *my* parentage that's in
question.'

'Phew,' she says.

'Thanks for the sympathy, Edie.' I can't believe that Miranda
wasn't really my mother. How could she keep it secret all those
years? How could Dad? He should have told me. *They* should
have told me. The woman I knew as my mother was in fact my
stepmother. So who exactly was my real mum? 'I've just found
out that everything I believed in was a lie.'

'I know that,' Edie says. 'It's a biggy.'

'*A biggy*? Not only have I found out that my mother isn't who I think she's been all of my life, but you've just inherited my home and my business, while I've been kicked out into the cold. What am I going to do?'

Edie sucks in her breath. 'Tricky.'

'*Devastating*.'

'You might be able to buy me out,' she suggests.

'Half of it?'

'Erm . . .'

'If the boot had been on the other foot, if she'd left everything to me, I would have split it with you half and half.'

She gives me a petulant look. 'How do I know that?'

'Because I love you. We've been brought up as sisters. Whatever this letter says,' I shake the blue paper angrily, 'we're family. We should look after each other.'

I want Edie to come and give me a cuddle, to tell me that everything will be all right. Yet she stays firmly rooted in her chair. My world has been rocked and Edie doesn't seem to give tuppence.

'I don't want the stupid house,' Edie says. 'I hate it. As far as I'm concerned, you can have it lock, stock and barrel. All I want to do is get back to Brandon as quickly as I can, but you know my situation. I'm broke. He's out of a job now too. We could buy our independence. He could leave his wife. This is the answer to all my prayers.'

'And a nightmare for me.'

She frowns at me as if she doesn't understand what the problem is. 'The only thing I need out of it is the money.'

And there's the rub.

'There's no way I could raise the cash to buy you out completely. The banks would never give me a mortgage that big.' I put my head in my hands. 'There must be options. There must be something I can do.'

But at the moment, I can't think what.

298

Chapter Sixty-five

It's three o'clock in the morning and I'm wide awake. I lie on my bed, hot and bothered, covers thrown back, legs restless. I stare blankly at the ceiling. I don't know what to worry about first, so I'm trying to resolve all of my anxieties at the same time.

It's not working.

My mum, who I've loved as a daughter would all of my life, turns out not to be my mother at all, but my stepmother. I'm struggling to get my head round it.

Has she cut me out of her will because she's harboured a secret resentment of me all these years? I was always Dad's favourite, that's true enough. But Edie was always Mum's favourite. I didn't think there was anything complicated behind it. Aren't all families like that? Even just a little bit? How I wish I could have a conversation now with Dad. Only he could tell me who my real mother was. He could tell me how she died, how he came to be with Miranda. Was it too hard, I wonder, for him to manage alone with a baby? I should be grateful that Miranda was willing to take me on: it can't have been easy for her taking on a young child like that. And I can't complain that

I had an unhappy childhood – quite the contrary. I always knew that Dad adored me. Yet sometimes, when I was feeling down, I felt as if there was a hole at the centre of me, and I wonder if, subconsciously, it was my mother that I was missing all along?

And what of Dad's situation? Was his first wife, rather than Miranda, the love of his life? Is that why she's chosen to punish me now? I try to reach back into my childhood for memories of my real mother, but I have none at all and that makes me profoundly sad. I must find out who she was as soon as I can. I'll probably never sleep again until I do. But, for now, I have more pressing matters.

On top of the worry of my newly discovered parentage, I've still to come up with a brilliant solution for hanging on to my family home, my little cake shop-cum-café. I tried to talk to Edie about it again this evening, but she is strangely quiet on the subject. As soon as we'd eaten dinner, pretty much in silence, she scuttled off to her room and spent most of her time talking transatlantically to blasted Brandon.

First thing in the morning, I'll have to ring the bank and see if I can organise a loan to buy her out. I'm also hoping that she might have a change of heart overnight and realise that the estate should, by rights and all that is fair, be divided equally between us. If she would see her way to doing that, then I could perhaps – at a stretch – afford to stay here. If I can't get a mortgage, perhaps I could even pay her a monthly rent. But she's made no mention of any such magnanimous gesture. I know Edie only too well. She hasn't said as much, but I know full well that she'll want the house gone as soon as is humanly possible and the money burning a hole in her hot little hand. I wouldn't mind if Edie even liked this place or planned to live in it, but she doesn't. I'm the one whose home it is. I'm the one who loves it here.

In the solicitor's office I did, for one moment, believe that

Mum had left everything to me. I'd been her sole carer for years and Edie hadn't even visited. Does that count for nothing?

It seems so.

In the reverse situation I would never have seen Edie cut out and stood by while it happened. I would have moved heaven and earth to give her a fair share.

The other thing that I could do is marry Anthony. Not that he's asked me. But we've been together now for long enough to know that we could do this on a permanent basis. If we got married then he could sell his place and we could, with a big jump, afford to buy this together. I know he loves this house. Perhaps not as much as I do, but we could surely make this our home. He'll understand my need to stay here. I know he will. He could secure our future. And he's been wonderful, marvellous since Mum died. What more could I ask for?

Then my stomach knots with a pang of longing and I'm ashamed to say that it isn't for Anthony.

Getting up, I go to the open window and look out over the canal. There's hardly a breeze to stir the air. The water is a steel-grey ribbon in the moonlight. I feel as if it's all that's connecting me to Danny now. Somewhere out there, he'll be deep in sleep on *The Dreamcatcher*.

I miss him. God, how I miss him. I'd love to talk to him now. Tell him what's happened. But what could he do? How could he help my situation? Danny's right, my future isn't with him. It's with Anthony. I shouldn't be throwing my heart away on someone completely inappropriate. I should be with someone settled, someone who's here, and supportive. I should marry Anthony. That's exactly what I should do.

There's no point in trying to sleep, so I go downstairs, thinking I'll start the preparations for the day. The café needs to be ready for customers again but, for once, my heart just isn't in it. As soon as the bank is open for business, I'll call them and see if they can come up with a solution to my predicament. I'm not holding my breath.

Instead of doing all the things that need to be done, I sit at the table with a pot of tea, staring at it as if it will provide me with all the answers. It doesn't.

I'm still sitting there when Lija arrives at eight o'clock. She throws down her bag and sits opposite me at the table.

'Tea?' I say.

She nods. Pushing a mug towards her, I pour her some.

'You look like shit,' she observes.

'I feel like it.'

'Can I help?'

I gaze up at her wearily. 'Only if you can find half a million quid, or thereabouts, to give to my sister.'

She waits patiently for an explanation.

'I had a bit of a bombshell yesterday,' I continue when I find my voice amid the welling tears. 'My mum, who it turns out wasn't really my mum, has left her entire estate to Edie. The house, everything in it, all the money.'

'What?' Lija is incensed. 'How could she do that? Wicked old bag.'

At the moment, I don't feel I can disagree.

'She is not your mother?'

'Stepmum.'

'You did not know?'

'No idea. Turns out that my dad was married before but he was widowed. Miranda took me on when I was a baby. It seems that all along she didn't view me as her "real" daughter.'

'You have run your arse ragged for her.' I can see that Lija is seething. 'She is not treating you fairly.'

'Oh, I do get the *Maid of Merryweather* though.' I love that boat, dearly. But, at this moment, the thought doesn't necessarily cheer me.

'Why?' Lija says. 'Why has she done this to you?'

'It's something I've asked myself every moment since we heard it from the solicitor yesterday, and I still can't give you an answer.'

'What will you do?'

'I'm going to phone the bank, see if I can sort something out. If it's possible I need to try to raise the money to buy the house from Edie.'

'I do not know what to say. Surely your sister would not see this happen?'

At that moment, Edie comes down. I would have expected to see her in her pyjamas at this hour, but she's already dressed.

'I know this is difficult, Fay,' she says.

I wonder how much she's heard of our conversation.

'Very,' I agree.

'I need to go into town,' she says. 'Can I borrow your car?'

'Yes. Of course. The keys are on the hook.'

'You cannot let this happen to your sister,' Lija says, impassioned. 'Where will she live? How will she earn her money?'

'This isn't of my creation,' Edie answers loftily. 'It's the wishes of a dying woman.'

'Our mother,' I say.

'*My* mother,' she corrects.

Edie picks up the keys and leaves, but at least she has the good grace to look embarrassed as she does.

Chapter Sixty-six

I ring the bank. They laugh in my face. Clearly Plan A, Borrow the Money, isn't going to run.

Next, I ring the solicitor.

'Isn't there any way I can contest this?' I ask Mr Crawley.

'You could try,' he advises. 'But I don't think you have strong grounds and it will cost a lot of money. If you decide to take Edie to court you could be tied up for years with it.'

Indecision gnaws at me.

'For what it's worth,' Mr Crawley says, 'I think this is very unkind of your mother. I did advise her against it, but she was adamant that it was what she wanted. She could be a very difficult woman.'

I'm now learning just how difficult.

'Edie might come round,' he offers. 'Money, inheritances, they always bring out the worst in people. When she's had time to think about it, she might feel differently.'

I'm afraid I don't hold out much hope.

Lija is making fresh soup in the kitchen for this lunchtime when I go to deliver the bad news.

'The bank won't lend me a penny,' I tell her. 'It's not as if I've even got enough for a deposit.' And that's mainly because Edie has gone through all the money I did have saved up in my *Maid of Merryweather* fund. I think it's wise not to tell Lija that bit.

I fret about it all morning and I'm sure I'm more of a hindrance than a help to Lija, but she doesn't complain as she normally would. She just mutters 'Fuck' under her breath at regular intervals.

Of course, when we could least do with it, the café is really busy today. All of the tables are taken at the moment and, now that the school holidays have started, there are a few children running around the garden.

'Here's Stan,' I tell her when I see him coming through the side gate.

'Cream of mushroom,' she says as she dishes out his soup.

'His favourite,' we say together, and then we laugh. It's the first chink of brightness today.

'What will Stinky Stan do?' she asks. 'If you are not here to look after him?'

'I don't know.' I can't bear to think of that either. 'I have one other cunning plan.'

She raises an eyebrow. I probably shouldn't tell her, but I have no one else to confide in.

'I'm going to ask Anthony to marry me.'

Lija looks aghast. 'You can't,' she says.

'We've been together long enough. It would do us both good to make an official commitment. He could sell up and move in here.' If Anthony got a good price for his place, then we might just have enough to buy Canal House together. 'It would be the perfect solution.'

'No,' she says. 'No.'

'I'm going to be with him for ever, Lija. We might as well put it on a more formal footing.'

'No,' she counters. 'You love Danny.'

'One night I had with him, Lija. One *ill-advised* night. And where is he now? Anthony is here for me. He's my future.'

'Don't be fucking idiot.' Lija bangs her palm against her temple in frustration. 'You are thinking like crazy woman.'

'It's the only answer.' I should never have told her. I knew she wouldn't approve. Hastily I pick up Stan's soup. 'I'd better take this before it gets cold.'

As I hurry out into the garden, Lija follows me to the door and bawls after me: 'You cannot marry Anthony because you don't fucking love him!'

All the customers in the garden stare open-mouthed at me.

My cheeks are on fire. 'Sorry,' I say sweetly to the mothers who clap their hands over their children's ears and look at me, horrified. 'So very sorry.'

'What's all that about then?' Stan asks when I deliver his soup.

I fill him in on the disaster that has befallen me in the last twenty-four hours.

'That Edie doesn't have the backbone that you do,' he says. 'But I'm sure she'll see you right.'

I'm not so certain, of course. 'Everything I thought was definite, assured in my life, has proved to be unreliable, so I'm not holding out much hope.'

'Miranda did love you,' he says. 'In her own way.'

'I'm struggling to see that too.'

'I wish I could do something to help.'

How is it that people who aren't related to me want to do so much for me, when those who are seem to be intent on treating me badly?

'If I had the money to buy her out, I would do,' I tell him. 'But the bank told me to take a running jump.'

'If I had the money, I'd give it to you.'

'That's very kind.'

Then his eyes light up. 'You can have my medals,' Stan says. 'Sell them.'

'Stan.' I'm overwhelmed. 'I couldn't possibly do that.'

'That Victoria Cross should raise a pretty penny,' he continues unabashed. 'There are people who specialise in collecting them. Take them, Fay. What good are they to me? I have no family left to leave them to.'

'It's so very thoughtful of you, but I couldn't possibly. You've earned those through your courage and valour. I could never sell them.'

'It would make an old man very happy if you did.'

I shake my head. 'Wouldn't dream of it. Somehow I'll sort this out myself.' Then I stand. 'I'll take your soup back and get it warmed up. I've chatted on so long that it'll be cold now.'

'What is it?'

'Cream of mushroom.'

'Oh, lovely,' he says. 'My favourite.'

And that makes me want to cry.

'I'll eat it cold,' he says. 'I don't want to upset Lija. She seems a little grumpy today.' Stan glances nervously back at the kitchen, where the sound of clattering pots and pans is unmissable.

'She's only worried about me,' I admit. 'And her job too, I suspect. That still doesn't mean you have to eat cold soup.'

'I think I'd rather.'

I laugh at him. 'Stan. You're brave enough for a little skirmish over the soup. You've got the Victoria Cross. You must have faced down the Luftwaffe single-handedly or something to get that.'

'Ah, yes,' he says. 'But this is Lija we're talking about.'

Chapter Sixty-seven

As usual Anthony drops in on his way home from work. He looks harried, and I'm not sure that I want to be having the conversation we're about to have.

Edie hasn't returned all day and, though I called her mobile repeatedly, there was no reply. I ushered Lija off early so that Anthony and I could be alone.

'What a day,' Anthony complains. 'What a day!' He throws off his jacket and tosses it over the back of a chair.

I'm sure the world of planning misdemeanours will pale into insignificance when I tell him what the day has held for me.

He pecks my cheek and then sits down, sturdy legs planted firmly on the kitchen floor. I give him a glass of red wine that I've already poured in anticipation.

'Lovely,' he says. 'Do I look like I need it?'

'Yes. And if you don't need it now, then you will do in a minute.'

He lowers his voice. 'Trouble with your sister?'

'Sort of. But she's not here now.'

'Oh. Where is she?'

'I don't know,' I admit. 'She left first thing this morning and

I haven't seen her since.' I suppose I could have tried texting her, but I confess that I haven't.

'Have you had an argument?'

'More than that, Anthony. I think you need to drink some of that wine before we start.'

He does as he's told.

Briefly and as succinctly as I can, I fill him in on the contents of Mum's will and her letter to me.

He sits, mouth ajar, unspeaking as he takes it all in. Occasionally he eases the process with a gulp of his wine. I refill his glass.

'I can't believe it,' he finally gasps. 'I simply can't believe it.'

'Me neither.'

'We must be able to do something. This really isn't cricket.'

I'm glad he said 'we'. 'The will can't stand as it is, surely?'

'Mr Crawley said that it probably would. She was in sound mind, blah, blah, blah. He said that it would cost a fortune to contest it and could tie up the estate for years.'

'Good God.' Anthony pours himself more wine.

'I want to buy Edie out,' I tell him. 'And there's only one possible way I can do it.' I take a deep and rather unsteady breath. 'This won't be the most romantic proposition you've ever heard, Anthony, but I think you and I know each other well enough by now.'

Anthony looks vaguely terrified, but I plough on. If I'm having any second thoughts about this, I push them aside. I know I haven't been the perfect partner, but I am determined to put that behind me. Everything else in my history has been rewritten, so why can't I write Danny Wilde out of my life? Anthony would forgive me one transgression, I know he would. It's the only time I have even looked at another man in our ten years together. Danny was an aberration, nothing more. I will be true and faithful to Anthony for the rest of my life.

'I love you,' I say. 'I do. You know that.'

He nods uncertainly.

'One of the ways that we can get over this crisis, together, is to pool our resources,' I press on. 'I know that it's asking a lot, but I wondered if you'd consider throwing everything in with me to save my home, my business.'

Still Anthony is speechless.

'I guess this is what I'm trying to say.' I cross the kitchen to where he's sitting. With another steadying breath, I go down on one knee on the floor in front of him. My heart is in my mouth and my palms are damp with sweat. 'Anthony Bullmore, would you do me the very great honour of marrying me?'

His jaw drops open.

Then there's a screeching noise in the lane outside, followed by an almighty bang. I dash to the window and look out.

'It's Edie,' I say. 'She's hit the gatepost.'

310

Chapter Sixty-eight

My sister is drunk. Horribly so. Anthony and I both rush out to her as she opens the car door – *my* crumpled car door – and falls out into the drive.

'Hi, honey,' she slurs. 'I'm home.'

'Oh, Edie. Where have you been?'

'Sampling the pubs and bars of the Costa del Keynes.'

'It seems as if you've done rather a good job of it.'

Her eyes try to focus on me and fail. 'Sorry, Fay. So fucking sorry. Will pay for car.'

Her legs are as much use as jelly, so we hitch her up between us and Anthony and I half carry, half drag her into the kitchen. We plonk her into a chair and her head lolls back.

Anthony looks at her with distaste. 'Should we not put her straight to bed?'

'What if she's sick? She might choke.'

'Coffee then,' he says. 'She needs black coffee.'

I go to flick on the kettle but, as soon as I try to move away from her, she starts to slide off the seat.

'She can't even sit upright. We need to lie her down,' I say. 'Let's put her on the sofa and prop her up with some cushions.'

So together we haul her out of the kitchen and manhandle her to the sofa. For someone so waif-like, she weighs a ton when she's lifeless. Once upon a time, I was well used to this. Edie regularly used to get drunk as a teenager and I was the one who used to try to help her to her room without Mum noticing.

'We need to talk,' she mumbles.

'Later,' I say. 'When you've sobered up.'

'Now,' she says. 'Noooow. Things I need to say.' But she flops back like a rag-doll.

I plump the cushions around her so that she's comfortable and rearrange her skirt to give her a modicum of decorum. Though with the drool coming from her mouth and her hair like a scarecrow, I'm not sure I make her look much better. She seems to be missing a shoe.

'What a mess,' Anthony mutters.

'I'm sorry about that,' I say. Though exactly why I should apologise for my sister, I'm not sure.

'Where were we?'

I try an uncertain laugh. 'I'd just asked you to marry me.'

'Oh, right,' Anthony says. He runs a hand through his hair and his cheeks turn scarlet. 'Right.'

He doesn't seem to be very forthcoming.

'How do you feel about it?'

'Er ...'

I giggle anxiously. 'Do you want me to go down on one knee again?'

'I ... er ...'

Edie pushes herself up from the cushions. Her gaze wanders round the room until it settles more or less on us.

'She fucked someone else, you know,' she announces. And then she falls back on the pillows again.

Anthony looks as if he's been slapped.

I feel the blood drain from my cheeks.

312

He stares at me open-mouthed. 'Fay?'

I let out a shuddering exhalation of breath. You could cut the air that hangs between us with a knife. I stand, shame-faced, waiting for the fallout.

'Well?' Anthony demands. 'Is it true?'

'Yes.' What else can I say? Why Edie chose this moment to spill the beans, I have no idea. It must be the drink talking. Yet there's no doubt that she has me bang to rights. My guilty secret is out.

Anthony looks as if he's struggling to breathe. He rocks back on his heels slightly and, voice tremulous, he says, 'I think I need the rest of that red wine.'

'Me too.' On the way out of the living room, I point a finger at the comatose Edie. I have no idea if she can hear me or not when I say, 'I'll talk to you later, young lady.'

So, together and in awkward silence, Anthony and I go back to the kitchen.

'Let's take the wine and go outside. It's a nice evening.' Which is a totally moronic thing to say. This evening could not actually get any worse.

I carry the glasses and Anthony brings the bottle. Neither of us speak. At the bottom of the garden, we take the two chairs that face right on to the canal. Stan's favourite spot.

There are still quite a few people on the towpath, enjoying the evening sun. We look at the canal, still in silence. Anthony pours us both a glass of wine and sips his pensively. I sit here feeling wretched. The tension between us is tangible.

'I'm sorry,' I say eventually, when it's apparent that words are required. 'I don't know how I can apologise enough.' I can hardly bring myself to look at him. I feel sick with guilt. How can I have done this? 'I don't know what came over me. If I could undo it, really I would.'

'Has it been going on for long?' Anthony asks tightly.

'One night,' I say. 'Just the one night.' Even in this moment of darkness, this critical time for Anthony and me, I'm having to push the images of my time with Danny away from my mind.

'Who with?' Anthony frowns at me. 'You don't do anything or go anywhere.'

Scarily, that accurately sums up my life.

'It wasn't Stan, was it?' He laughs uneasily.

'It was Danny,' I confess, head hung in humiliation. 'The young man from the narrowboat, *The Dreamcatcher*.'

'Him?' Anthony looks slightly startled at my revelation.

I nod. 'I promise you that I've never looked at another man in all our time together.'

'And it was just the one night?'

I nod again.

'When?'

'The night of my birthday. I felt so alone,' I say. 'I know you had to be at the hospital for Deborah, but ... well ... there are no excuses.'

'It's so out of character for you, Fay.'

'I spent the evening with him and I got drunk and stoned.'

He recoils at that even more than he did when he learned that I'd had a one-night stand.

'My judgement was compromised,' I add, in case he's in any doubt about that.

Yet the truth is that I may regret the outcome, I may regret the hurt that it's caused to Anthony, but nothing will ever make me regret that night.

Anthony, the man I have known for so very long, lets out a wavering breath. 'You realise that the answer's no, don't you?'

'Of course.'

'I can't marry you, Fay.'

'I did hope you'd be able to forgive me, but I can see that you

314

can't possibly. I'm so very sorry, Anthony. I did an unforgivable thing.'

He looks directly at me and sighs. 'I can't marry you because I'm in love with someone else.'

And, for some reason, that isn't a surprise to me at all.

'Deborah,' I say. Of course. Now everything fits into place. All those extra practice sessions, the lifts home, the text messages, the hospital visit. 'You were the person she turned to on the night of my birthday because you were the one there with her.'

'Yes,' he admits.

I put my head in my hands. 'Why did I not see that?'

Anthony's face colours. 'It seems as if we're both guilty of indiscretion.'

All the time I was feeling wretched over my feelings for Danny, and Anthony was doing just the same thing – for much longer, I suspect. It's no more than I deserve. 'I'm not going to ask for whys and wherefores, Anthony. I don't feel as if I have the right. But I feel that this relationship of yours has been going on for some time, hasn't it?'

'Since she first joined the Village Belles.' His eyes brighten. 'I loved her at first sight.'

It makes me sad that I didn't realise that my Anthony was capable of such fervour. 'What about Internet Man?'

'She was trying to move on. She thought I'd never leave you. I am very fond of you, Fay. I didn't want to hurt you.'

Fond. It seems I have given over ten years of my life to fondness. That's hard. Yet you should never marry someone you're 'fond' of.

'Deborah makes me feel as if I'm on top of the world.' Anthony's face lights up. 'I can be completely myself when I'm with her.'

'I'm pleased for you,' I reply sincerely. 'I really am.'

'I'm sorry, Fay. I didn't know how I was ever going to tell you.'

So, I have made it very easy for him. In one drunken sentence from Edie, ten years of my life have crashed around my ears. 'Could we have done more, Anthony? Should we have done things differently?'

'I don't know, Fay. I didn't realise there was anything missing until I met Deborah. We could have plodded on together well enough.'

That doesn't sound like a way to live a life. Plodding on.

Anthony clears his throat. 'Does he set your heart on fire?' he asks. 'This Danny?'

It's an uncharacteristically emotional question for Anthony. My dear Anthony, who eats the same breakfast cereal every single morning, who will wear only black, lace-up shoes and white shirts. Yet here he is talking of love setting my heart aflame. It brings a tear to my eye. How heart-rending that in all the years we were together, we were never able to find that in our relationship.

'He does,' I answer truthfully.

'Then you should be with him.'

Perhaps that's so, but at this very moment I don't even know where he is.

Anthony pulls his chair next to mine. He wraps his arms around me and I lay my head on his shoulder, possibly for the very last time.

'I think we did love each other, Fay,' he says. 'In our own way. But we simply didn't love each other enough.'

So Anthony is in love with someone else, someone who deserves him more. He's not going to be riding in on his white charger to save me, save my home, save my business. Instead, I've lost yet another thing that's dear to me.

When I said that this night couldn't possibly get any worse, it seems I was wrong.

Chapter Sixty-nine

You know when you lie awake all night and you can't quite make your eyes close and you can't quite make your brain shut up and you can't make sleep come? That.

I'm bleary-eyed and exhausted when Lija turns up the next morning. I have a small mug with three spoons of instant coffee in it. Currently, it's not helping.

'You look as if you have been beaten round head with shoe,' she observes.

'I've not had the best of nights.'

'Still grieving for mother?'

'Yes, but that's only the half of it.'

'Will I need coffee?'

'Probably a good idea.' So Lija makes herself a drink and cuts a huge slice of the carrot cake that's left over from yesterday. Then, in what seems to be turning into our morning ritual, she sits opposite me. It's actually quite a nice way to start the day. I just wish I had good news to tell her instead of it always being about my life falling apart.

Lija takes a hearty gulp of her coffee. 'Tell.'

'I asked Anthony to marry me last night.'

Lija splutters out her carrot cake. It's not a pretty sight. 'What! You are mad woman!'

'So it seems.'

'You cannot marry him. I forbid it. I hope he said no.'

'Actually, he did.'

'Then one of you is not idiot. Thank God.'

'My sister came home drunk and drove my car into the gatepost.'

Lija massages her forehead. 'How can I possibly leave you alone for five minutes?'

'It gets worse,' I explain. 'Edie told Anthony that I slept with someone else.'

'Bad. Very bad,' Lija concludes. 'But not end of world.'

'Then Anthony told me that he's been having an affair with Deborah.'

'Fuck me to hell!' Lija exclaims. 'This is better than *EastEnders*. How can I have missed all this fun? I hope you kicked their no-good arses out of here.'

'No, of course I didn't.' I look up at Lija and sigh. 'Anthony and I took Edie up to bed and I sat with her for a while to make sure that she wasn't going to be sick.'

'Too kind,' Lija spits. 'You are always too kind.'

'It's for the best, I believe. I'm not one for subterfuge. Everything is out in the open now.'

'Sometimes I think you are too very stupid to live,' she tuts at me.

'Unfortunately, this also means that my great plan to get Anthony to marry me and live here happily ever after has collapsed like a house of cards. It was never really going to be a goer.'

'That's why you asked him?'

'I couldn't think of any other way to keep the house and the café, Lija. I don't have any money, the bank won't lend me any and Edie seems intent on selling it.'

That makes me cry a little bit.

'What got into Edie's head?' Lija asks crossly. 'She is being so cruel.'

'She was drunk,' I say. 'Very much so. I'm sure she'll feel terrible today.'

'You must not let her walk over you. She has to change her mind. You must fight for your home,' Lija urges. 'It is very important to you.'

'I don't think Edie did it deliberately.'

At that moment, Edie comes down the stairs. She's wearing dark glasses and has her suitcase at her feet.

'Did what deliberately?' she says, voice croaky.

'Last night, while you were drunk, you told Anthony that I'd slept with someone else,' I tell her flatly. 'And now he's left me.'

I'm not sure that I owe her the explanation about Anthony's own infidelity with the lovely Deborah. Not yet, anyway. Edie deserves to suffer a little.

'Oh,' she says. 'I'm very sorry, Fay.' For a moment she looks quite chastened. 'I can only apologise ... ' Then she runs out of words and stands there looking sheepish.

I glance pointedly at the suitcase at her feet. 'How are you feeling this morning?'

'This is all very awkward,' she says.

Try as I might, I can't offer her any words of comfort as I'm so very angry at her and how she's dealing with this. She should be supporting me and yet I feel as if she's dismantling my life bit by bit.

'I'm moving out,' Edie says. 'To a hotel. For the rest of the time I'm here. I think it's for the best.'

Then my heart squeezes. She's my family. My *only* family. I can't watch her walk out like this. 'Don't go, Edie. We can work this out. There's really no need for you to leave like this. I'm hurting and you're hurting. The situation is very painful for both of us.'

However, the look on her face tells me that it's not quite as painful for her.

I try another tack. 'You're my sister. We need to sit down and work out what's going to happen. This is our home.'

'This is *my* home,' she emphasises. '*Mine*. And I've put it up for sale, Fay.'

I feel the blood drain from my face.

'I went into the estate agent's yesterday.' Like a spoiled child, her chin juts defiantly as she talks. 'They're coming to put a sign up this morning. He said it should sell really easily.'

'Oh, Edie,' I say. Weariness threatens to overwhelm me. I could lie down on the kitchen tiles and weep. 'How could you do this to me?'

'You know my situation,' she says.

'And you know mine,' I counter.

'I don't think a discussion will get us anywhere.' She picks up her case. 'That's why it's best if I go.'

'You'll have to get a taxi,' I say. 'You crashed my car yesterday. I don't think it's safe to drive.'

'Oh.' Her voice is small. 'I'd forgotten that.'

'You seem to have forgotten a lot of things in the last few days, Edie,' I say tightly to her.

Her answer to that is to pick up her case and leave.

Chapter Seventy

A man comes to put up the estate agent's sign before the morning is over, while Lija and I are busy dashing about the kitchen filling early lunchtime orders. He asks if he can put one in the garden, down by the canal, to catch the eye of people walking on the towpath, but I won't let him. A small and possibly pointless act of defiance. But it makes me feel as if I'm doing *something*.

Edie is selling my home from beneath me and I am totally powerless to stop her.

'Bastard,' Lija mutters under her breath, giving a death glare to the poor man, who is only doing his job.

I'm absolutely sure Edie won't go through with this. She'll come to her senses. She must. I'm certain. When she realises exactly what she's doing, she'll treat me fairly. Why wouldn't she?

Then I realise that I'm in this situation entirely because my own mother hasn't treated me fairly. Well, the woman I *thought* was my mother. That threatens to set my brain into a tailspin again.

As a distraction technique, I dish up Stan's soup and walk down the garden to take it to him.

It's overcast today and the café is very quiet. Heavy black clouds sulk above us. The forecast has threatened rain and there's a chill breeze in the air. Even the canal looks miserable, grey and unwelcoming.

Stan is wearing a much-loved tweed jacket and a scarf. He's got his walking stick with him today, which normally means that he's feeling a bit tired.

'Don't you want to come indoors, Stan? It's a bit chilly. I don't want you catching a cold. We can set you up in the dining room, if you like? It won't take a minute.'

'No,' he says. 'Thanks, Fay, but I prefer to sit outside whatever the weather, if I can.'

'Lija's made lentil and bacon soup today, Stan. That will keep you nice and warm.'

'I bloody hate lentils,' he says brightly as he peers at it. 'But don't tell Lija. I'll eat it anyway.'

I laugh at him. 'Let me get you something else.'

'I wouldn't dream of it,' he says. Then he nods towards the front of the house. 'I saw the man putting up the For Sale sign.'

'Edie's work, I'm afraid. She's determined to have the money from this place, and I'm not sure what I can do to prevent it.'

'That's so very sad.'

'I'm sorry to let you down, Stan. Where will you get your lunch every day?'

'Oh, I'm sure I'll manage. Might even be forced to open a tin or two myself.' He touches my arm. 'The offer of my medals still stands, Fay. I don't know how much you'd get for them but, if you could sell them, you should. I do wish you'd at least consider it.'

I shake my head. 'You're so very kind, but no. I couldn't possibly do that.'

'What will you do when the house sells?'

'I really don't know, Stan,' I admit. 'It's not much of a strategy,

322

but at the moment I'm simply hoping that everyone who sees it will hate it on sight.'

But they don't. Of course. The sign hasn't even had a chance to settle in the ground before the estate agent is ringing to make an appointment for the first viewing. The house, he explains, has been priced to sell and he's expecting a lot of interest. In my language that means they've marketed it cheaply so they can get shot of it quickly without having to do too much work.

This is all moving so fast, I can hardly catch my breath.

A Mr Wakeman arrives at three o'clock, accompanied by the youngest estate agent I've ever seen. He shakes my hand, but his eyes slide over me as he takes in Canal House, my home.

Mr Wakeman is a smartly dressed businessman and he goes through the house with a ruthless efficiency, his facial expression never changing. I trail behind him and the child estate agent like a spare part, clearly as welcome as a fart in a spacesuit.

In the garden, Mr Wakeman looks at the canal impassively. Then he points at the *Maid of Merryweather* on its mooring. 'Will that be going?'

'Yes,' I say, the words sticking in my throat. Which I suppose it will. But where to, and how, with no engine?

'Good. I don't want to have to get rid of it.'

Me neither, I think.

Shortly afterwards, at four o'clock, when I've barely had time to pull myself together, a horrible couple arrive with two pretentious children – Mabel and Eli – in tow. Mr and Mrs Everson-Green poke and prod at my house, they look in my cupboards, they turn their nose up at my ancient bathroom suite, at my working, work-a-day kitchen with its ramshackle range of cupboards.

In the garden, Eli is completely hyperactive and tries to climb the apple tree. He grazes his knee and much screaming ensues. I should get him some kitchen towel and antiseptic to put on, but I can't. I'm just too worn down by it all. Maybe they'll hate the garden now they realise it's a hurty, scratchy place. Mabel pulls the heads off some of the flowers. I want to kill her. Mrs Hoity-Toity doesn't even apologise.

The Everso-Grating family all march down to the canal and give it a cursory glance.

'Having water at the end of the garden is a terrible hazard for young children,' I point out.

Said children scowl at me.

The parents look like they couldn't care less about the place. I'm so overwhelmed with relief that I make some tea and Lija and I have a slice of banana cake that's going begging.

'They hated it,' I tell her with a broad grin.

Lija high-fives me. 'No shit, Sherlock.'

Chapter Seventy-one

By six-thirty, the Everson-Greens have put in an offer for the house that's ten thousand pounds under the asking price. Half an hour later, the agent calls me to say that my sister has accepted it.

It's fair to say I'm in a state of shock. I honestly didn't even think they'd liked the house.

'You're in a chain,' the agent says, but I barely comprehend what he's saying. 'Their home is still on the market, but we have a very interested buyer. I foresee no problems with their selling.'

'What about the cake shop and café?' I manage to ask. 'Will they run it as a business?'

'Oh, no,' he says loftily. Clearly running such a lowly establishment would be beneath them. 'It will be purely a residence.'

So my home is under the hammer and lovely Fay's Cakes is to fade into oblivion.

'I'll be in touch,' the agent says. 'It should all progress quite quickly.'

You've made me homeless, I think. I've lost my livelihood. Do you have to sound so very brisk and businesslike?

Instead of venting my spleen, I say politely, 'Thank you.' This man is only doing his job. My spleen-venting should be saved for Edie.

Hanging up, I sit at the kitchen table, head in hands, stunned into silence. I don't think I've ever felt such bone-numbing misery. How can this all have happened so quickly?

'What?' Lija demands. 'What?'

'It's gone,' I tell her. Just like that. 'Edie has accepted an offer on the house.'

'She can't.'

'Those dreadful people are buying Canal House,' I reiterate. It's too awful to contemplate.

'The ones with horrible kids?'

'Yes.'

Lija stomps off to the fridge and when she comes back, she slams down a bottle of wine.

'We will get very slaughtered,' she says.

I shake my head. 'What good will that do?'

'None,' she admits. 'But I have nothing else to offer you.'

I have no better plan either, so I say, 'OK. Let's do it.'

Lija pours us out two glasses of cheap white wine and we knock them back without speaking. Then she fills them right up again. We slowly but steadily work our way through the entire bottle. And then another.

'I wish I had Danny's mobile number,' she slurs as we hit the second bottle. 'I would call him for you.'

'What could he do for me?'

'He could make you smile,' she says. 'It seems that I cannot.'

'You're making a good stab at it,' I offer.

'I will stay tonight,' Lija says. 'I don't want you to be alone.'

'I'd like that,' I say. 'I don't want to be alone either.'

'We will find rubbish film on television and stay up late.'

So we go through to the living room and curl up together on the sofa, as Edie and I did just a few days ago.

326

Lija finds *Forgetting Sarah Marshall*, which is a truly terrible film, but I let it go past my eyes and, every now and again, join Lija – who seems to be less discerning than I am – in a weak laugh, to seem polite. Then she roots through my meagre stash of DVDs and puts something else on, but I can't even tell you what.

My mind is filled with anxious questions. How long will the sale take to go through? Mr and Mrs Everson-Green have yet to sell their house and we are in a chain; I know nothing more than that. They're not interested in taking over Fay's Cakes though and that grieves me. All my hard work – all of Lija's hard work too – and it will simply fizzle away to nothing. I'm so angry at Edie. She's giving me no time to put anything else in place for my future. Where will I go? What will I do? How will I earn my living once the café is closed for good?

I reach for the wine again. This was a good idea. A very good idea.

It's gone midnight when the second film finishes, but I'm still too wired to sleep.

Lija picks up her crumpled packet of cigarettes from the coffee table. 'Make tea,' she instructs. 'I am going out for smoke.'

So Lija goes outside and I put on the kettle and, while I wait for it to boil, I lean on the windowsill and gaze wistfully out of the window and into the garden.

My dear spiky girl is marching up and down, puffing furiously on her cigarette and speaking animatedly into her phone. The orange tip of her glowing cigarette and the whiteness of her milk-bottle skin stand out in the darkness. I hope she'll find another job. I hope another employer will see through her brittle surface to the lovely, kind person she is below. Perhaps I should let her go sooner rather than later? Selfishly, I want to keep her here until the bitter end. But that's hardly fair of me.

I'm going to miss her, I think. I'm really going to miss her.

Then I get a piece of kitchen roll and cry quietly into it, hoping I'm finished before Lija comes back inside, or she'll tell me off again.

Chapter Seventy-two

A week goes by and I haven't spoken to Edie at all. We are communicating only through the estate agent and the funeral director. My texts and calls go unanswered and you don't know how sad that makes me. She's all I have left in the world and I have never felt more estranged from her. At the same time I could cheerfully throttle her for being so bloody-minded and selfish. She's cutting a swathe through everything in her path and I know that, at some point, she'll regret her selfish actions. At least I hope she will.

In the meantime, Mum's ashes are being buried with Dad's in the cemetery today and I don't even know if her own daughter is going to be there. The funeral director assures me that she's been informed, and I've texted Edie myself – yet again – but have had no reply.

I suppose I could phone around the local hotels to see if I can find out where she's staying, but, to be perfectly honest, I really don't have the heart. I feel as if I'm deep underwater, moving sluggishly, struggling to kick for the surface. I wish I could be sharp and bright, then I might find a solution to this dastardly mess, but I'm not.

So, at the appointed time, on a day that's far too bright and sunny for the occasion, I turn up at the crematorium. I've left Lija in charge of the café for a few hours. I have to say, she's been unusually quiet for the last couple of days. Perhaps she too is brooding on what the future holds.

I'm already standing at the entrance to the Oak Chapel with the funeral director, the place he suggested we meet, when a taxi pulls up and Edie climbs out. I can't read the expression in her eyes for her dark glasses.

She's wearing the same black dress that she wore for Mum's funeral and looks every inch the movie star. You'd think she was at a film première in Cannes rather than the crematorium in Milton Keynes.

I wonder where she's been staying since she moved out of the house, what she's been doing. Perhaps she'll tell me, perhaps she won't. You never know with Edie, and I find that I'm now even more wary of everything she says.

'Hello, Edie.'

My sister studies her designer stilettos. 'Fay.'

'Whenever you're ready,' the funeral director says tactfully as he moves towards the cemetery.

He's carrying the casket that contains Mum's ashes and we drop into step behind him. Both of us are silent as we walk through the pretty gardens and into the cemetery itself.

The grounds here are modern, well-tended, but the head-stones feel a little crammed in. When we make our way to Dad's, a small hole has been dug in front of it.

'Would you like to say a few words?' the funeral director asks in hushed tones.

'No, thank you,' I reply.

'Bye-bye, Mummy,' is all Edie can manage before she begins to sob.

Then the funeral director lowers the casket into the hole and moves away.

Both Edie and I stand and look at the ground, lost in our own thoughts. I still can't quite marshal mine. The woman who I thought was my mother for all of my life wasn't, and I don't know if I'm grieving for that or for the loss of Miranda herself. With everything else that's going on, I feel as if I'm just firefighting and can't even begin to unpick my feelings.

I stare at the casket containing Mum's ashes and feel numb, nothing at all. It's as if all this is happening to someone else. Next to me, I hear Edie sobbing more loudly; tears run down her cheeks, and I should comfort her, I know I should, but I can't bring myself to put my arms around her.

A moment later the funeral director clears his throat, which I understand is our signal to leave. He turns and escorts us back to the Oak Chapel.

'I'm very sorry for your loss,' he murmurs. 'If we can ever be of service again, please don't hesitate to call.'

'Thank you,' I say. 'Thanks for everything.'

He shakes our hands and leaves us alone. Edie and I stand there, unmoving.

When it's clear that nothing else is about to happen, I say to Edie, 'Well. That's it then.'

My sister dabs at her eyes with a tissue. 'I don't know what we're supposed to do now.'

'Me neither.'

'Shall we go and get a drink somewhere?' she ventures tearfully. 'I could really do with a brandy.'

I nod. 'If you want to.'

'We have things we should discuss,' she says.

As my poor car is still crumpled and I've done nothing about getting it fixed yet, we have to call a taxi. I'll have to do something about getting it repaired pretty soon though, as we're running low on supplies for the café and I'll need to do a run to the wholesaler. Then I remember. In a few months, a few weeks perhaps, there'll be no café anyway.

I dial the number of the taxi company that brought me here.

Fortunately the cab only takes a few minutes to arrive, during which Edie and I stand together awkwardly. We both sit in the back, but make sure there's plenty of space between us.

'Can you take us to the nearest pub, please?' I ask. 'It doesn't matter which one.'

So the driver turns on to the busy road and heads off to the nearest pub. As fortune would have it, it's not a very salubrious one. Still, it doesn't matter. We're not really here to have a convivial lunch together.

I pay him and we go inside.

It's one of a chain, but very much a man's pub. There's a group of blokes in grubby checked shirts and work jeans huddled round the bar. The carpet is sticky with stale beer.

We find a table and Edie sits while I go to the bar and order a brandy for her and a pot of tea for me. I haven't asked her if she wants anything to eat, but the food looks dreadful anyway. There's no waitress service so I stand and wait until my tea is ready and then carry our drinks back to the table.

I push Edie's brandy across to her and sit down with my tea.

'That was quite nice,' Edie says. 'No fuss or anything, but nice all the same.'

'Yes,' I agree, even though it wasn't nice for me; it was very uncomfortable.

Edie sips at her brandy, hands cupped around the small glass. She looks like she wishes I'd got her a double.

Then we have a few moments of embarrassed silence before I eventually say, 'I understand that the house sale's going through.'

'Well,' Edie takes another swig of brandy. 'There's been a development. Just this morning.'

I can tell she's trying to look suitably solemn, but it's difficult for her to hide her excitement. That immediately makes me suspicious.

'What kind of development?'

'We have a cash buyer,' she says, and there's the underlying tone of glee again. 'They've gazumped the Everson-Greens. An extra five thousand pounds and no chain. So I've gone with that. I hope you agree.'

'I don't seem to have any say in it, Edie.'

She breezes on, oblivious to my comment. 'That means we'll be able to complete really quickly. The money's already in place, apparently. They had to prove it to the agent.'

We've only had two viewings, so I'm assuming it's Mr Wakeman, the businessman who came alone, who's bought it. I knew it would be a desirable property but, as I've never sold or bought a house before, I hadn't realised how quickly things could move.

'All we have to do is complete the formalities.' Now she can't help but smile. 'It could all be done in four weeks. Possibly less.'

In a month that's been full of shocks, this is yet another one.

'And where does that leave me, Edie?' I ask when I've found my voice. 'Where *exactly* does that leave me?'

'I know it's difficult for you, Fay,' she says tightly. 'But it can't be helped. I'm only complying with Mum's wishes.'

'She didn't want you to sell the house, Edie. She wanted you to come back and live in it, to keep it in her family. That, apparently, was her misplaced reasoning for cutting me out of her will.'

'That can't happen, can it?' Her face takes on a petulant expression. 'My life is in New York. With Brandon.'

'I could have taken it on. Given a bit more time, we could have worked it out somehow.'

'I don't see how,' Edie notes loftily. 'Besides, this is for the best.'

'For you. Not for me.'

'You'll have a few weeks to vacate the house,' she says.

'Thanks for that.'

And then, somewhat belatedly, she does look guilty. 'What will you do?'

'I don't know, Edie. But thanks for asking.'

'There's no need to be funny with me, Fay,' she says. 'This is Mum's doing, not mine.'

'You're literally going to leave me homeless and penniless, aren't you?'

'I can repay the money you've lent me when the sale goes through. I'll get that to you as soon as I can.'

'Have you heard yourself? I sent that money to you to help you out when you had nothing and were in danger of losing your apartment. I sent you money when I didn't have any to send. You've had all of my savings and I gave them to you gladly.'

'It's only about ten grand,' Edie grumbles. 'I can pay that easily now.'

'Yes,' I say. 'You can. Because you'll have nearly half a million pounds from the sale of Canal House.'

'I could give you extra, if you want,' Edie says reluctantly. 'To tide you over. Another ten grand or so.'

'Don't trouble yourself,' I tell her. 'You can repay what you owe me. Other than that, I'd rather manage alone.'

I finish my tea and stand up. 'I hope you and your money will be very happy together, Edie.' My voice catches on a sob. 'Take care of yourself.'

I walk towards the door.

'Fay!' she shouts after me. 'Fay! Come back!'

But I don't. I keep on walking.

Chapter Seventy-three

So. This month I have lost my mum, my sister, my boyfriend, my home, my business. And almost my sanity.

The house sale has whistled through. The one thing I prayed would crash around my ears has, of course, gone without a hitch. Contracts are exchanging today and, if that happens as planned, we're due to complete at the end of next week. The knowledge is weighing heavily on my heart. How I wish there was someone to hold me, to tell me that everything will be all right. But Anthony is gone and so is Danny. I'm in this alone.

I lie in bed at night thinking of Danny. I'd like to tell you that it makes me feel better, but the longing and yearning I feel for him only serve to make me feel more bereft, more lonely. I feel as if I'm dragging myself through the days.

I've done some desultory searching for accommodation on the internet, but without a job, how will I pay for it? To be honest, my heart isn't in it anyway. I could camp out on the *Maid of Merryweather* while the weather's warm, but she'll need a lot of money spending on her to make her habitable again. Plus I'd have to pay a mooring fee somewhere as I'm sure the new residents won't want me sulking at the bottom of the garden.

The customers, completely unaware that the café will soon be closing, are still coming along in droves. We are cake central. This is our best summer so far, helped in no small measure by the fabulous weather we've enjoyed. Lija and I haven't stopped since first thing this morning and the lunchtime rush is at its height now. It feels like such a sin that a great, thriving little business like this will go to waste. In the right hands it could go from strength to strength, and perhaps I wouldn't feel so bad if I knew someone else was willing to take it on and do all the things that I wanted to but never got round to.

I also feel bad that Lija will soon be out of a job, especially as she doesn't seem to have made any moves to find another one. She's certainly not asked me for any time off for interviews. But then, I think, she will probably walk straight into something else – as long as she's not too stroppy. I do worry about her. Underneath that abrasive exterior there is a lovely, caring girl. She's been with me for a long time now and I feel responsible for her. How will she manage to make ends meet without the café? Then again, how will I?

'Chin up,' Stan says when I take him his soup. 'Can't be all that bad.'

'It is,' I assure him. Putting down the bowl, I fuss with setting out his cutlery, his plate of crusty bread. Then I drop into the seat next to him. 'Contracts for the house sale are due to exchange later this afternoon. My days here are numbered.'

'Ah.'

I would love Stan to have turned out to be my fairy godfather. Wouldn't it be wonderful if he stood up and announced that he was a secret millionaire and had been swept away by all the soup and cakes he'd consumed at Fay's Cakes over the years and wanted to repay our brilliance with pots of cash which I could use to save my home, my business? Then, with a wave of his wand, made all my wishes come true? But this is real life and all that's happening is that Stan's soup is getting cold.

'Something will turn up,' Stan says optimistically. 'It always does.'

'You're right,' I say, even though I don't think in this instance it will. 'I'd better get back to the kitchen or Lija will tear me off a strip. I'll leave you to your soup.'

'What have we got today?'

'Spiced butternut squash, Stan.'

'Oh,' he says, his lined face lighting up. 'My favourite. Very exotic.'

I have to get up and leave before he sees my tears. How I'm going to miss this place, miss Lija, miss Stan.

I cry all the way back to the kitchen and have to stand in the corner of the veranda and wipe my tears on my apron so that Lija doesn't see me weeping again.

Yet I'm no sooner through the door than she scowls at me. 'Crying again?'

'No, no,' I insist. 'Pollen. Very high count today.'

She raises her eyebrows, but before she can quiz me further, her phone rings. She wipes her hands and peers at the caller display. 'I must take this,' she says.

Lija marches out of the door and I watch for a moment as, head bent in concentration, she strides up and down the driveway while she talks. I busy myself with an order of sandwiches for the family under the apple tree. A couple of regular weekend customers pop in to buy some cakes and I stand and chat for a few minutes while I serve them.

When I get back to the kitchen Lija is leaning on the counter, arms folded tightly across her chest. Although her facial expression rarely flickers from stonily impassive, she looks anxious.

'I have to speak to you,' she says.

'Whatever it is can't be that bad,' I offer. 'That's a hell of a frown.' I'm expecting she's going to tell me that she's found a job. Perhaps she needs to start tomorrow and doesn't want to leave me in the lurch. Well, if that's the case, so be it. Lija has to do what's best for her.

But before she can say any more, my phone also rings. It's the estate agent. My heart sinks.

'A moment,' I promise Lija. 'I'll be just a moment.'

I take my phone and walk into the living room.

'Hello, Miss Merryweather,' he says cheerily. 'Just wanted to let you know that the contracts have exchanged today. All successful. The completion date is set for next Friday. So, congratulations!'

He's obviously still completely unaware of my situation and how devastating this is for me.

'Thank you,' I say.

'Your sister says you'll be vacating the property in the next few days.'

Does she? How very kind of her. Well, there's nothing else to be done now. It looks like I will be. There's going to be no last-minute reprieve. No miraculous change of heart from Edie. My head is on the block and she's happy to swing the axe. My own sister, who I've always been there for, has completely abandoned me in my hour of need. I'm sadder than I've ever felt before.

'Yes,' I say.

Then I hang up. I want nothing more to do with this. Edie is the one who has been so very eager to sell, so she can deal with the rest of it. All I have to do now is pack up and leave.

I sit on the sofa, head in hands, stunned into a state of shock. It's happened. I'm homeless.

Chapter Seventy-four

I don't know quite how long I've been sitting there, catatonic, when Lija comes through to the living room.

'Sorry, sorry,' I say, wiping my face on my sleeve. 'I'll be with you in a second. I just need to collect myself. The orders must be stacking up.'

'Fuck the orders,' Lija says.

Yes, I think, fuck them indeed. Why should I be bothered? The place can go to hell in a handcart for all I care. Except that I still can't kid myself. I do care.

Lija gnaws at her fingernails. 'I have something to tell you.'

'Not now, please, Lija. I don't think I could cope with any more bad news. Can't it wait?'

'No.' She kneels on the floor in front of me. 'It must be now.'

Sighing, I mentally brace myself. 'OK. Hit me with it.'

'I do not know how to say it.'

I dab away my tears with the back of my hand and solemnly she hands me a piece of crumpled kitchen roll. 'Let me guess. You've got another job?'

'No. Is worse. Or better.' Lija takes a deep breath and her dark eyes are troubled. 'I do not know.'

'You're not going back to Latvia?'

She shoots me daggers. 'Do not be stupid.'

'Oh, OK.' The suspense is killing me now, so I say, 'Spit it out.'

She screws her fists into tight balls and blurts, 'I have bought house.'

My head snaps up. 'A house? Which house?'

'This house.'

'*You* have?'

'I have.'

'Are you sure?'

'Yes. I am cash buyer.'

I let out a teary and somewhat perplexed laugh. 'What? How? Why? When?'

'I have borrowed money from dodgy aunt in Russia who has dodgy business.'

'How dodgy?'

Lija shrugs. 'Very dodgy?'

I laugh more. A bit hysterically now. 'Is this true? It can't be.' She nods.

'Why have you done it? *How* have you done it?'

'I did not want you to lose your home. I did not want you to lose your job.'

'I thought the businessman that came to see it had bought it. What was his name? Mr Wakeman? Wasn't he the one who's come in with the cash offer?' Admittedly, since Edie has been dealing with it all, it didn't occur to me to actually ask. As we'd only had two viewings, I simply assumed that it was him.

'No. Was me. What could I do, Fay?' Her voice is unusually impassioned. 'I couldn't let it go to that horrible family with their horrible children.' Lija can't quite meet my eyes when she says, 'I love this house too. And you.'

That's quite an admission for Lija.

I massage my temples. 'Wow. I can't quite get my head round this. Are you sure?'

She nods. 'You can stay now. I thought we could run the café together.' She bites nervously at her lip. 'You could help me pay off the loan and we could be partners.'

Another unhinged-sounding laugh comes from me.

'Are you angry?' There are two scarlet spots on her snow-white face. 'I thought that it was the best thing to do.'

'You've done this for me?'

'For me too,' she admits. 'I will have share in business. A nice home as well.'

'Oh, God.' I don't know what to do. I don't know what to say.

'We can live here together, Fay.' Her dark eyes are troubled and imploring. Then she wrinkles her nose. 'Though I am not having room that Old Bag slept in.'

'Oh, Lija.'

'You are not pleased?'

'I'm delighted.' Though my brain is so confused, it might go into meltdown. 'Why didn't you tell me?'

'I didn't know how you would feel. I thought perhaps you would tell me no.'

I look at her ruefully. 'I would have.'

'We can do this,' she says. 'I know we can. I have many ideas.'

It's the first time I've heard Lija sound passionate about anything.

'I have borrowed extra money from dodgy aunt for makeover too. Danny could come back and help us.'

Danny. Even Lija is thinking of ways to bring him back here. That makes me smile. I wonder where he is now, what he's doing. Perhaps he's found another job that will suit him just as well.

'I must get back to kitchen.' Lija glances anxiously over her shoulder.

'Let me give you a hug first,' I say.

So I stand and my sharp, snappy and very kind friend lets me put my arms around her.

'You are not cross?'

'I'm pleased,' I say. 'So very pleased.' Yet I still can't quite believe that she's really done this.

Who knew that my fairy godmother would come, and it would be in the shape of a skinny and rather stroppy young Latvian lady? I feel a rush of warm affection for her. I'm so glad she wants to settle here, to make this her home and continue running the cake shop and café. 'I love this place. I can't think of anyone better to own Canal House.'

She grins hesitantly. 'It will be same as always. Nothing will change.'

But as I watch her bustle briskly back to the kitchen, I know in my heart that she's wrong. Everything has changed. Nothing will ever be the same again.

Chapter Seventy-five

I walk along the towpath, lost in thought. It's another blistering hot day. Although it's not yet noon, the sun is fierce, blinding.

Last night I didn't sleep. It seems to be a recurring thing now. The latest cause for insomnia was Lija's revelation that she will very soon own Canal House and Fay's Cakes. It might not even be Fay's Cakes anymore. It could be Lija's Cakes or she could rebrand and come up with something altogether more snappy.

I'm pleased for her. Of course I am. If the house had to be sold, and clearly it did, then who better for it to go to? I'm touched that Lija even thought of doing it to help me, but I hope she's primarily doing it for herself. I only wished she'd discussed it with me – but then, as she said, I'd only have tried to talk her out of it. The house is huge and the café a big responsibility. Lija is so young and I don't want her to be bogged down with responsibilities and worries, as I have been. She should be out enjoying life.

Despite this latest turn of events, I still feel as if I'm rudderless. Everything that anchored me to this place – Mum, Anthony, the café – has been kicked from under me. Can I really stay here now and work for Lija? Do I even want to?

My brain is buzzing with a thousand conflicting thoughts and I just can't make sense of anything. I've had to get out for a few hours to try to clear my head, and there are things I need to take time to do.

When I get to the lock gates at Cosgrove, I sit on the beam, arms wrapped around my knees, and watch the world go by. I'm at my most relaxed when I'm either on or by the water, and I start to feel myself settle, some form of equilibrium returning.

You can never be lonely on the canal as there's always something happening. I wave to all the cyclists and joggers who puff and pant past me. Then I watch a duck trying to marshal all seven of her babies round the lock and back into the water at the other side, and marvel at her skill. It all brings some much-needed light relief into what has been a relentlessly dark period of my life.

The only other high spot has been Danny, of course, who is never very far from my mind. I wonder whether he'll come back one day; whether I'll even be here if he does.

A few minutes later a narrowboat approaches – not one that I recognise. It's still the height of the holiday season and the canal is busy with boats from all over the country. Lija's been having a job to keep up with the constant demand for cakes both to serve in the café and to sell in the *Maid of Merryweather*.

The boat – *Four Winds* – drifts up to the gates. It's manned by a couple who look as if they're regular canal dwellers. The dreadlocked man on the back calls 'Hey' to me and I wave. The woman, with pink hair and dungarees, jumps out to work the locks.

'Hello,' I say as she approaches. 'Come far?'

'Up from Warwickshire,' she answers as she opens the sluices. 'What about you?'

'Local.' I nod towards Dad's narrowboat further down the canal. 'I run the cake shop on the canal.' And then I remember

344

that I actually don't any more. The café is now under Lija's tender loving care. It's hers and hers alone.

'Nice part of the world,' she says. 'We haven't been this way for a while.'

'Do you live on the canal?'

'Yeah. Have done for ten years or more now.'

'You must like the life.'

'I don't think I could go back to a house now. Though I sometimes have to remind myself of that when we're chipping ourselves out of the ice in the winter. I like the freedom the canal offers. We felt like a change of scenery and here we are.'

'You haven't seen a boat called *The Dreamcatcher* on your travels?'

She laughs. 'About ten of them.'

'Oh, right.' It *is* a very common name.

I jump up and help the woman to push open the gates. Her husband holds up a hand in thanks as he eases the boat into the lock.

'Were you looking for a particular boat?'

'One with a very handsome man on board.'

She laughs. 'I think I'd have noticed that. But, no, I didn't see that particular *Dreamcatcher*.'

It was too much to hope for really. Danny could be anywhere on the canal system by now. I don't even know which way he was headed. The Grand Union goes all the way down to London or, if he'd gone north, he could be in Shropshire or Leicestershire. Anywhere really.

When the *Four Winds* has passed through the lock, I wave goodbye to the couple and carry on walking up to the Two Barges, hoping to clear my head.

On my way, I pick a bunch of the wild flowers that are blossoming in the hedgerows, much as Danny did for me on my birthday – tansy, cow parsley, feverfew and meadowsweet.

When I reach the Two Barges, I get a diet cola from the bar and then find a table in the sunshine. I call a cab to come and collect me, then, while I wait, I lean back on the bench, eyes half closed, letting the sunshine warm my face.

A few moments later, I catch sight of a couple coming towards me. They're hand in hand, laughing and look very much in love. When I fully open my eyes and shade them from the glare of the sun, I see that it's Anthony and Deborah. He looks happier than I've seen him in a long time.

They're close when they finally stop looking at each other and notice me. They both stop in their tracks and their faces freeze.

'Hi,' I say as breezily as I can manage. 'Lovely day.'

'Hi.' Anthony looks anxiously at Deborah.

'It's nice to see you both,' I say. 'Are you going to sit outside?'

'Yes,' he says. 'We're just here for a bite of lunch.'

'You can have this table,' I offer. 'It's a lovely spot. I'm leaving in a minute or two.'

With only the slightest hesitation, they come over and sit with me. Deborah fiddles nervously with her hair which is fluffed out to 1980s proportions. Not only is she in full slap, she's also wearing her signature body-con dress with matching high heels and nails. Today's shade is electric blue. I feel distinctly underdressed in my shorts and crumpled white cotton shirt. Frankly, I'm not even sure whether I combed my hair this morning.

Anthony looks proud to have her on his arm and there's a light in his eyes for her that I know he never had for me.

'I'm so sorry—' Deborah begins, but I hold up a hand.

'No need.' I don't want to hear an apology or an explanation. I don't want sympathy either. 'There's nothing to say.'

If they feel there will be any sort of repercussions for their affair, then they're both wrong. I wish them nothing but happiness together. Anthony looks relaxed with himself and is wearing a very trendy shirt that it's clear he hasn't chosen for himself. It's taken years off him. He's sporting mirrored aviator shades too, which makes me smile. Deborah has obviously taken him shopping, though Anthony and his money are not easily parted. She might have him in a onesie next.

'I'm happy for you both,' I offer. 'Genuinely.'

I see them both unwind a little.

How can I possibly begrudge them their happiness? They do make a lovely couple. Plus, Anthony and I were together for a long time. Despite how it ended for us, I hope we can salvage some sort of friendship. But I do look at him now and wonder how I could have thought we could make a marriage work. I'm fond of him, but I don't love him. I know that now. He doesn't, in his own words, set my heart on fire. That privilege belongs to someone else. I've had one small taste of what love can feel like and know now that I'd rather spend the rest of my life alone than settle for anything less.

'How's the house sale going?' Anthony asks cautiously. 'Has Edie relented?'

'No,' I say. 'It's all gone ahead. She was determined to get the money out of it.'

'That's a shame. I'm sorry, Fay.'

'Me too.' I pick at my bunch of flowers, rolling a petal absently between my fingers. 'Lija's bought it.'

'Lija?'

I nod. 'With money from some dubious Russian aunt.'

'How are you with that?'

'I'm happy for her,' I say honestly.

'But what will you do now?'

I could make up something wonderful, tell him that I have exciting plans for my future, but even I'm not that imaginative. My brain still seems to be in shock and has stopped

347

functioning on all but a basic level. 'If I'm honest, I don't really know.'

'If there's anything I can do to help ...' Anthony's sentence trails away.

'I'll be fine, really.' My problems aren't his problems any more and I won't trouble him with them. 'But thank you.'

My cab pulls into the car park. 'This is mine.' I gesture at it. Finishing up my cola, I say, 'I'd better be going.'

Briefly I kiss Anthony's cheek, and then do the same to Deborah. She smiles warmly at me. She's a nice lady and will suit him just fine. She'll be better for him than I ever was.

'You should come along to the next performance by the Village Belles,' he says in a rush. 'I'll put a ticket aside especially for you.'

'That would be really lovely.' And I think that hell would have to freeze over before I ever felt compelled to listen to hand bells again.

'I wish you luck, Fay,' Anthony says.

'Thanks.' And, as I walk towards my waiting taxi, I know that I'm going to need it.

Chapter Seventy-six

I make my way up from the Oak Chapel towards the cemetery. This time, as I'm alone, I take in more. Some of the memorial stones have only a few blooms beside them, which are wilting in the heat, others have a more graphic catalogue of the deceased person's life – toy cars, bottles of beer, miniatures of whisky, medals, photographs in torn plastic covers taped to the marble that tell something of the person who lies there.

The heart-breaking ones are the headstones of children, covered in faded teddies, weather-worn dolls. There's one with a shiny happy birthday banner draped over it, bright cards with greetings such as *Our Special Son*, *Darling Grandson*, *Favourite Nephew* scattered around. Garish, hopeful tokens mark the grave of a baby who was 'born asleep' ten years ago and that makes me want to cry. A life that was over before it had even begun.

There's a bench at the top of the lines of stones and, over the years, people have hung small memories in the trees – wooden hearts carved with names or woven in willow, glass orbs or spinning copper wind chimes. They sway in what little breeze there is.

Eventually, I stand at the spot where Mum and Dad's are now buried. Together for ever. I wonder if that's what they really wanted? I wonder where my real mother is buried, and it's something I'm suddenly determined to find out. Did Dad ever visit her? I wonder. He could have taken me too.

The headstone has obviously been taken away at some point and has now returned with bright new engraving on it. Below my dad's name it now says, *Miranda Merryweather, much-loved mother and wife*. Then it states the dates of Mum's birth and death. That really tells so very little about her. But then how could such a minimal memorial begin to encompass Mum's life?

Sitting on the grass in front of the stone, I stare at it, trying to think of something to say. The only sounds are the birds in the trees and the steady thrum of the traffic on the busy road behind the cemetery.

Eventually, I manage to marshal my thoughts into something vaguely coherent.

'Why?' I ask her. 'That's all I need to know. Why did you do this? You've pitted Edie and me against each other when there was really no need. I loved you and I cared for you as any daughter would. And yet all that time you didn't think of me as your own child. How could you be so unkind?'

It would be nice to have some sort of divine sign to tell me that somewhere my stepmum, the woman I always believed was my mother, Miranda Merryweather, is up there listening. Perhaps a ray of sunshine illuminating a rose, a colourful bird on a branch, a white feather. Something like that. But there's nothing at all. Mum's gone for ever, leaving chaos and pain in her wake.

'Did you even love me?' I press on. 'After what you've done, I don't think you could have.'

I sit again, unspeaking, but when it's clear that there are no answers to be had here, I stand up, ready to leave.

'I forgive you,' I say. 'You've hurt me. Of course you have. Perhaps that's what you intended. But I think you've actually hurt Edie more. She'll take the money and blow the lot in no time at all. Then what will she do?'

Shaking my head I say, 'You've ruined our relationship, perhaps for good. I'm the one who looked out for her. You had no idea what her life was really like, and maybe that's my fault for trying to keep it from you. She wasn't the perfect daughter that you thought, Mum. Far from it. I could have given her a solid foundation. She could have always come back to me, to the house. Now that's gone and I'm frightened for her.'

I lay the wild flowers that I've picked at the foot of the headstone.

'Anyway, I still love you and I'll still bring flowers for you. To me you were my mum. The only one I've known. But I'm going to look for my real mum too. I want to know all about her, who she was. I wonder if you thought that Dad had always loved her more than you?'

Then I don't know what else to say, so I turn and head back towards the chapel. It was always difficult having a conversation with Mum when she was alive. It's considerably harder now that she's dead.

Chapter Seventy-seven

Fay's Cakes is closed today, but Lija and I need to make some strawberry jam as we're running short. I'd love to be able to go to a pick-your-own farm nearby, but these days there aren't any as most of the farmland has had houses built on it. The other option is that we try to find a way to grow enough to keep us supplied in the summer. I'm sure we could set a patch aside in the garden. However, that's something for Lija to decide now.

As it stands, we currently go to one of the local farmers' markets to stock up on our summer fruits. It's the turn of Woburn today. It costs more to do it this way, obviously, but I'd rather pay extra and support the local economy than go to a supermarket and pay to have my strawberries imported from Spain or Mexico or somewhere. This is good local produce and we make good local jam with it.

I know that from tomorrow, when the sale of the house is completed, all of these things will be Lija's decisions. But I want to make the handover as easy as possible. I want her to look forward to the future with excitement and not with dread. Perhaps my heart should feel heavy at the prospect, but for some reason I feel surprisingly light. I slept well last night and that always helps, doesn't it? I also dreamed of Danny – as I so often do – and that didn't hurt either.

'We'll have to take a cab,' I tell Lija. 'My car's still out of action.' The crumpled wing, courtesy of my sister, has yet to be repaired. 'You should learn how to drive. You'll need to so that you can go to the wholesaler. If you have to take a cab all the time, it will cost a fortune.'

'I know. I can drive,' she says. 'I do not like to. And I have no car.'

'I'll have to get mine fixed. I'm sure I could put you on the insurance.' I don't know why we've never addressed this before.

Lija remains stony-faced.

'We should put the Kilner jars in the dishwasher,' I add. 'So they'll be sterilised ready for when we get back.'

'I know,' she says tightly.

'I'm sorry,' I say. 'I'm just trying to help you settle in as owner.'

'Nothing will change,' she says. '*Nothing*.'

'Right.' So we load up with carrier bags and set off.

Lija is quiet in the taxi as we drive out to Woburn. It's only a short journey and we go through some of the prettiest countryside around here. She stares out of the window. When we reach Woburn, I pay the taxi and we set off down the High Street towards the market square. Lija drags her heels like a sulky teenager.

I link my arm through hers. 'Before we go shopping, let's get a cup of coffee and a cake. It will make a change for us to be served. Will that cheer you up?'

She smiles reluctantly. 'Might do.'

'We'll call it research,' I tell her. 'There's no harm in checking out what the competition is doing.'

So we stop at the first tearoom we come to. There are a couple of tables outside and one of them is vacant. Lija and I make a beeline for it, pleased that we've scored a prime seat.

The waitress comes to take our order, and it does feel very strange to be on the receiving end, for once. We both order lattes and gingerbread cupcakes.

'It'll be fine, really,' I say. 'There's nothing to worry about.'

Lija turns to me and her face is bleak. 'I am taking on big commitment,' she says. 'I am frightened, Fay. I never wanted to run café. I am happy just working for you.'

'I'll be here to help you. We should go through the books this evening, so you know the ropes. We could do it over a glass of wine.'

Lija bursts into tears. 'I feel terrible. This is your business. I am stealing it.'

'No, no, no.' I put my arm round her. 'You're saving it. Just think: the house could have gone to those awful people and the café would have closed. You're keeping it alive.'

'I feel like shit. I thought it was best thing. Now I am not sure.'

I wrap my arms around Lija and she sobs on my shoulder while I pat her soothingly.

'Hush, hush,' I coo as if she's my child. 'It *is* the best thing. I swear. You're just feeling a bit daunted. We'll work it out,' I promise Lija. 'You and me.'

She takes her napkin and blows her nose noisily. 'Fuck,' she says, making a little old lady who's passing by jump.

The woman looks at us both in disgust. 'Sorry,' I say. 'Sorry.'

She harrumphs and marches on. 'Younger generation,' she mutters over her shoulder.

But she doesn't know this particular member of the younger generation, who is fabulous and supportive and has done so much for me. More than my own sister.

Chapter Seventy-eight

We take our not insignificant haul of strawberries back to the house. We're both starving now and I make a quick sandwich and run one down the lane to Stan's cottage for him.

When I knock, it takes an age for him to answer and I stand there, heart in mouth, until he comes to the door. One day he won't open up, and I can't even bear to think of it.

His hair is tousled and he looks a little bit dazed. 'Snoozing in the garden,' he says with a yawn.

'Good for you.' I hand over the plate covered in cling film. 'Just a sandwich today, Stan. Cheshire cheese and our own onion marmalade.'

'Oh.' Stan's eyes light up. 'My favourite.'

'Lija and I are on a jam-making mission. We've got to crack on.'

'I'm grateful for whatever you bring me, Fay. You're so very kind.'

Some days he looks more frail than others, and today is one of them. His skin looks pale and his eyes slightly cloudy. I have to remind myself that he's ninety-three and won't go on for ever. But I hope that won't happen soon, as I couldn't face yet another loss.

'Walk up later, if you feel like it, and have some cake. The kettle's always on.'

'Not today,' Stan says. 'I'm a little tired.'

'You rest up then. Shall I bring you some supper later?'

'No,' he says. 'I've got something out of the freezer.'

'Are you sure?'

He nods.

'OK. But call me if you need anything. Promise me that.'

'I will.'

'We'll see you tomorrow for lunch in the café?'

'Nothing will keep me away.'

Slowly I walk back to the house, glancing back at his cottage over my shoulder, trying not to worry about him.

As soon as I'm in the kitchen, I have to concentrate as Lija and I set to with our mammoth jam-making session. The WI have nothing on us. We are lean, mean jam-making machines. It's something that we both love to do. We wash all the fruit and then I make a big pot of tea. We sit at the kitchen table, mugs at the ready, and start to hull the strawberries – in for the long haul.

We're going to make four smaller batches, since if you make too much in one go then you can have trouble getting it to set. I pour us some tea and turn on the radio to give us some music to hull to.

Lija seems happier now. Not smiley, obviously – that would be a step too far. She works quickly with her sharp knife, cutting away the sepal and the hard core from the strawberries.

'What?' she says when she catches me looking at her. 'What are you staring at?'

'Nothing,' I tell her with an affectionate smile. 'I just can't believe how far you've come since you first started here. I'm very proud of you.'

'Stop it,' she says. 'Or I will cry again.'

'You mustn't. You should only think of the future. I'm sure you'll do great things with this place.'

'The sale is completed tomorrow.'

'I know. That does feel a bit weird, but you'll be in the driving seat then.'

'You'll stay here?' Lija asks. 'You must. I want you to. I thought we could both live upstairs. Which bedroom do you want?'

'I'd like to stay where I am, if that's OK?' It seems weird having this conversation about what has been my home for so long. 'Will you move into Mum's room? It's the biggest one. I'll clear it out before you go in there. Freshen it up. And we can decorate. It's in desperate need of it.'

'Yes, I will take Miranda's bedroom.'

I note that Lija doesn't call my mother 'the Old Bag' now that she's no longer with us.

'Now I feel selfish. This is your house, not mine. I'll move in there if you'd rather have my room.' I wonder how long we'll feel that we have to tiptoe around each other.

'No,' she says. 'Is decided.' Then she chews her lip anxiously. 'I thought maybe . . . we could make Edie's bedroom into office and have living room in large spare bedroom.'

'Gosh,' I say. 'That's a good idea.' I'd never have thought of that.

'Perhaps when downstairs living room is clear, we could make that extra space for café. Expand. Make shop work harder.'

'Wow. You *have* been thinking about this.'

'I think about nothing else.'

I laugh. 'You'll be fine, Lija. You'll see.'

Emboldened, she's on a roll now. 'We could open in evening too. Do supper. Perhaps have dinner club. Not every night, but some nights. We have to maximise asset.'

This is the closest I've ever seen Lija to being excited. Her pale face is positively animated, and that makes me smile. But it also makes me realise that my business is very definitely slipping away from me.

'I'll support you in whatever you want to do, Lija,' I tell her honestly.

'We must have meeting,' she says solemnly. 'Do blue-sky thinking.'

I hide a smile. She's turning into Alan Sugar before my very eyes.

All the strawberries are hulled now and I get out our four big preserving pans so that we can set them to cook on the stove. I put one on each ring of the hob. We'll soon get them hubble-bubbling away.

Lija brings the fruit and tips it into the pans.

'What's Edie doing with all the fittings and furniture?' I ask. For all I know, she could be intending to sell this lot off, and then where would that leave Lija? I've done nothing about emptying the house out. If that's what Edie wants, then she hasn't said anything. All of Mum's things will need to be disposed of, and even Edie's room hasn't been changed since she left. There must be some things she wants, but as far as I'm concerned, it's her problem now. 'You'll need the kitchen equipment at the very least.'

'I have bought it all from her,' Lija tells me. 'Everything. She gave me a good price.'

'Oh.' My sister really has kept me firmly out of the loop on this.

'If there's anything special that you want to keep,' Lija hurries on, 'it is yours. Just say.'

'No.' I shake my head. 'There's nothing I want from this family. I'm happy for you to have it all. I'm sure you don't want Mum's stuff, so I can sort that out.'

'There is no hurry, Fay.' Hesitantly, her hand touches my arm. 'We must do this softly.'

'Of course.' But, in my heart, I feel that the sooner we do this, the better.

I add the sugar to the pans and we set it to boil. Lija is the one with the perfect touch when it comes to jam, so I let her take control of the cooking while I lift the sterilised jars out of the dishwasher and line them up on the counter ready to be filled. Then I reload the dishwasher with another batch of jars.

'It's ready,' Lija says over her shoulder a few minutes later. She lifts the pans from the heat and puts them on the kitchen table.

'Looks lovely.' The scent that fills the kitchen is heavenly. 'We just need to wait for it to settle and then we'll put it into the jars.'

'We should have glass of wine to celebrate,' Lija says.

'Sounds like a marvellous idea.' A wave of weariness washes over me. 'I'm absolutely exhausted. Let's have ten minutes down by the canal.'

Chapter Seventy-nine

So Lija and I take a bottle of white from the fridge and go and sit on the jetty, feet dangling above the water. I pour out some wine for us. It's taken us the best part of a day to make the jam and I'm feeling tired. Not surprisingly, I'm sleeping erratically again. One night fair, the next I'm wide awake until dawn. My eyes are gritty and heavy. The past couple of months have been such a strain and now I just want it all to come to an end. Once Edie returns to the States and Lija takes over, I'll be able to get on with my life.

Lija chinks her glass against mine. 'To us.'

'To us,' I echo.

I sigh and try to let some of the tension out of my body. My neck's like a concrete post, my shoulders feel as if there's a coat hanger in them, but the wine is certainly hitting the spot. It's a lovely evening, the sun still warm in the sky. There's no breeze at all and the air is still. Dragonflies flit through the rushes that line the canal and a busy little moorhen bustles in and out between them. The towpath opposite us still has its fair share of dog walkers and joggers and couples strolling hand in hand, probably heading to the Two Barges.

'These days I only seem to be relaxed when I'm down by the water,' I say to Lija. 'I do love it here. Edie and Mum were never as fond of it as me and Dad.'

'I wish I met your father. He sounds like nice man.'

'He was.' The wine is going down too well and I top up our glasses. 'I'd love to get the *Maid of Merryweather* working again one day. Dad would like that too.' I offer a prayer of thanks that Mum did actually leave the narrowboat to me. If she'd left that to Edie too, my sister probably would have sunk it out of spite.

'We'll have to find somewhere else to put cakes and jam.'

'A summerhouse would be nice,' I offer. 'And not too expensive.'

'That would work, but I think people like novelty of shop on boat.'

'I'm not going to be cruising away in her tomorrow, Lija,' I reassure her. 'It will be a long time before I can afford to renovate the poor old maid.' Much like myself.

I fill up our glasses again and then lie back on the jetty, enjoying the sun on my face. Lija kicks off her Doc Martens and lies down next to me. Her impossibly slender legs, despite one of the warmest summers in history, are still ghostly white, and I think that she will never, ever tan.

'The jam will be cold now,' Lija says. 'I will have to reheat it.'

'Let's do it in the morning. I've had too much to drink now to bottle jam. My ladle skills will be all squiffy and it will only end up all over the floor.'

'We will take rain check,' Lija agrees. 'We have deserved rest.'

'I second that motion.' So we lie there and gaze at the azure sky some more. We should make the most of it, as summer will soon be coming to an end and the canal and garden will change to their winter garb.

361

'Do you miss him?' she asks as we both study the fluffy white clouds drifting slowly above us.

'Anthony?'

'Don't make me want to kill you.'

I gather by her retort that she's referring to Danny.

'Yes. Every day.' Despite the fact that he's been gone for weeks now, I still think of him all the time. He's always there at the back of my mind.

Lija turns on her side to face me. 'He will come back. I am certain.'

'I hope so.'

'You are free to love him now, Fay.'

'Yes.' The prospect actually frightens me. I have nothing to hide behind. 'What if he never comes back, though? What if he finds a great job, a great girl somewhere else, miles away?'

'Then you will die lonely old woman or have to marry Stinky Stan.'

'Thanks for that, Lija.'

Though it scares me, there's a very real truth in that. Danny and I may have enjoyed a fleeting moment, but it will last with me for ever. It's not a prospect that thrills me, but if I can't be with Danny, then maybe I will end up alone.

Chapter Eighty

Lija and I have hangovers. She stayed over last night in Edie's room and we're having a later start than usual.

We're both still in a state of undress as we have our break-fast. I'm in my sensible pyjamas and dressing gown. Lija is in black, barely-there underwear, but at least I know that it's clean, and she's brushed her teeth too.

We both have a bowl of cereal and a strong black coffee.

'Do not crunch so loudly,' Lija complains.

'Sorry,' I say. 'Sorry.'

'Jam is still in pans,' she notes.

I know this as I've already pushed them to one side so that we could sit at the table.

'We can reheat it in a minute and then put it in the jars.'

'Is a little runny.' Lija glares at it. It's a face that would curdle milk, but I'm not sure that it will set reluctant jam. 'I would like it to thicken more.'

'We'll make it our very first job.' Then I remember, through my haze of stale alcohol, that Lija will become the owner of the house and the café at some point today. A new phase of my life is starting whether I like it or not. Despite being genuinely pleased that Lija is taking over rather than anyone else, my heart sinks a little bit.

It sinks even further when I hear a cough and turn to see Edie standing there at the open kitchen door. She's wearing a sunshine-yellow tailored dress and her designer sunglasses. Over her arm there's about fifteen hundred quid's worth of designer handbag – a new purchase, I'm sure, and Edie doesn't even have the discretion to hide it. My blood boils.

'Hi,' she says hesitantly.

I haven't seen her for nearly a week.

'I just came to say goodbye,' Edie offers. 'My flight back to New York is booked for this evening.'

'So soon?' I manage.

'There's nothing to keep me here now.' She fidgets and comes into the kitchen.

Lija stands up so that Edie can take her seat, but Edie breezes past her.

I should offer her tea or toast or something, but I am failing in my duty to be civil to my sister. Everything about me hurts when I look at her. She has taken everything from me and yet she has no shame.

She tips her sunglasses onto her head. 'The sale should complete today. The solicitor has said everything's in place. I'm just waiting for his call.'

This is it, I think. This is how it ends.

Behind Edie's back, Lija has picked up a knife and is making stabbing motions at my sister's neck. I put my hand over my mouth to smother my smile and silently thank Lija for bringing a bit of brightness to this moment. Without her, I'd be completely rudderless.

'I thought you'd be packed and ready to go,' Edie says. With a coolly disdainful look, she takes in my pyjamas and Lija's underwear. 'I understand that the new people aren't moving in

364

immediately but, in a very short while,' she glances pointedly at her watch, 'this house will no longer be yours to live in.'

'I'm staying here with Lija.' If we'd had a sensible, adult conversation about this over the last few weeks, then Edie would have known this. She clearly thinks I'm being turfed out of Canal House today. That makes me even more angry. She had no idea where I was going to go or what I was going to do and simply didn't care.

'You can't stay here,' she bristles.

At that moment, her mobile rings and she puts it to her ear. 'Yes,' she says. 'Thank you. I'm delighted to hear it.' She purses her lips at me as she clicks off her phone. 'The sale has gone through without a hitch.'

'I'm pleased to hear it too,' I say. 'I hope you're happy now.'

'None of this is my doing,' she says loftily. 'It's what my mother wanted.'

'Well, you can head straight back to New York safe in the knowledge that you've carried out her last wishes.'

'I don't think you fully understand my situation,' Edie says tightly. 'Brandon and I need the money. I haven't enjoyed any of this, you know.'

'Really.' I'm too exhausted to even argue with her. 'It seems to me that you have. I'm just happy that the house has gone to Lija.'

Edie spins round at that and stares at us both agog. 'What?'

'I'm relieved that Lija will be staying here,' I repeat. 'At least she'll carry on the business I worked so hard to build.'

My sister glares at Lija. 'How? How are you staying here?'

At that moment Lija's phone rings. She has the same conversation as Edie did. 'Yes. Thank you. Am delighted to hear it,' she mimics.

Lija hangs up. 'I am now owner of Canal House.' She can't help her smile.

'Congratulations.' I go to give her a hug. 'I'm so very pleased for you.'

'*You*'ve bought it?' Edie rages. Her hands are balled into fists at her side and her face is puce with anger. 'You can't have. It's a man called Robert.'

'Roberta,' Lija corrects, barely suppressing her grin. 'Roberta Lija Vilks.'

'Is this a trick?'

'No,' I say. 'Why would it be?'

'I had no idea that the buyer was Lija.'

'Why does it matter? You got what you wanted.'

Edie narrows her eyes. 'You think you're so clever.'

'Shouldn't you be pleased that I still have a place to live?' I remind Edie. 'You've taken everything else from me. Lija has paid cash. The sale has gone through much faster than it would have otherwise.'

'I don't know what kind of stunt you're trying to pull, Fay, but I won't have it.'

'There's no stunt, Edie. It's just that everything hasn't gone entirely your way this time. That's all.'

'I hope you'll both be very happy here together,' she spits.

I turn to Lija. 'We'll try to make a go of it, won't we?'

'Yes,' she says.

'But I think we've forgotten one last thing, Lija.'

'We have?'

My gaze flicks to the preserving pans filled with jam on the table.

Instantly, Lija is on board. 'Oh, yes.'

Together we lift the heavy jam pan.

My sister looks at us as if we're both mad. Which we may be.

'One, two, three,' I say, and we advance on Edie, who straight away recognises the mischief in our eyes.

'Don't you dare.' Edie backs away from us, but she's blocked by the counter behind her.

We are, however, unstoppable. All shred of conscience has gone from my mind. This is petty revenge and I'm thoroughly enjoying it.

As one, Lija and I tip the runny strawberry jam all over Edie's head. She stands and splutters with impotent anger as it runs down her immaculate auburn locks, her flawless make-up, her designer handbag. Her sunshine-yellow dress looks as if someone has bled to death on it.

'Oh!' Edie cries. 'Oh!' Frantically she wipes the jam with her hands, trying to get the sticky mess from her hair, her face. She smears more of it on her dress. Her new swanky handbag is slick with it.

My breathing is hard and my heart is pounding. I feel mean, so very mean. But I can't say I didn't enjoy it.

'You and I are finished, Fay,' she says. 'You're no longer my sister.'

'I think we were finished long before this, Edie,' I say regretfully.

Edie marches to the door, slipping and sliding on the jam that sticks to her shoes as she goes. 'Don't ever call me, Fay. I will *never* speak to you again.'

Then she slams the kitchen door and is gone.

'She is evil cow.' Lija looks at me uncertainly. 'Are you OK?'

'Yes,' I say. My heartbeat is returning to normal. Edie is another person to add to the growing list of those who are now out of my life. I feel sad, terribly so, but not utterly distraught.

I lick some jam from my fingers and turn to Lija. 'You were right,' I say. 'That jam was a bit runny.'

Chapter Eighty-one

The café is busy today, and in the kitchen Lija is multi-tasking to her heart's content. She has a cake in the oven and is making sandwiches as if she's on a production line. Already it doesn't feel like my house, my business. Though I'd like to say that all is back to normal, I can't help but feel slightly cast adrift.

I feel that Lija is still tiptoeing around me, and she's definitely been looking at me anxiously all day. Perhaps she thinks I'm going to bolt for the door now that the keys have been handed over, but where else would I go? It's just that this new arrangement is going to take some getting used to, and we both know it.

Lija will be the boss now, and, though she's been the one who's ordered me around since the minute she started working here, it will be on a different footing. But I'm glad. If I had to lose the business, then I'd rather lose it to my dear Lija than anyone else.

'Smoked salmon for the people under the apple tree,' Lija says. Then adds, 'If you don't mind.'

She's definitely not herself.

Scooping the order up, I trot outside. It's the Fensons, who I normally love to see, but today I have to force myself to stay chirpy as I chat to people. When I set their sandwiches out on the table I somehow feel that my heart isn't in it. This isn't my baby any more, it's someone else's, and try as I might, I feel a little piece of me has been taken away. I think of the hours that I've toiled here, the blood, sweat and tears – and for what? I did it all for Mum, for us. Yet, without a thought for me, Mum handed it all over to Edie who, in turn, has sold me down the river. It looks as if my relationship with my sister is finished too. I don't think I can forgive her for making me homeless. And I don't think she'll ever forgive me for the jam incident – which I feel pales into insignificance by comparison.

It's hot, hot, hot. The air is heavy and humid. People are starting to grumble about the continued heat as only the population of sun-starved Britain can. The Met Office are warning of temperatures over a hundred degrees, and water companies are still threatening hosepipe bans. Whenever I feel overheated, I love to sit by the canal for five minutes and cool off. That's all it takes. The garden is suffering though, all the blooms wilting for lack of rain. Soon the weather must break.

The canal is busy too, yet the narrowboats that pass seem lethargic in the water and many of the tourists who've rented them are as red as lobsters from the relentless rays. It's relatively easy to keep a boat warm in the winter now as the majority of them are fitted with central heating and wood-burning stoves. In the summer, when we have a hot one, it's harder to keep them cool. Sometimes, on the *Maid of Merryweather*, we had to keep the doors open at night and even take the windows out, as it was difficult to get a breeze through.

I wonder where Danny is now. Has he moored up somewhere in this baking heat, or is he making his way steadily around the network of canals? I hope he's enjoyed his summer on the water.

My sister will be back in New York now. I hope she had a good flight. It makes me sad that I wasn't the one taking her to the airport, waving her off. I also hope that she and Brandon will be happy with Mum's money and will use it wisely. But that might be a hope too far. With Mum and Dad both gone and Edie and me estranged, I realise that I'm all alone in the world. The nearest I have to family now is Lija and Stan.

'Could we have more tea please, Fay?' the Fensons, under the apple tree, shout out and break into my reverie.

'Yes, of course.' I go back to the kitchen and sort it out for them.

When I return, Lija says, 'I will bring my stuff over later today. If that's OK.'

I take hold of her bony shoulders and squeeze them affectionately. 'It's your home, Lija. Of course it's OK.'

'Ashley has borrowed van from friend to help me.'

That's the lovely barman from the Two Barges. I haven't heard any mention of him since the night of the Canal Festival, so this is a turn-up for the books. And I do believe that Lija flushed slightly as she said his name.

'Is there anything I can do?'

Lija shrugs.

'I could strip the bed down for you.' I know Lija was a bit reluctant to have Mum's old room, but I'll make sure everything's cleared out for her and it's nicely aired. 'Have you got clean sheets for a double bed? Or you can use some of the ones already here.'

'Yes. I will bring. I would like to go as soon as we close up, if that is OK?'

I laugh. 'You don't have to ask me now, Lija. You can come and go as you like. *You're* the boss.'

And I'm the employee.

We haven't actually discussed how much I'll be paid, but it's a conversation we must have soon, as I'm getting quite anxious. What little money I have won't last for very long.

Chapter Eighty-two

Ashley the barman comes to collect Lija in his friend's van. He's a nice chap. Caring. I watch them bounce off down the lane, skirting the many potholes, suspension groaning in complaint as it goes.

Then I head upstairs to strip Mum's bed so that it's ready for Lija when she comes back. It seems strange, but I haven't really been in here since the funeral and there's so much more to do than I thought. Mum's stash of tablets are lined up on her bedside cabinet, her book open at the page she was reading. The wardrobe still holds her clothes, some of them not worn for many years. I need to clear those out for Lija too, and empty the chest of drawers. The room smells stuffy and, frankly, of old lady. That brings a lump to my throat. I draw back the curtains and open the windows wide to let in some of the heavy evening air. Dark clouds are mustering on the horizon and it looks like rain.

I'll put everything in Edie's old room for now and then I can take it to one of the charity shops in the city when I've sorted through it. There's not that much in the wardrobe really. A few musty old coats that haven't seen the light of day for some time, a couple of smart dresses from the days when Mum used to be out and about and took pride in her appearance. The dust makes my eyes prickle. I picture Mum propped up here in her bed, like a queen on her throne, and it's a crying shame that my memories of her have been so soured. When I die I'd like people to remember me kindly.

Scooping the clothes out of the wardrobe, I take them through to Edie's room and pile them on the bed. I follow them up with her shoes and the couple of handbags she owned. I empty out the chest of drawers in the same way. In the top one is her underwear, and I'll find a separate box or carrier bag for that. The next one holds the nighties that were her sole attire in recent times. All that goes through to Edie's room too. In the bottom drawer there are a few sweaters. When did she last wear a sweater? I wonder. Aeons ago. I should have cleared these out long before now, but then there was always the hope that she'd rally at some point, leave her bed and join the world again.

The paper that she always insisted lined her drawers is ripped and in need of replacement. I'm sure Lija won't want this. So I pull it out and there, right underneath it, is a black and white photo.

Dropping the sweaters on to the bed, I pick up the print. It's yellowed with age, torn at the edges, and there are creases across the paper. It's a picture of a man and woman standing in front of the *Maid of Merryweather*. The woman, little more than a girl, has a baby nestled in her arms. The couple are both so young and look very happy. The man has his arm round the woman's waist and they're posing for the camera. I recognise Dad instantly, even with a full head of hair, but I know that's not the woman I've called Mum all my life.

This woman is curvy, with blonde hair that tumbles to her shoulders, and it's like looking at myself. This is my real mother. Without a shred of a doubt. And I offer up a silent prayer that

I'm the baby in her arms. My mouth goes dry as I turn over the photograph. In Dad's flowing handwriting it says, *Me, my darling Jean and baby Fay.*

I sink to my knees on the carpet. It *is* my mother and it *is* me. The date is there too, in Dad's hand. I would have been tiny, about three months old. Jean looks as if she's about twenty, probably not much older.

My finger traces the outline of her face and I feel tears course down my own cheeks. This is my mum. My real mum.

'Oh, Dad,' I murmur. 'Why did you never tell me? I would have loved to have known all about her.'

I look at the photograph again and see that she and Dad are looking at each other with adoration. How hard it must have been for him to never talk about her. I wonder if he married Miranda to give me a home, a mother. I wonder if he never loved her as much as he did his darling Jean, and if Miranda always knew as much. No wonder Miranda never liked the narrowboat. It always reminded her of Dad's former life, his first love. My real mum was the maid of Merryweather, I realise that now.

I wish I'd known her. She looks lovely and kind. I sit there with my head on my knees, the photograph clutched tightly in my hands, and I cry and cry. But I don't know who I cry for. Are my tears for the mum that I've lost or the mum that I've found? Or are they for me, for never having known either of them?

Chapter Eighty-three

I'm still staring at the photo in my hands, blinded by tears, and I'm just starting to think that I should move myself before Lija returns, when there is a huge clap of thunder overhead. Looks like the weather has just broken. The temperature drops, the sky darkens to black, and suddenly the curtains in Mum's room balloon in the breeze. Within seconds, rain pelts down in stair rods.

Quickly I pull myself together and go over to close the windows before the rain soaks the sill. Leaning out, I grab the catches and, as I'm pulling the windows towards me, I notice that there's a boat coming in towards the jetty behind the *Maid of Merryweather*. Then my heart skips a beat. It's *The Dreamcatcher* and Danny is standing on the back, getting thoroughly soaked as he steers in.

My knees are shaking as I stare out into the darkness. He's back.

I should finish tidying the room, make sure everything is nice for Lija, but I want to go to him. I so desperately want to go to him.

I could act calmly, sit here and wait for him to come up to the house. He's here to see me. He must be. But what if he doesn't want to disturb me? What if he waits until tomorrow? It would be just like Danny, and I think I might go slowly insane.

So I take the last of Mum's clothes through to Edie's room, then I go through to my own room and prop the photograph of my dad and real mum on the dresser. It's something I have to cherish.

Then I skip down the stairs and scribble Lija a note, which I leave on the kitchen table.

Danny's back! I write. She needs no further explanation.

Then, just as I'm about to leave, I hear a key in the front door and Lija has returned.

'Hello,' she shouts.

I glance anxiously out of the kitchen window. *The Dream-catcher* has moored now and I can see Danny tying her up, Diggery running up and down the jetty in the rain.

This is her first proper night here and, as a friend, I should stay and help her settle in.

Lija comes through to the kitchen with Ashley close behind. 'We are pissing wet,' she says with a tut. Then she looks at me. 'What?'

'Danny's here,' I tell her, unable to contain my excitement. 'He's back.'

'Then go to him.'

'I can't. I ought to help you.'

'Go, stupid woman,' she says. 'I have muscle.' Lija flicks a glance at Ashley.

'You don't mind?'

'No.' She makes a shooing movement with her hand.

'I won't be late,' I promise.

'You have nothing to rush back for,' she reminds me.

No mother. No Anthony. Nothing.

'Just be here in time to bake in morning,' she says.

'I will.'

Lija nods towards the window and the sheeting rain. 'You have umbrella? You have cardigan? You have emergency pants, toothbrush?'

'No, nothing.'

She grins at me. 'You are crazy in love.'

'I think I am.' So I rush out of the back door and into the teeming rain. It's coming down harder than ever and the thunder crashes around me.

As fast as my middle-aged legs will carry me, I run down the garden. Lightning illuminates the sky and the rain bounces madly from the surface of the canal. Danny's just finished tying up *The Dreamcatcher* and is about to climb on board. I see him turn and glance up at my bedroom window.

'Danny!' I shout. 'Danny.'

Then he lowers his gaze and sees me. Even from here I can tell that he's pleased. Diggery starts to bark a welcome. And my legs, suddenly weightless, carry me to him.

My hair is plastered to my head and the rain runs down my face, mixing with my tears of joy.

He holds open his arms and I run straight into them. On the jetty, he lifts me up and spins me round and round, holding me to him tightly, until we're both dizzy and breathless.

'I couldn't stay away,' he whispers to me. 'I couldn't stay away.'

Chapter Eighty-four

There's a flash of lightning and another crash of thunder right overhead. It makes me shiver, but I don't know if it's fear or excitement.

'You're soaked,' Danny says. 'Let's get on board.'

So I follow him on to *The Dreamcatcher* and we go inside where's it's cosy and warm. Water drips from us. Danny's hair is wet through, his T-shirt plastered to his skin. He's still holding my hand when he turns to me. We lace our fingers together and our eyes meet. The passion in mine is reflected back at me in Danny's. Without speaking our lips come together and his mouth is hot, searching.

His hands, burning on my chilled skin, rove my body and he crushes me to him. I peel off his T-shirt and he's more beautiful than I remembered, even in my dreams. I run my fingers over his chest, his damp skin.

Then we're like starving people let loose at the best banquet in the world. We fall on each other, feasting. There's no finesse in our foreplay. We stagger together towards Danny's cabin, stumbling, tugging at each other's clothes, stripping, bumping into the walls, the furniture. We stop to kiss, to touch, to explore. There's no vodka this time, no pot, but I am drunk and high all over again.

Diggery barks as we go, snapping playfully at our ankles, thinking that it's a wonderful game.

We fall on to Danny's bed and kick and tear off what little clothing remains until we're naked, skin against skin. I feel as if I'm in heaven when Danny enters me. He makes love to me like a thirsty man who's found all the water he'll ever need.

'I love you,' he murmurs. 'I love you.'

The storm rages above us. The rain lashes at the windows. Our bodies move together. Diggery nods off in the corner.

Later, much later, the storm is spent and so are we. We kiss softly, gently, as the thunder rolls and grumbles on its way. Then, in a delicious tangle of limbs and sheets, we fall asleep in each other's arms.

Chapter Eighty-five

We're shy with each other when we wake.

'You're glad to see me back?' he teases.

I shrug my feigned nonchalance. 'A little.'

'Would you say a lot, if I made you some tea?'

'Yes,' I concur, 'that would do it.'

His lips graze my bare shoulder and I quiver with delight. Danny climbs out of the bed and pulls on his jeans over his bare thighs, and even that makes me thrill with desire. He pads into the galley and I listen to him whistling cheerfully as he makes tea. Moments later there's the smell of toasting bread too.

I sit up, pulling the sheet around me. Diggery stirs and then jumps on to the bed. I ruffle his ears, his neck, and then he settles happily in the far corner at the foot. The dark clouds have moved on and the sky is lightening again now, even though it's late in the evening.

Danny comes back with a tray with two mugs of tea and a heap of buttered toast.

'Dinner in bed,' he says.

And I wonder, anxiously, hopefully, whether it will be the first of many.

He slips off his jeans and is naked again when he slides in next to me. The thought of eating this toast and drinking this tea really, really quickly is quite appealing.

'I couldn't believe you'd come back,' I tell him.

'I was making my way up the Grand Union Canal,' he says. 'I'd only got as far as Market Harborough.' He laughs at that. 'Not exactly the great adventurer. The further I went away from you, the more I knew I needed to come back.'

He puts his arm around me and I lean in to him, happy to be nestled against his warm chest. 'I'm glad you did.'

'In case I needed an excuse, I even picked up that reconditioned engine for the *Maid of Merryweather*.'

'You did?'

Danny nods. 'There's still a bit to do to it, but I think I can manage. I had a good chat with the bloke. He'll lend me a hand if I need it. That's if you want me to do it.'

'Of course I do.' Then I realise he knows nothing of my changed circumstances. 'There might be one small problem though.'

He raises an eyebrow at that.

'There have been a lot of changes in the last few weeks … I'm not entirely sure where to start.'

'At the beginning?'

'I'm not even sure where that is. But, anyway,' I dive in. 'Anthony and I are no longer together. He's in love with someone else and I'm very happy for them.'

'Wow.'

'We were never suited. It just took me a very long time to realise that. His new love is another handbell ringer. His protégée,' I tell him. 'It was love at first clang.'

'At least you're laughing about it.'

'Yes. But unfortunately, that's all there's been to smile about.' Then I tell him about Mum's contentious will and how I found out that she isn't my real mother at all. While he's still reeling, I go on to fill him in on how Edie has sold the house and how I'm now lacking my own home and business. 'Currently, I don't have a bean to my name. So the renovation of the *Maid of Merryweather* will have to wait.'

'But the boat's still yours?'

'Yes.' That would have been the final straw. 'At least that's still all mine.'

He rakes his hair and there's a slightly stunned expression on his face. 'All this has happened while I've been away?'

'Yes. And more. Lija now owns the house and the café. Lock, stock and barrel. Fortunately, she has some dubious oligarch aunt tucked away in Russia who has lent her the money. All of it. I did try to keep the place, but the banks wouldn't even entertain me. It seems they'll only lend you money when you don't actually need it.'

'How do you feel about Lija having the café, everything?'

'Pleased. I'm glad that someone I love has taken over. It would have been awful to watch it go to strangers or to someone who would simply close it down. And she'll make a great job of running it. Already she's full of ideas that would never have occurred to me.'

'What are you going to do now?'

I smile at him ruefully. 'That's the million-dollar question. I'll probably just stay here and help Lija out. I promised I would.' I let out a sigh. 'I do feel a bit disenfranchised at the moment though, and this place isn't holding good memories for me.'

Danny sits up sharply. 'Come with me,' he says. 'Lija can manage without you. I'm loving life on the canal, Fay. You would too. I know it. I've only explored a fraction of what the waterways have to offer. We could wander our way up north, over to Wales and back again.' His eyes shine with excitement.

'It's a totally different pace of life, and, after all you've been through, you could do with an extended break.'

It sounds so very appealing. My heart pitter-patters at the thought of drifting along the canals with Danny on *The Dreamcatcher*. It would be an idyllic life.

Then reality starts to encroach. 'But what about Lija?' I say. 'I can't simply leave her in the lurch. She needs my help. And Stan? What would happen to Stan?' I think of how tired he looked yesterday. 'He's ninety-three. How much longer will he be with us? He'll need someone to look after him – he has no family.'

'You're free, Fay. For the first time in years. You're not tied to your mum or to the café. Don't build up new barriers. This is your moment. We could do this.'

His dark eyes are so earnest, so imploring, that I feel I can't refuse him. And yet ...

'I have no money, nothing.'

'I've got enough to keep us going for a while,' he counters, 'and I can pick up some casual work along the way. You could carry on baking cakes and sell them as we go.'

'I don't know ...' Now there's a feeling of panic building in my chest. How can I just up and leave? I have promised Lija. I'm worried about Stan. 'You could stay here,' I suggest. 'Find some work locally.'

'I could,' he says softly. 'But that's not my dream.'

I feel the pull of responsibility. How can I just walk away and leave them to it? Even now I'm worrying about having left Lija alone for her first evening.

'I should probably get back,' I say. It's dark now. I don't know how long I've lain here in the comfort of Danny's arms, but I should probably make a move. 'Lija will be wondering where I am.'

'She's not a kid, Fay,' he points out. 'She's a grown woman and, believe it or not, she can cope without you.'

'I don't want her to be by herself for her first night in the house.'

'Oh, Fay.' Danny sighs at me. 'When are you going to put yourself first?'

'I don't know,' I answer. 'I don't know if I ever can.'

Chapter Eighty-six

Reluctantly, I leave Danny's bed and get dressed. The grass is wet as I make my way up the garden and back to the house in the darkness. Already I'm missing the warmth of his arms, the feel of his lithe body next to mine.

The lights are off downstairs and it looks as if Lija has gone to bed, so I tiptoe upstairs, trying not to wake her.

It seems I've worried needlessly. I stand frozen on the landing, not knowing what to do. The noises emanating from Mum's room – Lija's room – tell me that Lija isn't alone. It sounds as if she and Ashley have decided to celebrate, energetically and enthusiastically. So much for me fretting about her being by herself. I should have known better.

The moans and murmurs of pleasure grow louder and I try to block my ears with my fingers. Oh my goodness, I hope that isn't going to go on all night long. In fairness to Lija, she probably expected me to spend the night on *The Dreamcatcher* with Danny – that's what she'd have done in my circumstances. I curse myself for being so stupid. Danny's right. Of course Lija can cope without me.

There's yet more rampant groaning. Maybe I should text Lija

to let her know that I'm in the room next door. But then, this is her home now. She's free to do whatever she likes in it. If she brings home a different man every single night of the week, then there's absolutely nothing I can do about it.

As quietly as I can, I creep into my bedroom. I cross it to look out of the window at the canal. All the lights are off on *The Dreamcatcher* now: it seems as if Danny and Diggery have settled down for the night. I blow them both a kiss.

I love him. I'm in no doubt about that. So why am I finding it so very difficult to be with him?

I had a fitful night's sleep, but it was nothing to do with Lija's nocturnal passion, I simply couldn't turn off my brain. Until the wee small hours, I was going over and over in my head all that has happened recently, replaying it, regurgitating it and, ultimately, getting nowhere fast.

The very last thing on earth I feel like doing today is working in the café and, I have to say, it's probably the first time I've ever felt like this.

I have a long, hot shower and get dressed. When I go downstairs to the kitchen Lija is already there. So is Ashley. They're sitting next to each other at the kitchen table feeding each other morsels of toast and giggling like school kids. Lija is still in her underwear and Ashley is barefoot and bare-chested in just his jeans. They both jump when they see me.

'Sorry,' I say. 'Sorry.'

'I thought you would stay with Danny,' Lija says, not unreasonably.

'I ... well ... I didn't want you to be alone.'

'Fay.' She smiles at me. 'You do not have to worry about me.'

'I know.' I wring my hands, uncomfortable. 'I mean, I realise that now. Old habits die hard.'

'Come. Sit. I make you toast.'

385

'No, no. I don't want to intrude.'

She comes and steers me to a chair, pressing on my shoulders until I sit down. 'Shut up. Drink tea.'

Ashley pours me out a cup. 'Morning.'

'Good-morning.' I pick up my tea. 'Thank you.'

He smiles shyly at me. He looks like a man who wishes he was wearing a shirt.

I'm in the way, playing gooseberry. Then it hits me like a sucker punch: Lija doesn't need me here at all. It would be so much better if I were out of the way and she could put her own stamp on this place without feeling that she always had me looking over her shoulder.

'I'll be back in a minute,' Ashley says and he bolts out of the kitchen.

'Now you have driven him away,' Lija says as she puts some toast down in front of me.

'Sorry,' I say.

'Joking,' she tuts. 'He has to go to work. And we do.'

'I need to talk to you about that, Lija.'

'I know. We must sort out wages and go through books. It is all on list.' She waves a piece of paper at me.

A list. I didn't know Lija was a list maker.

'I have master plan,' she says.

'I might not be here to see it implemented, Lija.' Clutching my courage with both hands, I take a deep breath and plunge in. 'Danny's asked me to go away with him. On *The Dreamcatcher*.'

'For holiday? Is good idea.' She nods enthusiastically.

'Not for a holiday. Not exactly.' I hesitate before I say, 'Permanently.'

She recoils at that. Her usually white face blanches even further. 'No,' she says. 'You cannot go. I need your help here. I have done this for you, for us.'

'He's leaving again soon. To travel the canals all over the country.'

386

'He can stay here now,' she insists. 'Why not?'

'His dream is to move on, and take me with him.' My throat nearly closes as I murmur, 'I think I'd like to go.'

'No.' Lija clutches at my hands. There's panic in her eyes. 'Not now. Stay. I am not able to do this without you.'

'You can. You practically run this place already.'

'No!' She is distraught and I've never seen her look so scared. 'Don't go now. Stay. Just for six months. Let me settle. Help me to learn how to do this. Don't fuck off into blue yonder when I need you.'

'Oh, Lija.' Instantly, I'm sent into a tailspin of doubt.

'Six months,' she says. 'A year. No more. Then you can go.'

I can feel my resolve crumbling.

'Danny will understand.'

But will he?

I was sure, so sure that I could go with Danny. Simply sail away into the sunset. But Lija's right. How can I let her down? I know in my heart that I can't.

If I was like Edie, I could walk away and not look back, but I'm not like that. I don't ever want to be like that. I have a responsibility towards Lija. She's like family to me now. The only family I have. As she says, she has saved my home and my business. It will benefit her, I know that, but she's done it with me in mind. How can I turn my back on that when I know how hard it is to be let down by people you thought loved you? I could only go if I knew I had her blessing.

'Of course I'll stay,' I tell her. I try a laugh, but it sounds flat, disappointed. 'I don't know what I was thinking.'

Her relief is palpable. 'You won't regret it. Thank you, Fay.'

'I'll tell Danny that it was a silly idea. And he'll be back sometime. I'm sure he will.'

I glance down the garden towards *The Dreamcatcher* and feel hollow inside.

387

Chapter Eighty-seven

The café is busy all morning and we're run off our feet. Lija's cakes are becoming more and more in demand. She took a call from a restaurant in the city earlier asking her to supply them too. Proof, I suppose, that I'm needed here. Lija is still firmly in control, but does seem slightly more harried than usual. I'm trying to stand back and let her run the show as she's always done.

Stan comes in early for his lunch and I'm so glad to see that he's looking much more like his sprightly self today.

He takes up residence under one of the shades that Danny put up on his first visit here, and I follow him down the garden.

'Hello, Stan. All right today?'

'Oh, lovely,' he says. 'What a day! I'm thankful for every morning I see, and one with glorious sunshine is such a bonus.'

I sit in the seat opposite him, glad to take the weight off my feet for a moment. I thought the storm might have brought the temperature down today, but it seems as warm as ever.

'I came to see what you fancied today. We've got a tasty *salade niçoise*, if you fancy that instead of soup while it's so hot.' One of Lija's first changes to the menu.

'Oh, my favourite,' Stan says. 'That would be champion.'

'Don't you want to hear what else we've got?'

'No, no,' he says. 'That will be absolutely fine.'

'I'll be back with it in a minute.'

'You look a bit downcast today, Fay,' Stan notes.

I stay seated. 'A little matter of the heart,' I confess. 'Nothing that time won't heal.'

Stan glances towards *The Dreamcatcher*. There's no sign of Danny or Diggery this morning. 'I notice that young Danny's boat is back.'

That makes me smile. Not much gets past Stanley Whitwell. 'How very astute of you.'

'The course of true love never did run smooth, according to Shakespeare. And he knew a thing or two about it.'

'He wants me to go travelling on the canals with him,' I confide. 'But I need to stay here and help Lija.'

'Do you?' he ask. 'Are you absolutely sure about that? She's a very capable young woman.'

'She's asked me to stay. I can't say no.'

'That's your choice,' Stanley says. 'But, my dearest Fay, be wary of making a decision that might close the door on a wonderful opportunity. Don't get to my age and wonder "What if?"'

But how do I do that and still keep everyone happy?

'We'll both miss you terribly,' he says. 'But people have an extraordinary capacity for adapting to changed circumstances. Don't underestimate that.'

'I'll go and get your lunch ready,' I say to Stan. 'Thanks for the advice. I do appreciate it.'

I ponder what he's said all the way back to the kitchen.

The last of the lunchtime-rush customers have finally gone and there's a little lull. Lija is making a list of what cakes we need to bake for tomorrow.

'Shall I go down to the *Maid of Merryweather* and check what we've sold there? I could probably do with running a duster around too.'

'Yes,' Lija says. Then, after a moment, she adds, 'That would be very kind.'

She's been walking on eggshells around me all morning. Given a few days, I'm sure she'll be back to her abrasive self.

'I won't be long.' I get a duster and the Mr Sheen out of the cupboard and head off down to the *Maid of Merryweather*.

It feels as if this halcyon summer will never end, but all too soon the nights will start closing in, the brisk winds of autumn will appear and business at the cake shop and café will slow down for the winter season. Will Lija need me so much then? I wonder. In all truth, I probably could have managed on my own most of the time, especially if I hadn't needed to look after Mum. It's just that I never really wanted to. Despite her spikiness, Lija's always been a good and loyal companion. The least I can do is return that kindness.

I climb on board the *Maid of Merryweather*. As always, my heart lifts when I can spend time here, no matter how briefly. I've always loved this boat, but now it feels even more special now that I know that this is where my dad and my mum were so very happy together, where we were once together as a family. It's a great comfort to me.

The shelves are looking a little empty and I jot down what we need in my phone's notepad – Victoria sponge, lemon drizzle cake, gingerbread, all the standards that go so quickly. There's plenty of our strawberry jam, despite the full pan that was emptied on to my sister's head. I sigh at the memory. Edie will be home now and settled back into her troubled life in Manhattan. My eyes prickle with tears at the thought. It's difficult not to be able to call her and find out how she is, but I don't suppose she'll want to hear from me.

Sitting down at the table, I put my head in my hands. 'I'm sorry things turned out like this, Dad,' I say. 'I've always tried to look after Edie. I'm not sure where I went wrong.'

Sometimes I feel so close to my dad here, I think that if I opened my eyes, he'd be sitting there right next to me. Even the warm, musty scent of the boat reminds me of him.

'I've seen the photograph of you and Mum – my real mum. I found it in one of the drawers under the lining. I wonder if you hid it there? She looks nice,' I say. 'Did you love her more than Miranda? You look so in love with each other. I wish you could talk to me, Dad. I certainly could do with some help now.'

Just a word. That's all I need. A hint of Dad's voice on the breeze. Instead, the silence that encompasses me makes me sad.

Then I look up and see Danny and Diggery climbing out of *The Dreamcatcher* and on to the jetty. My heart flips a complete somersault, just seeing him. I knock on the window and wave to him. The way his eyes light up when he turns and sees me sends a thrill through me.

'Sorry, dusting,' I say to no one. 'You'll have to wait.' And I rush out to see him.

Chapter Eighty-eight

Danny holds out a hand to help me climb out of the boat to stand in front of him on the jetty.

'Hi,' I say, feeling ridiculously bashful.

'Are you busy? Come for a walk.' He's bright, animated. 'It's as hot as hell on the boat and Digs is sorely in need of liquid refreshment, so we were going to take a stroll to the Two Barges.'

I glance back at the house. I should go straight back and help Lija bake for tomorrow, but I don't think she can begrudge me an hour's absence, when Danny and I need to have a difficult conversation.

'It should be OK. But I have to ask Lija if I can pop out.'

'Is it strange having her as a boss now?'

'A little,' I admit. 'I'm sure we'll settle down in time.'

The expression on his face is unreadable as he gazes at me. 'That sounds as if you're intending to stay.'

'Let's walk,' I say.

So he takes my hand and we amble up the garden. When we reach the veranda, I stick my head round the back door. Lija is already up to her elbows in flour.

'Hey,' Danny says and holds up a hand to her.

'Hey, lover boy.' She responds in the same way and he grins at her.

'Danny has asked me to walk down to the Two Barges with him for a drink,' I say. 'Is that all right with you?'

'Of course,' she says.

I feel really guilty leaving her when there's always so much to do. 'I won't be long.'

She stares at me and purses her lips.

'What?' Does she not want me to leave right now?

Lija shakes her head. 'Nothing. Go, go.'

'Do you need me to stay and help? I'll stay if you want me to.'

'Clear off.' She flicks her floury fingers towards the lane. 'Do not hurry back.'

'OK.'

So Danny and I go out of the gate and down the lane, Diggery following close on our heels, trotting happily. On the humpback bridge over the canal we stop and lean on the aged brickwork and look down into the water beneath us. Danny slips his arm round my waist and turns me towards him.

He kisses me deeply and I cling to his body, enjoying the feel of it along the length of mine. My head swims. How can I possibly do without this feeling, now that I've found it?

'I've missed you,' he says when we break away from each other.

'We've only been apart for a few hours.'

'I know,' he says.

This is torture, tragedy. I don't want the conversation that we have to have. I want to stay in this moment for ever, putting off the inevitable. The words from Stan about missing opportunities ring in my ears.

We walk down to the towpath, hand in hand, and head

towards the Two Barges. Soon the blackberries will be fruiting in the hedgerows and Lija and I will come out and collect them for another mammoth session of jam-making. We've had so little rain this summer that the crop may not be a bumper one. The fruits may be small and dry rather than fat and juicy. But even thoughts of the vagaries of nature don't distract me from the feel of Danny's skin against mine.

'This feels weird,' I say to him.

He laughs. 'How?'

'I don't know,' I admit. 'It just does.' You're too young, too beautiful for me, my heart says. But it also whispers to me that it loves him all the more for it.

'We could be like this all the time, you know.'

I squeeze his hand. There's no easy way to break this to him. 'I can't leave Lija.'

He smiles at me sadly. 'How did I know you were going to say that?'

'Because I'm a terrible coward.'

Stopping dead in the towpath, he puts his hands on my shoulders. 'Because you're a kind and loyal woman, who would never consider putting her own needs before those of others.'

As he tilts my chin, I look into his sad eyes and ask, 'So what do we do now?'

'That's entirely up to you, Fay.'

'I can't just up and leave. Not now.'

'And maybe not ever.'

'I don't know.'

'You have a hard job leaving her for five minutes,' he points out.

Which is true enough.

'She wants me to stay for six months, maybe a little longer. To help her get on her feet. That's all.'

'I understand, Fay,' he continues. 'Of course I do. But what if

394

she asks you to stay on again after that? Or what if Stan takes ill? Would you be able to leave then?'

'I don't know.'

'There'd always be something, Fay. Now you're as free as you're ever going to be. Is it too much to ask you to give me a chance and put me at the top of your list?'

'No. Of course it isn't.'

He sighs wearily. 'Just as you can't leave, I don't think I can stay. No matter how much I might love you.'

At this moment, I suppose I could beg, throw myself on Danny's mercy, use a bit of emotional blackmail, dredge up some feminine wiles from somewhere and employ them to get my own way. Guilt him into staying, as I have been. But what does that achieve? I've seen all that in action from Edie and my Mum and I don't like how it feels. Someone should stay because they want to, nothing more. I have no right to hold Danny here simply because that's what I desire.

'You want to travel,' I say to Danny. 'And I want you to do that. I want you to have a fabulous life, enjoy your freedom while you're young.'

'Without you?'

'You can come back any time you want to visit. You know that.' I try to stay bright and breezy but inside my heart is breaking.

'It could be six months or more,' Danny says. 'I'm still getting used to the pace of life, so I've no idea how long it might take me to meander my way round the country.'

'Depending on where you are, I could come for a weekend or a holiday.'

'Yeah?' He raises an eyebrow at that. 'When exactly did you last take a holiday, Fay?'

'Well . . . let me see,' I bluster. 'Not for a long time.' Not for as long as I can remember. Anthony always used to go off on golfing holidays with his pals as I was always too busy caring for my stepmother and with work. 'But there was Mum, the café ...'

'And now there's Lija and Stan.'

'I could try.'

Then we both fall quiet as we know that's not what either of us really want. What I want is for us to be starting a new life together, and I'm sure that's what Danny wants too, but you also have to take into consideration what everyone else wants. Don't you?

We reach the Two Barges and, even though it's early in the afternoon, the garden is bustling.

'I must be getting too used to the peace and solitude of the canal,' Danny notes. 'Even this looks mad busy to me.'

I can't believe how nice that must feel, to spend your days drifting alone along the waterways, but I tear my mind away from the image.

Taking Diggery into the garden, I find a table tucked into the corner on the terrace right by the water. A handful of narrowboats from the local rental company are moored up alongside the pub and families are making good use of the kiddies' playground area. There are a few groups who look like they should be at work but have sneaked out of offices in Milton Keynes to catch a few rays of afternoon sunshine.

A few minutes later, Danny comes out with our drinks. He puts a glass of chilled white wine in front of me and takes a swig from his bottle of beer.

The wine tastes sour, but I think that's me rather than there actually being anything wrong with it.

'I'm going to leave later,' he says.

'Oh. So soon?' It hits me like a hammer blow. I thought he'd stay here for a week, maybe longer. I don't think I can bear the thought of him going again today, just when I'm so very glad to have him around.

'I don't want to draw this out, Fay. That would be too diffi-cult.' His hand covers mine on the table. 'You do understand?'

'Of course.' That doesn't make the pain of separation any easier. I feel nauseous at the thought.

'I don't even have your phone number,' Danny says.

'Well, that's one thing that's easily sorted out.'

We both pull out our phones and exchange numbers. We're acting stiffly, like strangers.

'You'll have to bear with me,' Danny adds. 'You know what it's like, the mobile reception on the canal is ropy at best. This phone is often three-quarters useless. Don't panic if I don't return your calls straight away.'

I can't believe we're even talking like this. He's come back into my life and has shaken it up. Soon, so very soon, he'll be gone again. I can feel him slipping away from me. It's hardly like he's going to be out nightclubbing every evening, but what if he meets someone else on his travels? Someone who doesn't have an over-heightened sense of responsibility, who can be with him all the time?

Danny drains his drink. 'Let's get you back.'

I finish my wine and together we walk back along the tow-path to Canal House. We take the steps down on to the bank and go along to the jetty to *The Dreamcatcher*.

'We can make this work,' Danny says. 'If we want it to.'

He's so young, so optimistic. I'm older, nowhere near wise, and know how much life gets in the way of your plans, your dreams.

'Of course we will.'

'We'll miss you. Won't we, Digs?'

The little dog wags his tail and even that tears me in two.

'What time are you going?'

'Not for a few hours.'

I glance back at the house. 'Lija will need me to help for a while, but I could come back later to wave you off.'

Danny shakes his head. 'No. Don't do that. It would be too sad.' He tries a smile, but I can tell that he's miserable too. By pleasing one person, I make another one unhappy. Is that one of the unwritten laws of the universe? 'Just kiss me and wish me on my way.'

So I step into his arms and feel his warm lips on mine. How can I let him go? Tears squeeze from my eyes and he brushes them away with his thumb.

'The months will fly by,' he whispers against my hair.

'Like the wind.' But I know in my heart that I'm risking losing him. Once he has flown free this could really be goodbye.

Chapter Eighty-nine

I walk briskly to the house, gulping back tears. I know Danny will be standing watching me. Diggery barks. But I can't turn round. If I did, I'd be lost.

I want to keep the picture of them both on the jetty, right next to *The Dreamcatcher*, firmly fixed in my mind. That will see me through the lonely days and nights without them.

By the time I get to the veranda, I've just about composed myself. I put on my happy face and get ready to slip back into the usual routine, to help Lija bake for tomorrow. I'll have to check on my phone for the list of things we need to replenish stocks on the *Maid of Merryweather*.

Distracted, I head into the kitchen, but when I see Lija standing at the cooker, her face looking even whiter than white, my head snaps up and I'm shocked to see my sister sitting at the kitchen table. Her eyes are red-rimmed and she's another one whose face is pale and drawn. Her suitcase is by her feet.

'I thought you'd be back in New York by now.' My first thought is that something has happened between her and Brandon. 'Is everything all right?'

'I couldn't get on the plane, Fay,' she says uncertainly. 'Not without talking to you.'

I look at Lija. 'I'm sorry, but can I have some more time?'

She nods at me.

'Let's go out on to the veranda then,' I say to Edie.

My sister gets up and follows me.

'I will bring tea,' Lija says. 'You both look as if you need it.'

'Thank you.'

Edie follows me out on to the veranda and I pull up two chairs nestled beneath the fading clematis. Lija brings us two mugs of tea and puts them down, then discreetly closes the kitchen door behind her. Edie and I both stare towards the canal, not daring to look at each other.

'There's just the two of us now, Fay,' Edie begins. 'I couldn't leave it like that between us. When I got to the airport I couldn't bring myself to check in.' She sighs wearily. 'I queued up – every step taking me further away – but when I actually got to the desk, I couldn't leave. I turned away and stood there for hours in the concourse, not knowing what to do, torn between leaving and staying. Eventually I came back to Milton Keynes and checked into to the hotel. It's taken me until now to pluck up the courage to come and talk to you. I wasn't sure if you'd want to see me again.'

'You're my sister.'

'And I've treated you really badly.' She breaks down and cries. 'You've lost all this.' She waves her arm to encompass the garden. 'I've destroyed our home and your business. You love it here so much, and it's all my fault.'

'You have, Edie. I can't deny that. You've taken everything I had.'

'I don't know what to do,' she wails. 'How can I put this right?'

'What can you do? Nothing can salvage Canal House. It's gone for good. Everything belongs to Lija. She took it on – thank God – when you turned your back on me.'

400

'I can see that now.' Edie is distraught. 'I wasn't thinking straight. I've rushed into this and I should have thought it through more.'

'All you saw was the money. You didn't think of the consequences.'

She hangs her head. 'You must hate me.'

'I don't like you very much,' I admit. 'But despite it all, I still love you. We're family. Nothing can change that.'

'I'm sorry,' she sobs. 'So sorry.'

I shuffle my chair against hers and put my arm round her. 'Shush, shush,' I murmur. 'Don't cry.'

'How can I make amends?'

'It's too late for that now, Edie. We just have to make the best of what we've got.'

'I can't manage without you, Fay. I was so excited to be going back to Brandon, but then I thought how shallow my life is with him. We do nothing together. I don't even get to go out to dinner with him. I thought if I could help him with money then that would make him want to be with me more, but what kind of basis is that for a relationship? All I was doing was trying to buy his love.'

Perhaps Edie is finally growing up.

'I'm thinking of coming back to England. Maybe I could even move back to the village and work in London.' Then the tears start again. 'I could have come back to the house.'

'I think we could have had some fun running this together.'

'If only I'd listened to you.' She sniffs her tears away and, in the absence of a tissue, wipes her nose on her arm. I get a glimpse of Edie as she was twenty or more years ago, and my heart contracts. 'You've always been the sensible one.'

Perhaps too sensible for my own good.

'And now you're doing it with Lija.'

'Yes.'

'I want to make things right between us,' Edie continues. 'You've always been there for me and I've been such a selfish cow.'

'I'm not going to argue with that either,' I chide.

'I'll split the money with you,' she says. 'I haven't seen any of it yet. Mr Crawley says it will take a little while to tie up the loose ends of the estate and complete the probate. But, as soon as I have it, half of it is yours.'

'You don't have to do that, Edie.'

'I've asked the bank for an overdraft in advance and I can give you a few thousand pounds now.'

'There's no need.'

She pulls a fat envelope out of her designer handbag and pushes it across the table to me. 'Take it,' she says. 'It's yours.'

'Thank you.' I might have my pride, but there's also necessity to consider. And I don't want to snap Edie's olive branch.

'I mean it, Fay. I want us to get back to how we were. We're sisters, even though we now know that your mum was a different one to mine. We were brought up together, we should stay together.'

'I found a photo of my real mum,' I share. 'It looks like Dad had hidden it under the lining in one of the drawers in their room. I look just like her.'

'Oh, Fay. Mum should never have done what she did. It's set us at loggerheads, and that was so wrong.'

'She must have had her reasons.' Though I don't know how anyone could deliberately cause their own children such pain. 'But I'm going to find out everything I can about my real mum as soon as possible. I want to know all about her.'

'I'm sure you do.' Edie looks at me hopefully. 'Are we sisters once more? Can you forgive me?'

'We were always sisters,' I tell her. 'But I'm glad we can be friends again.'

'Me too.' We stand up and hug each other tightly.

I give a teary laugh. 'You've forgiven me for pouring jam over you?'

'It was actually very funny,' Edie says, with a sniff. 'Not that I saw it at the time. It ruined my favourite dress.'

We giggle together like schoolgirls and she hugs me again.

'When the money comes through, perhaps you can buy into the café again, something like that.'

'Perhaps.'

'I'm sure Lija would let you. She did this for you, Fay. That disagreeable little girl has treated you better than I have, your own sister. I'll never forget that.'

I'm sure Lija would let me buy back into the café, but it's her business now, and somehow I feel as if my heart has gone out of it. I could stay here and carry on with it, but at what cost? Plus, I'll wait and see if Edie does as she promises. I hope she doesn't change her mind when she actually gets back to Brandon. I'll keep my fingers firmly crossed; it would certainly take a weight off my mind. And, do you know what? If she does offer again, I'll take the money from her and bank it gladly. If nothing else, then I'll be able to restore the *Maid of Merryweather* to the most beautiful condition, and that would make my heart so very glad.

'I'm sorry about what happened with Anthony too.' She looks even more shame-faced.

'It doesn't matter. It was never really meant to be. He was in love with someone else. They seem very happy together.'

'And what about you? What happened to that handsome young stud you'd kicked up your heels with?'

I glance down at *The Dreamcatcher*. 'Danny's here,' I say. 'But he's about to leave. He wants to go off travelling on his narrowboat and I don't feel I can stop him.'

'Go with him then,' Edie says. 'Why not? I can't see the attraction in it myself, but you've always loved Dad's old tub and the canal.'

'He's asked me to. But – well, I can't leave Lija.'

She frowns. 'I'm the wrong person to give relationship advice, but I thought you had something special. There were definitely sparks flying between you.'

'I do like him. I love him.'

'That kind of love doesn't come around too often. If I were you, I'd grab it with both hands and hold on for the ride.'

'I can't just drop everything and leave.'

'Only you can decide that, Fay. But, talking of leaving,' Edie glances at her watch, 'I have to go or I'm going to miss my flight. Again. I rebooked it for this evening and if I don't get a wriggle on right away, I'm going to struggle to make it.'

'Stay a little longer,' I beg. 'Another couple of days? This has been a terrible time for both of us.'

'I can't change it for a second time,' she says. 'Besides, I should get back to New York and sort things out with Brandon. He should stay with his family and make things right there. I have to tell him that face to face. I'll visit soon, though. I promise.'

'I'll take you to the airport.'

'I hate to remind you, but your car's all busted up. My fault too.' Edie looks stricken with guilt. 'I'll get a taxi.'

'It might not look pretty, but the car still runs,' I say. 'Just about. The wing is about to fall off and it's making some alarming graunching noises, but I think it'll get us there. We should risk it. I want to take you.'

'OK,' Edie agrees. 'I'd like that.'

So we dash back inside and grab her suitcase.

'I'll explain everything when I get back!' I say to Lija, who's looking very perplexed at this turn of events.

Then, sisters again and laughing together, Edie and I rush to the car, jump in and I gun the engine as we head off to the airport.

Chapter Ninety

With much swearing and sweating, accompanied by a plethora of groaning sounds from my car, we make Edie's flight in the nickiest-nick of time, despite having hit the rush hour on the M25.

She's checked in and now we're clinging together in the concourse as she's ready to go through security to the departure lounge. She has very little time to spare. We hold each other tightly.

'I'm going to miss you,' I tell her honestly. 'I'm glad you came back to sort it out. I would have hated for us to fall out permanently.'

'I can't even bear to think of it.'

We hug again.

'Let me know when you get home safely.'

She looks at me earnestly. 'Think about what I said,' she says. 'You're forty-two, Fay. Don't let Danny slip through your fingers. If you want to go with him, then you should do. Even if it doesn't work out, at least you can say you tried.'

'I'll think about it.'

'Don't think about it for too long. He's young. Men of his

age are impatient and impetuous. He might not wait.' Edie kisses me on both cheeks. 'I'll speak to you soon. Wish me luck with Brandon.'

'I love you,' I tell her. 'Of course, I wish you every luck in the world. Promise me that I'll see you soon.'

'I'll be back before you know it. Love you, sis,' Edie says and then she reluctantly peels herself away and disappears through the security gate.

As I head to the short-stay car park, my brain is buzzing, completely in overdrive. On autopilot, I pay my parking fee, get in my crumpled, grumbling car and drive towards the barrier.

Then, as I reach it, I stop short and stay there in the middle of the lane, staring at the yellow-and-black-striped barrier. Out of the blue, it strikes me: I've put so many barriers in my own way, and life is far, far too short to do that.

It's suddenly very clear to me that I need to be with Danny. I need to be with him permanently. Not just for the odd grabbed weekend or waiting anxiously until he next comes back to visit the café, but always and for ever. Everyone else can cope without me, and they will.

Then I experience one of those moments that he talked about when he decided to buy *The Dreamcatcher*. One of those moments that I never thought I'd be lucky enough to have in my whole quiet and ordinary life. But here it is, hitting me like a ton of bricks, at an exit barrier in a multi-storey airport car park. There's no choir of angels, no hallelujah cloud with the sun bursting from behind it and lighting up the sky, nothing of any great note at all – unless you count the robotic voice on the ticket machines saying over and over 'Please insert your ticket.' Yet somehow the planets align and, all at once, it seems so very clear. I need to throw in my lot and be with him. I need to be with him now and, if he'll have me, for the rest of my life. It seems so blindingly obvious. Why on earth *wouldn't* I? As Danny described it to me, I know deep down in my bones, my soul, my whole being that what I'm about to do is absolutely right.

I love him. I have to go to him. And he's leaving tonight.

The sound of a horn blaring behind me brings me to my senses. I pull over to let the impatient driver past and fumble my phone out of my handbag. No service. Of course there isn't, I'm in a multi-storey car park.

So I drive forward, nearly dropping my ticket in my haste to get it into the machine, then I screech out of the car park. In the very next layby I come to, I park up again and punch Danny's number into my phone.

'The number you are calling is temporarily unavailable.'

Damn it. I bet Danny hasn't got a signal down on *The Dreamcatcher* either. There's nothing for it, I'll have to put my foot down. I'm not sure this car is even able to break the speed limit, but I'm certainly going to give it a go.

Feeling stressed but lighter than I've done in years, I floor the accelerator and join the flow of traffic heading on to the motorway. Two junctions down and I hear the most dreadful noise. Oh God. What now?

Then I see that my crumpled wing has decided to semi-detach itself and is hanging off dangerously. Why do these things happen when you're in the biggest rush you've ever been in? There's nothing for it. I have to stop. Negotiating the stream of heavy traffic, I pull over to the hard shoulder and jump out of my car to inspect the damage.

The wing has peeled back and is now hanging down by the tyre. I can't drive like that or the next thing will be a puncture. Terrified by the cars and lorries hurtling by at tremendous speed, I try pushing and pulling it, not sure whether I'm attempting to push it back into place or to pull it off altogether. I have no idea which would be the best thing to do. Every time I try to fix it back into its proper place, it just droops down perilously. Clearly something quite crucial is missing.

Time is passing and my frustration is mounting. So, accompanied by the open-mouthed stares of passing motorists, I treat the wing of my car to a few well-aimed roundhouse kicks, which don't appear to make things any better. Yet eventually, with one final killer blow, the wing comes off altogether and drops on to the tarmac with a forlorn clang. The car looks like some sort of nightmare machine with its innards showing, but at least it still runs. I hope. Picking the wing up, I totter along the hard shoulder with it, sticking close to the car while the speeding lorries skim past my bottom. I open the back door of the car and with a heartfelt 'Ouff' heave the mangled piece of metal on to the seat. I flop back into the driver's seat, grateful to be relatively safe once more. I try Danny's number again, but still can't get through.

I ease back into the traffic, nerves shredded. It's getting even heavier now as I'm right in the rush hour. Crawling along, I barely get out of third gear. We're inching along the M25, four lanes of cross drivers who all want to get home quickly, all vying for position, while my anxiety level racks up. How lucky Danny is never to have to deal with this now. Well, hopefully, that will be me soon too.

At this rate, it's going to take me hours to get home and I don't know what to do. Danny said he was leaving later, but not exactly when. I can't miss him. It's very important that I go, and go now.

I could call Lija and get her to go down to the jetty and ask him to stay, but I want to have time to talk to her about it first. You can't break something like this over the phone. But if I give her time to think about it, then I know that she'll come up with a million arguments that mean I should stay. I love her and I love that she's bought Canal House and the café, but I can't live my life for her.

Danny's leaving tonight and I can't let him go without me.

Chapter Ninety-one

Eventually, a frustrating two hours later, I'm bumping down the lane in my battered car when I see Stan stooped over in his front garden, picking some roses. I stop the car and get out.

'Hello, dearie,' he says. 'You look a little harried.'

I open his white gate and go into the tiny and immaculately kept garden. 'I've just taken Edie back to the airport, Stan. That was more than a bit emotional.'

'Lovely,' he says. 'I take it that you've made up?'

'Yes.'

'I'm so pleased.'

'Me too, Stan. I've been rushing to get back but my car decided to fall to bits on the way home.'

'There's always something,' he agrees amiably.

'I wanted to talk to you, Stan.'

He holds his back and straightens up. 'I'm all ears.'

His cardigan is done up all wrong, so I undo the buttons and redo them. Stan stands and lets me.

'My Elsie would never allow me to go out of the house unless I was properly dressed,' he says. 'Thank you.'

Then I lower my voice, even though I'm not within earshot of the house. 'Stan, I'm thinking of leaving to go with Danny on *The Dreamcatcher*.'

His rheumy eyes sparkle. 'How very exciting.'

'I'm worried about leaving Lija,' I confess. 'Do you think she'll be able to manage?'

'Perfectly,' he says without hesitation. 'I've told you before, Fay, you must grab every opportunity that comes your way in life. That way, when you reach my age you'll be content. I take my pleasure in the small things: a colourful dawn, the song of a bird, the scent of a beautiful rose.' He offers a rich scarlet bloom that he has in his hand for my appreciation and the perfume is, indeed, heavenly. 'Hmm?'

'It's lovely.'

He indicates that I should keep it.

'I never once wonder, What if I'd done this or what if I'd done that? Because I simply chose to experience everything that was on offer. I can highly recommend it as a blueprint for an excellent life.'

'I wish I had your courage. I'd never get a Victoria Cross. I always seem to be living in fear.'

'Then this is a time for courage,' he says. 'Lija grabbed the opportunity that was presented to her with both hands and she'll make it work. She might frighten a few customers in the process, but I'm sure that's the only harm that she'll do.'

'So you definitely think I should go?'

'I think you should live your life for *you*, Fay. You must do what *you* want to do.'

I kiss his dry cheek tenderly, and my eyes fill with tears. 'I'll miss you, Stan.'

He laughs. 'Wait until you're on that canal with that handsome young man. You won't even think of us.'

'I will. I'll never forget you.'

Then we hug each other tightly. He feels small and frail in my

410

arms. I wonder how much longer he will be with us. Perhaps I should stay after all and look after Stan in his final years?

'You won't be far away,' Stan says. 'If there's an emergency, you can come back – if that's what you're worried about.'

'Of course I'm worried,' I sob. 'I could worry for England.'

'When are you thinking of heading off?'

'Now,' I say. 'Danny said he's leaving this evening. I need to try and catch him.'

'Then you'd better get a move on.'

'I'm dreading telling Lija. I don't want her to think I'm deserting her.'

'She'll be fine. She might swear a lot, but she'll be fine.'

So, shaking inside, I leave Stan and drive the few hundred metres back to Canal House. I sit in the drive and try Danny's number again, but I just get the same message. Number unavailable.

Chapter Ninety-two

I could walk straight down to the jetty and tell him of my decision, but I feel I must talk to Lija first. I owe her that much.

She's still in the kitchen when I walk in, which makes me feel even more guilty. There's always so much to do and she's been my loyal wingman for the last few years.

'Hey,' I say.

'Did Wicked Sister get away OK?'

'Yes,' I reply. 'I think she's had a change of heart. I hope so, anyway.' I'm still anxious that once she gets back to New York and Brandon she'll change her mind. But currently I'm thinking the best of her and praying that she'll do right by me.

'I want to talk to you,' Lija says.

'That's fortunate, because I want to talk to you. Let's sit.'

So she wipes her hands on her T-shirt and we both sit down at the kitchen table.

'I am going first,' Lija says. 'As I am now boss.'

I smile at that. 'Go ahead.'

'I want you to leave,' she starts. 'You must go away with Danny. I want you to. I have arranged for Krista to come and work here. She will give up her room and move in so that I will not be alone.'

Then she bursts into tears.

'Oh, Lija.' I go to her and hug her tightly. 'You know I won't go if you don't want me to.'

'Go,' she says. 'Clear off out of here. Have fun. Live life. Leave your fucking cardigan behind.'

We both laugh at that and Lija blows bubbles of teary snot from her nose.

'I want you to be happy here. As I have been. I could ask Danny to wait,' I suggest. 'Maybe we could go in a few weeks' time.'

'No,' Lija says. 'Go now or you will not do it. If we get too busy or Stan is ill, then there will be another excuse.'

That's the very same thing Danny said, and I know there's a truth in it.

Lija fixes me with a death stare. 'Go.'

'Are you absolutely sure?'

'Yes. I can phone you every day and be a pest. You will feel guilty and come back regularly.'

'I will,' I promise. 'Of course I will.'

'Then pack your things.'

'Spare pants and emergency toothbrush?'

'Everything. Pack as if you are never coming back.'

That makes my eyes well with tears. 'Edie has promised to share the money from the sale of the house with me. If she does, would you let me invest in the café again?'

'I would,' Lija says decisively. 'But for now, I want you gone, crazy woman.'

I hug her tightly. 'You don't have to tell me again. I'm going.'

So I fly up the stairs and into my room. I look out of the window to see if *The Dreamcatcher* is still there, and thankfully it is.

At the very bottom of my wardrobe there's a backpack that I bought many, many years ago. Years ago, when I thought I would have the nerve to travel to Peru, to Nepal and to China. I ferret about under all the abandoned shoes and handbags until I find it. Pulling it out, I brush off the dust.

It looks as if, finally and long-overdue, it's about to be used.

Chapter Ninety-three

I stuff my backpack with anything I can lay my hands on. A few T-shirts, some jeans. Socks. Underwear. I won't need much else. My business suits have been gathering dust in my wardrobe for years anyway. Lija should throw them all out. I look longingly at my favourite cardigan. Hard as it is, it's staying behind.

My new life will be a cardigan-free zone!

Scooping my potions and lotions from the bathroom, I fill a carrier bag with those too. If I've not got all I need, I can buy or send for what's necessary. I'll be spending my life cruising along the Grand Union Canal, not emigrating to the moon. The thought turns my tummy with excitement. Now that I've finally made the decision, I just want to be gone.

Lastly, I take the photograph of my mum and dad from my chest of drawers, kiss it quickly, and put it in the breast pocket of my blouse, close to my heart. Soon, when I have the time, I'm going to find out all I can about Jean Merryweather. But for now that will have to wait: there are more pressing matters needing my attention.

I rush downstairs, dragging my over-filled pack behind me and clutching my carrier bag of toiletries.

Lija is standing with her back to me at the cooker, but I can tell that she's crying.

I drop my bags and go to her. 'Don't,' I say. 'Please don't cry.'

She turns and falls into my arms, sobbing. 'I will miss you.'

'And I'll miss you too.'

We hold each other tightly. 'You'll make a fabulous job of this,' I assure her. 'Just don't tell the customers to fuck off.'

She sniffs. 'I will try not to.'

'Stan will help. He'll be here. He's seen more of life than either of us could ever imagine, Lija. Trust him.'

At that, there's a gentle knock at the door, and Stan is standing there.

'I just wanted to give you these, Fay,' he says shyly. 'To wish you on your way.'

He hands over a smart mahogany box. I know what's in it without needing to look.

'I can't accept these, Stan.'

'Yes you can. What use are they to me? I don't want to be buried with them and I don't want them to be lost if someone clears my house when I'm gone. I'm giving them to you for safe-keeping.'

I open the box and inside, sure enough, Stan's war medals are all neatly laid out.

'Thank you.' I hug him to me. 'That means a lot to me. I promise I'll always treasure them.'

'Come back to see us soon, Fay.'

I place Stan's medals carefully in the top of my carrier bag. 'I'll find a safe and special home for them as soon as I'm on board.'

Then I look up and point out of the window. 'Oh no,' I say. 'Oh no!'

Lija and Stan's heads spin towards the jetty, where *The Dreamcatcher* is pulling away.

'He's going without me,' I say.

'Then run!' Lija instructs. 'Run as fast as you can.'

Snatching up my bags, I take off down the garden as quickly as my legs will carry me.

Chapter Ninety-four

I'm halfway down the garden, Lija chasing behind me and Stan following as fast as he can, leaning heavily on his walking stick.

Danny is standing on the back of *The Dreamcatcher* as it putters away, Diggery at his feet. The dog barks at me happily. Danny's gaze stays firmly ahead and he doesn't look back.

'Danny!' I shout across the water. 'Danny! Wait!'

But he's wearing earphones: I can see a wire disappearing into his pocket, where it must be attached to an iPod, and it's clear that he can't hear me at all.

'Danny!'

'Run, Fay,' Stan encourages. 'Run.'

So I sprint along the jetty, up to the bank, taking the steps two at a time, and fly over the humpback bridge. I would say I was travelling light, but my backpack seems to weigh a ton. The carrier bag of toiletries clangs along at my side and I'm aware of Stan's medals perched precariously on top.

Over the bridge, and I'm on the towpath. *The Dreamcatcher* isn't too far ahead of me, but it might as well be ten miles. My breath is hot in my lungs and I don't think I've run like this since I took part in the egg and spoon race at primary school.

Lija and Stan have reached the jetty now.

'Danny!' They stand at the edge of the canal and shout out together. 'Wait!'

Diggery, caught up in the clamour, starts to bounce with excitement.

Yet Danny cruises on oblivious.

'Faster,' Stan yells, waving his walking stick in the air. 'Faster, Fay!'

But I'm going as fast as I can. My face is hot, sweating. My lungs are fit to burst. My heart is pounding so hard that it might explode.

Then, as Danny reaches the first bend, I can see the Fensons' narrowboat, *Floating Paradise*, wedged firmly across the canal. Hurrah! I can't believe my luck. My dear *Floating Disaster* might well come to my rescue.

I offer a silent prayer: Thank you, God!

Then, just in case, I offer up another prayer. Please, God, let them stay stuck there until I reach *The Dreamcatcher*!

On the bow, Miriam is standing, white cotton sunhat askew. She's pushing feebly against a boat moored by the towpath. 'I can't move it, Ralph,' she shouts back to her husband.

'Just give it a bloody good shove, Miriam,' he hollers back while he leans on the tiller, not doing very much at all.

I hear the engine note of *The Dreamcatcher* change and Danny slows down. He's stopping to help them. Of course he is. He's a kind and caring person and will want to lend a hand. Danny starts to manoeuvre the boat towards the towpath and that's my cue.

Grabbing the box with Stan's medals in, I clutch it to my chest for courage and valour. Then I drop my backpack, drop my carrier bag of toiletries. I need nothing in my life but this man.

I put a spurt on and start to pump my legs. My blood is

rushing in my ears. My eyes are like lasers focused only on *The Dreamcatcher*. I am Jessica Ennis powering her way to victory. I am Mo Farah on the home straight at the Olympics going for double gold. I am the unbeatable Usain Bolt. I am a nearly middle-aged, nearly menopausal woman whose legs are light and flying beneath her. Suddenly, I begin to eat up the towpath, striding out as if I'm on performance-enhancing drugs.

Ahead of me, Danny takes off his earphones and I hear the bow thrusters working to help him to steer to the bank to moor up *The Dreamcatcher*. Frantically, Diggery barks again. I think the little dog is getting desperate too.

Finally – thank God! Thank God! – Danny turns round and sees me racing after him.

'Wait,' I shout out. 'I'm coming with you! Wait for me!'

'Seriously?' he shouts back.

'Yes!'

Then he double punches the air in joy, turns his face to the sky and cries, 'Yeesss!'

And he waits for me while I, with the sun on my face and the wind in my hair, run, run, run to catch my dream.

Chapter Ninety-five

Lija and Stan stand on the bank and wave furiously after Danny and Fay.

Lija gazes after *The Dreamcatcher* as it moves further away from them. 'I'm frightened, Stan,' she says. 'What will I do without Fay?'

'You will take it all in your very competent stride, dear girl,' Stan replies. 'And you have me. I'll be here for you.'

Lija lays her head on Stan's shoulder. He has on his soft cable-knit cardigan, his best one, the one with the fewest stains. She thinks that he smells fusty, but comforting and not all that stinky.

'You'd better not die.'

'I don't plan to,' he says. 'Not yet.'

'I will hold you to that.'

'She'll be back before too long,' Stan adds. 'I know Fay. She won't be able to stay away. She loves this place, the café, making her cakes. When they've had their fill of travelling, they'll both come back here to work on the *Maid of Merryweather*. You mark my words.'

'I hope you are right.'

Now the sun starts sinking in the sky and *The Dreamcatcher* turns the bend and cruises out of sight.

'Do you want to stay for supper?' Lija asks. 'I have fresh spinach quiche. Is good for your old-man creaky bones.'

'How lovely.' Stan turns to her and rubs his hands together. 'My favourite.'

Acknowledgements

To Dean and Chris who looked after Sue and me so well on their narrowboat.

Remember, Sue is the completely useless one who did nothing but sit around with a glass of wine in her hand. Carole is the really helpful one who dashed about opening locks and was most excellent with a windlass.

Gentlemen, we leave at dawn!

Delia, Mary and My Love Affair with Baking

Whenever you turned up at my nana's house, there was always the scent of home-baking coming from her little kitchen. There'd be a meat and potato pie, or an apple one, in the oven and her first job after you'd taken your coat off would be to feed you. Once she'd done that, she could relax.

She was working in a bake house by the time she was twelve, so I guess that baking was in her blood. Her pastry was always as light as a feather and her pork pies sensational. In the school holidays when my mum was at work, she used to look after me. It was then that she first started to show me how to bake. But how I struggled to follow her! She was of the generation when there were no scales and everything was a pinch of this, a handful of that, a spoon of something else. Her results were always wonderful. Mine less so.

I still continued to enjoy cooking, but I didn't really bake cakes for many years after I started working as I never seemed to have the time and, when I did bake, we'd always eat the cakes so quickly. I can resist shop-bought cake much more than I can home-baked, so it was a good way to watch my weight! But I missed the lazy Sunday afternoon comfort that only home-made cake can bring and also the therapeutic relaxation that making it can provide.

Then Saint Delia Smith arrived on our tellies in the nineties and my love of baking was rekindled. I discovered that I can't bake by feel – I'm the type of baker who needs a precise recipe and I have to measure everything to the nth degree. That's why I loved Delia's recipes – follow them to the letter and they never go wrong. Some of them are still my favourites all these years later. I love her delicious puddings too – her tiramisu or dark chocolate and cherry trifle are always sure-fire winners.

Again, my cake-making skills lapsed a bit as I concentrated more on savouries. If I was baking, I always seemed to be doing it against the clock and that takes a lot of enjoyment out of it. Someone said to me recently that the most important ingredients in cakes are time, air and love – they might well be right.

Then two things happened, I suppose. One was the explosion in the popularity of cupcakes in this country. I thought they looked like a fun thing to bake and went on a few cupcake decorating courses and adored it. You could get some fabulous looking – and tasting – cupcakes with very little effort, a box full of cutters and some sugar paste. I love making them and have experimented with lots of different types and flavours over the years. There's nothing nicer than spending all of Saturday afternoon making cupcakes.

Also the popularity of baking had a real resurgence as people embraced all things retro and vintage. The time was ripe for a programme such as *The Great British Bake Off* and, like many people, I was hooked. Never has cake been so tense or exciting! My fingernails have all gone by the end of each series. And, of course, I'm a huge Mary Berry fan. If I'm going to bake a cake, her recipe books are now my first port of call. Like Delia's recipes, they just never go wrong. Being a home cook rather than a trained chef, I think she understands how the person at home bakes. She doesn't use ridiculously expensive or trendy ingredients. The recipes are all tried and tested. It's all straightforward – no bish, bash, bosh – and everything tastes fabulous.

It was a great pleasure to meet Mary a few years ago when I went to a book signing of hers in Costa del Keynes. Fortified by a couple of glasses of Prosecco (at lunchtime!), I also gave her a copy of *Calling Mrs Christmas* and told her that my readers and I get a lot of pleasure out of watching and chatting about *Bake Off*. She was utterly delightful and has then gone on to read several of my books. Go, Mary!

Recently, I had my biggest cake-baking challenge. Last summer, the eldest son of my partner, Lovely Kev, was getting married and he and his bride-to-be asked me to make their wedding cake. I was thrilled. Of course, I would. It was something I'd always wanted to do and I was honoured that they trusted me to do something so important for them. Goodness me, did I underestimate the work involved. It stretched me to the outer limits of my cake-baking skills. I made a two-tier cutting cake and also one hundred and fifty cupcakes. It was certainly a step up from knocking out a dozen cupcakes or a Victoria sponge. I made all of the roses, petals and cupcake decorations by hand and, the day before the wedding, started baking at eight o'clock in the morning and finished packing my last box at nine that night. I'll be eternally grateful for the encouraging advice of two top cake-baking ladies, Kerry Lillis from Vintage House Bakery and Jamie Kalek of Jamie Bakes Cakes. I don't think I could have done it without them. I take my hat off to anyone who bakes cakes on a professional basis. Man, is it stressful! I think getting the cake to the venue in one piece – contending with traffic accidents and a monsoon-like downpour en route – was one of the most nerve-wracking experiences of my life.

I always try to take cakes to my book events if I can – even if that means baking a couple of hundred in a week. Thank goodness for my Kenwood K-Mix! The hardest thing about writing a book like *The Cake Shop in the Garden* was that it left me craving cake at the end of each day and, of course, I had to try out the recipes myself. So, I hope you've enjoyed the book and also hearing a little bit about my love of cakes. Now I'm going to try to find a real-life cake shop in the garden to visit as I think that would be just fabulous.

Totally Gooey Triple Choc Brownies

185g butter
185g dark chocolate
275g golden caster sugar
3 large eggs
85g self-raising flour
40g cocoa powder
100g milk chocolate, chopped

Heat oven to gas mark 4, or 160°C fan oven, and line a 23cm x 23 cm tray with baking parchment.

Place the dark chocolate and butter in a heatproof bowl over a pan of gently simmering water. Heat until melted. Set aside to cool.

Beat the sugar and eggs together with an electric mixer until light and fluffy. This takes about 3 minutes.

Slowly add the cooled chocolate and butter to the egg mix. Then, gently fold in the flour and cocoa.

Finally, stir through the chopped milk chocolate.

Pour into the tin and bake for about 25-30 minutes or until the middle has just a slight 'wobble'.

Leave to cool completely (preferably overnight) before turning out and chopping into either 16 or 24 squares. (Lovely Kev complains if I cut them into 24!)

This is a *very* gooey brownie to cut so have a bowl of hot water to clean your knife with as you go. Whatever you do, the top will crack! We often call them drop brownies as they look as if they've been dropped on the floor, but they taste absolutely wonderful.

Sprinkle with a generous coating of icing sugar (to disguise the cracks!) before serving.

My favourite songs …!

I can't tell you how pleased I was to be invited to be interviewed by boogie-woogie pianist, Tom Seales, as part of his Tom Seals Presents series. The deal with this series of interviews is that you choose three songs that mean something to you. How hard is that! I had a lovely time going through Spotify and listening to some of my favourite songs over the years. In the end, I did manage to narrow it down. As part of the interview, Tom's band then play the songs in their own style.

If you haven't heard of Tom, he's the new 'piano man' on the block. Think Jules Holland and double it. His talent is quite incredible and Tom has supported artists all over the world. He also happens to be very funny and a natural interviewer.

Here are the songs I chose:

The Man Who Can't Be Moved – The Script
From reading *The Cake Shop in the Garden* you might have guessed that I have a soft spot for Danny O'Donaghue from The Script. I used to love watching him on The Voice and the hero in my book, Danny Wilde, is a thinly-disguised, romantic version of him.

Chocolate Girl – Deacon Blue
With my penchant for chocolate, how could I not pick this? Tom is joined on stage by fabulous jazz singer, Martyna Wren, for this amazing song and we talk about my *Chocolate Lovers'* series of books which have been my most popular worldwide.

Paperback Writer – The Beatles
My theme tune! I was brought up in St Helens just outside Liverpool so it's obligatory to love The Beatles and I have done all my life. This is a fantastic version of the song and I felt quite emotional to hear it played just for me (and the rest of the audience too!)
    Do take a look. I'm sure you'll enjoy it.

Carole x

Search for Carole Matthews' interview
with Tom Seals on Youtube!

Did you enjoy *The Cake Shop in the Garden*?

Don't miss Carole's gloriously festive sequel …

Out Now

HAVE YOU READ THEM ALL?

Discover the bestselling books by

Carole Matthews

LET'S MEET ON PLATFORM 8

Teri literally runs into Mr Right in Euston Station – but he might not be Mr Available . . .

....

A WHIFF OF SCANDAL

Aromatherapist Rose's new life in a quiet village is thrown into chaos when someone catches her eye.

....

MORE TO LIFE THAN THIS

Sort-of-happily-married Kate is determined to find herself – but finds a distracting man called Ben first . . .

....

FOR BETTER, FOR WORSE

Although she arrives without a plus one, Josie finds herself torn between not two but three handsome wedding guests.

....

A MINOR INDISCRETION

When Ali's head is turned by another man, her marriage is on the rocks – but should they let a minor indiscretion come between them?

....

A COMPROMISING POSITION

After Emily's boyfriend posts compromising photos of her online, her best friend tries to mend her heart – but they both wind up falling for the same man.

....

THE SWEETEST TABOO

Sadie is flown to Hollywood by a producer who wants to win her heart – but he's not the only man in LA who has his sights set on her.

....

WITH OR WITHOUT YOU

Lyssa embarks on a trekking holiday in Nepal in a bid to get over a broken heart, but meets someone new instead . . .

....

YOU DRIVE ME CRAZY

Meeting in their divorce lawyer's office was bad enough – and then Anna and Nick's ex-partners show up . . .

....

WELCOME TO THE REAL WORLD

A new job as an opera star's assistant could be Fern's big break, but only if she can keep things strictly professional.

. . . .

IT'S A KIND OF MAGIC

Emma wishes her long-term boyfriend would change – until he meets another woman, and she's the one to change him . . .

. . . .

ALL YOU NEED IS LOVE

Single mother Sally is on a mission to give her son a better life – but is the charming Spencer Knight the answer?

. . . .

THE DIFFERENCE A DAY MAKES

William and Amy move from the city to the countryside, but when tragedy strikes Amy finds herself living Will's dream . . .

. . . .

THAT LOVING FEELING

When the man who left her at the altar arrives to shake up Juliet Joyce's tired marriage, she finds herself with a difficult choice.

. . . .

IT'S NOW OR NEVER

Twins Annie and Lauren have very different lives – until they decide to make a change.

. . . .

THE ONLY WAY IS UP

When Lily and Laurence suddenly lose everything, will they get back to their old luxurious life, or learn to love their new one?

. . . .

WRAPPED UP IN YOU

After one too many questions about her love life, Janie books herself the holiday of a lifetime, and meets a gorgeous tour guide.

. . . .

SUMMER DAYDREAMS

Nell is inspired to swap the chip shop for her own business making handbags, but success doesn't come without a price.

. . . .

WITH LOVE AT CHRISTMAS
THE SEQUEL TO
That Loving Feeling

Juliet Joyce loves Christmas, but this year everything is spiralling out of control . . .

. . . .

A COTTAGE BY THE SEA

Grace and Flick jump at the chance to go on holiday to their best friend Ella's seaside cottage – but this week will change all their lives.

. . . .

CALLING MRS CHRISTMAS

Cassie's love of Christmas turns into the perfect business. But when millionaire Carter enlists her help to make the day special for his kids, where will it lead?

....

A PLACE TO CALL HOME

Ayesha and her daughter leave London for a fresh start, and find refuge with a reclusive popstar.

....

THE CHRISTMAS PARTY

Louise has no time for romance, until she meets her company's rising star Josh, and the office Christmas party suddenly looks more tempting . . .

....

THE CAKE SHOP IN THE GARDEN

Fay runs her dream cake shop from her garden, until love, life and family collide and she has to choose what matters most.

....

PAPER HEARTS AND SUMMER KISSES

Single mother Christie has a flair for crafting and design, and it's not long before opportunity – and love – come knocking. But can she really have it all?

....

CHRISTMAS CAKES AND MISTLETOE NIGHTS
THE SEQUEL TO
The Cake Shop In The Garden

Baker Fay is called back to her old life, putting her relationship with Danny to the test . . .

....

MILLION LOVE SONGS

Should Ruby break her no-strings-attached rules for Joe, with his beautiful ex-wife and two teenage kids, or let her boss Mason charm her?

....

HAPPINESS FOR BEGINNERS

When handsome actor Shelby enrols his son in Hope Farm's school, Molly realises they're going to be a handful, but this could be the start of something wonderful.

....

SUNNY DAYS AND SEA BREEZES

Jodie heads to the Isle of Wight, ready to leave London behind – but her new houseboat life isn't as solitary as she'd imagined.

....

CHRISTMAS FOR BEGINNERS
THE SEQUEL TO
Happiness For Beginners

Molly hopes a family Christmas will bring Shelby and his son together – but Hope Farm's animals aren't the only ones causing trouble this year.

....

THE CHOCOLATE LOVERS' QUARTET

1 THE CHOCOLATE LOVERS' CLUB

For Lucy, Autumn, Nadia and Chantal, there's nothing chocolate can't cure – and with troublesome boyfriends and bosses, there's always plenty for their Chocolate Lovers' Club to discuss . . .

2 THE CHOCOLATE LOVERS' DIET

Lucy thought she had her happy-ever-after, but life is throwing a few more twists and turns at the Chocolate Lovers' Club.

4 THE CHOCOLATE LOVERS' WEDDING

Lucy, Nadia, Autumn and Chantal are gearing up for the wedding of the year, but life keeps getting in the way.

3 THE CHOCOLATE LOVERS' CHRISTMAS

With Christmas just around the corner, the women of the Chocolate Lovers' Club have more to worry about than shopping for presents.

SHORT STORIES

SUNSHINE, WITH A CHANCE OF SNOW

Beth is faced with her biggest challenge yet while on a beach holiday with her family.

WINTER WARMERS

Curl up with a collection of three short, festive stories.

THE SILVER COLLECTION

A collection of heart-warming short stories.

A CHRISTMAS WISH

Broken-hearted Hannah is about to discover there's a little Christmas magic coming her way . . .

Love books? Love chatting? Love competitions?

JOIN
Carole Matthews
and her fabulous fans online

f CaroleMatthewsBooks 🐦 @CaroleMatthews
📷 @Matthews.Carole

OR VISIT: **www.carolematthews.com**

To sign up for her newsletter and read
the latest news, reviews, gossip and more